A TIME TO KILL

Jack Murray

A TIME TO KILL

DI Nick Jellicoe Book One

Jack Murray

Jack Murray

Books by Jack Murray

Kit Aston Series
The Affair of the Christmas Card Killer
The Chess Board Murders
The Phantom
The Frisco Falcon
The Medium Murders
The Bluebeard Club
The Tangier Tajine
The French Diplomat Affair (novella)
Haymaker's Last Fight (novelette)

Agatha Aston Series
Black-Eyed Nick
The Witchfinder General Murders
The Christmas Murder Mystery

DI Jellicoe Series
A Time to Kill
The Bus Stop
Trio
Dolce Vita Murders

Danny Shaw / Manfred Brehme WWII Series
The Shadow of War
Crusader
El Alamein

A Time to Kill

Jack Murray

ISBN: 9798509435898
Imprint: Independently published

A Time to Kill

For my mum and dad and Rina. For parents everywhere…

Jack Murray

A Time to Kill

To everything there is a season, and a time to every purpose under the heaven: ... A time to get, and a time to lose; a time to keep, and a time to cast away; A time to rend, and a time to sew; a time to keep silence, and a time to speak; A time to love, and a time to hate; a time of war, and a time of peace.
Ecclesiastes 3:11

We have no right to assume that any physical laws exist, or if they have existed up until now, that they will continue to exist in a similar manner in the future.
Max Planck

A Time to Kill

Prologue

January 1959

It's all just physics; matter that moves in time and space. However, our existence is relational. No man is an island said Donne and it's true. We are atoms that live in relation to other things. That relationship defines us. A mother is a mother only because she's had a child; sadness cannot exist without happiness; a hunter must have its prey; a murderer requires a victim. More than this, each must observe and recognise who they are. But the act of observation makes us a participant. Then it becomes real. We interact and by doing so we leave traces of *our* presence.

It was odd to think about such things while skulking through the shadows. The feeling that he was being hunted overwhelmed him. Yet he knew, at that moment, it was not entirely accurate. In another's reality, he was the hunter. That other person would not know this, of course; at least, they would not know this until the very end. Their final act would be this observation.

He moved forward, collar up, initially towards the front door but then round the side of the building and then the back. The sky was a deathly black. As black as a heart set on murder.

Jack Murray

The window at the back gave way easily. He was inside now and moving through the house. He heard a radio in another room. His heart was beginning to race now. Breathing became shallower. Light-headed, he clutched the table. Sadness enveloped him, not for what he would do but for what had been done already. It emboldened him though, and air began to reach his lungs.

The sounds of the other man were all too human, yet this made his hatred all the greater.

He waited.

His senses were at a pitch now. The clock's ticking deafening.

Then the man came at last. An old man. Stooped like an old man. He grumbled as he moved, like an old man. He reached for the light and missed it. Never mind. He felt his way forward and found what he wanted on the sideboard.

He was still unaware of the other. A movement perhaps, or a sound? And then he saw him. He stopped. Fear in his eyes. His legs turned to stone. The other man came to him. A shaft of light fell across his face.

'Remember me?' asked the man.

A slow shake of the head. Decades of memories as vast in number as the stars in the heavens or grains of sand on a beach or atoms in a body raced around inside his head. Then he knew who it was. He knew why he was here. And he turned away.

The man came at him. Something was in his hand. It was raised over his head now. And it came crashing down.

'Remember me…?'

A Time to Kill

1

9ᵗʰ January 1959

'Not exactly Agatha Christie, is it?'

Detective Inspector Nick Jellicoe swung around to the person speaking. His gaze fell on a rotund male somewhere between fifty and sixty. The man in question had a ruddy face and a beaming smile which seemed somewhat at odds with the grisly scene before them. The look on Jellicoe's face quickly wiped the smile from the other man's face.

'Sir?' said Jellicoe, one eyebrow cocked like a duellist's pistol.

The man shrugged, 'Dead body, in a library. Bloody candlestick.'

Jellicoe knew exactly what his boss had meant.

'You're thinking of that game, sir,' pointed out Jellicoe, coldly.

'Ah yes. Good point, Jellicoe.'

They both turned their attention to the dead body. It was lying face down on the floor, with arms splayed out as if he'd completed an inelegant belly flop in a pool. There was a candlestick by the dead body.

The head was a bloody mess. Jellicoe forced himself to take in the sight of the horrific injury that had been inflicted, almost certainly, by the heavy gilt candlestick. The murder weapon was at least two feet long with a wide, square base that had, at some point in the last six hours or so, met with the skull of the dead man. A single, fatal blow.

Just a single blow. It was not a mad frenzied attack. It felt pre-meditated. Jellicoe logged this away before switching his attention away from the candlestick. He crouched down to get a better look. The body was near the French window, facing away. Jellicoe studied the floor between the man and the window. There was no sign of any footsteps. No such luck that the murderer had stepped in the blood and left convenient footprints. A sixth sense told Jellicoe that Chief Inspector Burnett was more interested in what he was doing than the crime scene itself. He sighed.

'Thoughts?' asked Burnett.

Jellicoe rose up and looked out of the French window.

'Murderer came in through the window and either surprised Colonel Masterson or, at least, was known to him. It could have been spur of the moment, but this feels planned. He knew what he wanted to do. The choice of weapon was, perhaps, the only aspect of this that feels spontaneous. Obviously, we need to know if anything was stolen but everything looks to be in order.'

The two men looked around the library. It was tidier than a spinster's cottage.

Jellicoe continued a moment later, 'He struck the colonel once and left him to die.'

'You don't think he died instantly?' asked Burnett.

'There's a lot of blood.'

There was certainly a lot of blood, like someone had decided to douse a fire on the Persian carpet with red paint.

'What a way to go,' said Burnett. There was sadness in his voice. 'Survives two world wars. Gets beaned in a library by a coward sneaking up behind.'

'Yes, sir,' agreed Jellicoe. He stood back from the dead body to allow a photographer to capture the scene. Someone opened the French window and a blast of icy air rushed in. Burnett glanced up irritably at the new arrival. Jellicoe pulled his Burberry raincoat around him more tightly. The weather had taken a turn for the worse over the hour they'd been at the manor. The snow was falling thick and fast. If this kept up it would become more like an Agatha Christie after all.

The new arrival was younger than Jellicoe by half a dozen years. Detective Sergeant Yates saw the face on Burnett and quickly surmised his arrival had brought with it an ill wind. He quickly shut the window. Jellicoe smiled at this. At least he'd had the wit to realise why Burnett was so irritated. Although this was close to a permanent state.

It was Jellicoe's first week with this police force. The relative tranquillity of the first week had been brutally interrupted by the slaying of Masterson. Perhaps his transfer to 'the sticks' was not going to prove the break it was meant to be.

'Sorry, sir,' said Yates, aware he had incurred the displeasure of the chief inspector. He didn't seem too perturbed though. Jellicoe could see there was cockiness to the young man that might not sit well with an older man like Burnett. He waited to see how Burnett would react.

He didn't. This wasn't entirely a surprise. Although only his first week, it was apparent to him that Burnett was not a martinet. Jellicoe had encountered enough of them at the Met to know what they looked like. Instead, Burnett preferred sarcasm over censure and derision to dressing-downs. Jellicoe, oddly, quite liked him for it.

'Don't worry, son,' said Burnett nodding towards the open window, 'You can carry my coffin at the funeral when I die of hypothermia.'

'Will do, sir.'

'So?' asked Burnett, a hint of impatience was never very far away from his voice. Jellicoe suspected this was put on. A bit of show for the young whippersnappers. Keeps 'em honest, don't you know.

'No sign of forced entry. No footprints in the snow.'

Jellicoe looked out of the window. The wind was blowing snowflakes this way and that. This was a problem. The weather was busily erasing any trace of the murderer's arrival. This was assuming, of course, that he had come through the French windows. Jellicoe had not reached a conclusion on that point yet. Outside, in the distant field, a woman was walking a dog. She wore a headscarf and a dark tweed overcoat. She could have been sixteen or sixty. In this part of the world, dress codes were functional. The opposite was increasingly the case in London. Your dress was your tribe.

A man with grey whiskers appeared in the library, distracting Jellicoe from his reflections on fashion. Jellicoe assumed this was Dr Taylor. Old doctors always had whiskers, or so he'd been told once. The doctor was one of the few people he hadn't met in his first week. A murder scene seemed as good a place as any for introductions to be made.

'Hilary,' said Burnett warmly.

Hilary? Jellicoe supressed a smile. Why do parents do that? Did they hate their child so much that they would impose a name on him that was guaranteed to draw attention? May as well stick a target on his back and print 'bully me' on it. Taylor looked suitably serious.

The doctor shuffled into the library smoking a pipe. He wore a grey homburg which he removed and threw onto a nearby table. He and Burnett could have been brothers. They'd worked alongside one another for decades. Both were of a similar vintage which seemed an appropriate metaphor as Jellicoe suspected a friendship based on alcohol and mutual support against the true enemy, not criminals, but their wives.

'Without rupturing your imagination too much, what do we have here Reg?' asked Dr Taylor, crouching down to study the dead body.

Reg? It all seemed very bowls club to Jellicoe. He could just imagine what his former boss, Detective Superintendent Lane, would have thought of all this. He still remembered the curl of his mouth when he told Jellicoe that a spell away from London would do him good. Help him forget.

Now *there* was a martinet.

'Body was discovered this morning by the maid. I don't think it's suicide.'

Taylor glanced up at Burnett, a ghost of a smile on his face. There was obviously a history of gallows humour here, realised Jellicoe. Once more, Jellicoe found this strangely reassuring. No disrespect was intended. It was a way of dealing with the often-sickening reality, an unimaginable horror that most people never had to face. If the price of this protection was the occasional catharsis granted by humour, then so be it.

A Time to Kill

'No, I suspect death was as a result of this implement,' commented Taylor nodding towards the candlestick. 'We'll do the needful though and confirm this. Don't ask me time of death until you tell me if the French windows were open or not.'

'They were closed when the maid found the body,' said Yates, a little too keenly.

Burnett looked a little relieved at hearing this, which amused Jellicoe. He'd clearly forgotten to ask. Or perhaps he was at a point in his career where he managed cases rather than taking an overtly investigative role.

'If the window was closed then it will have slowed down the process of rigor mortis so we should have a better understanding of when he died. My estimate would be in the last eight hours to twelve hours.'

It was nearly nine in the morning now so the intruder or gang would have come after the staff had gone to bed.

'What time do the staff usually retire?' asked Jellicoe to Yates.

'Around ten or eleven,' came the immediate reply, 'but the colonel would often stay up later. He was listening to the third test in Sydney.'

'How did it finish?' asked Burnett, suddenly animated.

'Two hundred and nineteen all out,' said Taylor sourly. Burnett didn't need to ask if it was Australia or England who'd been batting. 'Benaud took five. Then we dropped McDonald first over.'

Burnett shook his head and muttered an oath under his breath. For the first time since seeing the dead body, Burnett seemed genuinely put out. Such was the importance of cricket.

Jellicoe wondered for a moment if Gilbert and Sullivan had been alive now how they would have written about the life-and-death importance of cricket for Englishmen. As if aware their conversation might be considered somewhat inappropriate by the newcomer, Burnett and Taylor resumed a more professional mien.

'When can you have the body with me?' asked Taylor.

Burnett glanced around. The photographer had just left. He looked at Jellicoe who nodded. Burnett turned to Yates.

'I'll see to it, sir,' said Yates, anticipating the order about to come his direction.

'I'm sure you will,' replied Burnett giving the impression that he was displeased with Yates' efficiency. Yates ignored him; no doubt inured to the chief inspector's permanent state of curmudgeon. Burnett turned to Jellicoe; eyebrow raised. A question hung in the air, or perhaps an order.

'I'll take statements from the staff, sir,' said Jellicoe.

Burnett made a show of rolling his eyes causing Taylor to chuckle.

'Looks like you're not needed here, Reg,' said Taylor.

The four men paused for a moment and looked at one another. There was one thought on each of their minds. The elephant in the room was not lying at their feet. Finally, Burnett asked the question on all their minds.

'There's no sign of the boy, I take it?'

'No, sir,' replied Yates.

'How old is he?' asked Burnett although he knew the answer already.

'Sixteen, sir.'

Burnett nodded and turned to Jellicoe.

'So, Jellicoe, do we think he is a murderer or…?'

10

A Time to Kill

Jellicoe glanced down at the bashed in head of the colonel. The case was barely an hour old and his new boss was publicly putting him on the spot. The new boy from London. From Scotland Yard, no less. Jellicoe could see the look in Burnett's eyes. It was somewhere between curiosity and envy. Curiosity because of his background; he was born to be a policeman. Envy because of his background and, perhaps, youth.

Let's see what you're made of sonny boy.

Jellicoe's mouth shaped into a half-smile; the gauntlet was accepted.

'Kidnapped. The boy's been kidnapped.'

2

Snowflakes fell gently onto Jellicoe, tickling his face. They melted on impact and ran down his face like tears. He put his hat back on. Yates joined Jellicoe at the front door. They watched Chief Inspector Burnett drive off down the long, tree-lined path. He left the questioning of staff to his subordinates and joined Dr Taylor in the car back to the police station.

Jellicoe glanced at Yates. There was a look of disdain on the young detective's face. One look from Jellicoe was enough to wipe away the smug superiority. Jellicoe knew what Yates was thinking for it was on his mind, too. A sense of irritation that the older man had elected to return to the warmth of the station. Perhaps it was just a good example of the art of delegation. Perhaps the older policeman wanted to give his younger subordinates a platform to show what they could do. Or he wanted to organise the search.

Either way, he was relatively happy Burnett wasn't there. He wanted to run this himself anyway. If Yates thought about it too, he'd realise the benefits. Unlike Yates, his desire to run the show stemmed not from ambition or any desire to prove himself. Jellicoe, by dint of his experience in London and more obviously, yet thus far unacknowledged, his birth right, was the natural person to lead this inquiry. After all, how many murders, never mind kidnappings, were there in this part of the world in a given year? Yet he, at thirty, had already handled, and brought to successful conclusions, over a dozen murder cases. Kidnapping was a new one, admittedly.

'Let's start to collect statements. Have you organised the lift of the body?'

'Ambulance is on its way.'

'Good, let's go back inside. I'm freezing.'

As if to underline Jellicoe's point a gust of icy wind whipped against their faces forcing both of them to grab hold of their hats. A rueful smile broke across both their faces.

'That was close,' said Yates.

They stepped in through the double oak doors of the manor house into a large entrance hallway. The black-and-white tiled floor came straight from a Vermeer interior; the walls were wood-panelled but surprisingly free of portraits of the previous occupants. There were some indications that paintings had once adorned the walls, however. It made Jellicoe wonder if they had been sold to pay inheritance taxes or for the upkeep of the estate.

'How big is this estate anyway?' asked Jellicoe as the two men walked into a large sitting room, away from the bustle of the library.

'One thousand acres, give or take.'

'Give or take what?'

'A cricket pitch or two,' said Yates with a grin. Jellicoe gave a half-smile in return. He wasn't sure about Yates. He didn't seem in command of the detail. Or perhaps he was becoming like Burnett, envious of youth and ambition. That had been him once. Yet, here he was, at thirty, transferred to the back arse of nowhere to recharge. Recover. Then return?

Jellicoe no more wanted to return to London than he wanted to be here.

Yates went off to organise a cup of tea and some breakfast. The call to come to the manor house had denied Jellicoe the opportunity to eat anything before now. The landlady at the bed and breakfast had stood at the door urging him to take something. Actually, he was glad to escape. The food was horrible. Fry-ups swimming in grease. Baked beans with a fried tomato. Jellicoe felt his stomach turn somersaults just thinking about it. Maybe he did miss London after all.

Yates returned a few minutes later with a tray containing two teas and a plate of toast. It smelled wonderful. The toast was made from freshly baked bread, as thick as a book by Tolstoy, the butter thicker still.

It was too early to know if Yates was any good, but one thing was abundantly clear already: he had a high estimation of his own abilities. Jellicoe had heard as much in the station. Following the transfer, Jellicoe was his boss now. Previously Yates had reported directly to another DI. A Welshman named Price. Yates had hoped for promotion. Jellicoe sensed some irritation at the new state of affairs. He'd have felt the same way.

'What do we know?'

Yates flipped open his notebook but then barely referenced it as he began to speak.

'I'll start with the boy, Stephen. He's sixteen and the grandson of the dead man. His father, Richard, is on his way over. The boy has been staying with the colonel since before Christmas. He'll be returning to school at Harrow next week.'

'What does the father do?'

'He's army. A major. These things run in families.'

This was met by a frown from Jellicoe. Was Yates making a point to him? Yates realised his *faux pas* or perhaps he was acting. He moved on swiftly.

'The dead man is Colonel Horace Masterson. He's well known in the town. Not quite the squire but close enough. He turned sixty-eight just before Christmas. Both he and the son fought during the war. The dead man finished the war as a colonel. The son was a captain then.'

'Wife?'

'Died two years ago.'

'Did he have other children aside from the army son?'

'No.'

'Does Stephen have any brothers or sisters?' asked Jellicoe.

'One sister. Phillipa. Nineteen.'

He thought about the woman he'd seen out of the window earlier. Draining the rest of the tea, he stood up and said, 'Right, let's get to work. Collect statements from any of the staff you haven't already spoken to.'

'Just the cook, Mrs Parrish. I've spoken with the butler, Fitch, and the housekeeper, Mrs Pickford.'

'Do we know when the major will arrive?'

'He's taking the train out from London. It may be another hour.'

'Very well. Have you spoken to the young woman yet?'

'No, she was quite upset, naturally.'

They separated and Yates headed towards the kitchen while Jellicoe headed back into the library. The door was open, and he walked straight over to the French window. The snow was falling at a forty-five-degree angle, heavily, too. It was already beginning to settle on the ground. There was a risk that they would be cut off at this rate. He saw the detective constable again and motioned him to come over. The constable came in through the French window.

'Yes, sir?'

'Are there any uniformed policemen around?'

The answer was no but they were on their way. Jellicoe nodded. They really were in the sticks. If this had been London, and given the rank of the person murdered, there would have been more policemen available to search the house.

'Very well, looks like it'll have to be you. Have you conducted a search of the house by any chance?'

'Yes, sir. Definitely no sign of the boy.'

'Take a member of staff, the housekeeper maybe, and do another search. They'll have a better idea of potential hiding places.'

'Yes, sir,' replied Wallace. He departed leaving Jellicoe staring out of the window. There was no sign of the young woman. He wondered if she'd gone to look for the boy herself. It seemed like a crazy idea and yet, was it so far-fetched?

Jellicoe walked out into the hallway and found Fitch. The butler looked at Jellicoe over his half-moon glasses.

'You are Fitch?' asked Jellicoe, knowing the answer.

'Yes, sir.'

'Has Miss Masterson returned from her walk?'

'No, sir.'

He needed to speak to her. Another thought occurred to him, a lot more pertinent. Was there a place she knew that her brother might have gone if he hadn't been kidnapped? He glanced down at his brown brogues. They were not ideal for tramping about snow-sludged woods.

A Time to Kill

'I'm sure we have spare boots, sir,' said Fitch, anticipating the next request. Jellicoe smiled and nodded.

'Size nine. I don't suppose you have a jumper I could borrow?'

'It is a little fresh outside,' agreed Fitch. 'Yes, I will find something.'

Fitch went off in search of something for Jellicoe. He returned a few minutes later clutching a pair of blue Hunter Wellington boots and an olive-green army jumper. Jellicoe nodded in thanks and went to change. The boots were a little tight, but he wouldn't need them for long. The jumper was a perfect fit for Jellicoe's lean frame. Donning his mackintosh, he made his way out of the front entrance at the same time as the police photographer.

'When will those be ready?'

'When you get back.'

An ambulance pulled in through the front gate of the estate. They would pick up the body soon. A thought struck Jellicoe and he turned back towards the photographer.

'Was the body officially identified, do you know?'

The photographer shrugged. Jellicoe headed across the front towards the wood where he'd seen the young woman walking with the dog. Snowflakes fluttered drunkenly in the icy breeze. Jellicoe's skin began to burn in the cold. He regretted not asking for a scarf. The ground now had a covering of snow but remained soft underfoot. He trudged forward into the sharp teeth of a stronger wind than he'd originally bargained for. The wood would give him some protection, so he increased his pace.

He reached the wood a couple of minutes later but was quickly disabused of any hope that it would offer a break in the icy tentacles of the wind slashing his face. The longer he stayed out in this hellish cold the more his respect for the young woman increased. It was bitterly cold.

He scanned the wood around him but there was also no sign of her. There is something about temperature, realised Jellicoe. Our patience wears out in direct correlation to the rise and fall of mercury in a thermometer. Not quite a general theory to put before the Nobel Committee, accepted Jellicoe, but it would do for a ghastly Friday morning. His hopes of exploring his new home over the weekend were likely to be dashed. He needed to find a place to rent. Another day in the hideous guest house he'd been given was too awful to contemplate.

'Miss Masterson,' shouted Jellicoe, prompted by an icy blast. He shouted again.

No response.

He went deeper into the wood, unsure of how well sound travelled. Twigs and snow crunched under his feet. There was a narrow path covered with snow. There were even some footsteps still visible. He followed them for as far as he could and then he lost them. Not exactly Davy Crockett, he thought ruefully.

To his left he noticed a drop. He went towards it. Then he saw a rope dangling from a tree with a plank of wood attached to it. He could imagine children using it as a swing during the summer. The drop was not too deep, only ten feet or so and then it levelled out. About fifty yards along it he saw an abandoned crofter style stone cottage. At least he assumed it was abandoned. The was only a hole where the window should have been.

He clambered down the ridge onto the level below and picked his way towards the cottage. It was made from large grey stones with thatch for the roof. It was in a very bad state of repair. There were holes in the roof and the stones had crumbled in some places.

But someone was there.

He could see tendrils of smoke curling upwards through the roof. His heart quickened. He inched forward towards the cottage trying not to make noise. Of course, the more one tries to tread quietly the more conscious we are of the snap and the rustle of feet over twigs and leaves. Utterly deafening thought Jellicoe. His membership of the Cheyenne tribe would certainly be at risk after this. By the time he reached the cottage he reckoned Beethoven would have complained about the noise he was making.

He peeked in through the glassless window. Sitting on an old wooden chair was a young woman. At her feet was a Labrador. To be more precise a snoring Labrador. There was a small fire in the hearth. She turned around and looked at Jellicoe. Clear blue eyes surveyed, assessed, and then dismissed him in space of a few seconds. Jellicoe realised that he seemed somewhat furtive standing with half his body concealed by the wall. He stepped forward so that she could see him better.

'Were you the one shouting?' asked the young woman.

3

Jellicoe stared at the young woman. Her eyes were red but there was a certain amount of defiance in her voice. The Labrador continued snoring. He left the window and walked around the front of the cottage arriving at a doorless doorway. He knocked the side of the wall.

The young woman frowned, then said, 'Come in.'

Jellicoe glanced down at the dog.

'Some guard dog.'

'He's deaf,' offered the young woman by way of explanation. There was a hint of defensiveness in her voice and Jellicoe instantly regretted his comment. It was a bad habit that, at thirty, he needed to grow out of. He nodded and watched as the dog, at last, became aware of his arrival. It opened one sleepy eye and offered a perfunctory growl.

'Are you Miss Masterson?' asked Jellicoe.

This question was met with some degree of surprise by the young woman. This amused Jellicoe. He realised that his voice was not typical of a policeman. She frowned a question which Jellicoe ignored.

'Miss Phillipa Masterson?'

'Yes. Are you a policeman?'

'Yes,' replied Jellicoe, taking one of the other wooden chairs. 'Detective Inspector Jellicoe, Miss Masterson. I'm sorry for your loss.'

She was still wearing her headscarf. It was a plain green and did nothing for her. Jellicoe suspected it was her mother's. At first glance it was clear she was genuinely grieving. Her eyes filled with tears again and she looked away, unwilling to show weakness.

'I need to ask you some questions,' said Jellicoe gently. This was met with a nod, so he pressed on. 'May I ask why you've come here?'

'I needed to get out of the house. Lottie needed a walk.'

Jellicoe stayed silent for a few beats longer than would have been considered comfortable. The implication was clear to the young woman.

'Do you think I'm lying?'

'No. I think you're telling me the truth. You are just not telling me the full truth. Did you come looking for your brother? Did you expect to find him here?'

She glared at Jellicoe. This was plainly what had happened. What was less clear was if she'd expected to find him or not.

'Why did you think he'd be here?' continued Jellicoe in what he hoped was a more sympathetic tone. He pulled his seat forward to be closer to the fire. Lottie the Labrador looked at him and then sank her head down. It was as if she sensed a tragedy had struck the house. A tragedy that she had been unable to prevent. A guard dog who couldn't protect her family. She was in mourning, too.

The young girl was silent for a moment. Whether this was emotion, or she was just trying to find the right words to absolve herself of some blame was unclear. Finally, she spoke, her voice barely a whisper. The tone somewhere between desolation and nostalgia. The gap is often narrower than we think.

'We used to come here. Play here. It was den. A bit like Swallows and Amazons but without the water and the boats.'

Jellicoe said nothing to this. As sure as they were sitting there, freezing, she would fill the silence.

'Then, when we were older, we stopped. It seemed too childish. Well, I didn't come much, anyway. I think Stephen still came here from time to time.'

'Did anyone else join you or your brother?'

'A long time ago. We had a bunch of friends. We'd all meet here. But I haven't seen many of them in years. I don't think Stephen had either.'

'I'll need their names,' said Jellicoe.

'Why? They probably don't even live in the area anymore.'

Jellicoe fixed his eyes on Phillipa and deliberately took a notebook and a pen out of his pocket. Seeing that there was to be no escape from this, Phillipa exhaled.

'Do you have a cigarette?' she asked.

Jellicoe shook his head. He glanced down at the floor of the hut. There were cigarette butts littering the floor. Many were recent.

'The names?'

She pressed her hands together so tightly they turned white.

A Time to Kill

'Sally Ross, Richard Croft and Billy Page. We were the Famous Five. Look, you're not going to start pulling them into a police station or something. They wouldn't have done anything like this.'

The thought of what had happened brought back the tears. Her body shook violently while Jellicoe stared at her, gripping his notebook, unsure of what to do. He hated himself at that moment. He hated this so much: questioning people in the midst of their grief. He knew that they knew he was looking for a lie, the inconsistency of narrative.

He knew what this felt like.

He put the notebook away. Perhaps he'd gone too far already. Rising from the seat he began to look around the interior of the hut. The wooden floor had rotted away, leaving a mixture of flattened earth and rock. There was an old table and some chairs. None of the chairs matched. It was as if the Famous Five had each contributed a chair. In the corner was an empty bottle. He picked it up using a handkerchief and turned it around in his hand. Then he showed it to Phillipa.

'Yours?'

Phillipa's eyes widened and then her brow furrowed. She seemed genuinely shocked to see it. She looked at Jellicoe, denial in her eyes. Jellicoe put the glass on the table and knelt down again. There was broken glass hidden under some leaves. He used a handkerchief to pick up some pieces.

Aside from this makeshift furniture and the bottle, there was nothing else of note in the hut. Jellicoe was unsure of its purpose as a den other than a place where they came and smoked cigarettes. He glanced at Phillipa unsure of whether to comfort her or to leave her be. She was still sobbing quietly.

Finally, he knelt beside her and put his hand over hers. Then he took out another handkerchief, silk this time, and handed it to her. She nodded in thanks.

Lottie the Labrador was, by this stage, aware that Phillipa was in distress. She rose gingerly to her feet and rested her head on her lap. Jellicoe looked at the old dog in wonder. He stroked her head. It was easier to comfort a sad dog than a person. Phillipa became aware of her Labrador and began to stroke her head, too. This seemed to satisfy Lottie. Her job had been done.

'Perhaps we should head back to the…' Jellicoe paused to find the right word. House seemed too small, and mansion felt like he was making a point. He decided on, 'your home. It's snowing rather heavily now.'

Phillipa nodded and rose from her seat. A thought occurred to Jellicoe.

'Is there anything missing here or is there something here that shouldn't be?

'The radio's gone. We had a radio. Music usually. Sometimes those BBC comedy shows. It's gone. The whisky bottle shouldn't be here.'

Jellicoe nodded and noticed some cigar butts on the floor. He knelt down and used his handkerchief to pick them up. There were three. All had been smoked recently in Jellicoe's estimation. He looked up at Phillipa, a question framed in his eyes.

'We never smoked cigars. My grandad does, though. Perhaps Stephen took these from the library. Grandad has a box of them there.'

Jellicoe pocketed the cigars and some of the cigarette butts and looked underneath the table. There was nothing to speak of elsewhere in the hut. He rose up to his full six foot. He towered over the young woman.

'Is there anywhere else that your brother might have gone?'

This question was loaded with so much implication that Jellicoe turned away from the young woman. He didn't want her to see his face. The look of urgency; the hunter.

'I don't know,' replied Phillipa, between sobs.

The answer was frustrating, but Jellicoe felt enough of a bad as it was to push her further. They left the smoky warmth of the hut; Jellicoe kicking earth over the small fire as they went to the doorway. An icy blast through the trees greeted them like a long-lost enemy.

Jellicoe clambered up the hill first and offered his hand to Phillipa. She took it and he helped pull her up. Then they trudged through the forest in silence. Phillipa dabbed her eyes while Jellicoe wondered why she was lying to him. He always assumed this, and he was almost always right. It was depressing. He could never understand the logic of lies. Obviously if you had committed a crime or wanted to save someone from embarrassment then it made sense. As often as not the truth came out. When it did the liar was seen in a harsher light than they might otherwise have experienced had they simply owned up.

Phillipa Masterson was certainly lying.

Thoughts raced through Jellicoe's head as they made their way back to the mansion. She had come to the hut expecting to see her brother. Had the boy really been kidnapped? What did she know about this and about her grandfather's murder? He wondered if he should ask her to view the body. It might jolt the truth out of her. Every part of him rebelled against doing this, yet it was part of the job. A job that he had once been remarkably good at.

The snow was noticeably thicker on the ground now. Jellicoe glanced upwards at the snow falling heavily and wondered if there would be problems returning to the town. The estate was three miles outside of town and the thought of driving through the snow was not an enticing prospect.

Lottie was noticing the cold, too. She began straining at the leash to get back inside, pulling the slight figure of Phillipa Masterson back towards the house. She began to whimper. At first Jellicoe thought it was the cold. Then he realised it was something else.

The body of Colonel Masterson was being loaded onto the ambulance. He heard a gasp from his granddaughter. She stopped in her tracks and knelt down to comfort Lottie. Or was it the other way round? They were now ten yards from the ambulance. Jellicoe strode forward and met DS Yates standing by. The young policeman glanced at Phillipa Masterson.

'Miss Masterson?'

'Yes,' answered Jellicoe on her behalf. He turned towards the young woman and then back to Yates. 'Have you spoken with the other staff?'

'Yes. There are only three of them. Have you seen DC Wallace, sir? He should be here.'

Jellicoe shook his head and motioned with his head towards the house.

'I asked him to conduct another search, this time with a member of the staff.'

A Time to Kill

Yates turned his attention to the young woman. She was kneeling with the dog, looking at the ambulance preparing to depart.

'She was looking for her brother,' said Jellicoe in answer to the unasked question. He was happy when Yates did not ask if they'd found anything. He wasn't ready to share his thoughts on what she wasn't saying. The truthful lies. What she was omitting to say. What she was supressing.

Phillipa Masterson's face was hidden behind the Labrador. It was as if she couldn't bring herself to look at the body being taken away. She only looked up as the ambulance drove off. Then she stood up and marched in the direction of the house. Her red-rimmed eyes filled with tears; her body seemed to shrink beneath the weight of her sadness. The sight of such desolation reached through to Jellicoe. He thought he'd lost that capacity to feel empathy. He was wrong. It was still there. He wasn't sure if this made him happy or sad.

They followed the young woman inside through the large double doorway and watched Phillipa run upstairs to her room. DC Wallace met them in the entrance hall. He was with the housekeeper, Mrs Pickford.

The housekeeper was around sixty years of age. She was a war widow who'd never remarried. Her eyes showed signs of grief, but this was someone who had spent close to a quarter of her life in a state of sorrow. It was yet another burden to be faced. Wallace answered the question in Jellicoe's eyes.

'No sign, sir. Mrs Pickford took me to all of the places the young man would have used in the past when they played hide and seek.'

Jellicoe doubted that Mrs Pickford knew half of them. He would have to check with Phillipa Masterson on that. She would know.

'Thank you, Mrs Pickford,' said Jellicoe. He indicated the stairs where they'd seen the young woman disappear. 'Perhaps you should organise a cup of tea for her.'

A grim smile appeared on the housekeeper's face. When she replied, Jellicoe was, unaccountably, surprised to find out she was Scottish.

'Miss Masterson is not really a tea drinker. She prefers coffee.'

This was said with enough disapproval to make Jellicoe think that Mrs Pickford would have made a fine head mistress at a girls' school. The idea that tea could be usurped by a faddish American drink seemed to signify to Mrs Pickford everything she suspected about the decline of Britain since Suez.

Jellicoe was momentarily amused by the evident annoyance of the housekeeper but decided it was not worth adding anything to what he'd suggested.

'Mrs Pickford, are there any other ancillary staff? For example, who looks after the estate? Who maintains the grounds? Was the colonel a landlord to any tenants on the estate?'

'Things have changed,' said Mrs Pickford, who had now cast aside any attempt to hide disapprobation about the state of the modern world. Jellicoe noted the arms folding across her ample bosom, her lips pursing.

'Meaning?' asked Jellicoe, fixing his eyes on the housekeeper. For a moment, the intensity of Jellicoe's stare upset Mrs Pickford's complacent discontent at the idea of change. However, she soon regained her sure-footed distrust of all things modern which, at that moment, encompassed insolent young policemen.

'Meaning that we, that is the colonel, had had to sell off much of the land to pay inheritance taxes. We only have a handful of tenants. All of them have been with the estate since long before I arrived and that was twenty years ago. One of the tenants, Mr Gilbert, is a groundsman. We haven't had an estate manager since Mr Mackenzie passed away in 1947. By then there was hardly any estate, that could be so named, to manage. The colonel kept him on because of his age and service.'

As she said this, the memory of the man who'd lost his life so violently overcame her. She began to sob. Yates looked at Jellicoe either in desperation or expectantly. Jellicoe had nothing to offer her. Instead, he studied her, trying to decide if the tears were for a man she had admired or fear at yet another sign of a world that would just not stop changing. In the end, he settled on genuine grief for a man she had venerated. But that would have to be proven. There was no reason for them to discount her as a possible suspect in the murder quite yet.

'Can you supply us with names and addresses of these tenants, Mrs Pickford?'

The housekeeper nodded curtly.

'Sergeant Yates, can you go with Mrs Pickford and get the names. Then go and speak to them. Get their statements.'

Jellicoe could have done without the 'what-are-you-going-to-do?' look from Yates but he ignored it. He turned away and made his way up the stairs. As he did so he cast his eyes out at the blanket of white that had formed on the estate lawn outside. He passed Fitch on the way up.

'In which room will I find Miss Masterson?'

'Second on the left, sir.'

Jellicoe thanked him and continued up the stairs stopping for a moment to admire a de Laszlo portrait of a soldier. He guessed this was the colonel. The uniform seemed to be from the Great War. Moments later he was outside the room. He knocked.

'Yes?'

'Miss Masterson, it's Detective Inspector Jellicoe. I have just a couple more questions.'

'One moment.'

One moment from a woman can often turn out to be many minutes in the life of a man. He was used to how men and women very often had a different conceptions of time. His wife had been the same. The door opened at last. Phillipa Masterson peeked her head out to check who was there. Seeing Jellicoe, she opened it fully and invited him in.

It was Jellicoe's turn to feel awkward. The young woman was dressed in a bathrobe. 'I asked Fitch to run me a bath,' she said by way of explanation.'

'I see,' said Jellicoe trying his best to keep his eyes fixed on hers. He saw a photograph of the family sitting on her dressing table. He turned his attention to it. The framed photograph was just in front of the mirror. This positioning offered little or no protection from seeing Phillipa in her silk dressing gown. This was becoming intensely uncomfortable for the detective. He sensed that Phillipa knew he was looking at her. He picked up the photograph and studied it. There were five people in the photograph: Phillipa and her brother along with her father, mother, and the murdered colonel.

'That was taken two years ago,' said Phillipa, who was now sitting on the bed. Stephen Masterson was fair-haired and seemed like a son to be proud of. He gazed at the camera, his smile was warm and genuine. It had been difficult to see what Phillipa looked like under the headscarf and with the teary eyes. Since arriving in the bedroom, he'd studiously avoided looking at her, fearful of being seen. It was clear from the photograph, notwithstanding her unwillingness to smile, that she was attractive and knew it. The two children seemed to take after their mother who was fair-haired, blue-eyed, and clearly effortlessly elegant.

Alive, the dead colonel was every inch a military man; from the cut of his hair to the trim of his moustache he was an officer. Richard Masterson seemed like a younger version of the man. The likeness of the two men, their stiffness, their detached superiority felt like they were playing a role. This was probably a requirement of being an army officer.

'What are you thinking?' asked Phillipa. Then she added a moment later, 'Or am I not meant to ask?' There was an almost kittenish purr to the question that was as unmistakable as it was surprising given the circumstances.

Jellicoe turned to answer her. Her state of dress was still alarmingly less than he would have liked. Flustered, he looked away, just catching the hint of a smile on the young woman's lips. This would not do. He was clearly in a difficult situation. A strategic withdrawal was called for before he lost all credibility.

'I should leave you until you're ready,' said Jellicoe, keeping his eyes fixed on the falling snow outside. 'I'd like to question you further though if I may.'

'You may.'

It was there again. The purring sound of a beautiful young woman playing with the lesser-spotted mortified English male. Beads of sweat formed on his forehead and he felt his throat tighten. He tried to keep his eyes away from her but was aware she was sitting on the bed, shrunken, sadly beautiful and untouchable. It was a combination that made him feel utterly impotent. He escaped through the door, running into Mrs Pickford.

The housekeeper took one look at the detective and read him like the Bible she knew by heart. Her lips pursed again but there was something else in her eyes. She was laughing at him.

'I think she's ready for her bath,' said Jellicoe as calmly as he could.

Under the circumstances, this was probably not the most appropriate comment to have made if he was wishing to maintain some degree of standing. It met with the fate it deserved. Mrs Pickford raised an eyebrow. This was enough to send Jellicoe scuttling off downstairs screaming silently at a world that was laughing at him.

4

Jellicoe tore down the stairs like he was escaping Beelzebub himself. He passed Fitch who looked at him rather strangely. Another good impression formed, thought Jellicoe grimly. He wanted nothing more than to be away from the house now. The front door opened as he reached the foot of the stairs, bringing with it a welcome chill and the sight of snow falling.

'Damn,' snarled Jellicoe, not caring who heard him. As it transpired only Wallace did. He'd just entered, almost banging into Jellicoe as he did so. The young DC was worried he'd done something wrong. Jellicoe shook his head and pointed at the door.

'What's it like out there?'

'Hellish,' replied Wallace, in a relieved voice.

'Come with me,' said Jellicoe. He headed towards the library.

The room was now empty. This was a surprise. Where was the man from the Fingerprinting Department? Then he remembered the snow. He turned to Wallace and said, 'No one can come in here. While we're waiting for the fingerprints to be collected, take a look around. Don't touch anything obviously.'

'Is there anything I should be looking for, sir?'

'Can I ask you a question, Wallace?' Jellicoe pressed on without waiting for an answer. 'Do you want to be a detective?'

'Yes, sir. It's always been my ambition to be a detective. My grandfather was a policeman all his life.'

'Mine too,' replied Jellicoe with a half-smile. He might have added his father as well. Then he turned his attention to the room. 'Look around the room for any sign of the intruder, if it was an intruder that is. You have two lenses to use, Wallace. The first is to look for something that may have been left behind by the murderer. Do this without any preconceptions. Look closely at everything, should it be there? The second lens is to think about afterwards. Is there something that was not there that should have been?'

'The staff said there was nothing stolen.'

'That's not what I meant,' replied Jellicoe. 'I mean something in the wrong place. It doesn't matter how small or seemingly immaterial.'

Wallace nodded. The brief was clear and simple, its execution nigh on impossible in the young man's view. But he would do his best.

'I'll be back in a minute,' announced Jellicoe. He went out into the corridor in search of a telephone. He remembered seeing one near the foot of the stairs. He picked up the phone and dialled a number. A minute later he was speaking to a police sergeant at the station.

'It's Detective Inspector Jellicoe. I'm at the Masterson house.'

'Yes, sir,' replied the sergeant. 'How can I help?'

'Is someone coming here from the Fingerprint Department?'

A Time to Kill

'Yes, sir. He left twenty minutes ago. Probably the snow.'

Jellicoe thanked the sergeant and returned to the library to find Wallace on his hands and knees. All he needed was a magnifying glass; he couldn't have looked any more like a fictional detective.

'Seen something?' asked Jellicoe, genuinely curious.

'Yes sir. Some soil. You can barely see it but definitely there.'

Jellicoe joined him on the floor by the window. There was a blood stain on the carpet but, next to it there were unmistakable signs of someone who could only have come in from the outside.

'Very good, Wallace. What do you conclude from this?' asked Jellicoe.

'Well, I think someone came in from the outside through the French windows. I think they may have tried to tidy things up a bit. However, because they only had light from the table lamp, they probably missed some of the smaller bits of soil.'

Jellicoe nodded. This was his thought, too. It led to another thought, though. Who had opened the French windows? Was it the colonel inviting someone in that he knew or had the windows not been locked in the first place? This was not to discount the possibility that the intruder had access to keys or, and this stretched credibility for Jellicoe, they had come from the inside but were trying to make it look like an outsider. Try as he might, he had pretty much discounted the staff of being either capable or, indeed, motivated to murder the colonel. And even if one of them had, what happened to the boy?

'Why take the boy?' murmured Jellicoe to himself.

'Perhaps he witnessed the murder,' suggested Wallace. 'Perhaps he was the murderer.' The young detective constable's tone of voice suggested he didn't believe this himself.

Their musings were interrupted by the arrival of man who Jellicoe vaguely remembered being introduced to on his first day. The new arrival was called Vaughan. Patches on the arms of his Harris Tweed jacket and a certain distractedness lent him the air of a maths teacher at a Grammar school.

'Hello, sir, sorry I'm late. Tricky going out there now. I wouldn't advise staying too much longer or you'll be stuck.'

Jellicoe had been wondering as much himself. He was keen to get back to the police station.

'You should make a start then. We'll get out of your way.' Reaching into his pocket he took out the handkerchief holding the glass, cigar, and cigarette butts as well as the whisky bottle. 'I found these in a den outside. Not sure if you can get prints from them. Can you try? Check the cigar box in the library, too. I think they may have nicked a few cigars from it.'

'Will do. Are there many staff?'

'Just the three. There is a granddaughter here, too,' replied Jellicoe. He turned to Wallace. 'Have you taken prints before?'

A half-smile and a nod confirmed he had.

'Vaughan, would you be happy if Wallace here fingerprinted the staff and Miss Masterson?'

'Good idea. It'll save time.'

Vaughan took some cards and the inkpad for stamping fingers and gave them to Wallace. The two men left Vaughan to his job. Fitch was suspiciously near the door when they came out, but Jellicoe couldn't care less if he'd been listening. At least it would save explanations.

'DC Wallace needs to take elimination fingerprints from you and the rest of the staff. Wallace, when you've finished with the staff can you do the same with the tenants? You're about the same size as me. I'm sure Mr Fitch can lend you the wellington boots he gave me.'

Wallace, escorted by Fitch, headed towards the stairs leading down to the servants' quarters and kitchen. Jellicoe watched them before going to the drawing room. He'd not yet looked around the other parts of the house. He wasn't sure what he was looking for, which suited him as it ensured he'd have an open mind. It was often a mistake to look specifically for one thing when in doing so you might miss something previously unconsidered that might be more important.

The drawing room was large with a fireplace that was bigger than his flat in London. There was a large equestrian scene above it painted by Munnings. In front of the fireplace were two large settees and a coffee table. The room looked as if it had been unused in the last day or two. The windows were locked, and it was spotlessly tidy.

The dining room proved to be a similar story. It had clearly been cleared up on the previous evening. No one would have been in here save for those who had searched for the boy.

Towards the back of the house was the games room. It seemed like something from the Raj. Trophies adorned the walls in the form of animal heads that Jellicoe judged would have looked better on the animal than on a wall. The room was full of black and white photographs showing the colonel as a young man in India. The centre of the room was dominated by a billiard table. There was nothing to suggest anyone had been in the room overnight.

One photograph sitting on the mantlepiece attracted his attention. It had been taken in North Africa. The date read Cairo, April 1942. It was quite wide and showed a regiment. The men were lined up in three rows with the officers sitting, as ever, at the front. All military policemen. Jellicoe recognised the son of Masterson sitting in the front row alongside the regiment colonel. He scanned it for a minute or two. The men were squinting into the sun. He set down the photograph and returned to stalking the room like a hunter. The prey was proving illusive.

He left the room and returned to the hallway in time to see Wallace leaving. There was a grandfather clock near the stairs. The time was just after midday. He checked his watch. The clock kept good time. He knocked on the library door and on hearing a response entered. Vaughan was finishing up by the window. It looked as if the desk had been dusted.

'Many prints?'

'Yes, some good ones. I'll be another hour probably.'

'I'll see if I can get some sandwiches sent up.'

He wondered if Phillipa Masterson had finished her bath yet. He certainly wasn't about to check for himself. If she was anything like his wife then it could be an hour or more. Frustration was building. He felt he should be at the station helping coordinate the search for the boy. Hopefully Burnett had this in hand. All he could do here was develop a timetable of events; make background checks on the staff, and tenants; then wait for either a ransom note or some news of the boy.

A Time to Kill

The colonel's son was due in soon. Weather permitting. Jellicoe gripped the chair tightly and stared out of the window. The snow was going to get in their way, no question. He could feel its icy tentacles encircling them all, slowly squeezing the life out of their chances of bringing about a swift conclusion.

Of course, the press would soon hear of the murder. At first it would be the locals and then the nationals. As soon as it became apparent there was a kidnapping, they would descend like vultures. Not least because it was him on the case.

After fulfilling his promise to rustle up sandwiches for Vaughan and himself, Jellicoe sent word via Mrs Pickford to Phillipa Masterson that he would see her in the drawing room. The message, of course, served two purposes; the chief one being to hurry the young lady along.

It was nearing one o'clock before she appeared. Despite wearing a shapeless woollen jumper and a tweed skirt, it was difficult to see anything other than a frightened child. She sat down opposite Jellicoe. The eyes retained their reddened sadness.

'Thank you for seeing me again. I appreciate this is tremendously difficult.'

Phillipa fixed her eyes directly on him. He found this disconcerting and once more wished to be away from the house. Perhaps he'd come back to work too soon. Being around the grief of others was hardly going to help him.

'Are you married, Inspector Jellicoe?'

Whatever he thought she was going to say, this probably ranked somewhere near the bottom. His face coloured. For a moment she was amused by this but then she saw something else. Pain.

'I was, Miss Masterson.'

Her mouth fell open and it was as if she recognised something. A news item, perhaps. Her throat tightened. Jellicoe could see recognition filter into her eyes swiftly followed by guilt.

'I'm so sorry. I don't know what I was thinking. Forgive me.'

Jellicoe shook his head as if it was nothing. He wanted to move on. Outside there was a commotion in the entrance hallway. He tried to ignore it.

'Miss Masterson, we must expect at some point today the possibility that the kidnapper will get in touch with us about Stephen.'

The door to the drawing room opened. Phillipa's glanced at the door, her eyes filled with tears. Jellicoe kept his attention on the young woman as she finally confessed the truth.

'Stephen wasn't kidnapped.'

A Time to Kill

5

12 hours earlier:

Stephen Masterson lay in bed reading Dr No by Ian Fleming. He loved the James Bond books, although his father was less enamoured. Thankfully, he was always able to catch up when he came to his grandfather's house. He'd spirited this copy away from the library a few days ago.

It was nearing ten in the evening. He lay on top of the bed, fully dressed save for his boots. The sign came, as arranged, at ten thirty. He heard a rattle at the window; the sound of small stones thrown with unerring accuracy. He was on the second floor and his window was quite small. He set the book down and skipped over to the window. Down below, on the lawn, was a young man. He saw Stephen and waved up to him. Stephen gave a thumbs up.

A minute later he was on the landing outside his bedroom, clutching his coat and wellington boots. The coast was clear. He padded down the stairs and headed directly to the library. He could hear the sound of the radio in the drawing room. His grandfather was listening to the preamble leading up to the third test against Australia. Stephen stopped by the door. The rich Hampshire accent of John Arlott filled the room.

41

Jack Murray

Stephen detested cricket, or so he'd convinced himself. Sixteen-year-old boys develop firmness of prejudice and principle that can sometimes last as long as an ice cream in summer. He left the door and darted over to the library. The staff were in bed now. He would not have been observed.

He made for the French windows. Standing outside was the young man who he'd seen earlier. He was clad in an overcoat, scarf, hat, and boots. He stamped his feet and beat his arms on his chest. Stephen opened the door and the young man stepped in.

'Freezing out there.'

'Snow,' said Stephen.

The young man looked around the library and whistled. He'd like to have spent more time in a room like this. A different world.

'What's in there?' asked the young man, pointing to a box on the table by the window. The young man was taller than Stephen but very slight. He seemed underfed. His voice lacked the refinement that Stephen was usually surrounded by at school and at home.

'My grandad's cigars. Cuban.'

'Bloody hell,' grinned the young man. 'D'ya think he'd miss a few?'

Stephen wasn't sure but to back down now was only marginally more appealing than admitting he was feeling decidedly uncertain about this adventure. 'Only a couple, mind,' added the young man, trying to press the case.

Stephen nodded and opened the box. The young man reached into the box and grabbed three cigars. Another stab of worry. This was becoming a worse idea by the second. He said nothing. They went out through the French windows.

A Time to Kill

'You'd better leave it open for when you return,' said the young man.

Stephen nodded. It was so cold it felt like his eyes would freeze. He let out a string of oaths which made his friend grin. Stephen reddened then smiled, too. It was ridiculous but, oddly, he felt more relaxed now.

'Snow coming, all right,' said Stephen looking up at the starless black shroud overhead. They made their way across the lawn towards the copse.

'Yes, a bit parky. Come on.'

Unseen by them was a figure at the window of an upstairs room looking down.

-

Phillipa Masterson had heard her brother in the corridor. Unable to sleep, she switched on the light and picked up the book on her bedside table. She'd bought 'Venetia' by Georgette Heyer in town, earlier that week. It was the story of a young girl growing up in the country with an over-protective father and a brother.

After a few minutes she heard the voices outside. Setting down the book, she went over to the window. Despite the lack of light, she could see her brother and his friend walking across the lawn towards the wood. She shook her head and thought, for the thirtieth time that day, of what an idiot her brother was.

She wasn't particularly keen on his friend. He looked at her sometimes in a manner she didn't like. Oddly, it wasn't in the way she'd become used to. Most young men were transparent. She knew what they were thinking and, despite herself, she enjoyed the attention. Mostly she would ignore them but sometimes the men in question were a little too old to be doing this. Or, in the case of Stephen's friend, simply the wrong *sort*. He was different. It wasn't just a question of class, although she acknowledged that was part of it. It was something more unsettling. He seemed to be assessing her but in a different way from the other boys.

She smiled at her own haughtiness. Perhaps she was reading a too much Georgette Heyer and not enough John Braine or Alan Silletoe. Not that she'd be allowed. She could just imagine the kerfuffle that would ensue if grandfather caught her with a novel from one of the 'Angry Young Men'. She'd tried, of course. What self-respecting young woman wouldn't. The library had been out of their books and the reservation list went beyond the school holidays.

Perhaps one of the girls at the school would smuggle in one of their books. There was usually contraband like this floating around. She'd finally read *Lolita* during the previous term. There'd been a long queue for that one.

She returned to the bed and switched out the light. If Stephen wanted to be out on a night like this then more fool him. They'd probably just go down to the hut for a smoke like they usually did. Like she did, sometimes.

-

'Ever smoked a cigar?'

'No,' replied Stephen after a few moments. He'd thought about saying yes but quickly realised the humiliation of not doing it properly outweighed the risk of seeming inexperienced and young in the eyes of his friend.

'Me neither,' admitted his friend.

Stephen felt relieved at hearing this and glad he'd decided to be honest. Perhaps it really was the best policy as his grandfather always said. Perhaps everyone wasn't laughing at him. Phillipa was usually the one to tell him this. She said no one cares about you. They're only thinking of themselves. Don't try to be something you're not.

Easy for her to say. It was different for girls. Different for her. Soon she'd have boys, young men, even old men chasing her, and she wouldn't have to lift a finger for it to happen. It was different for him. The world had different expectations. His father had different expectations. He had to be strong. The first step in being strong was the pretence that you were. He'd worked that out a long time ago. School's biggest lesson wasn't something taught in class, it was what you learned outside the safety of the classroom. Yes, pretence was everything. Don't let anyone see what was behind the mask. Even James Bond was scared sometimes.

If not quite scared, Stephen was feeling distinctly uneasy as they picked their way through the wood towards the hut. The ground underfoot was semi-liquid. Rotting leaves and mud formed a sludge that made their boots squelch as they walked. The chill had infiltrated his clothing, bringing up goosebumps. Or was it anxiety? Quite why he'd agreed to this was as unfathomable to him as it was regrettable. Would Ben really have cared if he'd said no? He looked at Ben and said, 'Nearly there. Do you want to smoke the cigars?'

'Damn right I do,' replied Ben with a grin.

Stephen smiled and thought about when he'd first met Ben a week and a half earlier. It was strange to think that back then, before Christmas, the two of them had been so close to fighting. Such was the way with boys, he supposed. He'd found Ben in the woods, their woods, and demanded to know what he thought he was doing. Public school and wealth lend a certain peremptoriness to things you say that sound normal in the halls of a school or with servants. Somehow with rough boys they are decidedly a great deal riskier.

He'd seen a look of anger flash in Ben's eyes but, thankfully, he'd backed down. Stephen was honest enough to acknowledge this was less to do with fear than it was his essential good nature. Ben was a couple of years older and had a harder edge. If push had escalated to shove then Stephen doubted, he'd have stood much of a chance.

Ben had offered him a cigarette. The pipe of peace had sealed their friendship. Over the Christmas holidays they'd met regularly for a conspiratorial smoke. Phillipa joined them sometimes. They even went into town to meet him.

Ben treated his sister well. It was strange that even rough boys understood that sisters were out of bounds. They all would have a smoke in the hut and walk down to the brook. Phillipa was as uninterested in Ben as he was in her, so she rarely stayed long. If anything, she seemed relieved that Stephen had some company.

'Here we are,' said Ben marching through the doorway.

Stephen walked in. It was then he realised that this adventure was really something he shouldn't have embarked upon. There was a man sitting on one of the chairs.

'Who are you?' demanded Stephen hoping to hell the fear in his voice wasn't as evident to them as it was to him.

'This is Sol,' explained Ben taking the cigars out of his pocket and handing one to the man.

6

Major Richard Masterson strode into the room like The Duke of Wellington on the eve of battle. He glared at Jellicoe for a moment, making a point of sizing him up, being seen to size him up, impressing upon the policeman who was in charge. Jellicoe read all of this on his face in an instant and then had to choke back a smile when Masterson asked, 'Who is in charge here?'

You, by the sound of it, thought Jellicoe. He rose from his seat and walked towards the major. Phillipa Masterson's father was as tall as Jellicoe, in his forties with fair hair receding slightly at the temples. Were it not for the seriousness of the situation, Jellicoe would have been amused by the pencil-slim moustached decorating his upper lip like a painted eyebrow.

'Are you Major Masterson?'

'Of course, I'm Major Masterson,' said the new arrival in a voice that was several decibels above what was necessary given their proximity. 'Who the bloody hell else would I be?'

Jellicoe nodded, keeping his eyes steadily on Masterson.

'Chief Inspector Burnett has returned to the police station. I am Detective Inspector Jellicoe. I'm taking statements along with a few of my men.'

'Why isn't he here?' The voice was loud and deliberately provoking. It was clear Masterson was ready to explode and Jellicoe was likely to be caught in the blast.

Jellicoe sighed and reminded himself the man had just lost his father. Shock and anger were inevitable, although he'd reached the latter rather more quickly than normal.

'We had reason to believe that your son had been kidnapped. The chief inspector left me to handle the initial inquiries on the murder while he coordinated the efforts of the police in the county and beyond in the search for your son.'

Masterson paused for a moment to take in what had been said. This made sense and Jellicoe saw the anger slowly dissipate to be replaced by fear and grief. He finally realised his daughter was in the room. He strode over to her and they hugged one another tightly.

'Thank God you're all right. Your mother and I have been at our wit's end.'

Phillipa buried her head into her father's chest and sobbed. Jellicoe stood looking at them feeling useless. He turned to Fitch and asked the only question that could be decently asked in such trying circumstances.

'Can you arrange some tea?'

-

Jellicoe went outside to give the father and daughter some privacy. The last thing both would want at that moment was the presence of a policeman intruding on their grief. The anger and resentment at his presence was natural. It would eventually give way to gratitude and hope. Then, depending on how things went, other emotions would intrude: fear, anger, desolation.

A Time to Kill

The snow had stopped falling which was a blessed relief. The sun peeked out from behind the gun-metal clouds. The carpet of snow was thick on the ground ribboning the trees on the estate. It had settled on the road but had compacted making it drivable if not particularly safe. Jellicoe stared at it and felt a flutter of concern at the prospect of their journey back.

The return of DS Yates and DC Wallace distracted him. They were making their way across the lawn from cottages a quarter of a mile away. It hadn't taken long for the interviews to be conducted. He turned back towards the house and glanced up at the icicles hanging from the guttering like glass on a washing line. A pearly cloud of vapour surrounded him as he exhaled the cold air.

He went back inside just in time to see Fitch bring tea into the drawing room. He would give them few more minutes, then he would have to interrupt them and find out an answer to the question screaming inside his head.

What exactly had happened to Stephen Masterson?

For a few minutes he spoke with one of the constables assigned to stay at the house and then he knocked on the door of the drawing room. Pausing for a moment, he entered without waiting to be asked. Father and daughter were sitting on? the settee. If anything, it seemed as if it was Phillipa who was comforting her father. His eyes blurred with tears and anger.

'Do you mind, Inspector? I've just lost my father and my son is missing. It's not as if we are suspects.'

'No, sir. And I am sorry for your loss. However, I do need to ask your daughter some questions. It won't take long.'

Masterson could hardly show anger at the policeman who was obviously doing his job and who displayed such a degree of sympathy. He nodded curtly. Jellicoe turned his attention to Phillipa Masterson.

'Miss Masterson, you were on the point of telling me that your brother hadn't been kidnapped.'

'What?' exclaimed Richard Masterson, staring at Jellicoe before jerking his head towards his daughter. 'Is this true?'

Phillipa nodded her head. Tears welled up in her eyes and she gripped her father's hand. Masterson's brow furrowed deeply. To Jellicoe's eyes, he appeared fearful. Of course, why wouldn't he? But was there something else?

'I saw him. He was with that boy Ben.'

'What boy Ben?' asked the two men in unison.

'I don't know. He said his name was Ben. He's from the town.'

'Do you know where?'

'No,' admitted Phillipa. 'That's what he told us. We never asked.'

'How did you meet him?' pressed Jellicoe.

'Stephen came across him in the woods down at the hut I showed you, Inspector. I think the boy was surprised but didn't seem a bad sort. They began to meet up. I met him, too.'

'Can you describe him?' asked Jellicoe.

'About Stephen's height and build. Dark hair. Not well-spoken but not stupid either. He was a year or two older than Stephen. I didn't have much to do with them to be honest. I don't know much about him. They seemed to get on well and it was company, I suppose.'

'What happened last night?'

A Time to Kill

'I saw the two of them heading off to the woods around ten, maybe closer to ten thirty now that I think of it. I was surprised but it was too cold to run out and stop him.' Phillipa began to cry at this point. 'It's my fault. I should have stopped him going. Why did he go?'

Why indeed thought the two men. Masterson held his daughter's hand and tried to reassure her that she'd done nothing wrong. Men said such things but never really meant them. If anything, it was to stop themselves saying something that would inflame the situation further. This was probably not the moment to point that out that she really should have stopped him.

'Why would he have gone with this young man?' asked Jellicoe gently.

'I don't know. He's never done it before.'

Jellicoe thought of the cigar butts. 'Was there anyone else with them?' he asked.

'No. It was just the two of them. They were walking across the lawn.'

'You don't think Stephen was being taken against his will.'

Phillipa shook her head before dissolving into tears again.

'Inspector is all this really necessary?' snapped Masterson.

'One more question, Miss Masterson. Where were they coming from? At the house I mean.'

Phillipa Masterson looked up from behind her hands. She stared in horror at Jellicoe. Her head began to shake, and her mouth formed the word no, but she couldn't speak. Perhaps it was fear of implicitly accusing her brother of murder. Masterson's felt no such obligation to be quiet.

'What are you implying, Inspector?' he snarled, teeth bared liked an animal fighting for its life.

Jellicoe looked at Masterson and said quietly, 'I am implying nothing. Your father was alive after ten thirty. We know this because Mr Fitch saw him. However, if the two boys exited from the library, then it's possible that someone else may have entered via the French windows and committed the murder after this. Can you inspect your father's papers and safe, Major Masterson? We need to understand the motive. For example, was it robbery? Or perhaps, notwithstanding what Miss Masterson has told us, is this a kidnapping case which accidentally resulted in a murder?'

Phillipa's hands were gripped knuckle white. Her fingers intersected with one another and she twisted them so much that even Jellicoe could feel her pain. Finally, she spoke. It was barely a whisper.

'It looked like they were coming from the library. My room is directly above it.'

'Can you tell me more about why Stephen formed such a close friendship with this boy?'

'He's not really a boy. He seems older than Stephen. We love, loved, being down here with grandad. But sometimes it's nice to be with people your own age. I think Stephen and Ben got on because they like the same music and shows on the radio.'

Jellicoe looked up from his notepad. He'd been scribbling things down as Phillipa spoke.

'Not that bloody *Beyond Our Ken*,' said Major Masterson.

Jellicoe glanced at Phillipa for confirmation.

'Yes, they both loved the show and *The Goons*. They'd start talking like the characters. They have their own language.'

A Time to Kill

'Polish,' said Masterson. 'All a bit queer if you ask me.'

'Polari,' replied Jellicoe. His eyes were now fixed on Phillipa; however, she was resolutely not looking back at the detective. Jellicoe wondered if *Beyond Our Ken* was on BBC radio that evening. He'd listened to it before. It was amusing after a fashion. A *particular* fashion if his memory served. More food for thought on Stephen.

'Did Ben say what he did?'

Phillipa thought for a moment and then replied, 'He didn't say exactly. I think he had his own business. He talked about having a few regular clients. He said that he did odd jobs for them.'

"I see,' said Jellicoe. He saw all too clearly but stopped himself from racing too far ahead without evidence. 'How was he when he said this?'

'How do you mean?' asked Masterson, affronted at such a tangential question. It seemed to him to be irrelevant. In fact, too many of the questions seemed to him to be a waste of time. The police should be out looking for his boy. He would say as much to the Superintendent when he saw him.

Jellicoe ignored the major and kept his attention fixed on Phillipa. This further enraged the army man who was on the point of speaking when Phillipa replied, 'He just laughed. It all seemed a bit of a joke. Then he talked of something else. Ben was a very chatty type of person. Gossipy. He changed subjects quite quickly. A bit like a butterfly flitting from leaf to leaf.'

Masterson's patience finally snapped.

'Look here, Jellicoe, why are you asking all these damn questions. You're not going to find my boy sitting in here asking what type of person this friend of his is. Shouldn't you be out looking for Stephen and finding my father's killer? I was a military policeman during the war. I know a little bit about this.'

The major's face was turning red with anger as he glared at the object of his contempt. Jellicoe stared back at Masterson but kept his voice even and calm.

'At the moment we don't not know if we are dealing with one person or more than one. They may be working together or separately. You may wish to consider this, major. If we are not dealing with two people, then it means Stephen is directly implicated in his grandfather's death. Two people at least gives us the possibility that Stephen was unaware of what took place after he left. I have to investigate both possibilities.'

'I hope you're not suggesting that Stephen was working with these people.' This was almost a snarl. The major was like a cornered animal. All Jellicoe could think was what a useless military policeman he must have been. He paused for a moment unsure of how much to reveal to the major. In the end he remembered how he'd felt when it was him: when he'd had to confront and deal with the violent death of someone close to him.

'I'd be surprised if Stephen was involved in your father's death. However, it's possible he's been used by this person or these people to gain access to the house. It's important that we understand the motive involved. Was this a kidnapping that went wrong or a kidnapping to enable a murder to take place? Was the murder planned in advance or was it the result of a robbery that was interrupted by your father? There are a number of avenues we must explore sir. It would be a great help if you could check the library now. We need to understand if this was a robbery or not.'

Jellicoe rose to his feet. This prompted the army man to do likewise. He seemed unhappy at being rushed along. They left Phillipa behind and went into the library.

'Who the devil are you? What do you think you're doing?' exclaimed Masterson when he arrived in the library to find Vaughan on all fours collecting prints. Jellicoe glanced at Masterson and wondered if this was one of the stupidest people he'd ever met. Any child would have worked out what Vaughan was doing, and this was a former military policeman.

Jellicoe introduced Vaughan in a manner that could not disguise his wonder that the major needed the forensic process explained. Masterson picked up on the tone, but embarrassment prevailed over anger at Jellicoe's manner towards him.

'Many prints?' asked Jellicoe.

'Yes. I did the cigar box as you asked,' answered Vaughan.

'Very good. Carry on,' responded Jellicoe. Then he turned to Masterson. 'Can you check if anything valuable or important is missing, sir?'

Masterson started with the desk drawers. They were locked. Jellicoe had earlier noted that the drawers showed no signs of being forced. He opened a small Indian chest sitting on the desk. Great security thought Jellicoe sourly. There were no signs of dusting on it. He glanced over at Vaughan who was looking at them and pointed to the chest.

'Hold on a moment, sir.'

Vaughan dusted the drawer keys and took what prints he could. Finally, Masterson was able to inspect the drawers. Everything seemed to be in order. The drawers had little of consequence in them explained Masterson. Next, he went to a painting on the wall. Another Munnings, noted Jellicoe. Any *thief* would have hit a goldmine if he'd focused on the art. Masterson removed the painting and open a safe in the wall with one of the keys taken from the Indian chest. He glanced inside and inspected the papers it contained After a few minutes he turned to Jellicoe.

'I don't believe anything has been taken.'

Normally Jellicoe had people double check by asking them 'are you sure'. He decided against doing so here. Masterson was already in enough of a state. For some reason Jellicoe was not surprised. Looking around the room he could see there a number of things of potential value for a thief. No, this was an attack on Masterson himself for reasons yet to be determined.

'How much longer?' asked Jellicoe to Vaughan. Jellicoe motioned to Masterson that they should leave the fingerprint man to his work. The major followed meekly, still burning with mortification at not recognising the forensics process.

The telephone was ringing outside in the hallway. Fitch looked up at Jellicoe. 'Sir, it's the police station. They wish to speak with you.' He held out the phone towards Jellicoe.

'Jellicoe.' He listened for a moment and then his eyes widened. 'Can you send the police artist up here. Yes Heathcote-Willoughby. Sorry, is there anyone else? All right.' Then he put the phone down and looked at the major.

'Someone has just contacted the police. They left a short message. They claim to have taken Stephen.'

'How do you know? Is my son all right?'

A Time to Kill

'We don't know. A typewritten message was dropped off at the police station a few minutes ago. We don't know who left it in.'

Masterson looked fearful and shook his head.

'What did the message say?'

Jellicoe did not have to look at his written note. He looked at Masterson in the eye and said, '*A wise son makes a glad father, but a foolish son is the grief of his mother.*'

The eyes are a window to the soul; Jellicoe studied the eyes of Masterson as he said this. The major's pupils dilated two or three seconds after Jellicoe had spoken. This was the amount of time it had taken for Masterson to understand the provenance of Jellicoe's words. Changes in pupil size are involuntary. The nervous system controls pupil size. Something about the words had triggered the reaction. The colour seemed to drain from his face. And then he was back in control.

'Nothing else?' demanded Masterson.

'No, sir.'

'What does it mean?'

'Does it mean anything to you?'

'No, Detective Inspector. It does not.'

He was lying.

7

Eleven hours earlier:

'Go on, try some,' said the man. He put the cigar back in his mouth and puffed contentedly. He picked up the mug and showed it to Stephen. Ben had called him Sol.

Stephen looked at the mug. Smoking was one thing but stealing the cigars had escalated matters somewhat. Now drinking seemed not so much to be crossing a Rubicon as leaping over it and performing a war dance. There was no going back now. Besides which, he'd look a tremendous clot if he didn't. He wasn't very keen on the man either. What was someone of his age doing here? With them? The voice was educated, at least. Perhaps it was something in the eyes.

Stephen judged the man to be in his late thirties, perhaps older. It was always hard to tell. His dark hair was greying a little. He had a way of looking at you that was somewhat disconcerting. Stephen felt he was continually being assessed, judged, even. He hated this at the best of times. Now, in the middle of a wood close to midnight with people he hardly really knew, Stephen was becoming horribly aware of a singular fact. He was afraid. The man poured a little whisky into the mug and held it out. Stephen paused a second then took the mug. He studied the golden liquid trying not to show his distaste.

'Here he goes,' said the man named Sol, smiling encouragement.

Stephen glanced at the whisky bottle. It had an unpronounceable Scottish name. He put the cup to his lips. There was a decision to be made here. Sip or neck. The former would make him seem weak. The latter risked seeing him choke. He elected for a half-way house and took half a mouthful.

The bitter taste was like an unwelcome medicine foisted on him by nurse. Did people really drink this muck for pleasure? His throat felt like it was being rinsed in acid. Eyes watering, he could not stop himself screwing up his face. Then the coughing started further. His throat was aflame. It was horrible. The other two were in hysterics at this which added further to his misery. His own temperature gauge was rising. Who the hell did these people think they were? Then Stephen felt a hand on his arm.

-

'There you go. Takes a bit of getting used to, doesn't it?' said Sol. There was some sympathy in the voice, at least. 'Here, sit down, young fella.' Stephen didn't need to be asked twice and he sat down. He wiped his mouth and made no attempt to hide his distaste for what he'd imbibed. Ben patted his back. This riled him. It helped not a jot and was merely patronising. He hated Ben at that moment.

Another sip. Less this time. They smiled encouragingly at him. He noticed they hadn't taken any. And then another. He began to cough again. The mug was removed from his hand.

His two companions were silent while they waited for the coughing to abate. Then Sol said, 'Perhaps you'd better skip the drink, my boy. Bit strong.'

As much as Stephen hated what he'd been drinking, he was at that age when nothing can be worse than loss of face.

'Let me try some more,' he croaked. This made Sol smile and he shook his head.

'Nonsense, son,' said Sol. 'I'm sorry, I should never have given you this to drink.' There was remorse in his voice. This made Stephen angrier. He would not be pitied.

He took matters into his own hands, literally. He reached over and grabbed the mug from Sol's hands and threw the liquid down his throat. The coughing began immediately.

'I told you he had spirit,' said Sol, chuckling away. He took the mug back off Stephen and placed it on the table. For the first time, Stephen noticed Sol was wearing gloves. The whisky began to kick in. Stephen felt the first signs of disorientation. It was almost as if he was disassociated from himself. Despite the burning sensation in his throat, he began to understand, at last, why alcohol was so appealing to adults. His head was swimming in the cold air. No, floating. He was rising out of himself; a separate entity observing the scene dispassionately. Ben and Sol were looking at him strangely. Expectantly almost. They were waiting for something.

'Are you feeling all right?' asked Sol.

'What's wrong,' asked the boy beside Stephen. Stephen looked around to see who'd asked the question. Then he realised it was himself. He frowned. His movements became slower. He tried to form some words to convey what he was feeling.

Then all went black.

A Time to Kill

-

A tickling sensation on his face woke him. He may not have known how long he'd slept, but he recognised a headache when he had one. But this was the least of his worries. There was something infinitely more serious to consider. His hands and feet were bound with rope. He wanted to scream. Only he couldn't. The gag in his mouth was wrapped so tightly it was cutting into his cheeks. Tears filled his eyes as the full horror of his situation became apparent to him.

There was no light, yet it was not quite pitch black either. It was silent save for the rustling which may have been the trees outside. He looked around. His eyes slowly began to focus. It was cold but not quite the chill he'd experienced in the hut in the forest. He was inside a room, but it was still cold. He looked around. The floor beneath him was concrete. He tried to shift position and realised he was propped against a wall. A corrugated metal wall. He looked up. He could barely see the ceiling. It was like he was in an enormous metal container.

He succumbed first to anger. Then he tried rolling around trying desperately to loosen the binding on his hands and feet. It was useless. The bitterness of recrimination set in. His stupidity knew no limits. What had he been thinking? He'd been kidnapped. Someone who he thought was a friend had tricked him. Oh God had he ever been tricked. The shame was overwhelming. He tried to scream again, but it was useless.

Fear gripped him now. He couldn't escape and he had no idea where he was. But that was not what terrified him.

Another thought loomed large and unbidden. A thought so horrifying that he, initially, tried to block it out. But it refused to stay hidden. The more one tries to stop thinking about something the more likely the brain will latch onto it to the exclusion of all else. The thought becomes more powerful; it dominated every sense. And Stephen couldn't stop thinking about it now.

Neither Ben nor Sol had made any effort to conceal themselves.

Worse than this; Ben, in particular, would easily be identified by Phillipa. Had they kidnapped her, too? Either way, Stephen could not think why it would be in the interests of the kidnappers to keep him alive. The realisation that these men could, in fact were highly likely, to kill him mugged his senses. He wept without restraint. His body jerked as the sobs wracked his body.

As he lay there, fully abandoned to his own misery, he felt the first pangs of hunger. A further addition to the growing evidence that he was a fool of the first rank. The rustling seemed louder now. In fact, unless his ears were deceiving him, it was coming from inside the container. He looked around in confusion. Then he saw a rat scuttle across the far end of the container. Then another. This was a new low for Stephen. He thought things could not get any worse than this.

He was wrong.

8

'I'd like to see Stephen's room, if I may, sir,' said Jellicoe to Masterson.

'I'll show you,' said the major. His tone was somewhere between fear and sulky schoolboy. Jellicoe remembered how he'd felt. To be fair to the major, it had been exactly the same. The anger at the crime, the desolation of loss and the resentment at the intrusion on your grief by the police. Yet he had to be firm. He had to be professional and distance himself from the natural human reaction one felt when confronted by grief.

'No, sir. If you don't mind, I'd like to go there alone,' replied Jellicoe. He looked at Masterson and recognised the aggravation on his face. The major didn't like him; that much was clear. Whether it was because he wanted someone more senior to deal with or it was a transference of his anger from the criminal to him, he couldn't decide.

Jellicoe knew Masterson's type. He was a martinet. Men like this were dangerous because they were, fundamentally, unintelligent. The danger wasn't that they were unaware of this, often they were all too aware; no, it was that they still wanted to be in control despite their obvious lack of qualification for this role.

Masterson's face betrayed his irritation, but he directed Jellicoe to the room anyway. It was not like there was an alternative. He watched the detective climb the stairs. Then he heard a door open and shut. He climbed a few steps to check that Jellicoe was in the room then he quickly came down and went to the phone at the foot of the stairs.

'Put me through to the police station,' said Masterson to the operator.

Moments later he was connected. Standing as if on parade, Masterson's face took on the aspect of a scowl.

'This is Major Richard Masterson. Put me through to the man in charge of investigating my father's murder.'

-

The room was quite warm, certainly warmer than the rest of the house. It was large with a dormer window that overlooked the lawn and the wood which Stephen was last seen walking towards. The rich green wallpaper was a little dark for Jellicoe's taste but otherwise it was a room that reminded him of his own when he was a child.

The bed had not been slept in although he could see the wrinkled blanket where Stephen would have lay down. A hardback copy of *Dr No* by Ian Fleming lay open on the bed. Stephen was nearing the end of the book. Another book sat on the bedside table. *The Picture of Dorian Gray* by Oscar Wilde.

Jellicoe sat on the bed and looked around the room. It was quite spartan. A bed, bedside table with lamp, drawers, a wardrobe, and small bookcase. Jellicoe knelt down by the bookcase and scanned the titles. Stephen had long since left *'Boys Own'* stories behind. The books were all for adults. He seemed to have an interest in thrillers. A number of Patricia

A Time to Kill

Highsmith novels were present. The books were arranged by author.

Jellicoe had never read any of her work although he'd seen *Strangers on a Train* with Sylvia at the cinema. He picked out a couple of the novels and looked at the flap to see the subject matter. From the three on offer he took the one with the green cover and man wearing a yellow t-shirt, *The Talented Mr Ripley*. He put the book in his pocket.

There were no other items in the bookcase. On top was a picture of the family taken quite a few years ago in Jellicoe's estimation. Phillipa looked quite a lot younger. Stephen was very similar to his sister. His looks were quite feminine. Jellicoe imagined that he would be very popular with young women. Perhaps. His hair was fair, and he probably had the blue eyes of his father and sister. Stephen's mother was attractive if rather severe. She brought to mind Joan Crawford just moments after stubbing her toe at a house party.

The room was ordered. This was not significant in itself as there was a housekeeper. He looked around the room and tried to think about what was not there. One picture of his family was probably, just about, acceptable. There were no pictures of friends. Was he a lonely boy? Is this why he'd jumped at friendship with Ben?

As a sixteen-year-old, Jellicoe had been a keen sportsman. He loved football and cricket. Denis Compton had been a hero to him. He'd read magazines and books related to these sports voraciously. There was no sign of such interests here. He was clearly a reader. The choices were more adult than he'd expected. Perhaps it was a sign of the times. Boys grew up more quickly now. He grew up during the war. His father had been absent for long periods. He'd grown up with the fear that he would not return. He'd been lucky; so many of his friends had lost their dads.

Stephen was from a different generation. Brought up after the war, these boys were proving troublesome to say the least. Nothing in this room, or indeed Stephen's life, suggested explicit rebellion to Jellicoe, yet he was building a picture that suggested this was far from the case.

With young people, with children, rebellion has many forms. The most obvious of these is disobedience. But Jellicoe knew parents often missed signs of another form of revolt. This was quieter, less willing to draw attention to itself: non-conformity. Young people learned too late that the best way to irritate your parents was to imitate them.

It was too early to build a picture of youthful revolt. Furthermore, while it certainly explained the means and opportunity behind the crime, he suspected it was not a motive. As ever, finding the motive would provide the key to what had happened and who had committed these crimes.

-

'What were Stephen's interests?' asked Jellicoe. Yates and Wallace had returned now and looked towards Masterson, expectantly. Masterson was a seething cauldron of frustration. Rage burned freely in his eyes. His reddened face suggested a Vesuvian eruption was but seconds away. The answer from Masterson was curt and spat out as if he was suggesting his son enjoyed regular and consensual congress with poultry.

'Books. The arts.'

Jellicoe nodded and scribbled in his notebook. He held it away from everyone, like a schoolboy protecting an exam paper. Jellicoe changed tack after this and returned to the murder inquiry.

'Can you think of any reason why anyone would wish to have killed your father?

'No.'

Jellicoe looked up from his notebook. He studied Masterson and tried a different angle of attack.

'What about former comrades? Would anyone have held a grudge against him as a result of the war?'

Masterson looked askance at Jellicoe.

'Why wait until now?' Masterson said this slowly, emphasising with every syllable his contempt for the question. Doing this in front of Yates and Wallace angered Jellicoe, particularly because there were a number of reasons why this should be so. He decided to ignore both the answer and the contemptuous tone with which it had been offered.

'What did your father do during the war?'

'Oh, for God's sake, aren't you listening?' exclaimed Masterson. He glared at Jellicoe. Silence. Jellicoe had learned from his grandfather many years previously the value of silence in interviews. It creates a vacuum which needs to be filled. Jellicoe wondered if Masterson, as a former military policeman, would guess what he was doing. Apparently not. Masterson answered after a short pause.

'He was in North Africa working on Cunningham's staff and then under Ritchie. He returned to England when Montgomery took over from Auchinleck. That was 1942. He spent the rest of the war in England in charge of training in the county.'

Jellicoe closed his notebook and stood up, catching not just Masterson by surprise.

'Is that it?'

'Yes. For the moment anyway. Are you planning on staying here tonight, sir?'

'Of course, I am,' replied Masterson angrily. 'Where else would I go when my son is missing?'

It was clear to Yates and Wallace that Jellicoe was unhappy with this which seemed surprising. Did he really think that there would be a second visit from the people who'd kidnapped the boy and murdered the colonel?

'There will be a policeman stationed with you for the next day or two,' announced Jellicoe.

Before Masterson could make claims regarding what he would do to the beggar should he try to visit them again, Jellicoe walked away. Yates and Wallace hurried in pursuit while Masterson's jaw fell agape. He would be back on the phone to the Superintendent soon.

They left the drawing room and followed him to the library. Yates looked in amusement at Jellicoe.

'I don't think he's very impressed.'

Jellicoe glanced at Yates but ignored the implication. He opened the door to the library and saw that Vaughan was finishing up his work. He glanced at Wallace, but Vaughan answered on his behalf.

'Yes, the constable has passed on the prints that he's taken.'

'Have you done the major and Phillipa Masterson?'

'Yes, sir.'

They all left the library together and went outside to the front of the house. The sun was shining now. The sky was clear and a cerulean blue. Jellicoe breathed in the fresh air. So different from London, he thought.

'What now, sir?' asked Yates.

'You're aware that we definitely have a kidnapping case?'

'Yes, sir. Major Masterson mentioned as much.'

'How was it with the tenants? Was there anywhere that the boy could have been taken?'

Yates and Wallace exchanged looks.

'No, sir,' replied Wallace. 'The houses are too small and there were no sheds or cellars. I had a look around.'

Jellicoe nodded. Then another thought occurred to him.

'There must be farms around this area. We need to visit them'

'Today?' asked Yates.

Jellicoe shot him a glance, 'Yes, why? Have you something better to do?' The sharpness of Jellicoe's response silenced the Detective Sergeant. Jellicoe felt a stab of guilt momentarily. 'Actually, you have a point. Yates, you can return with Vaughan to the police station and make the reports on the statements you've taken. Wallace and I will visit nearby farms. Also, we need to have a policeman stationed here tonight. Can you ask that we have twelve-hour shifts set up for next few days? Oh, and can you give me the car keys?'

Burnett would love this, thought Yates as he handed Jellicoe the keys. He was about to say as much but Jellicoe was already heading outside into the crisp cold air.

'Can you drive?' asked Jellicoe to the young detective constable. Jellicoe realised this may imply something different to what he meant. He was about to apologise when he saw

Wallace smile and nod. Jellicoe threw the keys over to him and went to the passenger side of the car.

A minute later they were heading slowly along the driveway to the exit. The snow had hardened making travel more treacherous than either man would have liked. The road outside the estate looked no more inviting. At least it had stopped snowing.

'Do you know the area?' asked Jellicoe.

'Yes, sir. I grew up in the county.'

'Can you take us to the nearest farm?'

Wallace nodded and they turned right out of the estate.

'You grew up here you say?'

'Yes, sir. My father owns a small holding a few miles from here. Most of the farmers have small holdings. Not sure how long that will last. It's not really economic. My older brother will take over. He has a young lad himself so there was no room for me.'

'So, they sent you off to the police.'

'No, I always wanted to join. I never fancied the idea of farm work. There's an army of young lads the same as me. It used to be what you'd do. Leave school and work on the farm. Since the war that's begun to change. The fields used to be worked by teams of men. Now if you have one or two tractors you can farm three hundred acres. It's not just that. It's a hard life. There's not much money in it, either. My dad never took a holiday in his life. Pigs don't look after themselves, he'd say.'

Wallace put on a yokel-ish voice when he said this. In doing so he, perhaps, revealed the real reason as to why young people were abandoning life on farms for work in towns and cities.

'It must be a lonely life.'

70

A Time to Kill

'It is. My mum was a widow when dad married her. He wasn't young. Just an old bachelor then he married and had Alastair and me. Must have been a shock to his system.'

Jellicoe smiled at this. He knew the area well, too. The life Wallace was describing was familiar to him. He'd come down from London every summer to stay with his grandad and find work on the farms. It had been a wonderful time, but he couldn't envisage living that way. It was a holiday. He always knew that he'd step back out of it and return to boarding school.

Wallace drove sensibly, keeping good control of the car. Yet the drive to the first farm was quietly terrifying. The country around the estate was hilly. Going up or coming down presented equally dangerous challenges. Jellicoe was glad they'd encountered no other vehicles on their way there. Wallace seemed remarkably sanguine about the whole experience.

The first farm was composed of a small grey-brick farmhouse with a thatched roof and a large metal barn. The smell assaulted both men as they emerged from the car.

'Pigs,' said Wallace nodding towards the barn and the low rumble of snorting.

I suppose we are, thought Jellicoe with a grim smile, unnoticed by his companion. They knocked on the door. There was no answer. Jellicoe was glad of this as it gave them an excuse to explore further. They walked around the side of the house towards the barn. There walls were corrugated metal that looked like it was slowly corroding. The sound of the pigs grew louder as they skated and stepped towards the back of the farm.

Jack Murray

A man dressed in a brown wax jacket and wearing green wellingtons was smoking a pipe by a fence enclosing the animals. He looked up as the two men approached. The man was in his twenties, which surprised Jellicoe. He'd been expecting someone older. His greeting was confined to a nod. No words were spoken. Hard grey eyes studied Jellicoe; he ignored Wallace.

'Good afternoon, sir. I'm Detective Inspector Jellicoe. This is Detective Constable Wallace. You are?'

'Hobson. Eric Hobson.'

'Is this your farm?'

A nod.

Jellicoe suspected that this would be a short interview. 'Do you have anyone else working for you?'

A shake of the head, 'No.'

'Have you had any visitors recently or seen any strangers about the farm?'

'No.'

'Would you mind if we had a look around?'

'Why?'

Jellicoe explained that they were investigating a crime but added no details as to what that crime was or who it involved. Hobson listened in silence then shrugged and motioned with his head upwards. Jellicoe took this to mean that they could have a look around. He glanced towards Wallace. The young constable set off to inspect the farm buildings which comprised the barn where the pigs lived and another, smaller, brick building that Jellicoe suspected was a store.

'Would you mind if we went inside, Mr Hobson?'

'You want to search my house?'

A Time to Kill

Jellicoe did but did not want to admit this. However, Hobson started to march towards the house. Jellicoe followed him.

'Must be serious for someone like you to come along,' said Hobson when they entered the house. Jellicoe wasn't sure if he was referring to his rank or his accent that was clearly different from the farmer's.

The stone floor was covered in carpets. A warm fire blazed welcomingly. An Alsatian lay in front, sleeping. It stirred momentarily before deciding to ignore the arrival of its master. The farmer filled a kettle and put in on the Aga stove. He didn't bother asking if the policeman wanted tea.

'Take a look if you want.'

Jellicoe did so. There were two bedrooms that gave absolutely no indication that a woman had ever darkened the doorstep of this house. There were no books, no pictures on the wall. This was as solitary an existence as Jellicoe had ever encountered. He thought again about Wallace's comment about his father and the fact he'd never taken a holiday.

When Jellicoe returned to the living room-kitchen area, Hobson handed him a tea. Jellicoe sat down and drank the tea. Hobson eyed him curiously.

'What are you doing here?' asked the farmer.

He wasn't asking about the crime; he was asking about him. Jellicoe thought for a moment about how to answer such a question. He decided to be honest. If anything, he was curious to see how the farmer would react.

'My wife was murdered. I asked for a transfer away from London.'

Jack Murray

9

Jellicoe and Wallace arrived back at the police station a little after five. Night had drawn in and the streets were lit by a purplish glow reflecting the snow. The town was quiet as if people were reluctant to face the chill of the evening. Wallace let out a huge sigh of relief as he pulled up inside the car park. This was greeted by a half-smile and raised eyebrow from Jellicoe.

They got out of the car and hopped up the steps of the station. The entrance area was quiet. Perhaps even the criminals had elected to stay inside and avoid committing crimes until the temperature gauge broke into double figures.

Jellicoe gave a nod to the desk sergeant and then parted company with Wallace. Jellicoe made his way upstairs. At the top of the stairs, he went through double doors which led to a corridor. Burnett's office was at the end of the corridor. The lights were still on.

A single knock-on Burnett's door and then he entered. Burnett was sitting with Yates. Burnett looked over his half-moon spectacles at the new arrival.

'Mr Popular is back,' said Burnett. His tone was amusedly detached. Jellicoe suspected, correctly as it turned out, Masterson had been on the phone to the Superintendent and, no doubt he'd been on the phone to Burnett. He was unworried by this. Rank likes to deal with rank. Oddly, Burnett would have been in the firing line for not being at the crime scene as much as Jellicoe would have been a target for his manner with the major.

Jellicoe shrugged in response but clearly didn't care and Burnett decided to not to make a thing of it.

'Sit down. Yates has been updating me on the statements from the staff and the tenants on the estate. Anything new from you?'

'I spoke with the major and his daughter about the murder and the boy. I visited three of the nearest farms to check on them.'

'And?'

'Farms first. Nothing of interest. The three farms we saw before it became too dark didn't look to have many places that anyone could be hidden. The first one, Hobson, is quite young, a pig farmer. Unmarried. Hasn't seen anything or anyone strange in the area. Same with the Johnsons and the Lloyds, they have…'

Burnett held his hand up, 'I know them. They're not who we're after. What about Masterson and his daughter. What did you learn?'

'Stephen and Phillipa Masterson came before Christmas to stay with their grandfather. According to Phillipa Masterson, Stephen got to know another young man called Ben, no surname, when they came across him on their estate. Stephen and the other boy became friendly but as I told you earlier, he may have either kidnapped Stephen or, at least, led him to the kidnapper. Major Masterson added nothing to what I learned from his daughter.'

A Time to Kill

'Heathcote-Willoughby is there now with the girl,' said Yates. 'We'll circulate a likeness as soon as he returns.'

'What about this queer angle?' asked Burnett.

'It's hard to know if it's relevant beyond maybe helping us locate Ben, which almost certainly is not his name. We need someone to go to where Ben would be likely to pick up passing trade and show the likeness.'

Jellicoe was looking at Yates as he said this.

'Good idea,' said Burnett. 'Yates, go to the front tomorrow morning. Usual places. Don't even think about coming back unless you have a name and an address.'

Yates gave every impression that he was unhappy to be on this particular mission. This was further exacerbated by the look of amusement in Jellicoe's eyes.

'Well,' concluded Burnett, 'we await the likeness.' He glanced out of the window and saw more snowflakes lit like fireflies by the streetlight. 'I'm not holding out much hope that our road checkpoints will yield much. No one will be out on a night like this.'

'Who took the kidnapper's message?'

'Matheson on the desk. He has no idea who left the envelope. It could have been any one of half a dozen people.'

'Where is the note?' asked Jellicoe.

Burnett opened a drawer and picked out a folded piece of paper. There was dust all around it. Jellicoe did not ask if there were any prints. He unfolded the paper and looked at the typewritten message.

A wise son makes a glad father, but a foolish son is the grief of his mother.

Jellicoe studied the note for fully a minute, eyebrows furrowed. Burnett grew impatient when Jellicoe continued to say nothing.

'Well?'

Jellicoe was about to say "interesting" when he stopped himself. This would only have added fuel to the flames.

'King Solomon,' said Jellicoe. Burnett sat back in his seat; his eyebrows raised. He looked at Yates in irritation. The last thing he wanted was some fancy-dan cop from London showing them up as yokels. Yet, Burnett was already beginning to sense that this was exactly what was likely to happen.

'How on earth do you know that?'

A Time to Kill

10

It was nearing eight in the evening when Jellicoe returned to the guest house which was his temporary residence. It was a large Victorian villa converted into a small guest house with four bedrooms. Jellicoe's room was small and basic to the point that even the soldiers of Sparta would have been up in arms at their living conditions. However, the room was luxury compared to the food on offer.

Mrs Ramsbottom was a formidable woman in her late sixties. Robust of build, pursed of lip and incandescent of temper she stalked the house like a prison guard at Stalag 17. Her cooking was a B-movie horror show in a town that had little to offer those gastronomically inclined aside from fish and chip shops of which there were plenty. Jellicoe had already suffered through beans on toast, scrambled egg on toast and, the previous evening, tinned spaghetti on toast. Tonight, Mrs Ramsbottom proved that, if nothing else, she was versatile by throwing a steak and kidney pudding onto the table.

Jellicoe stared down at the re-heated creation trying desperately to disguise his nausea. This was a variation on that very British staple, rather than steak and kidney it was more kidney and kidney. Grey lumps of meat nestled unappetisingly in watery gravy. Oval globules of oil floated on top of the sauce like scum on a pond. Jellicoe knew he had to get out of the house otherwise Mrs Ramsbottom would have yet another reason to dislike him. His regular excuse was that he'd had a 'big lunch'. The only thing thinner than this rather obvious lie was the thin set of Mrs Ramsbottom's lips.

'Going out again?' asked Mrs Ramsbottom, standing dangerously close to Jellicoe in the corridor. She was as tall as Jellicoe with a husband who might have been a refugee from Lilliput. He stayed well in the background. Whether this was through fear or shame, Jellicoe could not tell. She folded her arms and stood with feet shoulder-width apart. Short of waving a knife, she could not have appeared more aggressive in Jellicoe's eyes. Her battle dress of choice was a pastel brown crossover apron. It would always be 1939 in this house.

'Yes, I do enjoy my walks along the front. A chance to get to know the town. Sea air.'

Mrs Ramsbottom looked at him sceptically. Fire burned in her eyes. This is probably what kept her warm because she certainly didn't invest much in central heating. Every shilling of profit that could be wrung from what few guests they had was done with a fanatical zealousness.

Jellicoe escaped into the cold night air.

-

'Your usual, Mr Jellicoe?' asked the chip shop owner Harry Harris.

This was his fifth consecutive day of visiting the chip shop.

'Yes please,' said Jellicoe, smiling ruefully.

'Don't worry, I won't tell Mrs Ramsbottom. You're secret's safe with me.'

Jellicoe rolled his eyes. He knew the chip shop owner by now. An East Ender called Fred who had escaped from 'the

80

smoke' to the sea and some of the clientele now. There was a conspiracy of amusement at the plight of the toff policeman from London. The fish supper arrived, and Jellicoe made for the sea front.

The night was relatively still, silent and free of any hypothermia-inducing breeze coming off the channel. The snow had stopped falling leaving Jellicoe to find a bench and gaze out at the incoming tide. The sea front was mostly deserted. The only sound was the rush of waves softly dousing the beach. The shore was lit by a warm glow that warmed Jellicoe's soul if not his feet or hands.

He breathed in ice-cold air and felt his eyes water as it hit his lungs. He wasn't sure how much good it was doing him but by God it was a marked improvement on the air of London. One of his earliest memories as a policeman was the Great Smog in London. This had happened a few years previously in 1952. A curtain of fog had descended om the capital so thick that you couldn't see but a few feet in front and to breathe was to take your life in your hands. The foul air had caused many deaths. Even he had been affected. He'd been ill for a week despite not having asthma. What must it have been like for those who had respiratory problems? The cold crispness of this air was the very opposite of that memory.

An odd sense of peace descended on Jellicoe. He liked sitting here in the evening. A month ago, this had seemed like a ridiculous idea of his father's. Now he recognised that it was rather inspired. His father was like that. He had great insight but had chosen no longer to employ it in detection. Instead, he'd taken a more political route in the police force. It was why he'd risen as high as he had.

Even when his fish and chips were finished, he stayed on the bench gazing out. He was in no rush to return to the claustrophobic confines of that awful guest house. He'd hoped to look for a small flat this weekend, but the murder and kidnapping had put paid to that. Perhaps the newspaper would have an advertisement for accommodation, assuming Commandant Ramsbottom hadn't disposed of it by now.

The visit to his grandfather would also have to be postponed. He'd understand. He was a former policeman, too. This case would not be over quickly. The kidnapping was a complication. A distraction even. Jellicoe thought it impossible that it was not connected to the murder but there was always the chance that it may not be.

Around nine the chill of the night was becoming too uncomfortable. With some regret, Jellicoe decided to return to his prison cell of a bedroom. At least the guest house was close to the sea front. Unfortunately, he had had no sea view. This partly explained why it was so cheap. That and the fact that it was obviously the worst of the worst. He made a point to find out who had booked the accommodation for him. A number of ways of killing him filled his mind on the way back but he settled for the most despicably inhumane.

He would invite him back to Mrs Ramsbottom's for dinner.
-

Jellicoe arrived back just as Mrs Ramsbottom was in full charm mode if the rictus grin across her otherwise demonic features was anything to go by. A new guest had arrived and was signing the book. It was too late for Jellicoe to urge him to save himself while he could.

The new guest was a male, in his forties. Jellicoe looked at the suit. It was clean, pressed and had hardly been worn. The cuffs looked like it had been purchased off the shelf that day. Yet, its cut and style suggested that it was at least ten years old, if not more. Jellicoe glanced down at the man's black shoes. They'd been shined to within an inch of their life. The man removed his hat. The hair was cut very short. When he stopped bending over to sign the guest book, he stood ramrod straight.

The man turned to Jellicoe and gave a brief smile.

'Good evening. Cold out, isn't it?'

When in doubt, talk about the weather. Jellicoe smiled and replied, 'Yes. Another minute and I was a goner.'

The man chuckled and said, 'I thought I'd be at the beach this weekend.'

'Good luck with that,' said Jellicoe to the man. Then he turned to Frau Ramsbottom and asked, 'Do you have an evening paper I can take to my room?'

As tempted as Mrs Ramsbottom might have been to tell the unfriendly 'nob where to go, Jellicoe realised she was caught by the fact that there was a witness present. She had to go against her natural inhospitable inclinations and maintain some pretence of being welcoming. Her smile grew wider as her eyes frosted over.

'Of course, I'll just get it when I've finished with Mr Montgomery.'

Mr Montgomery? Cheeky devil thought Jellicoe. If his name's Montgomery, then I'm Rommel.

'Thank you,' said Jellicoe.

A few minutes later Jellicoe was shivering in the fridge-like atmosphere of his room debating whether or not to sleep fully clothed. The light was on but either it was of a particularly low wattage or it was on its last legs. He almost felt like going back to Mrs Ramsbottom and demanding a candle. At least the candle flame would light the room, maybe even add some heat as well.

Around ten, Jellicoe decided to call it a night. Two properties had been identified. He made a note of their details but did not circle them lest the *Oberleutnant* guess his escape plan. Jellicoe put his head down on the thin, lumpy pillow and for the first time that night felt warmed by the thought that he would soon be leaving. This glow of satisfaction lasted three minutes. That was when the first drip of water from the ceiling landed on his nose.

A Time to Kill

11

Saturday 10ᵗʰ January 1959

The next morning saw Chief Inspector Reginald Arthur Burnett trudging through the snow like King Wenceslas returning back to his missus: slowly, with long, weary steps. The weight of the world was on his shoulders. Murder was rarer than warm weather in winter in this town. To have a murder and a bloody kidnapping at the same time felt like all his Christmases had come at once. And Burnett hated Christmas with a passion. He'd just survived another hellish holiday period at his wife's family home with all of his wife's hateful nieces, nephews, and assorted children.

Now this.

Saturday morning. By rights he should have been lying in after a night of listening to the cricket in Australia. Then there was the football later. Tottenham were going to be close this year. He could feel it in his water. But no, he'd get to enjoy none of it today. Instead, the Almighty was having one enormous joke at his expense. At that moment, Burnett doubted there could a more miserable man in the county than him. He paused for a moment when he realised there were probably a couple. Even so, this was an unhappy policeman heading to his miserable place of work to lead an inquiry that would no doubt be hellishly complicated.

There was one silver lining in all of this. Providence had gifted him a potential escape... he stopped himself and thought for a second. Jellicoe was obviously highly capable. His record at the Met was beyond reproach. The word he'd received from some old chums there was that he was highly thought of and had not achieved his promotions through family connections but because he was actually rather good. Unusual but good.

In what way is he unusual, he'd asked?

To a man they'd just laughed and said, *you'll see*. His chums were straight-ahead cops. Old school. No messing around. Burnett's stomach tightened as he thought this. This was the one black spot in the picture he was painting. Jellicoe was not old school. He was new. He brought new ideas. Burnett was a sly enough old dog to know that this could work as easily in his favour as against.

Give 'em enough rope, was a motto he'd lived by in his life. Keep back, let folk dig themselves in it or let them succeed. When things went well, the kudos were always shared. Kudos could be like a benign Hydra if handled well. Knowing looks to the man, the senior man who'd, no doubt, been pulling the strings quietly in the background. A man always happy to give credit to others. Good old Reg. Just smokes his pipe; lets the young ones think they're running the show.

Invariably the credit always reflected back on him in the end. You don't put in thirty years on the force and rise to Chief Inspector without being able to step lightly when needed. And on those other occasions, when a more vigorous approach was required; stick the boot in. Hard.

Burnett crunched through the snow with more purpose as he neared the police station. His back straightened. Always important to put on a show. Never knew who might be looking.

It was nearing seven in the morning. He was the first at his desk most mornings. Twenty-seven years of happy marriage had him escaping the home-haven as early as was humanly possible. Of late, though, well the last week to be more precise, he'd met someone who was even more desirous to escape his dwelling place.

A thin smile creased the features of the old Chief Inspector as he thought of Ramsbottom's Guest House. The place must have come as something of a shock to the young 'nob from London. A bit of your genuine seaside hospitality there. He let out a cackle before stopping himself lest anyone catch him laughing like a man minutes away from being sectioned.

He walked through the entrance of the police station, a nod to the desk sergeant then up the stairs to his department. He saw the lone figure of Detective Inspector Jellicoe standing in front of a board containing photographs of the key individuals. In the centre of the board was the artist's impression of Ben. Soon policemen would be on the streets with photostats of the likeness and the local newspaper would have it on the front page. The involvement of the press would, of course, be a two-edged sword.

Jellicoe stared at the likeness of 'Ben' and was thinking along similar lines to the Chief Inspector. He'd made a point of coming in half an hour earlier, and not just to avoid the culinary catastrophe that Mrs Ramsbottom served up each morning as breakfast. Jellicoe had found a seafront café that was open early. The breakfast served by this establishment was certainly hearty given that it increased the prospect of clogging the arteries to that important organ. It was still a vast improvement on Ramsbottom's Guest House.

Jellicoe's thoughts turned to the Press. Their cooperation did not come for free. By engaging their help, they were effectively making them partners in the hunt for Stephen Masterson. As Burnett was about to find out, there would be an additional complicating factor. He heard a noise behind him and swung around.

'You're in even earlier than usual,' said Burnett.

Jellicoe resisted the temptation to reply, 'so are you'. They regarded one another for a moment and then Burnett wandered over to the window. It was still dark outside, and the street was deserted. He stared down at the street.

'They'll be here soon.'

'The press?'

'Aye, the Press.'

'May even be some of the nationals,' said Burnett.

You can count on it, thought Jellicoe. He realised that Burnett hadn't considered how Jellicoe's presence would add to the potential frenzy that was about to envelop them. He watched Burnett head into his office and then returned his attention to the board.

The arrival to Ramsbottom's Guest House of someone clearly from the army was proof that Masterson did not trust the police to find his son. Jellicoe could not imagine how the major was feeling at that moment. The death of his father and the potential loss of a son. In similar circumstances, he would want to mobilise the forces of heaven and earth to find those responsible. Yet this sympathy was borne of his own experience.

Lurking behind all of this was the certainty that, like all victims of a crime, Masterson was not telling the full truth. Was there a skeleton somewhere in his father's cupboard that the son was trying to hide? But if so, why risk his own son's life? Surely it would be better to be completely transparent about the potential motives the killer and or kidnapper would have in order to catch them more quickly.

Finding who 'Ben' was would happen relatively quickly. But even when they found out who he was, it would be academic. The fact that he was identifiable suggested that he was either very stupid or not the man who planned the crime. Ben was a fall-guy as the Americans put it.

A few other policemen were beginning to arrive to the office including Yates. He joined Jellicoe by the board. There wasn't much to look at but that would change soon. Once the door-to-door work started, once the telephones began to ring as people read the morning newspaper. Everything would have to be followed up. This was merely the calm before the storm.

By half seven the office was full. Jellicoe was impressed by the turnout or perhaps the word had gone out. Seeing the number of detectives and uniformed policeman assembled finally brought Burnett from his office. He walked over to the board and pointed to it. Specifically. he pointed to Stephen Masterson.

'This boy, as you know, has been kidnapped. His grandfather, Colonel Masterson, a man many of us had met

89

before, has been murdered. There can be no doubt the two crimes are connected. Find the kidnapper and I'll bet you a month's pay you'll have the killer. To find the kidnapper, we need to trace the boy here. Goes under the name of Ben. If his name's Ben, then I'm Winston Churchill.'

This brought a few dutiful laughs from the men facing the Chief Inspector. Jellicoe looked on, unsmiling.

'You will all be given photostats of the boy. Some of you will stay here and wait for calls of sightings to come through but I want Yates to lead a team of uniform to hit Old Christchurch Road and start speaking to locals and businesses. We need to know who this boy is. If he was on the game, then someone will have seen him before. We need a name, and we need an address. Understand?'

'Yes sir,' came a number of replies although, noted Jellicoe, not from Yates. The detective sergeant seemed to be unhappy at having to go out into the cold.

'Is there anything you would like to add Detective Inspector?' asked Burnett, catching Jellicoe on the hop, somewhat.

Jellicoe stifled an initial desire to say, 'not really'. This was not so much because he was uninterested but more to do with the fact that Burnett had actually done a reasonable job in communicating the task. Jellicoe stood up and scanned the group. All eyes were on him. To say there was a degree of expectation in the office would be an understatement. They all knew he'd come down from 'the Met'. They all knew this was the family business. They all knew why he was here. He paused for a moment and then began to speak.

'As the chief inspector says, find the kidnapper and you'll probably find the killer. I would add to this; find the motive and you'll find the killer. What possible motive did this boy Ben have for kidnapping Stephen Masterson and possibly killing his grandfather? I would suggest very little. He is, in all likelihood, an accomplice. His job was to lure Stephen Masterson away. What we don't know is if the purpose of the plan was kidnap with the murder being a tragic accident or if the murder was planned all along. But make no mistake, this was well-planned and took weeks to effect. This is not your common or garden criminal. A plan like this is conceptually sophisticated and logistically difficult to execute successfully. Stephen Masterson was, for wont of a better expression, groomed to walk into the trap that was laid for him. This process took place over a number of weeks. Bear this in mind as we investigate. We are dealing with very dangerous individuals. Highly intelligent individuals. They have murdered once. They may do so again. Do not put yourselves in high-risk situations.'

Jellicoe's spoke evenly, without dramatic emphasis. He barely had to raise his voice for his words to carry to the far end of the room, to every man. He finished with a nod and then turned to Burnett.

Burnett was impressed and suspected most of the men would be, too. In the background a phone was ringing persistently. He was saved from having to say anything by a comment from the back that a crowd was forming outside. Burnett glanced at the window. A few pressmen he recognised had arrived. There was also the usual bunch of onlookers. It had begun.

The phone was still ringing.

'For God's sake would someone answer that damn phone. It might be a lead; it might be the damn kidnapper,' said Burnett grouchily. 'And get to work.'

A constable grabbed the phone and listened for a few seconds.

'Sir,' called out the policeman who'd answered the phone.'

'Yes,' said Burnett.

'It's the Assistant Chief Constable of the Met.'

'Bloody hell, that was quick.' Burnett began to move towards the phone.

'No, sir. He wants DI Jellicoe.'

Everyone in the office stopped and turned to Jellicoe. A half-smile appeared on his face and he rose from the table he'd perched on and walked over to the phone. The only sound that could be heard was the breathing of a dozen policemen of various sizes, shapes, and vintages. Jellicoe took the phone from the constable and put the receiver to his ear. He glanced out of the window and looked down at the scene below.

'Hello, father,' said Jellicoe

12

The newly appointed Assistant Chief Constable, James Jellicoe, glanced down at a photograph of his son on his desk. He heard a policeman's voice speak to someone nearby and say who it was. Some background laughter at the other end of the phone made him smile. Moments later he heard his son speak.

'Hello, father.'

'Have I caught you at an awkward time?' asked Jellicoe senior, knowing that he had. He remembered his wife waving to his son once at the school gates when they'd left him for a new term. The fleeting look of embarrassment that had crossed the boy's face as his friends began to wave to him too.

'One or two folk around, yes,' answered his son. The laughter in the background grew louder.

'Ah,' said his father. 'Forgive me. I should have thought of that. Is it true what I hear?'

'Sadly yes. It's a very serious case. Cases, even.'

'They couldn't have a better man in my view to help them,' said Assistant Chief Constable Jellicoe.

'Your objectivity does you credit, sir. Any news on the other?' Jellicoe doubted much would have changed in the last week, but you never knew.

Jack Murray

The older man glanced down at the picture again. His son was standing beside a young woman dressed in white. The photograph showed a moment in time. A happy time. White comets of confetti flew through the air around his son and Sylvia.

'No, son. No new leads. Until the killer makes another move, we've probably gone as far as we can go.'

They talked only briefly. Just enough time for Jellicoe to update his father on the events of the previous night. The call ended soon after and the Assistant Chief Constable stared out of the window of his office at New Scotland Yard. His was an intelligent, if sombre-looking, face. Like his father before him, and now his son, he was a serious man doing a very serious job.

Policemen lived every day of their working lives with the results of crime. The tragic consequences, however, invariably fell upon the lives of others: the victims and their families. The death of, or violence towards, policemen was still relatively rare. The scars of crime were another matter. They ran like a deep black seam through the hearts and minds of all the men who confronted crime's brutal reality.

But James Jellicoe and his family were victims, too. He picked up the wedding photograph and stared at it. A wave of sadness engulfed him. No one, no matter what position in society you held, was invulnerable, untouchable, completely protected from acts of random violence. He set the picture down just as there was a knock on the door. It was time for work again.

-

Jellicoe set the phone down and looked around at the policemen busy doing things that signally failed to convince him that they'd not been listening to every word. It was to be expected. If they didn't know who his father was before, they would now. He caught the eye of Burnett who was motioning for Jellicoe to join him in his office.

Jellicoe shut the door behind him wondering if Burnett would refer to the call he'd just received. However, the chief inspector was nothing if not unpredictable. He perched himself on the windowsill and glanced down at the small crowd outside in the cold. It was much lighter now, but this did not mean warmer. Burnett's office was a fridge.

'You and I will visit the Masterson's today. The major is going to be trouble. I can feel it in my water.'

Jellicoe thought of the man he'd seen the previous evening. He couldn't have agreed more. But more than this, he couldn't help but feel that the major was holding back something material. His reaction upon hearing the quote was visceral. He'd recognised the words. Furthermore, the implication worried him. This suggested that the communication had been directly targeted at Masterson and was meant to tell him who had sent it.

If this were the case, and Jellicoe was making an enormous leap here, then why wasn't Masterson sharing what he knew? This made no sense especially as he was potentially putting his son's life at risk. His thoughts were interrupted by Burnett.

'I will make it clear to Major Masterson that I have complete confidence in you handling this case. We'll mention that your father is the Assistant Chief Constable at the Met. You may not like this but it's important when dealing with a character like Masterson. Bloody army types are all the same.'

'I agree, sir,' said Jellicoe. It was said resignedly so Burnett knew it was genuinely meant.

Burnett nodded and said gruffly, 'I wasn't asking for your bloody agreement.'

Oddly, coming from Burnett, this did not sound as rude as it seemed. If anything, it was something Jellicoe might have said himself. In truth, it was academic. The press would see to that. Once the 'nationals' picked up on where he was and the case he was working on, then everyone would know who he was, who his father was and then it would start all over again. He could see the headlines now. The questions that would be asked.

'Detective Inspector Jellicoe, is there any connection between this murder and the murder of your wife?'

Jellicoe wasn't sure if he should speak about his suspicions regarding Masterson. There was nothing he could do to force the issue anyway. If the man at Ramsbottom's Guest House was army and if he was working with Masterson, then that would reveal itself in due course.

'I've arranged to see Dr Taylor this morning. We'll go there first then we'll head up to the Masterson house. Around eleven we'll speak to the press back here.'

It was clear to Jellicoe that the morning would be something of a waste of time. On his own he might be able to shake the tree with Masterson, but this would be impossible with Burnett. As soon as he tried to probe about the new arrival, Masterson would appeal to the chief inspector. That would have to wait. Burnett was on his feet and heading to the door now.

'Don't just sit there, come on. Let's get this over with.'

A Time to Kill

There was just enough of an edge in Burnett's voice to suggest that visits to the mortuary held little appeal for the older man. Perhaps he was squeamish. Alternatively, it was a reminder of his mortality. Burnett wouldn't see sixty again. He was edging closer to his three score and ten. Jellicoe's grandfather was over eighty now and going strong, though. People were living longer. This was no longer the Victorian era despite his grandad's ridiculous moustache.

They descended to the basement where there was a small mortuary where the dead body had been kept overnight. Dr Taylor was drinking tea and eating a slice of bread with a liberal spreading of marmalade on top. He dabbed the side of his mouth with a handkerchief and rose to greet the two men.

'Hilary, what do you have for me?'

'Death and misery, Reg, just death and misery.'

Taylor led them into a cold, tiled room with a long table in the middle. A body covered by a pastel blue sheet lay on top of the table, motionless. By the look of the large paunch on Masterson, his army days had given way to a fuller, less Spartan way of life. Jellicoe couldn't blame him. He'd heard much of what life in the army had been like. Hellish was one of the kinder descriptions. The man lying dead before him had gone through two World Wars in the defence of his country. Jellicoe felt anger rise within him at the briefly violent act that had brought an end to his life.

'The cause of death was severe trauma to the back of the head.'

They walked towards the covered corpse. Jellicoe sensed Burnett slowing down to allow Jellicoe first dibs at seeing the body. Perhaps he was using him to cover his own view of what was about to be revealed.

At this point Taylor drew the covers back. Jellicoe steeled himself to look at the horrific injury inflicted on the skull.

'A woman couldn't have done this,' said Jellicoe.

'No, not even with the heavy candlestick. It still took a degree of force.'

Did it ever, thought Jellicoe, looking at the result of the impact. He looked away and towards Taylor.

'Would this have required particular strength or could an average man or youth have inflicted such an injury.'

Taylor thought for a moment before replying, 'It would have required unusual strength in a young person, but I think any average man, taking a good swing, could have managed this. Do you play golf at all, young man?'

Jellicoe said he did, which prompted a theatrical eye roll from Burnett.

'Well, as a golfer, you will know that the speed with which you swing the club will impart greater force on the ball thereby making it go further. So, it is with this candlestick's impact on the head of the poor colonel.'

A number of questions flooded into Jellicoe's mind. Doubts, too. Since the previous evening, Jellicoe had been wondering if the attack was against the colonel or somehow connected to the son. The violence of the attack suggested a deep anger against the colonel.

'Time of death?' asked Burnett.

'I think he was killed around midnight, but you can add an hour or two either side of that if you want.'

They'd managed to get through the rest of their time in the mortuary without either of them revealing too much about the nausea they felt. Back at Burnett's office they ran into Vaughan who had finished his report. The unsurprising conclusion was that the assailant had left no fingerprints.

A handful of policemen were fielding calls from the public on the published picture of 'Ben'. One name featured prominently: Alfred Douglas.

'At least we have a name now,' said Yates.

'It's made up,' said Jellicoe.

'How do you know?' said Burnett, still unable to stop himself from seeming put out by anything Jellicoe said.

'Alfred Douglas was the name of Oscar Wilde's lover. "Bosie". It's made up but that's less important than having an address,' explained Jellicoe. Then he added, but without much hope in his voice, 'I don't suppose any of the callers left their name?'

Yates didn't deign to answer the question beyond raising his eyebrows in a *what-do-you-think* manner.

'They were all male callers,' added Yates. 'Last address they had for him was on Columbia Road.'

'Head over there now,' ordered Burnett. Then he turned to Jellicoe. 'You and I will get this trip to Masterson's over with.' He sounded no more enthusiastic about this than he had about the trip to the mortuary.

-

The car journey to the Masterson estate proved a much less nerve-wracking experience than the previous day's. There had been no further snowfall and the snow on the roads was slushy rather than slippery. For once Burnett remained fairly tight-lipped as they travelled to the estate. He was not a man who dealt with confrontation well if it was not him doing the confronting. Jellicoe often observed this in men with positions of responsibility. Their ability to absorb disparagement was inversely related to their propensity to dish it out. Perhaps if he ever got round to doing his PhD in Psychology this could be his subject. A snappy title like *A Study of behavioural and cognitive correlations related to dominance, prestige, and leadership components in the explicit power motive*, for example, would set the tone. Or perhaps not.

They parked in front door and marched towards the house. Burnett nodded to the young constable on duty then remarked to Jellicoe through the side of his mouth, as they went through the portico entrance, 'I'd have introduced you, but I can never remember the names of half these young lads now.'

They were met by Fitch and taken to the drawing room. Burnett took up the offer of a cup of tea while they waited for the major to make an appearance. The cup of tea was made and drained by the time Masterson appeared in the room. He paused after entering, somewhat surprised to see Jellicoe in attendance. This was noted by both detectives who stood up when he entered.

'Chief Inspector,' said Masterson walking over and briefly shaking the hand of Burnett.

'Major Masterson, may I once more convey my condolences on your loss,' said Burnett dutifully. His tone was markedly different to what Jellicoe was used to hearing.

This was briefly acknowledged; then Masterson asked for an update on progress. Sensing that the major was only interested in hearing from the man in charge, Burnett answered.

A Time to Kill

'The artist's likeness of Ben has already yielded a response which we are following up now.'

'Who is he? I presume his name is not Ben,' replied Masterson.

Jellicoe realised that this was something they would have to be careful of. Masterson might try and fish for information that he would pass on to his possible 'lieutenant'. He jumped in ahead of Burnett.

'The lead is being followed up as we speak. It is not appropriate to say more at this stage.'

Masterson looked fit to explode. So did Burnett, to be fair. The chief inspector glanced at Jellicoe and hardened his eyes in a manner that he hoped would convey his displeasure. Jellicoe understood all too well the undercurrent but did not care. He realised he would probably have to say something after all to the chief inspector about the new guest at Ramsbottom's.

'What DI Jellicoe means is that we have to be sure that this is a legitimate suspect and not some sort of retribution from people who do not like him.'

'I know what Jellicoe means,' snarled Masterson. 'I have done this myself before.'

And you're still doing it, thought Jellicoe, sourly.

'Did the message have any significance for you?' asked Burnett.

'No, why should it?' replied Masterson, stiffly.

Jellicoe saw it again. The dilated pupils. The hesitation that suggested concealment. He was lying all right.

'Just wanted to check, sir,' responded Burnett, backing down. This was as far as the chief inspector was going to push

Masterson, that much was clear. On reflection, it was probably no bad thing. It might give Jellicoe a freer hand in running things. The antagonistic attitude of Masterson had persuaded Burnett that the less time spent in his presence the better it would be for his peace of mind. The briefing was concluded in record time. Masterson accompanied the policemen to the door.

'Be sure to tell me of any developments the minute they happen.'

Burnett assured him he would as he hurried to the car to escape the scalding rage of the army man.

'Let's get away from this place,' said Burnett as he smiled at the angry major, standing at the entrance to his house. He stopped short of waving.

Burnett turned to him as they pulled out onto the road. Jellicoe sensed he was about to be upbraided for his earlier interjection.

'What on earth were you thinking of when you interrupted me earlier?'

Jellicoe realised he had to tread carefully on this point. There was a possibility that Burnett would have been smart enough to be circumspect. He turned to Burnett and decided to go full bore.

'Interesting guest house you put me in.'

Burnett looked confused then suspicious before a smile appeared and was then snuffed out. This at least confirmed Jellicoe's hunch that the guest house was not chosen for its hospitality.

'Not what you're used to then?'

'Not since boarding school, no.'

'What's wrong with it then?'

A Time to Kill

'Aside from my cold room, horrific food and a landlady who should have faced trial at Nuremberg, you mean?'

For a moment there was a look on Burnett's face that was unreadable. A sadness in his eyes perhaps but as quickly as it had appeared Burnett shrugged it off.

'What's all of this got to do with the price of milk?'

'Only this, sir. A new guest arrived last night. Army.'

Burnett frowned. He was silent for a moment and Jellicoe watched the cogs turning in the chief inspector's head. Jellicoe was curious to see if he would make the connection.

'So, you think because he is a military policeman, he's asked one of his men to shadow our investigation?' Jellicoe nodded. 'And when were you thinking of telling me about this?'

This was a good point and Jellicoe was impressed that he'd reached it in record time. Clearly Burnett was not a man to dismissed.

'I should have mentioned this morning, sir. Of course, I don't have any proof.'

'So why mention it at all now?'

Jellicoe broke into a sheepish grin and replied, 'He gave his name as Montgomery to Frau Ramsbottom.'

Burnett looked away but there was a ghost of a smile on his face but sadness, too. Jellicoe wondered if he should say something about the major's reaction to the kidnapper's note. However, he was curious to see if Burnett had noticed anything. The rest of the journey was made in silence as Burnett stared out at the white-blanketed fields. When they pulled into the carpark near the station, a crowd of pressmen were waiting.

'Here we go,' said Burnett as he spied the waiting Press.

13

They decamped from the car and were surrounded by half a dozen journalists. Questions were fired with machine gun rapidity and duly ignored by both men. Burnett held his hands up in front of him and pushed through, telling everyone they would have to wait until eleven. Jellicoe remained tight lipped. All of the men around him were unfamiliar. This would soon change. It might take a day or two but then the pictures of him alongside Burnett would make it down the press wires and then the second wave of press would arrive.

They made it into the police station and removed their hats. Burnett breathed a sigh of relief then headed directly up the stairs at a surprising speed for someone of his size and age. Jellicoe followed at a more dignified pace.

The office was a lot quieter now with many of the police officers out searching for leads on 'Alfred Douglas'. Jellicoe was ignored as he walked through the department. He headed towards Burnett's office.

'Close the door,' said Burnett.

'What do you make of Major Masterson?'

This was unexpected and welcome. It gave Jellicoe the opportunity he'd been looking for to discuss the major.

'He knows more than he's telling us, that much is clear.'

'They all do,' replied Burnett. 'Why do you say that?'

105

'You saw his reaction to your question about the kidnapper's message.'

'What did I see?'

Jellicoe paused for a moment. How much should he say? Everything, he decided.

'Yesterday when I related what the kidnapper had communicated, he reacted quite visibly. He did so again today. I think he recognised the quote. Furthermore, I think it meant something to him. I would even speculate that he may know who the kidnapper and murderer is or, at least, have a suspicion.'

'So why isn't he telling us?' demanded Burnett angrily. However, his anger was not directed at Jellicoe. Jellicoe's regard for his superior officer was rising by the hour. He was no fool.

'When I saw the murder scene yesterday, I assumed that the motive was based around the victim. It could either have been pre-meditated or accidental but either way, the victim was the reason for the killing: he'd either surprised an intruder or the murderer had always planned to kill him. The major's reaction to the kidnapper's note as well as this mysterious new arrival makes me think that we're looking in the wrong place for a motive. He's hiding something.'

'If he is, then we need to find out what. We need to know more about what he did as a military policeman. Who might hold a grudge? Why? Either we make him tell us or we speak to the military and see what they can tell us.'

'Or both,' added Jellicoe.

Burnett stopped for a moment and studied Jellicoe.

'Or both,' agreed Burnett. 'Do you think that the military will help us?'

A Time to Kill

Jellicoe had his doubts, and he could see that Burnett was similarly sceptical. Still, one thing was certain. Burnett was on his side on this matter. This would make things easier when the case started to become messy. And it would become messy.

-

The gentlemen of the press trailed into the small meeting room at the police station. Both Chief Constable Leighton and Superintendent Frankie had threatened to attend but, in the end, had decided to leave matters to Burnett. The two senior officers split their time between a few of the town police stations in the county. They were obviously too busy, thought Jellicoe. There were half a dozen reporters and two photographers snapping away like they were at the opening night of a West End musical.

Jellicoe sat alongside Burnett surveying the new arrivals. There was no sign of anyone from London. Burnett seemed to recognise the reporters and greeted them in a relatively friendly manner by name. The door shutting signalled the start of the press conference.

'Gentlemen, thank you for attending this morning. I will take some questions at the end, but I would just like to read from this prepared statement. You can have a copy of it afterwards.'

He paused and looked at the room. No one said anything. Pens were poised over notebooks ready to capture everything that was said.

'In the early morning on the 9th of January, a dead body was found in the library of the house belonging to Colonel Horace Masterson. I can confirm that the deceased is Colonel

Masterson. He was a man well-known to us all. The cause of death was a head trauma inflicted by a person or persons unknown. As you may have surmised, we are seeking a young man who identified himself as Ben to help with our inquiries. At the same time, we are also investigating the whereabouts of Colonel Masterson's grandson, Stephen Masterson. We have been given to understand by his father, Major Richard Masterson, that a reward of two hundred pounds will be given for any information leading to his recovery. Thank you. Any questions?'

There were. Everyone spoke at once leading Burnett to hold his hands up and wave them up and down.

'One at a time. Ed, you're the oldest. You go first.'

This brought a ripple of laughter from the assembled men.

'Has Stephen Masterson been kidnapped?'

Burnett was quiet for a moment and clearly seeking to choose his words carefully.

'We believe he has been kidnapped, yes.'

Another blaze of voices but they quietened when the reporter, Ed, held his hand up.

'Just one follow up. Have you received a ransom note?'

'Not a ransom note, no. We have received a communication which we are treating as genuine, but I cannot reveal anything more than that.'

This was greeted with exaggerated dismay by the newspapermen and duly ignored by Burnett as the conference descended into knockabout humour that is usually the outcome when members of the distaff side are not present to remind everyone of the gravity of a given situation.

The conference was ended when Burnett rose from his seat and added a warning on the way out.

A Time to Kill

'If I see anyone near the Masterson estate, I'll bang you and your editor up quicker than you can say "Jack Robinson", am I clear?'

'Yes, Chief Inspector,' chorused the newspaper men. Jellicoe suspected that they would be as good as their word. He doubted such threats would work so well with the 'nationals'. He was glad that Burnett had not introduced him but that was academic. When the photographs appeared in London, they'd be along.

They walked along the corridor to the large office shared by the detectives. Two men were manning the phones. Burnett and Jellicoe went into the Chief Inspector's. On the top of Burnett's desk was an envelope. Burnett's name was written in capitals.

Burnett frowned and was about to pick it up when Jellicoe stopped him. They looked at one another with one thought on their mind.

How on earth did the letter get there?

'The mail room,' said Jellicoe. He didn't wait for an answer from Burnett. He flew out of Burnett's office into the larger outer office. Then he was in the corridor, almost taking out a uniformed sergeant who let Jellicoe know in words consisting of no more than one syllable what he thought of him. Jellicoe wasn't listening; he was already at the end of the corridor and leaping dangerously down the stairs. He arrived at the mail room and burst through the door like a policeman.

There was a man in the room. The man in question was in his late fifties and happily occupying himself by dipping a digestive biscuit into a cup of tea. Jellicoe had not yet met a master criminal in his short career as a detective. He doubted he was staring at one now. The man looked up and smiled gently.

'Hello, sir. Is there something I can help you with?'

-

Jellicoe slumped down in the seat opposite Burnett. The chief inspector was seething, unable to speak. Jellicoe sensed there was some embarrassment that the police station had been effectively broken into by some person unknown.

'The boys outside saw nothing?' asked Jellicoe.

The answer to that, if Burnett's angry glare was any indication, was a resounding 'no'. Jellicoe decided not to kick the wasps nest any further. He sat in his chair and considered the implications of what had happened.

A man that no one in the office had seen entered with an envelope, walked into Burnett's office unchallenged and back out again. He'd even shared a joke with the two men manning the phones and left the building. No one knew how he'd got in. No one knew how he had passed himself off as a policeman delivering internal mail. Jellicoe glanced at Burnett again. He was still raging. The two men on the phones had probably been on the receiving end of a mother and father of a carpeting. The silence grew oppressive, so Jellicoe decided to speak.

'This is good news and bad.'

Burnett looked up slowly from the floor. His eyes widened alarmingly, and he snarled, 'What could possibly be good about this?'

Jellicoe met and held his gaze.

'He's overconfident. He thinks we're idiots.'

'He's not far wrong there,' replied Burnett glancing out of the window at the two men in the outer office.

A Time to Kill

'If he's overconfident, he'll make mistakes. He'll gamble once too often. But equally it shows we're dealing with an uncommon criminal.'

Jellicoe paused for a moment to take in the breath-taking audacity of what had happened. Uncommon barely conveyed the level of impudence that had been displayed. He became conscious that Burnett was studying him.

'This is no common criminal. He's smart. He's faced danger and risk before. Walking into a police station so brazenly and pretending to be part of the internal post suggests a level of self-confidence and willingness to take a chance that any normal criminal would avoid.'

'So, who is he then?' asked Burnett. 'You're the psychologist. That's what you studied isn't it? Cambridge? What are we dealing with here?'

When he'd first arrived at the Met, Jellicoe had encountered the usual barbed comments from 'old school' policemen wanting to show him they didn't care for his sort. In Jellicoe's case, 'his' sort were college-educated. The fact that his father was a senior member of the police force was both a protection and a burden. It protected him from outright mistreatment, but he did have to suffer the regular slings and arrows of coppers who'd come up from the beat. Jellicoe had never cared what they thought.

He'd not cared what they thought when he started to apply a psychological approach to his investigations. They'd laughed. At first. Then something strange happened; he began to solve cases. When this happened, his methods began to seem less like voodoo and more like something which worked.

'Have you heard of Césare Lombroso, sir?'

'No. should I have?'

'He lived in Victorian times. He developed a typology for criminals based on race, age, sex, physical characteristics. Basically, if you were a working-class male with a low forehead and funny ears you were probably a criminal. Lombroso tried to help Scotland Yard find Jack the Ripper. He was so badly wrong he probably set back profiling of criminals decades. But the funny thing is, sir. It works.'

'A psychiatrist named Brussels suggested that the Mad Bomber in that case in the States a few years ago would be a heavy, single, middle-aged man who dressed impeccably; a mechanic or some such engineering type. He also suggested that he would be from Connecticut because they had high concentrations of people of Slavic origin. Brussels believed Slavs favoured the use of bombs. He derived all this from his visits to the crime scene and the letters that the bomber sent. Do you remember the case?'

'Yes, I do. They caught him, didn't they?'

'They did. George Metesky was a single man, fifty-four years old. He was wearing a double-breasted, neatly buttoned up suit when he was arrested. He was a mechanic from Connecticut. My point is that crime scenes and notes like the one that this man is leaving us leave clues beyond potential fingerprints. They can tell us who and why if we choose to look.'

Burnett exhaled and said slowly, 'Fine. Who are we dealing with then Sigmund, and why is he doing all this?' Burnett threw his arms in an expansive gesture.

'Like the bomber case, I think we have someone with a grudge. He either knew the colonel or the major or both.

That means he is somewhere between thirty-five and fifty. He may have served during the war.'

'Brilliant, Sigmund, that only narrows it down to tens of thousands.'

Jellicoe had the grace to smile at this. He'd heard 'Sigmund before. He would again. It meant nothing to him now insofar as it ever had. They usually changed their tune. As with all things, it just took time. Like grief, time heals. It really does.

'So how do we narrow the field down? There's too many runners and riders here,' continued the chief inspector.

Jellicoe stood up. He needed to think. This was easier when he was standing, for some reason. It was different for everybody. One detective sergeant he'd known claimed he thought better when he scratched his arse. Each to their own he'd concluded from that particular revelation.

'Do you mind if I go to the board sir. I need to write this down.'

Burnett rolled his eyes but offered no objection. The two men rose and walked out to the outer office. The two men on the phones looked up sheepishly and Burnett glared at them angrily. He began to talk to Jellicoe although he was really addressing the two men.

'Once you're finished, Jellicoe, we'll get a description of the mysterious postman who waltzed in here and left the latest message. Oh, that's right these two men, two policemen I might add, didn't see his bloody face. Bloody shower.'

Burnett shook his head in disgust and then stared at Jellicoe waiting for the young DI to demonstrate something magical. Behind Jellicoe, Burnett could see DS Yates arrive back to the office with a young man of around twenty. Accompanying them both was a rather large constable who Burnett had occasion to get drunk with not infrequently. Unless he missed his guess, Yates appeared to be hobbling. Burnett turned back to Jellicoe with a look that suggested he get on with it

Jellicoe was studying the board with an intensity that bordered on manic. There were a number of pictures on the board now. The murdered man in life and death. His son dressed in his uniform. His grandchildren. There were also photographs of the murder scene with and without the dead body. Pinned up on the board was a photostat of the first communication from the kidnapper. The second note was with Vaughan to be fingerprinted. In its place was a note handwritten by Burnett. Jellicoe read the message and looked at Burnett.

'Is this from Solomon?' asked Burnett.

'I think so, yes.'

'How do you know? Are you religious?'

'Not particularly. It's the kind of thing Solomon would have written, if you believe that it was Solomon who wrote those books in the Bible. There is some disagreement on this point.'

Burnett's expression strongly indicated he could have cared less about this latter point. Jellicoe returned his attention to the message. It read:

Whoever digs a pit will fall into it, and a stone will come back on him who starts it rolling.

'This is about revenge, isn't it,' said Burnett.

A Time to Kill

'Yes, this is about revenge,' agreed Jellicoe.

14

He woke up cold and shivering. His first thought made him feel sick. *It hadn't been a*
dream.

He sat up and felt the chill bite deeply. It was dark. He was disorientated. It could have been day or night, yet he had no idea. Tears stung his eyes. Fear, worse, a sense of despair set in. He was going to die. There was no other way this was going to end. His body jerked violently as he sobbed. His wrists were red raw from the rubbing of the handcuffs which seemed to be made from a rubber-like substance. His back felt old-man stiff. And then there was the ultimate shame to compound his misery: an ammonia smell around his person.

Going to die? He wanted to die.

He lay against the metal wall for an hour. There was no part of his body that wasn't aching now. His shins were also bound but the captor had, at least, allowed for the possibility that he would want to stretch his legs. He'd tried to loosen the binding before falling asleep but with no success.

He rose to his feet but stumbled and fell. His second attempt was more successful, and he began to move slowly, carefully around the edge of the container. His hands were in front of him which helped aid balance. The prison was rectangular with corrugated metal all the way round. There was a door at the far end. He tried to open it. No joy. He banged on it, but the sound was deadened, and it hurt his hands.

He slumped to the ground feeling wretched with hunger. Then there was the headache brought on by dehydration. He was bored. The only thing he could do to stave off the boredom and the pain in his limbs was to keep moving. Keeping the circulation in his limbs might help warm him up too, he reasoned. This might help him feel better. Just like a prisoner, he began to make circuits around the edge of the building. It helped warm him up a little. Blood began to move around his body at last. It was on his twenty fifth lap that the door opened.

Light flooded into his prison; he squinted, momentarily blinded. A man stood silhouetted in the doorway. His hopes rose as he thought salvation had come. Then his eyes began to adjust to the light he saw who it was. The man he'd known as Sol, stepped forward. There was something in his hands. It was like a newspaper or something. Then the smell hit him.

It was fish and chips.

'I've brought you lunch. I'm going to loosen your gag. You make one noise then you go without this and water. Understand?'

He nodded.

Sol kicked the door shut. Darkness fell immediately but he was too hungry to care.

15

Detective Sergeant Yates's fingers were now sore. His decision to come out of the house that morning minus gloves was proving to be monumentally short-sighted. He'd remembered the forecast had promised sunshine and no more snow. On such a basis did he decide to forego his gloves. What a brilliant detective.

He and a middle-aged constable named Clarke had walked the length and breadth of 'the strip'. Bar after coffee bar, had been visited. In each one he'd been greeted with the usual snorting sounds and the word 'pig' coughed into a mug of tea, cappuccino, or espresso. If he'd had more time, he'd have dealt with the young men responsible. In a moment of rare reflection, he realised many were probably his age or not much younger.

Their morning had proved, so far, fruitless. No one claimed to recognise 'Ben' or 'Alfred' or 'Fred' or Freddie'. A conspiracy of silence about talking to cops or fear at being associated with someone who was a known male prostitute?

Yates was on the point of giving the whole deal up as a wasted morning when they finally struck gold. Clarke had, for the most part, demonstrated ably why he'd reached the aged of forty-five without any promotion. He was as slow of thought as he was of movement. Yates had grown increasingly irritable about the slow speed with which they walked. He was a young man who wanted to go places. Preferably quickly.

A Time to Kill

This applied as much to his career as it did to his life. The burly copper alongside him could barely catch a cold never mind some fleet-footed robber. He glanced once more at Clarke as he walked, no, make that pootled, along.

Clarke was immune to such looks. Either he was extraordinarily thick-skinned, thought Yates, a condition that went all the way up to his head, or he was genuinely that stupid. Yates hadn't reached a conclusion on this point. After a couple of unrewarding hours in his company, he finally proved his worth.

'Sir,' he whispered through the side of his mouth in the manner of an actor on stage helping someone who has forgotten his lines, 'that young chap over there.'

There were several young chaps 'over there'.

'Which one?'

'Black hair combed up like they do now. Blue jacket.'

The youth in question was wearing a bright blue jacket and drainpipe black trousers over unhealthily skinny legs. Yates was on the point of saying he would catch his death when he stopped himself and went for something more police-like.

'Let's split up you walk ahead. Don't look at him. Get to the other side of him. Pretend you're going for a sandwich.'

Looking at Clarke's rotund frame, this was an all too plausible ruse. Clarke made his stately way along the street whistling an old tune looking into the shop windows. Yates, meanwhile, shook his head at the obviousness of it all.

The groups of youths looked at Clarke pass. Conversation ceased for a few moments. Then it began again once they thought the coast was clear. In fact, by the laughter and the way they mimicked a Charlie Chaplin walk, Yates suspected that Clarke was the subject of some bad-natured lampooning about his un-policeman-like girth and gait. While Yates was no admirer of his temporary sidekick, he was certainly not the sort of man to see his beloved service made fun of. There was an added urgency to his step as he made directly for the group of youths.

Something about Yates attracted the attention of the group. Whether it was his mad staring eyes or his gabardine mackintosh and fedora that screamed 'I'm a detective and I want to speak to you', Yates wasn't sure. The group turned round and stared briefly like a gang of startled meerkats Yates had seen on a BBC Natural History programme presented by Peter Scott. Then they went their separate ways. As hoped, their target went in the direction recently occupied by Clarke.

At this point an unwelcome thought crossed Yates's mind like a tax reminder in the post. Should he have taken Clarke's position? He would never be quick enough to catch their quarry. Too late now. But they faced an all-too-likely scenario that the young man would easily evade the bulky and aging constable.

Their target turned his back and began to walk quickly away. Yates broke into a run once the young man's back was turned. Eyes straight ahead he sprinted as hard as it was possible to do wearing brogues on a slippery street. The full folly of his actions had yet to be revealed though. The boys were now running in all directions and, if Yates' eyes did not deceive him, Clarke was engaged in conversation with a young woman pushing a pram. The damn fool seemed entirely oblivious to the scene directly in front of him.

A Time to Kill

This presented a dilemma for Yates. Should he shout and attract the attention of the idiot plod or trust in his own ability to outpace his prey. Whilst in the middle of cogitating his options, the matter was rendered academic. One moment he was sprinting like Jesse Owens in front of the Nazis, the next he went arse over tit courtesy of an icy patch on the pavement. He hit the ground with a thump.

His one-word reaction to his pratfall was enough to send one old lady and a vicar scurrying away in shock. He groaned at his stupidity and raised himself up just in time to see something quite extraordinary.

Leonard Clarke was a constable of some twenty-seven years; it would have been thirty years but for a small matter involving a recalcitrant neighbour on the continent. Being a constable had been the very limit of his ambitions, especially after what he'd been through in Normandy and beyond. It gave him and his Deirdre a nice life. He could spend most of the day in the open air untroubled by the waves of crime lapping on the shores of British towns and cities around the country. For some reason his beat was remarkably crime-free. This was almost entirely due to the fact that he'd seen all of the children on his beat grow up. He knew their names. They knew his. Law and order had been instilled from the cradle. At its most severe, justice was summarily dispensed through the agency of a clip on the ear or, more often than not, a quiet word with the boys in question. Sometimes the threat of going to their parents did the trick. Justice was understood and respected.

But Leonard Clarke had another life. From about the age of fourteen, the future Constable Clarke had accepted he would never play for his beloved Manchester United. A fondness for cakes and, later, ale, put paid to that. Instead, his increasing waistline and upper body strength found an outlet in another sport more receptive to his burgeoning physicality.

Leonard Clarke took to rugby union as much as it took to him. From the age of seventeen he became prop forward for the local 'Spartans', a position he'd kept for over thirty years. A prop forward is to rugby what an anchor is to a boat. An anchor needs to be dense of constituent with sufficient heft to provide stability. Clarke was all of these things and more.

The detective sergeant knew nothing of Clarke's other life. What he saw made his mouth fall open. One moment Clarke was chatting to the mother, the next saw the corpulent constable pirouette like a Margot Fonteyn at Covent Garden and proceed to drive forward with a crunching rugby tackle that winded Yates just looking at it. The initial impact of Clarke on the young man-made Yates flinch; he closed his eyes as the constable landed on top of the young man, resulting in an audible groan from both him and half the onlookers gazing awestruck at the altercation. To a man and woman, they offered a silent prayer of thanks they were law-abiding. The young man was crying in pain which, at least, confirmed he was still alive albeit a little flatter for his unscheduled meeting with Clarke.

Yates rose painfully to his feet. He'd twisted something. A throbbing in his knee was agony and his ankle wasn't much better. There was nothing about the situation which was going to reflect well on him. He hobbled towards Constable Clarke and the stricken youth. Clarke looked up at Yates in confusion.

'Are you all right, sir?'

A Time to Kill

Of course, I'm not all right, screamed Yates in his head. He remained grimly silent realising an irritable reaction would seem somewhat churlish given Clarke's astonishing arrest. Clarke slowly rose to his feet leaving the youth on the icy ground. Yates restrained himself from pointing out that the young man might try to escape. One look at the boy confirmed he wouldn't be going anywhere in a hurry for a week at least. He was splayed out on the ground like Leonardo's Vitruvian Man. Just a for a moment, Yates had visions of him rising up completely flat, like in a *Tom and Jerry* cartoon. He'd always liked the cartoon and its extreme violence. It had never occurred to him he'd see something quite so painfully comic in real life.

Clarke, realising that Yates was not mortally injured, turned his attention to the young man lying on the snow. He took out of his pocket the photostat of 'Ben' and put it in front of the young man's face.

'Now son. You tell me who this is. If you don't tell me, I shall ask the constable here to jump on top of you again. Do you understand?'

He understood.

-

'Who's this?' asked Burnett as Yates entered the office accompanied by Clarke and the young man. Jellicoe noticed he was asking the constable, not Yates.

'Young fella by the name of Vincent March.'

'Vince,' said the young man defensively.

'No one asked you,' pointed out Burnett. 'Put him in my office, Leo.' He turned to the limping Yates. If there was any sympathy towards the young detective sergeant, then he kept it well hidden. 'What happened to you?'

The answer from Yates was a yelp of agony which certainly explained the problem but not how it happened. He looked at Clarke once more. It was Jellicoe's very firm impression that the two men were more than a little amused by Yates' discomfort.

'It's rather icy outside, sir,' replied Clarke dutifully. 'Detective Sergeant Yates fell while attempting to apprehend Vincent, sorry Vince, here.'

'Lucky you were there, Leo,' said Burnett. This comment, more than anything else, was the most painful moment of the morning for the mortified Yates.

Clarke led Vince into the office. Jellicoe noted that he did not push or bully the young man. He could imagine Yates pushing him, at least if he'd not injured his leg. Burnett followed his drinking companion into the office along with the two detectives.

At this point Burnett glanced up at Clarke who nodded and made for the door. He turned to Burnett and said, 'Bloody fielding let us down again, I see.'

'I know,' replied Burnett, 'Long way back now to win. Best we can hope for is a draw.'

Having discussed the latest on the test match in Australia, Clarke departed. Burnett turned his attention from a cricket match several thousand miles away to the young man in front of him.

'So, tell me what you know about him,' said Burnett pushing a photostat in front of the young man.

'Look I told the other two. I don't know nothing, all right?'

Yates leaned down very close to the young man.

A Time to Kill

'I'm not in a good mood. My leg is killing me and all I want to do is to hurt someone so that they can feel what I feel right now. I'm thinking to myself, who deserves it most? Perhaps it's the little so and so who's responsible for my pain.'

Jellicoe had some sympathy with the look of misgiving on the young man's face. The only person responsible for his injury was Yates himself. This, however, was not the time for pointing it out.

Vince's face reddened in fear and shame. His ribs ached from the force of the tackle he'd endured earlier. Fear, however, can sometimes be used to find courage. Why else do men march towards the sound of a gun? Jellicoe saw the fire grow in the young man's eyes. He leaned in.

'Vince,' said Jellicoe, his voice warm and unthreatening. 'We're not after you. You've done nothing wrong.'

Out of the corner of his eye he saw Burnett's eyebrows shoot up. Well, a little white lie was probably called for at that moment.

'The boy we're after is an accomplice to a murder and a kidnapping. Now, I'm sure you are not an accessory to this. Do you have any other reasons for keeping quiet? Is this boy a close friend of yours?'

Vince would have leapt out of the chair had Yates not held him down.

'What are you saying? He's not a friend.'

'Good, at least we've established that you know him,' said Jellicoe evenly. 'Can you confirm his name?'

Vince's face reddened again. This time it was definitely embarrassment as he realised, he'd been duped. Jellicoe fixed his eyes on Vince but did so without giving the impression that he was seconds away from dishing out a more traditional approach to interrogation.

'He's not a friend. His name's Freddie, I don't know his surname. We weren't friends.'

The last three words were said with great emphasis. This confirmed in Jellicoe's mind, insofar as it needed confirmation, what Ben / Freddie had been.

'All right, I understand what you're saying, Vince,' said Jellicoe. His voice was even and unaccusatory. 'But we both know what Freddie was. You clearly do. Did you see him with anyone regularly? This is important, Vince. A young boy's life hangs in the balance. I don't think you'd want to go through the rest of your life knowing that you might have been able to save him if only you'd mentioned something that might have helped. You don't seem that sort.'

Burnett shot a glance towards Yates. He wondered if Yates could ever have used such an approach, or would he have been more robust approach in dealing with the young man? He suspected the latter. Vince was looking more uncomfortable by the minute, just as Jellicoe had intended. Nothing about Vince suggested criminal. He was gambling that notwithstanding a natural suspicion of the police, he was probably not a bad sort. Youth wasn't a crime in his book, but it was a condition. Its cure was age and experience. Vince would need to grow up a little now if he were to be of any use.

Vince was confronting rather similar thoughts himself. His life thus far had been dedicated to messing around at school, messing around with his mates and, when he had the opportunity, messing around with the opposite sex. In this he was no different from any young man in the country. What he was facing now was a real life and death situation. Its acquaintance was a reminder to him of why he preferred messing around instead.

He shook his head. This time it was genuine. The look in his eyes was a combination of fear and something else. Jellicoe suspected it was helplessness. He kept his eyes fixed on Vince.

'Can you tell us anything, Vince? We need to know who Freddie has been hanging around with or if he had a regular client. Whatever you can add to our knowledge of Freddie will help us.'

'Look I don't hang around him, but he did have some mates. Y'know, similar to him. And, well, he hangs around people who are bad. You know the sort. He probably works for them. Look, I don't know, all right? I don't get involved with these people.'

Jellicoe pushed forward a piece of paper and a pen.

'Write the names down.'

Vince was allowed to leave half an hour later after Jellicoe was convinced there was nothing more to gain from keeping him. A constable led the young man out leaving the three detectives together.

'What do you make of him?' asked Burnett.

Yates looked to Jellicoe. Although he was itching to speak, he recognised that his rank precluded from him speaking first. Jellicoe, however, held his hand out palm upwards to allow Yates to speak.

'I think he's on the level. I know what a hardened criminal looks like and that isn't one. I don't think he hangs around with Freddie, that much is clear. When I was on the street waiting for Constable Clarke to get into position, he had his eye on every girl that passed.'

'Jellicoe?'

'I agree with Yates. I think these names will give us something more to go on. Do any of them mean anything to you?'

Burnett and Yates exchanged a look of recognition. Then Burnett smiled like a panther contemplating his next meal grazing nearby.

'Oh yes, lad, some of them do.' He pointed to a couple of the names and said, 'Start with them.'

Just as he said this there was a knock at the door. Jellicoe looked up and his jaw fell open.

A Time to Kill

16

Elodie Lumsden looked like Rita Hayworth trapped in a civil service job. Her auburn hair cascaded down wildly, at least in every man's dreams, although propriety was maintained in the ponytail she adopted. Jellicoe sensed Burnett's smile at his reaction although he couldn't actually see it himself.

'Detective Inspector, I don't believe I've introduced you to the chief constable and superintendent's secretary, Miss Elodie Lumsden.'

Introductions were made during which, and a little bit late in the day, Jellicoe remembered his manners and stood up. This was acknowledged by a half-smile from Elodie and an enormous grin from Burnett who was enjoying the scene immensely. Yates remained tight-lipped; struck dumb, as ever when the half-French, half-English lady appeared. His face fell somewhere between lust, a desire to impress and, unusually for him, self-doubt. Yates was one hundred and sixty pounds of pure ambition. One of those ambitions was standing a few feet away. He'd no doubt that he would one day be a chief inspector. He was less sure of his chances with Elodie Lumsden.

'The Chief Constable has just arrived. He'd like to see you in his office, sir,' said Elodie.

Her voice was cut glass finishing school but there was just the merest hint of an accent. Jellicoe guessed, correctly as it transpired, she had a French mother and an English father. His mind raced forward as to how they would have met. The war seemed the most likely. However, that would imply she was not his child. The mother was a widow. The father killed by the Germans. Mr Lumsden would have been the knight in shining armour who fell for the young Frenchwoman. If the mother was anything like her daughter, then he was to be congratulated.

Burnett, who had remained seated throughout, got up and started to follow Elodie out. Yates sat transfixed and mute. Burnett rolled his eyes and said to Jellicoe, 'Are you coming or not?'

Jellicoe was quite surprised by this but offered no objection. Another minute or two in Miss Lumsden's company was to be welcomed. Calling her Miss Lumsden felt wrong, however. Too prosaic. Elodie. He would think of her as; nothing else would do. With a name like Lumsden, he speculated, she would be in a hurry to marry.

In this Jellicoe was quite wrong although his suspicion that she detested the name Lumsden was correct. Name or not, she adored her adoptive father. He was her hero. Just a pity about the name. She eyed the new arrival with some approval. Unlike that gaping idiot Yates, he'd at least recovered himself sufficiently to stand up when she'd entered. Most men just sat there and stared. There was a seriousness about him though. He'd not smiled stupidly when she arrived. No, perhaps not seriousness, she decided: sadness.

Elodie Lumsden was well aware of the effect she had on men. She'd noticed it first when she was fifteen which was both a comment on her late arrival to puberty as well as shedding a less favourable light on the men. Unfortunately, the field for her was limited. She was caught between wanting to carve out a career for herself and fulfilling what mother nature, culture and education had suggested was her future.

They arrived at the chief constable's office. Elodie knocked and seconds later Jellicoe found himself in a surprisingly small room. The chief constable was either remarkably humble or he was weak. Then Jellicoe remembered that he was only at the station a couple of days a week. He split his time between this police station and the county headquarters. He'd never met Chief Constable Laurence Leighton before.

Leighton nodded to Elodie and left the office. He stood up and walked around his desk. This was something, thought Jellicoe approvingly. If ever he reached the lofty heights that his family inheritance suggested he should, then he would never be one of those senior officers who sat behind a desk and pretended to ignore new arrivals.

Leighton was a big, lumbering man, even taller than the six-foot Jellicoe. He stepped forward with all of the finesse one associates with the police service, hand outstretched. Thick square fingers encircled Jellicoe's hand and a smile beamed its welcome.

'So, you're James Jellicoe's boy. Pleased to meet you. And how is James these days?'

Jellicoe could just imagine Burnett rolling his eyes at this. He couldn't blame him. It made him feel like a schoolboy again, faintly ashamed of his father and then guilty for feeling so.

'He's well and sends his regards, sir.'

'Very good. How are you settling in?' he paused for a moment and looked uncomfortable. 'Of course, we're all very sorry about what happened. If ever you need anything…'

'Thank you, sir,' said Jellicoe. He was keen to steer the conversation away from the subject of his wife. Thankfully, so was Leighton.

'Sit down. Tell me what I need to know.'

Jellicoe and Burnett sat down in front of Leighton's desk, but the chief constable remained standing. He was an impressive figure. He more than filled his blue uniform. Definitely a rugby player, thought Jellicoe. Probably a lock forward at one time. He looked around fifty, so no longer a player if the slight paunch was anything to go by. The ears had more than a hint of cauliflower about them.

Burnett spoke first.

'We've identified the young man who was an accomplice in the kidnapping. His name is Freddie Douglas, probably an alias.'

'He's not the murderer then?' asked Leighton.

'No. He's on the game. Probably hired to reel in the boy but, no, he didn't murder anyone, nor did he plan this,' said Burnett.

Burnett raised his eyebrows and turned to Jellicoe.

'We have some theories which we are going to follow up.'

'Go on.'

There followed a moment of silence before Jellicoe realised this was his cue to speak. Fair play to Burnett he thought. He didn't hog the limelight or claim any idea as his own. Perhaps he'd misread his new boss.

'Given the nature of the murder, we are dealing with a quite tall and strong man. Freddie Douglas was seen accompanying Stephen Masterson towards the wood in the estate. The witness, his sister, was surprised but was not alarmed as Freddie was known to them, albeit under the name of Ben.'

'What should I read into the fact that the boy followed this other chap into the wood?'

Jellicoe exhaled and held his arms out. Burnett said nothing.

'Either way,' said Jellicoe, 'There is no suspicion that either boy could have killed Masterson as the colonel was seen by their butler soon after Stephen and Freddie had left. He was listening to the cricket apparently.'

Leighton turned to Burnett for a moment.

'Bloody Aussies have a lead of 139.'

'I know,' said Burnett despondently.

'Anyway, do we have anything on the man we believe committed the murder and, presumably, planned the kidnapping?'

'We're following up on Freddie Douglas' known associates and clients,' replied Burnett. 'There's another line of inquiry though. It may need your help.'

'Go on.'

Burnett turned to Jellicoe once more. The stage was his. What was it Shakespeare said? Life was a series of stages. You always had to be ready to perform, receive approval, move on. No one must see what's underneath. He paused for a moment then spoke.

'There's a possibility that although Colonel Masterson was the victim, the real target was his son, Major Masterson. We are keeping an open mind on this.'

Leighton frowned in response to this which Jellicoe took, correctly, to mean that he had better have a good reason for the suggestion.

'There's been no ransom note. This is unusual. Instead, we've had a number of cryptic notes taken from the Bible. Solomon, in fact. This leads us to suspect that the kidnapper has something other than a ransom in mind. Major Masterson was in the military police. He served between 1938 and 1949. It's possible that he may have made enemies over the years whereas Colonel Masterson has effectively been retired since the middle of the war. We believe the motive for the murder and the kidnapping stems from the major's time as a military policeman. This is about revenge, sir.'

Leighton looked sceptical. His brow was furrowed, and he shook his head.

'But if Masterson, is no longer in the military police and by the sounds of it he left them a long time ago, surely that undermines your theory. He's hardly likely to have developed enemies working in an administrative role, at least none who would be likely to want to commit these sorts of crimes. So, who are we dealing with? Why have they waited until now to kill his father and kidnap the boy?'

Jellicoe looked directly at the chief constable, yet Leighton could not help feeling that his mind was elsewhere. He'd met people like this before. Odd characters. Thinkers. They often thought out loud. Potentially they made good cops. The young detective inspector was working through something. Then he spoke as if a thought had just struck him.

'Because he's just left prison.'

Leighton noticed two things about the statement. Both equally gratifying. Firstly, Burnett's head had swung around at

134

such a velocity on hearing this that Leighton thought he'd
wrick his neck. And, more importantly, something about the
young detective's voice suggested the idea had only just
occurred to him. This meant his original assessment of Jellicoe
had been spot on. This was always a small win for any
policeman worth his salt. The old instinct. He could still read
'em. Perhaps he should get more involved in case work again.
Politics never resulted in any clear-cut wins. He missed the big
cases, the hunt. Most of all he missed the capture. That
moment when you could put a hand on the shoulder of the
miscreant and say, 'you're nicked'.

Silence followed this pronouncement. Burnett fixed his
eyes on Jellicoe hoping to hell the young upstart knew where
he was going with this. It only took a few moments for him to
realise Jellicoe was right. What other explanation could there
be?

'It makes sense,' said Burnett, 'Doesn't it, sir?'

'It does.'

'So, we'll need to ask the military to let us have a record of
Major Masterson's arrest records which led to trial and
imprisonment,' added Burnett, impressing both Leighton with
his grasp of the course they needed to pursue and rather
surprised Jellicoe with his boss's rapid speed of uptake.
Burnett looked at Leighton meaningfully. Perhaps there was
hope for the older man yet.

'I take your point chief inspector. Rank will be important
in dealing with the military.'

'Exactly. sir.'

-

'Next time you have a brainstorm, son, give me advance warning,' said Burnett as they descended the stairs.

'I'll try, sir,' replied Jellicoe.

'Have you had any other thoughts you haven't told me?' said Burnett stopping on the stairs to continue to his point. This threw Jellicoe slightly. It was apparent that they were not returning to his office until Jellicoe's mind had been well and truly emptied of every idea and thought on the case. Jellicoe thought for a moment.

'Don't think. Just speak,' pressed Burnett irritably.

'Well, sir, it's as I said earlier. Masterson has suspicions about who has the boy. He's going after him himself. It would make our lives easier if he just told us and let us get on with it.'

'Why isn't he telling us then? Why would he put his own child at risk?'

Burnett started to walk down the stairs as he said this.

'I can think of only two reasons, sir.'

Burnett turned sharply to Jellicoe which the young detective inspector took, correctly, to mean he should get on with it and sharpish.

'Firstly, he knows where to find this man, or this man has already told him in so many words.'

'Secondly?'

'He thinks Stephen is already dead.'

A Time to Kill

17

Two quid the man had given him. Two quid! A fortune. The only thing was what to do with it? His father would give him a clip round the ear 'ole and accuse him of thievin' and his mother would have a go at him. The house would be in uproar all because he had earned, honestly, some money. What a life.

Best keep it to himself, thought Jimmy. He looked once again at his hand. There were, if he was not mistaken, two crisp pound notes there. And the envelope the man had asked him to deliver. He'd not really had a good look at the man. The sunglasses and the hat made him look a bit shady. The fact that he didn't want to visit the cop shop himself made it even more dubious. What of it, thought Jimmy? Ours is not to reason why his teacher often said to him as a prelude to or after dispensing a slap. This invariably occurred when Jimmy had been utterly innocent of any crime.

The police station was quite busy looking today. There was a crowd milling around outside. Jimmy wasn't keen on joining the throng. A part of him wished it had been a bit quieter. Still, two quid was two quid.

Sensing that the man's eyes were on him somewhere, Jimmy steeled himself to execute his task. He marched forward towards the nick. There were few cars on the road because of the snow. He sprinted across the road and dodged in and out of the people at the front. A policeman posted on the steps tried to stop him, but the man had been insistent. He had to get past the defence. Jimmy was small, nimble, and right winger for his school football team. A big awkward plod like the one at the front would present no problems. He raced through the crowd, feinted one way and then darted the other, past the policeman. He jumped up the steps of the police station like a young gazelle evading a big cat. Moments later he was through the double doors.

The sergeant at the desk peered over his glasses down at Jimmy. What he saw was an eight-year-old boy who looked like he was up to no good. He was breathing hard, and his face was flushed. Obviously, he'd been running. Equally obvious was the fact he'd evaded the copper at the front. A bit of a scamp, in other words. However, he'd made it through and was obviously here for a reason.

'Hello, son. Come to turn yourself in then?'

-

'He wore sunglasses a hat and a scarf, sir. I'd never recognise him again'.

'Voice?'

'He was putting on a gruff voice. Wasn't his,' replied Jimmy.

'Height?' asked Yates.

'As tall as you,' replied Jimmy. Then warming to the task, 'Broader though. Not fat. He'd wider shoulders. Like a boxer.'

Yates was a little put out at the implication that he was somehow a lesser man than the criminal. Had the others not been there he'd have given the little imp something to think about when speaking to his elders and betters. Kids of today had no respect.

'What was he wearing? Can you be very specific, Jimmy?' asked the other policeman with the posh voice. Jimmy quite liked him. He seemed kinder, less hostile than the other one.

'He had a dark grey hat and grey scarf.'

'Matching?' asked Jellicoe much to the evident chagrin of Burnett and disdain of Yates.

'Similar colour, yes. His overcoat was dark blue.'

'Buttoned?'

'Yes.'

'Single or double breasted?'

'Double.'

'Shoes?'

'Brown.'

'Scuffed or new?'

'Looked new.'

Jellicoe nodded and sat back in his chair as if he was satisfied. The other two policemen glanced at one another and looked very dissatisfied. Another thought occurred to Jellicoe just as Burnett was about to speak.

'Let's go outside. He's still there.'

'What?' exclaimed Burnett. 'Are you mad?' But Jellicoe was already on his feet.

So was Jimmy. He was excited. The man he'd spoken to was obviously a criminal. Perhaps a master criminal. The nice policeman knew what he was about. It looked like the chase was on. Even with the man's two quid nestling happily in his pocket, Jimmy's loyalties were, mostly, with the forces of law and order.

'Bloody hell,' said Burnett and rose to his feet as well. Jellicoe was already out of the office and heading towards the corridor accompanied by the Baker Street Irregular. When Burnett reached the corridor, he realised two things; Jellicoe was taking the fire escape. This, he acknowledged, was good thinking. The kidnapper would know by now who was investigating him. He'd spot them immediately when they went out of the front entrance. Burnett followed them at a more dignified pace.

Jellicoe was leaping down the stairs and, impressively, so was his partner. Jimmy had no problem keeping up with the detective and they reached the fire door within a matter of minutes. Burnett and Yates reached them moments later. Jellicoe looked at the group.

'Yates, you and I will wait here. Chief, can you take Jimmy to the front and see if the man is still there? Once Jimmy sees the man, Chief, can you send a message on where he is? We'll go around the side of the building and try and nab him if he's there.'

'Yes, sir,' said Jimmy carrying off a military salute.

Jellicoe responded in kind. Burnett did, too, but Jimmy was unaware of the underlying sarcasm to the gesture.

'Come on, young man,' said Burnett, putting his arm around Jimmy's shoulder. 'We'll let the young officers give chase. You can show this old man who the baddie is.'

Jellicoe turned away and smiled at his Chief Inspector. The comments were positively dripping in acerbity. Burnett led Jimmy, who was now in a state of ecstasy over his role in the plan, up some steps to a door and then, moments later, out into the main entrance of the station.

A Time to Kill

'Ready son?' asked Burnett. 'Look for the man and when you spot him don't say anything. Just tell me where he is. Understand?'

'Yes, sir,' responded Jimmy trying to contain his excitement. What a day. Two quid and now on the chase after a hardened criminal. One thought crossed Burnett's mind as they went to the exit. The press outside would see him with the young lad and quickly put two and two together. Burnett looked around and spied a constable.

'Over here, son.'

The constable came over as ordered.

'Get ready to go to the back exit. Sharpish mind. Detectives Jellicoe and Yates are there. Carry a message when I tell you. And they'll need your help then too.'

'Once we're outside, stand at the entrance and look around you. I'll be behind the door. If you see him tell me where he is then come back inside like you've forgotten something.'

Jimmy went through the double doors while Burnett stood behind them, keeping one of the doors ajar just enough to see the young boy. Jimmy, meanwhile, scanned the other side of the street.

He was there. Jimmy saw him immediately. He was standing between the bank and the big shop next door.

'Standing between the bank and Woolworth's.'

'Tie your lace, son. Doesn't matter if it's already tied.' Jimmy bent down immediately. Burnett turned to the constable. 'Get down to Jellicoe and Yates. Tell them he's at Woolworth's.'

The constable burst through the fire exit door rather heavily, causing Burnett to roll his eyes. He stopped short of saying, 'young people'.

Jellicoe and Yates heard him before they saw him. He yelled at the top of the steps, 'Woolworths. He's outside Woolworth's.'

But the two detectives were already under starters orders and tore off round the building. Jellicoe considered himself fairly fit and had played as a back for the school fifteen. He quickly outdistanced Yates who was still suffering from his earlier fall.

He reached the side of the building in front of the main street. Jimmy was tying his lace. Through an open door he saw Burnett. Jimmy stood up and went back inside just as Jellicoe turned to the street and saw their quarry standing by the Woolworth's shop window. He started jogging hoping that he would not draw attention to himself.

The man in question was smoking a cigarette. He was as described. Tall, athletic with a neat blue overcoat and grey homburg. He could have been a banker. His face was obscured both by the brim of his hat and a pair of sunglasses. He had no facial hair.

Jellicoe crouched slightly as he ran. Behind him he could hear other footsteps. Yates and the constable had appeared. This was potentially a problem. The fact that he was jogging in a rather odd fashion as well as the presence of two other men doing likewise, might attract the attention of the kidnapper.

As it turned out he was both right and wrong.

The odd trio had, by now, been seen by the waiting pressmen. They turned to a man and started towards the three policemen. This action, as it was concerted, drew the attention of the man they were after. Unless Jellicoe was mistaken, he seemed to smile. Seconds later Jellicoe saw why. What followed next happened in a curious slow motion although it was probably only a matter of seconds.

First the press descended on the three men like a wave crashing over one of the local surfers. As they did so, a bus appeared on the main street and stopped in front of Woolworth's. Jellicoe saw the black bus driver chat briefly with their quarry as he boarded.

'Detective Inspector have you an update for us?' shouted one press man as they converged on Jellicoe.

Yes, you've just let our suspect escape. You're all under arrest thought Jellicoe sourly.

'Detective Inspector have you an update for us?' shouted one press man as they converged on Jellicoe.

Yes, you've just let our suspect escape. You're all under arrest. These were the first two thoughts that went through Jellicoe's mind. Then he saw the kidnapper taking a seat by the window. He turned to Jellicoe and saluted. A broad grin creased his face. Jellicoe could do little but look on in frustration. And then one other thing attracted his attention. Taking a seat at the front of the bus was another man. He couldn't place him at first but as the bus drew away, he remembered.

It was the man he knew as 'Montgomery'.

18

'I knew I should have set the dogs on them,' shouted Burnett angrily. Jellicoe was not quite convinced he didn't mean it and had to restrain him from arresting the press outside for aiding and abetting a criminal. It seemed churlish to point out that he probably wouldn't have made it to the bus in time anyway. Sometimes facts and evidence need to take a back seat to anger. This was one such occasion. The idea of the press being hounded away from the front of the police station did have some appeal.

Burnett ordered police to be sent to bus stops on the route of the number 82, but no one had much expectation of success. The appearance of Montgomery could not have been by accident. If anything, it made Jellicoe all the more certain that he had been sent by Masterson to find the kidnapper. Well, he'd found him. If Montgomery was any good, and Jellicoe suspected he was, then he couldn't be in any doubt as to what had just taken place and who the police had been chasing. But then again, shouldn't he have recognised the man?

Such were the thoughts crisscrossing Jellicoe's mind that he didn't hear Burnett speaking to him.

'Are you listening to me?' snapped Burnett which woke Jellicoe from his reverie.

'Sorry, sir,' replied Jellicoe and then proceeded to explain what he'd seen.

Burnett, already on a short fuse, exploded again.

'Right, let's get Masterson in and have him explain to us what the hell's going on.'

'Can I suggest, sir, that we wait until we know more? In the meantime, perhaps we can have a man watch this Montgomery character. They don't know we're on to him. If he's still at Ramsbottom's we can follow him.'

Burnett treated this idea the same way senior people treat all ideas that are better than their own: a gruff acknowledgment followed by making it seem that this is what they'd always thought.

The mood in the office was not helped when Vaughan returned with the message sent by the kidnapper and confirmed that it contained no prints. Burnett suggested he try harder next time. A chastened Vaughan left the office but not before seeing Jellicoe smile at him and roll his eyes. They placed the note on the table and examined it. It read:

Make them bear their guilt, O God; let them fall by their own counsels; because of the abundance of their transgressions cast them out, for they have rebelled against you.

'Solomon, I take it?' said Burnett.

'I suspect it is, but we can check,' replied Jellicoe. 'It's interesting though.' He sat back and pondered for a moment. This moment was a second too long for the already worn-out patience of his chief inspector.

'What is?' roared Burnett. Yates tried and failed to supress a smile which earned a warning glance from Burnett.

Jellicoe seemed unruffled by the explosion. He put his finger on the text and read it out, 'Make them bear their guilt.'

He looked at Burnett expectantly. There nothing on the older man's face except impatience and a look that one did not need to be a psychologist to interpret as 'get-on-with-it'.

'Three things strike me, sir. Firstly, why is there no ransom being asked? Secondly, why is he delivering the notes to the police and not Masterson, himself? It makes no sense unless we assume revenge, not gain, is the motive. This is where the third thought comes in. What if the notes are meant for Masterson and for us? Masterson knows who has his boy. The kidnapper assumes that he will either tell us or has a reason not to do so. In which case, he wants us to investigate Masterson. He wants us to find out what he already knows.'

'Which is?' asked Burnett wearily.

'Masterson is guilty of something in this man's eyes. He's giving us an opportunity to find this out for ourselves. Masterson knows this and has brought in his own man to stop him.'

Burnett sat back in his chair. To be fair to the young pup, thought Burnett, he certainly comes up with some plausible theories. He glanced at Yates and his heart fell. This is what he'd had to work with all his life. People like Yates quickly tired of investigative work because, fundamentally, they were not much good at it. They usually became politicians; figuring out how to get promoted into senior positions in the police service. Then they'd spend their days dealing with council leaders and other politicians, people with more ambition than brains. People like themselves in other words. The one saving grace from all of this was that at least they were out of the way.

'So why not just kill Masterson and have done with it?' asked Yates, aware that Burnett's eyes were on him and thus expecting him to make a comment.

'But then who would know of Masterson's guilt?'

'Why not just come out with what Masterson has done?' asked Yates, warming to his theme. 'That's assuming he's done something wrong in the first place. This may just be an attempt to discredit.'

'He's gone to a lot of trouble if it's just discrediting someone. No,' said Jellicoe, 'this is a serious grievance, and he wants Masterson to fall. Remember the earlier message - *Whoever digs a pit will fall into it, and a stone will come back on him who starts it rolling.* He sees himself as God, almost. The vengeful, wrathful God punishing the sins of the transgressor.'

'He's nuts,' said Yates.

'Thank you, Freud,' said Burnett drily. 'So, we need to dig into Masterson's past. Find out who he imprisoned, why, when and when they were released.'

Yates shook his head and said, 'I can't believe we're treating Major Masterson as a criminal. Have you considered that this is what the kidnapper wants? Maybe he's misdirecting us because he wants to waste our time.'

'Your time, son,' said Burnett. 'You're the one who will be investigating this. You, Jellicoe, can speak to the men Vince mentioned. Take Constable Clarke with you. He'll guide you right.' Burnett paused for a moment and looked at the two detectives. 'Well come on. Don't just sit there like garden gnomes. Get out!'

-

'How long have you been in the job?' asked Jellicoe.

'Twenty-seven years on and off. I had three years doing something else.'

Jellicoe glanced at Clarke for a second but said nothing. He didn't need to ask why he'd had time off.

'Where were you?'

'Normandy first then into Germany. They wanted me in the military police, I said no. I wanted to do my bit.'

Jellicoe nodded. He could see that the big constable was uncomfortable, so he let the subject drop and turned to the case.

'What can you tell me about Ronald Musgrave?'

'Ronnie and I go way back. He's always been trouble, of course, but he's old fashioned. He runs things along the front, there's a bit of smuggling cigarettes from France, but he doesn't like drugs and discourages their sale on his turf. This suits us, of course. He confines his activities to gambling, fencing and, although he won't own up to it, prostitution. High class, not your street walkers. We've never made anything stick. His lawyer is the best and witnesses usually change their mind mysteriously. Some of our boys were on his payroll.'

He saw Jellicoe raise his eyebrows at this which brought up a smile.

'The next we hear of them; they're living it up in the south of France. The man you replaced was one of his.'

'So, I heard. How did they catch him?'

A Time to Kill

'Reg, sorry, the chief inspector is no mug. He had his suspicions for a long time. He set a trap for him.'

The big constable clapped his hands together loudly and laughed. Jellicoe smiled and decided not to inquire further. They drove down towards the sea front. The buildings were stained as grey as the sky overhead. All except one. A burned-out amusement arcade. Probably an insurance job, thought Jellicoe grimly. Some men were carrying out the blackened arcade games and loading them onto a lorry.

They drove in silence for another minute then Clarke turned to Jellicoe and said, 'So your dad's the big cheese in London, I hear.' He seemed to be enjoying travelling in a car rather than walking the rather cold and certainly treacherously slippery beat.

'I wouldn't say he's the big cheese, but he is quite senior.'

'That'll be you one day then,' said Clarke, knowingly.

Jellicoe shook his head.

'I hardly think so. It's not really for me. I'm more like my grandad. I prefer the chase.'

He'd never said it like that before, but he realised it was true. He did enjoy the chase. In fact, he probably enjoyed it more than the capture. This case was actually proving to be just what he'd needed. Three months off on bereavement. It felt good to be back. More than this, it felt good to be back on a case that genuinely challenged him.

'Can you pull over here, sir?' asked Clarke following a few moments of silence. They were at the sea front now. Jellicoe saw a man standing on a corner just outside an amusement arcade. Jellicoe pulled the car up in front of the man.

Clarke rolled down the window and shouted to the man, 'Oi Smithy, over here, mate.'

The man's face creased into a frown and then he saw who it was. He came over grinning.

'Bloody hell, Clarkey, are you a detective now?'

'You can't keep talent back, Smithy. Where's the gaffer? We need to have a word.'

Smithy motioned with his head towards the arcade.

'Upstairs. What's the problem?'

'Nothing for you to worry about. Or him for that matter. Not this time anyway,' said Clarke getting out of the car. Jellicoe followed suit, assuming they'd reached their destination.

Smithy led them inside. The arcade was mostly empty. A few young men playing games that Jellicoe had lost interest in by the time he was nine. Music played from a speaker with a frog in its throat. The spinning, ringing sounds of the games competed against the jazz music. Thelonious Monk was fighting a losing battle against the ringing of the games, which was a pity. Jellicoe could have happily spent a few moments listening to the piece. Instead, the shrill sounds from the games and the harsh laughter of the young men made this a scene from Hieronymus Bosch. It was certainly Jellicoe's idea of hell.

They went through to a door at the back which led to a wooden staircase. They followed Smith up the narrow stairs and reached another door that led to a corridor. Dark wallpaper was peeling from the walls. It felt like the building and everyone inside was slowly decaying. It was unfathomable to Jellicoe how anyone would want to work in such a desolate situation.

A Time to Kill

They reached the end of the corridor and Smithy gave a knock. He waited for a response. An irritated 'yes' was enough for him to open the door. He noticed that Clarke took off his helmet. Jellicoe removed his hat, too.

It would be fair to say that Jellicoe's experience with the criminal underworld, in fact with anyone seeing him with a uniformed police officer was a mixture of suspicion mixed with hostility. It was not usually a beaming smile.

'Clarkey! What brings you here, old son.'

Clarke had the grace to be slightly embarrassed by the effusiveness of the greeting. He suspected, rightly, it might take some explaining to his new colleague from London.

'Hello, Mr Musgrave, sorry to land in on you like this.'

Jellicoe could see why he'd been sent along rather than Yates. This was a man that needed to be handled with a greater degree of tact than the young detective sergeant had thus far demonstrated.

Ronald Musgrave was of a similar vintage to Clarke and clearly had a similar appetite to the big policeman. He was taller, a little unkempt and would not have looked out of place in the kitchen of an Italian restaurant. His thick dark hair was greying and his face, which at that moment was full of Pickwickian good-fellowship, looked as if it needed to be shaved twice a day to keep the beard in check. His shirt was open revealing both a string vest and a veritable jungle of thick hair on his chest. The accent was from London.

The first thing that hit Jellicoe as he entered the office after the ice-cold trip up the stairs was the heat in the room. Musgrave was sweating profusely. There were not one but two, two-bar, electric heaters burning. The air was close and oppressive.

'Who do we have here?' asked Musgrave, fixing hard grey eyes on Jellicoe.

Clarke turned to Jellicoe and grinned like a proud father.

'This is DI Jellicoe. Newly arrived from the Met.'

Musgrave's smile widened and he said teasingly, 'Here to show the yokels how it's done?'

Jellicoe smiled at the rather predictable joke.

'I suspect it'll be the other way around.'

Musgrave hesitated a moment then said shrewdly, 'Somehow I doubt it. What can I do for you, Inspector? I take it this isn't a social call. Have a seat.' Musgrave motioned with his head to Smithy to move a couple of seats over to them.

'No,' admitted Jellicoe sitting down. 'You've heard about the murder of Colonel Masterson and the kidnapping of his grandson?'

'Bad business,' agreed Musgrave also taking a seat. 'I hope you don't think we're responsible.'

Clarke had been slightly concerned about this point, too. He'd tried to suggest earlier that while Musgrave was no saint, this was probably not his territory. Jellicoe put everyone's mind at rest.

'No, unless you want to confess.'

Musgrave exploded into laughter. It was genuine and he seemed to appreciate the cheek from the new DI. It also suggested, as it was meant to, that this was unlikely. Jellicoe continued, 'We're looking for a young man named Freddie Douglas.'

The smile evaporated from Musgrave's face.

'So are we.'

A Time to Kill

'Why?'

'Can't say. It's not relevant to your case.'

'How can you be sure?'

'We're sure.'

There was nothing in Musgrave's manner that suggested he was going to be more forthcoming, so Jellicoe moved onto another topic.

'Are you aware he may have information related to the murder and the kidnapping?'

In response, Musgrave held up the newspaper. The front page carried the picture of the young man they'd formerly known as Ben and the story of the crime. Jellicoe nodded and then leaned forward.

'If you were to find him first, would you hand him over to us?'

'Why do you want him?' asked Musgrave, avoiding answering the question directly.

The answer was a more delicate balancing act than it might have appeared. Jellicoe knew that Musgrave knew what Freddie was. By connecting him with Stephen Masterson he was potentially offering a known criminal the opportunity to blackmail the family.

'A witness saw him on the estate on the night of the murder and kidnapping.'

'He's no killer, is Freddie,' laughed Musgrave dismissively. But Jellicoe sensed something else in the laugh. Perhaps it was because he knew of Freddie's inclinations. Or something else, perhaps. Underneath the cheerful reaction to seeing Constable Clarke, Jellicoe felt he was looking at a man who was on edge.

'No, Mr Musgrave, but he may have been an accomplice to the kidnapping. You know, it would help us a lot if you could tell us more about why you want to see Freddie.'

'Not necessarily.'

'Why not?'

'It's our business. We'll take care of it. But if we find Freddie or the boy, we'll hand him back.'

'And Freddie?'

Musgrave did not answer but the veil had dropped a little. The man in charge of rackets on the sea front, the criminal, was revealed. The grey eyes fixed on Jellicoe grew harder. The answer to Jellicoe's question was to be found in that stare and in the deadly silence. Clarke began to shift in his seat. Jellicoe glanced at him. It was clear that the constable sensed the meeting had taken a darker turn. The question in Jellicoe's mind was no longer solely about why Masterson had been murdered and Stephen kidnapped. Something else was in the air in this coastal town. At the centre of it all was a young man called Freddie.

Jellicoe shot to his feet, which surprised the two older men. Both rose more slowly and shared a rueful grin that spoke of the loss of their youth. However, Jellicoe was in no mood to join in.

'Thank you, Mr Musgrave. We'll see ourselves out.'

His manner had changed, and the curtness was noted by both Clarke and Musgrave. The constable shrugged while Musgrave merely waved him away like it didn't matter to him what the cub thought.

Clarke raced after Jellicoe who was bounding down the stairs, two at a time, past a surprised Smithy and some people playing pinball. After the stuffy atmosphere of the back office,

154

the cold air hit Jellicoe like a slap across the face. Jellicoe crossed over the road to the seafront. Some hardy souls were swimming. One youngish man was trying to surf. Not exactly California thought Jellicoe. He sensed Clarke arrive beside him.

'Everything all right, sir?'

No, everything was not all right. The meeting with Musgrave had thrown up all manner of questions that no old pals act from Clarke would uncover. Jellicoe turned to Clarke and regarded the constable for a moment. He could see a man who was probably as honest a copper as he'd ever met. A man who upheld the values of the service and had unquestionably prevented more people becoming criminals than he, Jellicoe, would ever catch. Clarke's palpable decency was not at odds with the seeming affection he was held in and held for Ronald Musgrave. In fact, it was entirely in keeping. It was the likes of Clarke rather than punitive justice or aggressive policing that kept the likes of Musgrave in check.

'I don't know,' answered Jellicoe and he was being honest. 'There's something going on here. This is more than just about a murder and a kidnapping.'

Jellicoe spun around and faced out towards the sea. An icy breeze was whipped up causing sand and flakes of snow to swirl around the air, stinging Jellicoe's face and temporarily blinding him. He turned away from the front and rubbed his eyes. Then he opened them again, but his vision was blurred, his skin prickled and smarted.

'Come on,' said Jellicoe striding towards his car.

'Where are we going?' asked Clarke.

'To a shop,' replied Jellicoe. Clarke's frown was a question. 'To buy an electric heater,' added Jellicoe.

19

Burnett's eyes grew wider, and he was seconds away from his fourteenth explosion that Saturday. He should have been at home listening to the football. Or in a pub with friends. Anything except sitting in front of a 'nob from London complicating an already complicated case. Wasn't he supposed to bring solutions not more questions? Yet part of him was already beginning to trust the instincts of the young policeman. There was an otherworldliness about him that was as disconcerting. And irritating. He did not doubt he was perceptive, though.

'The only man you could call a rival to Musgrave is Johnny Warwick. They heartily detest one another but they also keep their distance. Warwick deals with the things that Musgrave has no interest in, drugs, booze, cigarettes. There's no overlap. Musgrave owns or has interests in everything on the sea front. The further you go into the town; the less interest Musgrave takes.'

'There's no gang violence, sir?' asked Jellicoe.

'I honestly can't remember the last time. Both know it's in their interests to keep things quiet. They each make enough money without trying to muscle in on the other.'

Jellicoe nodded but still seemed unhappy.

'What's this got to do with Princess Freddie and his boyfriend or the dead colonel for that matter?'

Jellicoe's face confirmed Burnett's worst fear. He had no idea. In fact, it was worse. He had too many ideas, each one more fantastic than the next. Realising that silence was probably not what Burnett needed at that moment, he pressed ahead.

'I still think that the murder and the kidnapping are revenge, pure and simple. But there's more to this than we know. In this regard, I think Freddie is the key. We need to know more about his movements, contacts and activities in the last few days.'

'Oh right,' said Burnett, sarcasm dripping from every syllable, 'Let me just call up all the officers not already checking on Masterson's past, shall I?'

'Have we been given access to the military's records?'

'Not yet,' said Burnett glumly. 'The chief is working on it but it's Saturday. I doubt we'll get near them before Monday.'

It was Jellicoe's turn to frown.

'What's Yates doing if that's the case?'

'You and DS Yates will spend the rest of the afternoon finding out about Freddie Douglas' whereabouts. Speak to the other people on Vince's list. And speak to Johnny Warwick. He's a lovely man.' By the tone of Burnett's voice, Jellicoe judged this to be unlikely. Burnett picked up the phone and nodded towards the door, 'Off. I'll tell Warwick's lawyer that Johnny-boy is going to get a visit. And then…'

Jellicoe paused and waited to hear what Burnett was going to do then.

'…and then I'll try and catch the second half of the football on the radio.'

A Time to Kill

Jellicoe looked at his watch. It was just after three thirty. He saw Yates arrive in the outer office and went to join him.

-

The foyer of the police station was quiet as the two policemen walked through. A couple passed them at the entrance. The woman was being comforted by her husband. Jellicoe glanced at them but thought better of inquiring. The desk sergeant could deal with them. They headed outside into the cold. The sun was shining, and the thaw was setting in.

As they walked towards the car, Jellicoe handed Yates the keys and the list of names provided by Vince. This was in anticipation of the question Yates was going to ask about where they were going. The list had four names; one had been crossed off.

'How was it with Ronnie Musgrave?'

Jellicoe smiled and replied, 'Interesting.' He didn't expand on why, much to the evident irritation of Yates.

'Shall we do Craig Woodward next?' asked Yates. 'He's not too far from here.'

They climbed into the car and drove off. Most of the press men had left by this stage. It was Saturday after all. They had lives, too, thought Jellicoe.

'Tell me about Woodward.'

Yates pulled out onto the main street and drove along a road that was virtually empty of cars but thronged with shoppers.

'He's a small-time hood. Independent. Has a foot in both camps so to speak. Musgrave and Warwick, that is.'

'Unusual.'

Yates smiled at this comment.

159

'We're not in the city now, sir. The pool is smaller. Woodward does his own thing, and they respect that.'

'His thing being?'

'He's six foot five and two hundred and fifty pounds,' replied Yates. 'Between him and Marciano, I think I know who I'd bet on.'

'Ahhh, I see. Will he talk to us?'

'Probably not.'

'Excellent.'

They drove for five minutes before arriving at a small pub on a street corner, *The Bricklayer's Arms*. Outside was a painted sign displaying a fairly tough looking gentlemen sporting biceps that he seemed, with some justification, to be inordinately proud of. A couple of men entered the pub. They were dressed in pea coats, wore butcher's boy caps, and looked as if they knew what the inside of a police cell looked like.

'Nice place. I don't suppose you have a machete underneath your raincoat.'

'They'd have it off you in no time, sir,' said Yates as he pulled over.

The two men got out of the car. Jellicoe and Yates exchanged looks. To be fair to the young sergeant, he didn't lack for courage. There was a hint of a grin on his face. Jellicoe could think of nothing to smile about so contented himself with a here-we-go raising of the eyebrows. He hoped he appeared outwardly calm because inside he was feeling distinctly 'windy'.

Jellicoe marched into the pub first as Yates stood back, politely. The interior of the pub lived down to expectations. Through the wall of smoke Jellicoe could see dark wooden

A Time to Kill

panelled walls adorned with pictures of boxers. The diminutive exterior was no disguise; it really was a small pub. What it lacked in square feet it more than compensated for in noise and atmosphere. A darts game was taking place which genuinely placed the spectators at risk of injury such was their proximity to the board. Because of the match, no one paid much attention to the arrival of the two policemen. At least they didn't for the first two seconds after they entered.

And then the first pig snort could be heard.

Slowly people turned around and all of a sudden Jellicoe felt like he was in the middle of a wild west saloon. The noise slowly ebbed away. Jellicoe headed towards the bar and the welcoming snarl of the barman who was glaring at them malevolently.

'What can I get you?' asked Jellicoe turning to Yates, ignoring the fact that everyone in the pub was looking at them.

'Bottle of Guinness.'

'Two Guinness,' said Jellicoe to the barman. The barman made no move. Jellicoe smiled congenially at him. 'Did you hear what I said?'

'I heard,' said the barman but continued to stand still.

'They're a friendly lot here, aren't they?' said Jellicoe turning to Yates. He put his hand in his breast pocket and extracted a wallet. From his wallet he pulled out two-pound notes and laid them out on the bar.

'We don't serve your sort here,' said the barman sullenly.

'You surprise me,' said Jellicoe in a voice that suggested he was not in the least bit surprised. He fixed his eyes on the barman. He was relatively young, perhaps the son of the owner. He was not especially tall, but it was obvious he fancied himself and more than this, he had an audience. This was a chance for him to earn the respect of people he was desperate to earn the respect of. Jellicoe kept his eyes on him and said nothing.

'Fair enough,' said Jellicoe at length.

Yates looked on, rapt at what was taking place. And a little guilty. He wasn't sure if Craig Woodward would be here or not, but he had been completely sure that, in a pub like this, a man like Jellicoe would detonate like a stink bomb in a classroom. The joke, insofar as these things are ever funny, was potentially going to backfire. What if the hoodlums in the pub turned on them both?

Jellicoe turned his attention to Yates. His cold blue eyes seemed to read the detective sergeant and he could not stop himself colouring a little.

'Any sign of our man?'

'No, sir.'

'Strange. You seemed so sure he would be here.' Yates's reaction to this confirmed Jellicoe's suspicions. The sergeant had deliberately brought them here to test the new man's mettle. He wondered if Burnett had suggested this or if it was his own initiative. They were here now. He decided he may as well introduce himself to the local 'roughs'.

Turning away from Yates he faced the pub. Everyone to a man, and they were all men, this wasn't a pub to bring a date to, stared back at him in a sullen silence. A half-smile appeared on Jellicoe's face and he stared back at them nerveless and implacable. He hoped so anyway. He stepped forward and decided to speak to them in the manner of a schoolteacher addressing unruly children.

A Time to Kill

'Good afternoon, gentlemen. I'd like to introduce myself if I may. My name is Jellicoe. Detective Inspector Jellicoe and I'm recently arrived from London to work with DCI Burnett and DS Yates, here.'

Silence hung in the air like a threat.

'I need your help,' said Jellicoe and then paused while there was derisive laughter. While the unwilling audience laughed, Jellicoe used this moment to take out a picture of Stephen Masterson and the artist's likeness of Freddie Douglas. He held the pictures up. Much to Yates's surprise this seemed to act to dampen their amusement. The silence that developed made Jellicoe's voice all the stronger. It filled the air, yet he was not shouting. He was speaking to them as if there was only one other person in the room. He was speaking to them as if, and this is what Yates found astonishing, they were adults, law-abiding adults.

'A young boy has been kidnapped and his grandfather murdered. I don't believe any of you had anything to do with this. I don't believe any of you would have much time for those that did. I believe that you would want these people caught.'

He paused for a moment to let this sink in.

'Equally, I don't expect any of you to come forward and provide us with information about this young man here,' said Jellicoe, indicating Freddie Douglas.

Jellicoe's voice dropped a little as he said this. It was said with sadness but also captured a sense of realism of the situation. It was not condemnatory, noted Yates with surprise. Then Jellicoe raised his arm up brandishing the artist's impression of Freddie.

'This is Freddie Douglas. Many of you will know who he is. Many of you will know what he is. To that let me add that he is implicated in the kidnapping of Stephen Masterson. The Mastersons are offering a reward of two hundred pounds for information leading to the recovery of Stephen.'

'Stephen is sixteen years old. He's just a boy. Stephen has barely begun his life. He deserves a chance to live. One of you may well have information that could help this happen. Please contact the police station and tell us what you know. We won't come to visit. We won't name you. It will be, to all intents and purposes, an anonymous tip off. No one gains from Stephen Masterson's death. Not you. Not Mr Musgrave. Not Mr Warwick. No one. Please help us find Stephen. Thank you for listening, gentlemen.'

Jellicoe nodded to Yates that it was time to leave. Interestingly, there were no snorts as they left. Yates had not expected this. But a more immediate problem presented itself and it was one Jellicoe addressed seconds after they emerged from the pub. He spun around to Yates and grabbed him by the lapels of his mackintosh.

'Don't ever pull a stunt like that again,' snarled Jellicoe.

20

Yates looked stunned by the vehemence with which Jellicoe had spoken to him. There was no mistaking the anger in the clear blue eyes of the detective inspector. Just as Yates was about to defend himself, Jellicoe held his hand up. This silenced Yates immediately.

'If you think we're going to save this boy with you wasting our time in places like that, think again.' This was said in a tone only just above a whisper. Then Jellicoe added the final insult, 'I take it Woodward wasn't there.'

'No, sir.'

Jellicoe didn't bother waiting for the reply, he turned around and marched to the car. Yates followed behind burning with rage. He was angry at himself. His attempt at putting the new man in his place was transparent. And it had failed. Worse, it had been seen to fail. This day was turning into an unmitigated series of personal humiliations.

'Where to?'

'Sir,' snarled Jellicoe who was now in no mood to let the sergeant off.

'Sir,' added Yates. He realised he sounded like a caricature of a teenager.

'Warwick.'

This was the last word exchanged between the two men as they took the main road that led out of the town. They passed through parts of the town that were being redeveloped. The anger Jellicoe felt at Yates was replaced by something else, deeper, and more intense because of its essential sadness. Up and down the country, town planners were creating housing estates that concreted over this green and pleasant land. Worse, they were erecting blocks of flats that were, to Jellicoe's eyes, demoralizingly ugly, inspired by an abstract architectural theory that was abhorrent. A house was more than a machine for living in. Jellicoe was sure that one day soon the social consequences of this experiment would soon be laid bare. The estates and the blocks of flats would become a breeding ground for crime as they had in London. Why anyone would want to live there was beyond him. He remembered the words of the Spanish philosopher: those who do not read history are condemned to repeat it.

They passed from the grey concrete to the country. Green grass peeked out from under the melting snow. The houses were bigger yet veiled behind walls and trees. This was a different form of ghetto.

Up ahead, a large white cottage with a thatched roof attracted Jellicoe's attention. A sign outside told him that this was their destination. It read *The Highwayman est. 1728*. This represented the other end of the hostelry spectrum. A quaint old English pub straight from a tourist guide. The name was neatly ironic given its present owner's occupation. Yates noted the smile when the detective inspector saw the sign.

'This is Warwick's pub but it's not like the last one.'

'So, I see. Was the other one a Warwick pub?'

A Time to Kill

'Yes, sir. He spends more time here, though. Most people don't know it's his. Anyone you saw in the last pub is pretty much banned from this one. This pub is strictly for locals. If they had any idea who owned it, I'm sure they'd have a fit.'

I'm sure they would, thought Jellicoe. The road they'd driven along was tree-lined with large houses with enormous gardens and high, manicured hedges. It had the feel of a village even though they were, in fact, on the outskirts of the town just at the point it meets the country.

It was interesting how the pub's ownership or, at least, the owner's reputation, had somehow remained either a secret or been accepted.

'Is Warwick a golfer?' asked Jellicoe, as they pulled into the car park adjoining the pub. This prompted Yates to look at him strangely.

'How on earth did you know that?'

Jellicoe felt like sighing. He was caught between his irritation at the young sergeant's attitude and a desire to help him. After only a week at his new police station, he could see just how immature his subordinate was; the mismatch between the young man's view of himself and Jellicoe's was an unbridgeable gulf at that moment. This was as dangerous for him as it was for colleagues. The Burnett-style of leadership was effective but from another time. It worked as much because of Burnett's personality as his experience. He was like an old lion: scarred from battles past, unafraid of the fight ahead, always confident of success.

Jellicoe turned to Yates. His voice was neutral. He could never carry off Burnett's sense of irritation and he wanted to avoid condescension. For someone as insecure as Yates, this would have been catastrophic for the future.

'I was guessing of course. We passed a golf course two minutes ago. Then we arrive to this very quaint village pub. If Warwick owns this, it's because he craves respectability. The *leif motif* of this man's life is to belong to a class that hates him. He thinks he's done the first part. He's wealthy and successful. I suspect he has many legitimate businesses. Ronnie Musgrave is small-time by comparison to Warwick. Probably Warwick has not bothered with the sea front because it is just too dilapidated and associated with crime. No, he wants respectability. Once you have the money, you use it. How? You buy the trappings associated with having wealth: big house, big car, beautiful wife, the right clothes. Then you need the right friends. So, you join a golf club. You have to understand what drives these men, Yates. Understand that and you become better at your job. You'll spend less time on the inessential and focus, instead, on what matters.'

It was difficult to tell if any of this was making an impression on Yates. His face retained its permanent look of dumb scepticism. This probably wasn't a bad thing in a policeman. Jellicoe left it at that. Lesson over, they climbed out of the car.

The two men walked into a bar that seemed to be from a different time, different planet, even, from the one they'd come from. The ceiling was much lower yet there an absence of the smoky-hostile atmosphere they'd experienced earlier. No wonder Warwick had taken an interest in this pub thought Jellicoe. The people here were just like him: newly minted middle class country gents.

A Time to Kill

The noise didn't alter when the two men walked in. There was no sense of intimidation. No one was interested because no one immediately identified them as policemen or, if they did recognise the species, no one felt threatened by their arrival. Why would they? They were all law-abiding.

It was nearing five now. This time Jellicoe would take a drink. He ordered two Guinness from the barman and joined Yates in a snug near the bar.

'What about Warwick?' asked Yates, as Jellicoe set the drinks down on the table.

Jellicoe glanced at the barman and said, 'Unless I've missed my guess, he'll be along soon.'

Yates looked at the barman. Jellicoe was right, he was possibly the only person in the hostelry who seemed nervous at the two policemen's arrival. Five minutes later Jellicoe spied a man talking to the barman. The man in question was short but well-made and quite dapper. He was also bespectacled which somewhat undermined the impression that they were dealing with a hardened criminal. Jellicoe was amused by this perception and knew he should discount it.

The man approached them.

'Gentlemen, may I join you?'

Jellicoe nodded and Yates edged along the seat to allow the man to sit with them.

'Another drink? On the house.'

'Thanks, perhaps some other time,' replied Jellicoe for both of them.

The man turned to the bar shook his head. Then he fixed his attention on Jellicoe. Close up he was man of around forty. His dark hair was short and neat but greying at the side. He wore a dark pullover with a shirt underneath and grey cavalry tweed trousers. The brown tortoiseshell glasses looked like something Jerry Lewis would wear when he wanted to appear stupid. But the hard blue eyes behind the lenses told Jellicoe this man was no fool. Warwick was busy appraising Jellicoe, too. Then he spoke.

'How can I help you?'

Straight to it; no introductions, no social niceties. He knew they were policemen; he knew they were here to see him. He was polite but the meeting would have none of the chumminess he'd witnessed earlier between Clarke and Musgrave. Warwick was a businessman and a busy man. Jellicoe smiled. The tone had been set.

He was, oddly, glad that there was no pretence. They were enemies. Nothing could disguise this so why try? They were forever to be engaged in a war. It had been so since the first law was struck. It was the reason why laws existed. There were police and villains; cops and robbers; goodies and baddies.

'Thank you for seeing us, Mr Warwick,' began Jellicoe. 'I am Detective Inspector Jellicoe, and this is DS Yates.'

'I know who you are,' replied Warwick. He offered no explanation as to why.

Jellicoe nodded.

'Stephen Masterson's abduction was made possible because of a young man called Freddie Douglas. We're trying to understand his movements over the last few days, who he would have seen. Can you help us?'

Warwick took off his glasses. Jellicoe did not for one second believe they were anything other than another totem of the respectability he desired so much. He stared at Jellicoe. This was something the detective had come across before in more powerful criminals. They imposed their presence on you through unblinking attention and taking an inordinate amount of time to answer even the simplest of questions. If he hadn't seen it so often before, he would have been intimidated. As it was, he was amused.

'No.'

Well, it was brief at least. Jellicoe took a sip of his Guinness and studied Warwick for at least as long again. Then he asked, 'No you won't or no you can't?'

'Both.'

'Why not?'

'Why should I?'

'A boy's life may depend on it.'

'Why should I care?'

Jellicoe sat forward; his face was less than a foot away from Warwick.

'Because you are probably not to blame. Someone else is. Why should you care who goes down? You and Musgrave have this town to yourselves. The last thing you need is an independent running loose, stirring up all sorts of trouble. Help us catch this man. Just tell us how we can find Freddie Douglas.'

Warwick rose from the seat. The meeting was over. He walked away and did not look back. Jellicoe and Yates exchanged glances.

'Have you come across him much before?' asked Jellicoe. He was clearly amused by Warwick flouncing off dramatically.

'Only with the Chief.'

'Was that typical?'

'Yes,' replied Yates before remembering to add, 'sir.'

The two men finished their drinks and left the pub unsure of whether they were any further forward or not. It didn't feel as if they had made much progress beyond introducing Jellicoe to the local criminal gentry. It rankled with the two men. Rather than chase after the third name on the list, Jellicoe suggested they return to the station in case there had been any ransom demand or further communication. There was always the faint hope that the door-to-door inquiries about Freddie Douglas's whereabouts may have yielded something.

Jellicoe did not feel like talking so they drove back in silence. The snow had cleared from the roads but still clung to rooftops and trees. It was dark by the time they pulled into the station car park. The streets were empty. Light reflected from the puddles made by the melted snow.

The office was mostly deserted. DC Wallace was manning one of the phones. Burnett had left as promised, no doubt enjoying what was left of the afternoon sport. Jellicoe and Yates checked the board. There was precious little to add, and nothing had been added by anyone else. It was as if criminals and snouts downed tools for the weekend.

'Any message from the chief,' asked Jellicoe to Wallace.

'No, sir. Nothing new from the inquiries today. Freddie has gone to ground. No one knows where he is. They haven't seen him in days.'

'Do they know why he's disappeared?'

'Aside from the kidnapping?' asked Wallace.

172

Jellicoe paused for a moment and wondered if the young man was being sarcastic. He wasn't and it was a legitimate question. He decided to take it a face value.

'Something Ronald Musgrave said suggested he may have had other reasons for wanting to disappear. Any ideas?'

Wallace shook his head. Clearly no one knew or, at least, was saying. Frustrating but unsurprising, concluded Jellicoe. He glanced at Yates.

'I think there's not much more you can do here. I'll see you Monday. First thing Monday I want to know more about the colonel.'

Yates turned to go and then stopped. There was something on his mind. Jellicoe looked at him and raised his eyebrows.

'Something on your mind?'

Yates looked uncomfortable. His fists seemed to be clenching or perhaps it was Jellicoe's imagination.

'I just wanted to say sorry, sir.'

21

The prospect of returning to the one-star luxury of Ramsbottom's Guest House on a cold Saturday evening was unenticing. Jellicoe went to the window and stared out at the street. The snow was turning to a dark sludge. One or two people scurried along the wet footpath, head down as if charging into a scrum of rugby forwards.

'Where is everyone?' asked Jellicoe.

'The Chief went home an hour ago and DI Price popped in. Apparently, some boy has gone missing. Well, eighteen. He was due to go back to his National Service camp. Probably gone AWOL.'

This seemed extreme. While he'd never particularly enjoyed his time doing National Service, it had never occurred to Jellicoe to run away either. If this was the case, what would have driven him to do such a thing? He wondered idly if it was connected to their case.

'Do you know if DI Price is checking any connection with Stephen Masterson?'

'The Chief was very specific on that point, sir,' confirmed Wallace.

Jellicoe nodded with approval and then approached the board pinned with photographs and bits of paper. He wrote down two names, Ronnie Musgrave, and Johnny Warwick, and pinned them to the board. Then he perched on a table and stared at the collage in front of him. His hands gripped the edge of the table tightly as if he was holding on for dear life. Soon he became aware of Wallace standing beside him.

'How were the meetings with Warwick and Musgrave?'

Jellicoe told him.

'So, we have no idea why Musgrave is after Freddie Douglas?' asked Wallace.

'None whatsoever. Of course, it may be entirely unconnected with the kidnapping yet if this was crime fiction, then we know it would be.'

Wallace took a step back. There was a grin on his face. Jellicoe looked at Wallace with curiosity. He frowned but there was a smile on his face.

'I'm just trying to imagine you in a movie, sir,' said Wallace. Jellicoe's grin widened and he shook his head.

'Who would play me?'

'Anthony Steel, I think.'

This made Jellicoe raise his eyebrows. Then he grinned and said, 'I'm more of a Terry Thomas man myself.'

'I say,' responded Wallace which made both men laugh. Wallace turned to the board and joined Jellicoe in studying it. 'What do you see, sir?'

'Confusion. It's always the way at the start of an investigation. Life would be so much easier if the men on this board would just come clean about what they know.' As he said this, Jellicoe scribbled something in capital letters and pinned it to the board. It read: Montgomery. Then Jellicoe explained the significance of the name to Wallace.

The young policeman was surprised and asked, 'But why don't you just come out with it to Major Masterson?'

The rationale for saying nothing appeared to be evaporating by the hour. Perhaps the direct approach was best. Jellicoe glanced at Wallace.

'Have you any plans right now?'

'None aside from going to see the major, sir,' replied Wallace with a grin. Jellicoe handed Wallace the keys of the police car.

'Let the desk sergeant know where we're going in case anyone needs to reach us.'

-

Wallace took the keys and climbed into the car. Soon they were travelling at speed, noted Jellicoe, out of town. They began to chat about matters other than the case. Jellicoe asked Wallace how he'd come to be a policeman.

'When I finished National Service, I had a choice between going to university or working. I didn't really fancy more school, so I opted for the police. That was three years ago. The Chief seemed to like me and suggested I move out of uniform. I think Clarkey, sorry Constable Clarke had suggested this to him,' said Wallace. The car snaked along the narrow country road that was now, thankfully, free of snow.

Jellicoe laughed and said, 'Constable Clarke seems to be quite a popular man here. Even the criminals like him.

Wallace smiled, 'He's the best. I feel proud to work alongside men like him and the chief.'

Jellicoe said nothing to this as they were about to pull into the estate. It was good to have the company, but it had occurred to him that Masterson would be less forthcoming if he had the young detective constable with him.

A Time to Kill

'It may be better if you speak to Miss Masterson again. I'd like to know more about Freddie Douglas and Stephen. Did they only meet at the estate? Did they go into town together during the day or night? Was Miss Masterson with them? We need to get a picture of who else would have known them or met up with them, not just in the last day or two but before then. I still can't accept that there isn't some connection to Ronnie Musgrave.'

Wallace looked happy enough about this. They stepped out of the car and chatted for a moment with the constable on duty outside the house then Jellicoe knocked on the door. They were greeted at the entrance by Fitch who managed to keep his excitement at their arrival well concealed behind a mask of dignified indifference. He led the two men through to the drawing room and asked them to wait.

Masterson, true to form, was a man you heard before you saw. He appeared a minute later, a demand to know what the hell they were doing perched on his lips like a vulture ready to swoop down on a rotting carcass.

'Hello, sir,' said Jellicoe all too aware of the ticking time bomb he was facing. He didn't doubt that an explosion was imminent. 'We have a few more questions if you don't mind.'

'I most certainly do,' snarled Masterson, with one eye on Wallace. Before he could enlighten the policeman to his what his objection might be, Jellicoe interrupted.

'I'd like DC Wallace to speak to Miss Masterson. Can Mr Fitch take him to see her?'

Fitch was duly called for and led Wallace away to another room, leaving the ring to the two combatants. Jellicoe stayed on his feet as did Masterson. He circled round the major which was calculated to anger him.

'I came here, major, in order to clear up a few matters that have been troubling me since the start.'

'What makes you think I can help you?'

Jellicoe stopped and faced the army man.

'You can tell me who has kidnapped your son, and why, for a start. Then you can tell me who the man calling himself Montgomery is, too, while you're at it.'

As he said this Jellicoe fixed his gaze on the major to see how he reacted. For three years studying psychology at university and six as a policeman, he'd interviewed hundreds of people in order to understand what they were thinking. He could read the face of someone the way a child read a picture book. The words and the image melded together to create a narrative.

'How dare you accuse me of holding back anything when my child's life is at risk,' stammered Masterson. He took in a roomful of air and his face twisted in rage. It all looked very impressive. The affronted anger. The fulminating expression.

'I don't believe you,' said Jellicoe calmly and sat down.

-

Phillipa Masterson sat facing Wallace. Her hands were clasped together tightly. They were in the games room. She shifted uncomfortably in her seat and gazed behind Wallace at the wall. There wasn't much comfort to be had there either. Wallace looked at the trophies but decided not to comment. He doubted she'd bagged any of them.

'Once again, I'm sorry about your loss, Miss Masterson. We just have a few questions related to Stephen. We've identified the young man as Freddie Douglas, so he lied to you.'

Phillipa Masterson nodded. If anything, her hands were more tightly clasped now. They seemed to be turning white.

'Did Stephen only ever see this boy on the estate, or did they go into town together from time to time?'

Phillipa looked up to the ceiling. It was as if by tilting her head she could stop the tears running down her cheek.

'We met him in town once. Along the front.'

'Was it just the three of you or was there anyone else?'

'Just us.'

'Where did you go?'

'We went to Timpo's Amusements. Played around there for a while and then we went for a walk along the sea front. We stopped at a Mario's Italian Bar and had a cappuccino. Then Stephen and I took the bus back home.'

'Freddie, sorry, Ben, never showed you where he lived?'

'No.'

'Did he meet anyone or speak to anyone when you were with him?'

'Yes, he seemed to know lots of people. He never introduced us though. You don't think one of them was the accomplice?'

'It's possible. Can you tell me about some of the people he spoke to?'

Phillipa sat back in the chair and unclasped her hands. She exhaled loudly. Then she formed a fist brought it slowly to her face.

'I should have said something. It's all my fault. I should have said something.'

Wallace moved towards the young girl unsure of police policy on the matters of young damsels in distress. He decided he would let instinct rather than training guide him.

-

Masterson remained on his feet, struck dumb with rage. He gripped the armchair in front of him. His face had turned bright red and a vein on the side of his head seemed on the point of popping.

'Who is he, Major Masterson? Why does he want revenge? We'll find out, trust me. The Chief Constable and the Superintendent have both been in touch with the army. We'll get hold of your arrest records and check these against recent releases. Please save us a job. And call off your man. This is a police matter.'

There was a moment of hesitation. A flicker of the eye, a frown even.

Something was on his mind. He walked around the sofa and slumped down. 'I haven't asked anyone to investigate. I don't know anything about that.'

This rang true but Jellicoe was wary of accepting anything Masterson said at face value. He remained silent and waited for Masterson to come clean on the other matter. The army man looked to be engaged in battle inside his mind. He could not look at Jellicoe. Rage and humiliation make for poor company. Jellicoe looked at him, fascinated. What could have prompted such a reaction?

'There is a man,' said Masterson. His voice was drenched in resignation. 'His name is David Solomon.'

Jellicoe's eyes widened. At first, he was surprised but this soon gave way to anger. Why hadn't Masterson said anything?

A Time to Kill

'I wasn't sure at first, but I made a call earlier. He was released from prison a couple of months ago.'

'Why was he in prison?'

'He was a deserter.' Masterson spat the words out like he was swearing. He looked up and stared defiantly at Jellicoe. 'He deserted his comrades, his friends during the war. We caught him and stuck him in jail. If I'd have had my way he'd have been up against a wall. Bastard.'

This was said with some feeling. Jellicoe sensed this had all been true and the name clinched it for him. The man they were looking for was David Solomon. Jellicoe waited to hear more. Instead, there was silence. Whatever he'd been expecting it wasn't this.

'Can you tell me more?'

'I made some phone calls today. I have someone looking for the file. They'll bring it down.'

Jellicoe felt his heart sink. Another day at the station.

'Do you know when the file will arrive?'

'No, I'm sorry,' said Masterson, his voice breaking. 'I've explained the circumstances but the files on Solomon are in the middle of nowhere, it's the weekend and, Jellicoe, you really have no idea how many files on deserters there are. Can you guess?'

Jellicoe had no idea.

'Thousands, I presume.'

'Nearly one hundred thousand men deserted, Jellicoe. We have a file on all of them. All of them. Every last coward. Many of them are living amongst us now under assumed names. Some stayed hidden like rats in a cellar in France. If they ever show their faces here, they'll be thrown in prison where they deserve to be. At least, they will be until some namby-pamby government decides to offer an amnesty.'

'You're not in favour,' said Jellicoe sardonically.

'Bloody right I'm not in favour,' exclaimed Masterson, clearly irritated at Jellicoe's tone.

'Very well,' said Jellicoe. 'And will you call off your man Montgomery. He could compromise this investigation.'

'I have absolutely no idea what you're talking about. Montgomery?' said Masterson witheringly. 'Was he with a chap called Rommel by any chance?'

This interview was proving to be full of surprises. Masterson's eyes had never left Jellicoe's. He'd not looked away when talking about Montgomery. Jellicoe was inclined to believe him. Not entirely though.

'We know it's an assumed name. The man I saw was around my height but larger in build. His hair was fair and clipped very short. He had a jaw like Desperate Dan.'

This made Masterson start. Or perhaps it was the sound of the telephone ringing in the hall.

'You know the man?'

'I know someone like you've described. I can't believe it's the same man. Must be a coincidence. I'm sure there are many men who look like this.'

'Can you give me his name?'

'Well yes, Weir. He was my sergeant when I was a military policeman. I haven't seen him in six or seven years. We stopped working with one another long before that.'

They were interrupted by a knock on the door. Masterson called for whoever was outside to enter. Fitch entered and spoke to Masterson although the message was for Jellicoe.

A Time to Kill

'It's the police, sir. They wish to speak to the detective inspector.'

Jellicoe excused himself and went to the entrance hallway. He lifted the phone. As he did so he saw Wallace emerge from the games room followed by a tearful Phillipa Masterson. He raised his eyes at Wallace, but the young man's attention was focused entirely with the girl. Don't blame you, thought Jellicoe.

'Jellicoe speaking, yes?'

Wallace looked up and saw Jellicoe speaking on the phone. He saw the detective inspector's head jerk up suddenly and his eyes widen. The conversation was brief and concluded with Jellicoe promising to return immediately. Masterson was in the corridor. His face seemed to turn white.

'What's wrong? Is it Stephen?'

Jellicoe put the phone down and looked at the major.

'No not Stephen. There's been another kidnapping. We need to return immediately to the station. Please excuse us.'

-

'So, I'm sitting in front of my bloody TV, Dixon of Dock Green has just solved another case of shoplifting and Billy Cotton sayin' "wakey bloody wakey" when I have to come here and look at you lot. I'm not bloody having it. A man's entitled to watch his TV on a Saturday night without all this. We've got to do something about it. Enough's enough.'

So ended the sermon from Burnett. He was standing in front of half a dozen men including Jellicoe, Yates, Wallace, and the other detective inspector with his team. Detective Inspector Ivor Price was as Welsh as he was uninspiring. Most of the Welshmen Jellicoe had met previously had been on his rugger team at Oxford. To a man they were men. Price had obviously missed this memorandum. The other DI edged over to Jellicoe, a mixture of a smile and grave concern on his face. He seemed unsure of where to pitch his reaction to the unfolding events.

'Hell, Jellicoe,' said Price in that curiously high-pitched voice. He talked quickly as if he feared that no one would listen if he spoke for too long. He wasn't a bad sort, thought Jellicoe. It was a surprise he'd made it so high up in the service. Perhaps there was something in the man he'd not seen. 'Bad business this,' continued the Welshman, writhing nervously.

'Yes,' agreed Jellicoe.

Superintendent, Ian Frankie entered the room. Aware that no one had noticed him, he took decisive action. He slammed the door. This achieved its objective. All eyes turned to him. Like Chief Constable Leighton, he split his time between two police stations. He marched to the front of the room. His face was set to grave. A guarded anger seemed to propel his movement as well as his speech. He gazed at everyone with an expression of controlled distaste, as if he was scandalised by them laughing at some innocent innuendo.

He was as tall as Jellicoe but much more heavyset. His face looked like someone had slapped two halibut on each cheek and glued them there. He brought to mind a pantomime dame but without the laughter; someone dressed up as a policeman, attempting to exude dignity and gravitas to a role that nature had never intended him to occupy. Jellicoe noticed a few eyes rolling when he'd appeared.

'As the Chief Inspector says, we have a serious situation developing that is going to explode in our faces. Your weekend is officially cancelled. I want every man jack of you out on the streets. Speak to every snout, in fact anyone that might have an opinion on what the hell is going on. I don't need to remind you that the last thing we need for a seaside town is to become known as the kidnap capital of the country. Any questions?'

'Is there any connection between the kidnapping of Tim Pemberton and Stephen Masterson?'

Superintendent Frankie turned to Burnett; eyebrows raised. Jellicoe wasn't sure if this was because they expected him to know the answer or the absolute certainty that someone was taking the rise out of him. His late appearance on such a significant case showed questionable judgement. Jellicoe's initial scepticism about Frankie was turning to outright contempt.

'Not that we know of. I want to know if there is,' replied Burnett tersely, trying to work out who'd asked the question in the first place.

'If there are no more questions, I will let the chief inspector take over,' announced Frankie. 'Thank you,' he added without a trace of gratitude. Frankie made for the door hoping that all eyes would be fixed on him so that he could ignore them.

After Frankie had left the room, Jellicoe stood up from his perched position on a desk. He looked at Burnett who motioned him forward. Behind him, a uniformed officer was handing out photostat pictures of the missing boy. Jellicoe took one as he walked forward to the front. He stood and faced the men in the room.

'We have new information on the Masterson kidnapping. We may be looking for a man called David Solomon.'

Jellicoe glanced at Burnett as he said this. It would be fair to say the chief inspector's jaw dropped when he heard this. Moments later there was a rage in his eyes which Jellicoe had more than a touch of sympathy for.

'Solomon was an army deserter. He deserted around 1945. Major Masterson was the arresting officer. The army are sending his file and it will be with us tomorrow or Monday. We'll have a photograph then. As the chief says, we don't know if this is connected with the other case. We shouldn't assume that it is nor should we discount any link. Solomon is an outsider. He has no connection with this town as far as we know.'

Jellicoe nodded to Burnett and stood down.

'Price, take Fogg, Lester and Wilson. Go to Warwick's pubs. Get the word out. Jellicoe, Yates, and Wallace hit the sea front. Usual places. Any questions?'

There were none.

Burnett stared at them for a moment and shouted, 'Well what are you waiting for?'

22

Jellicoe, Yates, and Wallace walked three abreast out of the police station like the Earp brothers going to face the Clantons in the movie Jellicoe had seen the previous year. The ice-cold air stung their faces as they emerged from the station. The OK Corral had looked warmer.

'Where to first, sir?' asked Wallace climbing into the driver's seat of the police car.

'I don't know about you but there's only one choice right now,' answered Jellicoe.

A few minutes later, Jellicoe stood in front of a man, dressed in white, who was sweating profusely. He had something Jellicoe needed. The man seemed eager to give him what he wanted. Jellicoe waved a few pound notes in the air.

'Three fish and chips, please,' said Jellicoe.

'Three fish and chips coming up, Mr Jellicoe.'

There was no one else in the chippy. While they were waiting, a thought occurred to Jellicoe. He held up photostat pictures of the missing boys.

'Have you seen these boys around recently?'

'No, Mr Jellicoe. That boy with the dark hair, he was in the paper.'

'Yes,' acknowledged Jellicoe. 'Have there been many new faces in here over the last week or two?'

'There's always new faces. They come for a while then you don't see them again.'

Yates reached inside his coat pocket and took out his wallet to pay. Jellicoe waved them away.

'These are on me.'

The fish supper arrived, and the three policemen walked down the hill and round the corner to the sea front. The street was deserted. Saturday night and it was empty. A clue as to why this should be so was blowing in from the sea.

'Bloody hell,' said Yates as the breeze hit the three men. They decided to retire to the car. It would be someone else's problem in the morning when they entered a car literally humming with the smell of fish. The windows stayed firmly shut.

'Do we know anything about Solomon?' asked Yates.

'He deserted in 1944. They found him in Paris. He spent the next fourteen years in jail.'

'For desertion?' exclaimed Yates.

'They shot quite a few in the Great War,' chipped in Wallace.

'I think they stopped this during the last war but many of the deserters were involved in crimes outside of desertion. Masterson told me to read the file. I still think he's being evasive but at least he's saved us a job.'

'You mean he's saved me a job,' said Yates with a grin.

Jellicoe laughed, 'Yes, I daresay that's true. You can use the time tomorrow to follow up on the father. I'm worried we haven't done any background checking on him.'

'Yes, sir,' replied Yates unenthusiastically. If Wallace hadn't been there, Jellicoe might have said something, but he decided against it.

A Time to Kill

'Right, hurry up and finish these,' said Jellicoe. 'The sooner we're out the better.'

'Shall we split up?' asked Wallace.

'Yes, good idea. Wallace, you're most familiar with this area. Can you suggest where we go?'

-

The front was not quite a mile in length. In the middle was a pier that extended three hundred yards out onto the sea. At the end of the pier there were outdoor amusements and some food stalls. They were shut at this time of year. The pier was just a long black tentacle reaching out into an inhospitable sea. Quarter of a mile past the pier, the coast arched round forming a small, natural harbour. There were a dozen small fishing boats as well as yachts. Jellicoe fixed his gaze on the horizon. Somewhere across the black sea lay France.

Yates and Wallace went down to the harbour and the surrounding area while Jellicoe investigated the other side of the pier. The next couple of hours saw them troop the length and breadth of the seafront. The plan was to meet up at the pier around ten.

By ten in the evening, Jellicoe was on his own, standing waiting for the two other men. There was no sign of them. In the distance he could see the harbour lights, just like the song. Boats bobbed gently in the sea near the jetty. Quite a lot to check even for two men, he conceded. Rather than wait any longer, Jellicoe decided to investigate the pier himself.

It was typical of many he'd seen that had been built in Victorian times to allow the town's inhabitants to promenade into the sea. Jellicoe felt tremendous admiration for those who'd created them. Engineers and entrepreneurs had built

189

what would have once been considered marvels. To Jellicoe, they still were. Memories of holidays by the seaside flooded though his mind as he set foot on the long boardwalk.

HIs feet were beginning to ache from all the walking. He made his way slowly up the pier. There were a couple of men fishing, legs draped over the side. They stayed far enough away from one another to fish freely but still close enough to chat. What was there to say though? A man alone, Saturday night, fishing on a pier perhaps had chosen a way of life that was a denial of company. Their blue-lit bearded faces puffed contentedly on pipes. Jellicoe sat down somewhere approximately in the middle of the two men. His arrival prompted no welcome.

'Good evening, gentlemen,' said Jellicoe, half sensing he was talking to himself.

'Evening,' said one of the men, without looking at Jellicoe.

'Sorry to disturb you, I'm a police officer.' This was met with silence. This was an old technique he would have used. They were using it on him. Nature abhors a vacuum like silence. It was human nature to wish to fill it. These two men were, perhaps, the exception that proved the rule.

'Two boys have gone missing. I don't suppose you've seen either of them?' He took out the two photostats, leaned over and handed it to the first of the two men. The man glanced at the two pictures for several seconds. Then handed them back to Jellicoe. He shook his head. The other man was no more forthcoming.

Jellicoe glanced towards the end of the pier. There were several huts and a couple of larger buildings. All had shutters up.

'Are they all closed for the winter?'

A Time to Kill

More silence. Waves broke onto the shore and Jellicoe waited for an answer. Finally, the second man cracked. A victory of sorts.

'Aye. They're shut.'

'When do they open.?'

'Another month or so.'

Jellicoe nodded towards the sea below them.

'Any luck?'

'No.'

Jellicoe decided against inviting the two men for cocktails some evening and nodded his 'thanks'. He rose unsteadily to his feet, limbs stiffening in the cold. Barely thirty years of age, he felt like an old man, with an old man's aches and an old man's sadness. Reluctantly he set off down the pier to inspect the huts. The further down the pier he went the colder it seemed to become. A stiff breeze beat his face relentlessly and at that moment he might just have welcomed being back in the relative warmth and comfort of the Ramsbottom's Guest House, although it was a close-run thing.

It took a few minutes to walk to the end of the pier. Every step felt like he was wading through thick soup. When he reached the end, the wind seemed to intensify. He moved towards the huts to shield himself. This partially succeeded but the cold had long since leeched through his gabardine mac and suit. He cursed his lack of foresight in not bringing warmer clothes down from London.

The wooden huts were painted an ugly green. Each had an electric sign, switched off. One was a sweet shop. Another served tea. Yet another promised the best fish and chips in the country. This may have been an exaggeration. The larger building was an amusement arcade. It looked like there may be dodgem cars in it, but it was unclear as the sign had been taken down.

There was no indication that these had seen any life since Christmas when, presumably, they'd have been open. Jellicoe was somewhat at a loss as what to do. He couldn't very well break into the huts. This was a pity as they would have made good places to hide someone. He made a lap around each of the huts hoping to see if there was some sort of window to get a look inside. There were none. He smacked the palm of his hand against the wooden walls. There was nothing for it but to retrace his footsteps down the pier. This would once more expose him to the icy blasts coming off the sea. He buried one hand in his pocket and kept the other firmly on his hat.

There was a tumult beneath him. Through the cracks in the boardwalk, he could see water rushing then crashing with a roar against the columns holding up the pier. It slabbered and spilled white onto the shore before being swallowed up again. Jellicoe kept his head down and ignored the two men on the way back. He just wanted off the pier.

Somewhere up ahead he heard the sound of sirens. At first, they were faint. Then they grew louder. He looked up. A couple of police cars pulled up on the roadside in front of the pier. To his right he saw Yates and Wallace running along the front towards the cars. Jellicoe stopped and wondered what was going on. Then he realised what it was. Burnett had emerged from the lead car. Jellicoe turned and began to sprint back down the pier.

A Time to Kill

23

His body felt stiff. If this is what it was like to be old, then he wanted no part of it. He tried to stand but this is not a simple matter when your hands are tied behind your back. He wanted to scream but try doing this when you are gagged. He'd seen a film once where the tied-up hero managed to free himself by pulling his hands over his feet and then finding a conveniently placed sharp object. At this point it was a simple matter of rubbing the rope against the object until it broke.

This was real life. He was so cold that his body had all but seized up. He could barely move his arms never mind pull off a trick that would test a circus contortionist. No, he was going nowhere anytime soon. For the tenth time that hour, tears stung his eyes.

He thought of Ben and felt the bile rise within him. He'd been taken in. If he survived this, he would make it his life's mission to see that Ben faced violent retribution. In fact, the only thing that kept despair at bay was the array of violent endings he conjured up for the boy he'd thought of as a friend. As something more even but that folly did not bear thinking about.

Poor Pippa. What must she be thinking? She knew. She's always known. Right from when they were children. Mother, too, had suspected not that she cared. Then she'd left. His father hadn't a clue. He'd never notice such things. He was too busy nursing his disappointment to wonder why he was feeling this way. Father never tried to hide the sense of let-down with his boy. But he'd never made the jump. There was no attempt to consider the implication of his son's persistent disinterest in the things that boys his age were supposed to be interested in. This was beyond him. Or perhaps he was in denial.

The wind was whistling outside. It compounded the chill he was feeling inside the metal prison. The rattling was intensifying as if it were a storm outside. Or perhaps there was someone there. Then he heard something near the door.

It was opening.

-

They met Jellicoe at the huts. Half a dozen uniformed men arrived followed by the chief inspector puffing behind them like an asthmatic bull elephant. Burnett's shirt was sticking out from his trousers and his tie was sat an angle unlikely to find its way onto the pages of Vogue. He put his hands up as Jellicoe went to speak to him then he bent double, hands on knees. Jellicoe was worried for a moment that he was going to topple over or worse, throw up. Thankfully this indignity was narrowly avoided. He was, however, breathing in great heaps of air. Finally, he straightened up. He looked thoroughly disgruntled.

'A few years ago, they wouldn't have seen me for dust.'

'I don't doubt it, sir,' replied Jellicoe trying not to smile.

In the distance, sprinting along up the pier, Jellicoe caught sight of Yates and Wallace. There was no sign of Price, but he was probably on his way.

'Which one?' asked Jellicoe.

A Time to Kill

'No idea, son,' replied Burnett. His head motioned towards a sledgehammer. They would break into each hut if necessary.

'What happened?'

'Anonymous tip off,' spluttered Burnett, still trying to recover his breath. He loosened his tie even more and the top two buttons of his shirt. Pink skin peeked out beneath the tie. Jellicoe realised that part of Burnett's problem was that he'd buttoned up his buttons in the wrong holes. There was always going to be a mismatch. Burnett didn't care. He'd given up on trying to look like Cary Grant a long time ago.

Jellicoe looked confused about the tip off. They were common enough but weren't always to be trusted.

'What did they say?'

'They said check out the end of the pier. Nothing else.' Burnett noted the look of scepticism on Jellicoe's face. 'I know, son, but we can't ignore it either.'

Burnett turned to the constable holding the sledgehammer. Jellicoe looked at the constable. He was well over six feet and that was just his shoulders. A sledgehammer seemed to be cheating. A man like this could have ripped the doors off with his bare hands, in Jellicoe's view.

The constable set to work with a violent glee. The first blow took off the door handle and lock. The second one seemed to be for fun.

The first hut was empty as was the second. This left two more huts and the large amusements building. They headed towards the tearoom. One mighty swipe saw the half the door taken away. Burnett put his hand up lest the rest of the building get obliterated. They pulled the door away and stepped inside.

Propped against the end of the hut was a body. Burnett shone a torch on the face. A pair of scared eyes stared back at him.

'Thank God,' said Burnett.

-

It was midnight before Jellicoe was able to return to the welcoming warmth of Ramsbottom's Guest House with a renewed hope in his heart brought on by the twin developments of the recovery of one of the kidnapped boys and having in his possession one electric heater. The house was quiet when he returned. Mr and Mrs Ramsbottom were early risers and thus, retired early.

Jellicoe made his way inside quietly for reasons other than a desire to avoid social or any other intercourse with the good lady of the house. He made straight for the desk at the entrance of the house. This was little more than a broom cupboard that had seen its doors removed and been converted into a one-star approximation of a reception. Underneath the counter lay what Jellicoe was looking for.

He knelt down and lifted the visitors book up onto the counter. It was a heavy affair, thick of page and with a surprisingly ornate cover. He opened it at the first page. The first visitor had been a Mrs Lyons and her son. The date read 7th August 1950. Jellicoe frowned for a moment and wondered if he'd picked up the wrong book. He hadn't. As he began to skim through the pages, he saw that the guest house spent long periods without any visitors. Sometimes eight months could pass by without a guest.

Jellicoe felt a stab of guilt at how he had acted with the couple. More than guilt, he felt shame. His attitude had varied between distance and a kind of superiority that, at that moment, he knew was not his to own. On and on through the pages he flicked, inflicting further discredit on his own conduct yet fascinated by the names, the dates, and the long gaps between guests. Some names reoccurred. One woman, a war widow perhaps, had come with her two sons summer after summer from Birmingham. For seven years they had visited and then it was just the woman on her own. Jellicoe could imagine how she had been abandoned by the two young men. He could see, more than that, he could hear them; their horror at the idea of returning to this place. He could feel the mother's sadness at making the trip alone. A trip she long knew she would make. But there would have been a warm welcome here.

Three quarters of the way through the book, he found the most recent entries. No one else had come since Montgomery. And he had signed out. This left Jellicoe as the sole guest. He realised he was not surprised by Montgomery's departure. Yet he was angry with himself now. The feelings of shame now mixed with this self-admonishment for not acting on his hunch about the man. The address was probably made up. He would have to check this. This one would not be delegated. He ducked down and replaced the book. When he raised his head, he almost had a heart attack.

'What do you think you are doing?' said Mrs Ramsbottom. She was tapping a rolling pin on the palm of her hand and she had a look on her face that a writer of pulp fiction might have suggested meant business. It certainly felt like a scene from an end of pier revue and Jellicoe knew she had him bang to rights. He could barely take his eyes off the rolling pin and the powerful arm holding it. There was enough combined heft to do significant damage if matters deteriorated. In fact, anyone capable of sneaking up in the manner she had was clearly someone not to be trifled with.

'Mrs Ramsbottom,' said Jellicoe, smiling nervously.

'I'm aware of my own name,' snapped the landlady. 'What are you doing looking in the guest book?'

Jellicoe realised that his choices were limited at that moment and he was never the most natural of improvisers.

'That man, Montgomery, when did he leave?'

'Why do you want to know?' asked Mrs Ramsbottom. Her manner did not quite soften but this had taken her by surprise.

'It was an assumed name. he may have something to do with the case I'm working on.'

This revelation did take the wind out of the rolling pin-wielding warrior's sails. She fixed a steely eye on Jellicoe.

'The kidnapping?'

'Kidnappings. There were more than one. We've just found one of them in fact.'

'The Masterson boy?' asked Mrs Ramsbottom, the arm holding the rolling pin dropped to her side. It was still in a position to be used but altogether the situation was rapidly becoming less threatening.

'No, a young man named Pemberton. He's safe now. They took him to the hospital. We'll speak to him when he wakes up. He's had quite a fright.'

'And the other?' asked the Amazonian landlady. Jellicoe shook his head. Mrs Ramsbottom nodded a little sadly and half turned away.

'Have you eaten?'

Another surprise question. It seemed so unlike Mrs Ramsbottom. More like a mother. Jellicoe had no idea if she was a mother or not. She'd never said anything and there were no family photographs in the areas where the guests sat or ate.

'I do feel a bit peckish,' admitted Jellicoe. The cold and the adrenalin of finding the boy had drained him. He felt like a cup of tea and something to eat.

'Follow me,' ordered Mrs Ramsbottom in a manner that brooked no insubordination.

They trooped through the dining room to an adjoining room that Jellicoe had not been in before. It was a small living area with a sofa two armchairs and a small television. Mrs Ramsbottom switched on the light so they could see better. The room was covered in framed photographs. Two boys were prominent. There were photographs of them playing football and then in their army uniforms.

Jellicoe turned to ask Mrs Ramsbottom about them but stopped himself just in time. There were tears in her eyes. She turned her face away and said, 'This way.'

She led him into the kitchen. A large white fridge dominated the small space. She opened it up and took out a plate sitting on top of which was some fatty bacon.

'Bacon sandwich?'

Jellicoe felt like gagging but smiled wanly and said, 'Toast maybe? With some tea?'

She looked at the bacon for a moment and seemed to colour. Jellicoe formed his hands into fists. His nails dug into his palms and he felt inhuman. It was too late to change what he's said. She returned the bacon to the fridge and cut some bread.

A few minutes later Jellicoe was sitting alone in the dining room eating his toast and drinking the tea. Jellicoe looked up at Mrs Ramsbottom. The rolling pin was once more back in the drawer. Her arms hung by her sides.

'This is lovely, thank you,' said Jellicoe.

'Do you need anything else?' asked the landlady.

'No, really, you've been too kind. My apologies once more for, you know…'

Mrs Ramsbottom nodded and then glanced down at the brown cardboard box at his feet. She frowned but said nothing. Jellicoe's face reddened as he realised, she'd seen the heater he'd purchased earlier that day.

'Well, goodnight, then.

'Goodnight,' replied Jellicoe in a voice he hadn't used in twenty years.

When she was gone, Jellicoe sat back in the dining seat and exhaled the guilt and the shame. He finished his toast and drained the remainder of his tea. Then he carried the plate and the cup through to the kitchen and washed up. It felt like the least he could do.

As he was now the only person in the house, he felt a little strange when he crept up the stairs. He opened the door to his room and was greeted by cold air. He'd opened the window as he'd left. Mrs Ramsbottom had obviously left it open. He screamed a few expletives in his head. Ignoring the light switch, he knelt down and plugged the electric heater.

Nothing.

He switched it on and off a few times.

Still nothing.

The screams in his head grew louder. There was nothing else to do except go to bed. He brushed his teeth in the sink and flopped down on the bed fully clothed, too tired to undress. He was asleep within a minute.

-

The next morning, Jellicoe bathed in some mercifully hot water, was treated to a breakfast comprising a pot of tea, a couple boiled eggs and yet more toast with homemade marmalade that was actually not bad. He felt quite human again as he marched towards the office.

News of the recovery of one of the kidnap victims had obviously not filtered through yet or perhaps because it was Sunday, the area in front of the police station was deserted. Price arrived around nine with Burnett, Yates and Wallace following closely after that. By ten in the morning the office was full. Burnett addressed the men for the second time in the last sixteen hours.

'So, we had a break. Lucky us. Let's not be complacent. We still have to find a murderer and the other boy. Tim Pemberton should be available to question soon, so get someone down there, Ivor, pronto. I want you to bring in Ronnie Musgrave. If you've any problems, let me know. He needs to explain how it is we found one of the kidnap victims in one of his huts.'

'Yes sir,' said Price.

Jellicoe frowned. He had not made that connection with the huts, but it made sense. However, he did not believe Musgrave capable of conceiving and executing such a ham-fisted crime. Musgrave would need to be questioned. In all likelihood, it was unlikely to lead them very far beyond discounting him as a suspect. Then again, one could never be too sure. It led to mistakes. Absolute certainty was a critical ingredient of negligence. It led to inattentiveness and missing key clues. He'd seen it before. Been guilty of it before. Keeping an open mind was always the only sure way of closing a case efficiently.

As Burnett, Jellicoe and Price agreed the tasks for the day a uniformed officer appeared and stood nearby the three men. After a few moments Burnett looked up irritably.

'Yes?'

'There's a military-looking man downstairs at the desk. Wants to speak to someone in charge of the Masterson murder and kidnap.'

'Well why didn't you say?' snapped Burnett. Go and see who it is. If it's Masterson take him to the large meeting room. If it's some "squaddie" find out what he wants.'

Jellicoe followed the constable downstairs and into the entrance area. Standing by the desk was a man in his thirties wearing an overcoat. Nothing could hide his military bearing although he was in 'civvies'. He turned to face Jellicoe as the detective approached him.

'Are you in charge of the investigation?' The tone suggested surprise that someone so young would be.

'Chief Inspector Burnett is, I report directly to him. I am Detective Inspector Jellicoe.'

'You're Jellicoe,' replied the military man. 'My name is King. Lieutenant King. I was asked to come down as soon as possible to assist in an investigation.' He held up a briefcase which Jellicoe guessed contained files related to the man Masterson had mentioned.

'Can I take the files? There seems no point in keeping you detained here at the weekend.'

A Time to Kill

'No, Detective Inspector. I'm not to let the files out of my sight. Major Masterson specified you as being the person who would most likely want to read them. You are to read them and return them to me. Then I shall be on my way.'

'Do you know anything about the contents?' asked Jellicoe, leading King through to the stairs.

'Nothing whatsoever,' answered King helpfully.

They went upstairs and Jellicoe deposited King in a meeting room. Then he went to Burnett to update him on the new arrival. The fact that the files were not to leave the person of the army man did not surprise Burnett unduly.

'It means you'll have to stay here and read the file,' concluded Burnett with a dry smile.

Jellicoe had suspected with a sinking heart that this would be his fate so was unworried by the lurking amusement in Burnett's eyes. He was, however, frustrated not to be involved in the ongoing search for Masterson and the questioning of the boy in hospital. The two kidnappings were connected but Burnett wanted more evidence that this was the case rather than a copycat effort by someone looking to profit while the police's attention was elsewhere.

The meeting between King and Burnett was as cordial as it was brief. Burnett was happy to leave this part to Jellicoe; this was a privilege of being the senior officer. The junior man would absorb the detail, assimilate with the current case, and seek points of convergence. It suggested that Jellicoe had already earned the chief's trust.

Jellicoe showed King to a meeting room. He returned a few minutes later with a pot of tea and some biscuits. An exercise like this would involve several pots of tea in Jellicoe's estimation. He set the tray down on the table and watched King remove a large, ripped manilla folder from his briefcase. Jellicoe stared at the file. King glanced at him with a smile that a romance writer might have described as cruel. This irritated Jellicoe and he said, 'I'm not sure why you're smiling, lieutenant. At least I have something to do.'

King said nothing. Instead, he took something else out of his briefcase. A novel. Jellicoe tilted his head to look at the cover: '*Murder on the Orient Express. Agatha Christie.*'

'Jolly good, I hear,' commented King, opening the book to the front page.'

'The butler did it,' said Jellicoe sourly.

'You can't get the staff these days,' tutted the lieutenant.

24

15 years earlier…

September 1944: Paris, France

Feet pounded off the street; the steps echoed around the walls. Behind him he could hear the posse. Only they weren't on horseback. The jeeps had been abandoned. They were on foot like him, racing through the narrow lanes of Paris.

Heart pumping, chest heaving, he was at desperation point. They would catch him. It was too easy, and they were too well trained. They'd split up and block off the exits. The remaining military policemen would drive round to the other side. They'd stop him reaching the river. Not that it would have saved him anyway unless he managed to reach a boat. A moving boat.

There wasn't time to stop and try a door. They were too close. They'd be on top of him in no time. Instead, all he could hope to do was to keep running. He needed to widen the gap and then, perhaps, he would get lucky. An open door. A window ajar. That's all it would take. Perhaps Father Christmas would dispense an early gift to a man in trouble.

And boy, was he in trouble.

Up ahead he saw two old French gentlemen sitting outside their house drinking tiny glasses of wine. They looked on with that expression of wry amusement that only the French can have. They certainly weren't going to help him. Instead, this would give them something to chat about for a long time. Perhaps they'd tell their friend that it was they who'd captured the English 'déserteur'. One of them lifted a glass as he passed them and toasted his success. He saluted back with a smile. And kept running.

When had he taken the decision to desert? Probably on the beach. As the bombs blasted the sand, bullets raking through his friends and comrades; he'd promised himself that if he survived this hell then the first chance he had, he was off.

It had taken just over three months, but he'd managed it. The request to take the jeep to carry a message to the American colonel had been the moment. The brass liked him. They could see he was smart. Promoted twice in as many months. Certainly not for his bravery. He wasn't like the other idiots. The idea of having his head shot off did not appeal. He was not in it for the glory. Only survival. And survival required extreme measures. Which was preferable, he'd debated? Survival and a life on the run or the daily misery of wondering if today was going to be the day you caught one?

There was only one answer for David Solomon. He kept his counsel. Bided his time. Had a word for everyone. Particularly the military policemen; the ones that brought back the deserters. It cost him a few cigarettes but the intelligence he gained was worth it. A number of things always did for them. Many deserters were poorly educated. They couldn't speak French or German. Either they were caught by the Germans or taken by the Resistance and handed back to the army. There were exceptions of course. Quite a few soldiers had joined the Resistance. But this was just going back to war with arguably lower chances of survival than being part of the bigger army. They'd helped them for a while before the creeping realisation set in that all they were doing was what they'd run away from in the first place. At least in the army you had your mates. The French cared even less for your life because you were a déserteur.

A Time to Kill

Avoid the enemy; avoid the Resistance. What could be simpler? Solomon knew he had certain advantages over the poor fools who'd been caught. He had been educated at Charterhouse, studied at Oxford. He spoke French fluently and even had passable German. The latter was of no use as he looked Jewish. The dark hair and eyes would be the first hint. Other things you couldn't hide. There was one other advantage he had. He had not reached desperation point. Too many who deserted did so when they were at their lowest ebb. This hindered thought; it made you grab at chances like a drowning man splashing in water. Not all opportunities were equal. Each would present unexpected challenges to overcome. The key was knowing this and not cracking when the time came.

He'd delivered the message then driven through the night, west of Paris before abandoning the jeep and making the rest of the way on foot. He'd hidden in a barn during one rainy night and avoided a convoy of American trucks in echelon. They all seemed to be heading into Paris rather than away. This seemed to miss the point. The battle for Paris had been won. Perhaps the brass were wanting to celebrate while the men at the front lay shivering and starving in foxholes wetting themselves not through fear but because they were pinned down by snipers.

He'd made it to Paris sporting a new set of clothes. A farmer had sold him garments that were probably out of fashion in 1900. He sported a frock coat and trousers that were slightly too large. They needed braces but as none were available, he'd used rope. His hat was something the Artful Dodger might have rejected. At least he could speak the language and he didn't look British. He would find a way to blend in.

Or so he thought.

It hadn't taken long for his rather outmoded attire to attract attention. Even in war-time Paris his apparel stood out. He walked through the outskirts of the city increasingly self-conscious, feeling like Raskolnikov after the murder. Everyone seemed to stop and look at him. He would say 'bonjour', but no one was fooled.

He pushed on and on. Each step an exercise in self-criticism. There were more army personnel around the city. All dressed in clean, pressed uniforms. They, of course, did not see him. You needed to be local to understand the exquisitely bad dress he was wearing; you needed to be British or American to be blind to it.

His face began to burn red as he passed Parisians glancing askance towards him. The hidden smiles. He'd thought about nothing else for months. Prided himself on his self-control, his intelligence. What a fool! How could he have been so stupid? Someone was going to give the game away soon. Either that or at least one of the damn desk-bound-office-wallahs from the army would spot a character from Dickens walking up the street.

He needed new clothes.

Money was short, though. He had enough to feed himself for a few days but that might all go on acquiring new garb. He sat down on the street near a lamp post and took off his ridiculous hat. It was a warm day and perspiration matted his dark hair. A mongrel dog approached him. He smiled at it. A friendly face at last. He stroked the dog behind the ears, and it sat down. As he sat there, he heard the sound of money being dropped.

He glanced up in shock, but the man was already walking away. He'd been mistaken for a beggar. Solomon wasn't sure whether to be affronted or pleased at his sudden good fortune. However, the funny side of it was all too plain. He had a penchant for gallows humour and what could be more absurd than this. He sat a bit longer. More coins came his way.

Unfortunately, his success began to attract the attention of some American army men. The army men began to walk over to him, double quick. It was time to exit stage left. Solomon was on his feet and began to walk away from the Seine. He didn't look back but once around the corner he broke into a jog. It was when he heard the shouts that he began sprinting.

The shouts were more distant now. Ironically, he'd always been a good middle-distance runner. Who knew it be so useful? The key was not going all out. Maintain a steady pace; stay calm when they drew close; wait for them to burn out. Sprinting was a sure-fire way to empty the tank. The streets echoed still but he sensed he was outpacing them now. This was gratifying but only for a few moments. There were still too many of them. They could surround the area. He'd be cornered like a rat.

He needed to get indoors.

He arrived at a small square. There was a fountain in the middle. Children were playing around it. The sound of children's laughter and the chattering of the water from the fountain filled his soul for a moment with a type of euphoria. Old people were gazing at the children, wishing they could be young and free again. They would be, one day. Then, slowly the people in the square became aware of him. There was no bemusement on their faces. It was as if this were a regular occurrence. Rather than finding his garb funny, there was another look in their eyes now. Sympathy. However, this did not appear to stretch as far as allowing him shelter inside. Pity was the worst form of sympathy. It offered nothing except a sense of humiliation to the pitied.

He stopped and looked around for where to go. If he didn't get his bearings, he'd soon be going round in circles. The net was drawing in. He bent over, hands on knees and glanced up to consider his options. He could still hear the footsteps. They were coming from two different directions now. There was a large number of men by the sound of it. All of them running. Had they nothing better to do? Didn't they know there was a war on? Or perhaps they did. This was desertion in another form. Avoid the enemy by policing the poor fools who'd been forced to fight. At least he'd faced the true enemy, killed them, forced them back. For the men running towards him now, he was the enemy.

Standing in one nearby doorway was a young woman. She was no older than him. Very pretty but also quite skinny. Their eyes met. Her eyes were dark and sombre yet sympathetic. Solomon smiled at her and shook his head. He wasn't trying to win her over. It was just a human reaction to the hopelessness of his situation.

The footsteps grew louder.

Solomon rose from his haunches and looked around. He had three streets to choose from. One of them was the one he'd come from so this was clearly out of the question. The other two were a gamble. One or both had his other pursuers. Then he heard it. It was like a 'Pssst' from a prompter in a theatre.

The young woman was motioning him over. He, stupidly, pointed to himself. She nodded. He bounded over like a happy Labrador and through the door. Seconds later, two groups of military policemen rounded the corner arriving at the small square. They found it empty of anyone save for the locals. They looked around them. Children, old people, and some mothers looked back at them and then returned to their business. A few oaths were uttered by the sergeants and then orders were given. They started to question the people in the square. Aggressively. The children were motioned back inside.

Within a few minutes, the only people outside were a dozen military policemen scratching their heads at the disappearance of the deserter and wondering why the inhabitants of the square were so damn French about it.

25

Two hours had passed in silence. The only noise was the sound of Jellicoe scribbling notes in a notebook. King was content to leaf through the pages of his whodunnit. If he was surprised at Jellicoe's reluctance to ask questions about what he was reading, then it was pleasantly so. It meant he could enjoy focusing his mind on what was happening on the train making its way through France, page by page.

Just after midday, Jellicoe decided it was time for a break. The question was where to go? Sunday in a seaside town in the middle of winter was notably deficient in places open to weary travellers in search of sustenance. Choices were few.

'Lunch?' he asked.

'Well, now that you mention it, old boy. I'm sure a sandwich wouldn't go amiss.'

That was the extent of Jellicoe's ambition, too, given his knowledge of the area. A cold chill descended on him when he spoke the next words.

'Perhaps we could prevail upon my landlady to make us a sandwich.'

'Well, I was thinking it would be an idea for me to check in to the hotel. Perhaps we can go there. The surroundings will be a little more congenial.'

'Where are you staying?'

'The Clifftops.

This was the best hotel in the town. It was situated, as the name suggested, at the top of a cliff. Jellicoe had often seen it from the front but had not yet had the time to pay a visit to the beautiful white hotel overlooking the town from on high. The two men descended the stairs and after Jellicoe left a message with the desk sergeant on where he was going, they set off to the hotel.

The snow was melting quickly leaving the streets damp and full of puddles. Jellicoe had to swerve on a number of occasions to avoid creating a lifetime of hatred for the police force by unnecessarily splashing pedestrians. The army man seemed to find all of this highly amusing, describing each episode as a 'near miss'.

Jellicoe waited in the bar while King checked in for the night. The bill, it had been agreed, would be picked up by the police force. Burnett strongly suggested that Jellicoe find all he needed as soon as possible. Budgets were tight enough without providing the army with a weekend pass by the sea.

Unfortunately, as King had taken his briefcase, Jellicoe could not continue reading the case file on Solomon. It was twenty minutes before the army man returned. In the meantime, Jellicoe had ordered some sandwiches and tea. He made sure to charge it to the room.

'Sorry old boy. Had to let the folk back home know I'd arrived safe and sound.'

'Do you mind if I ask you some questions?'

'By all means. I shan't know many answers, I expect.'

Optimistic chap thought Jellicoe.

A Time to Kill

'Did any British deserters face firing squads in the Second World War?' asked Jellicoe, biting into something that professed to be a ham sandwich on the menu.

'No, sadly not. They were court-martialled after they were caught and usually had a sentence of sorts. Hard labour,' answered King.

'And if they committed crimes?'

'Then they ended up in a civilian prison eventually.'

At this point Jellicoe set the sandwich down and dabbed his mouth. The food in this seaside town seemed to be uniformly bad. Fish and chips appeared to be the only exception to the rule. He was beginning to tire of this diet. The army man tucked into his ham sandwich with abandon.

'Try living on bully beef for years,' he explained between mouthfuls. 'This is bloody luxury; I can tell you.'

Just as Jellicoe was about to ask for the file, he spied a waiter coming over towards them. He was obviously looking for someone, and as they were the only people in the bar, the odds were that he'd find them.

'Excuse me, sir,' asked the waiter, 'but is one of you Detective Inspector Jellicoe?' Jellicoe nodded by way of response. 'There's a telephone call for you at reception.'

Jellicoe excused himself and followed the waiter out to the hotel foyer. He was handed a telephone.

'Jellicoe here.'

'I need you here,' said Burnett. 'Now. Some developments. Leave the army angle for the moment.'

The call did not last longer than the transmission of these instructions, so Jellicoe hurried back to King and explained that he would be off.

'What shall I do?'

Jellicoe thought for a moment and then replied, 'Stretch your legs. You're by the sea. I'm sure the air will do you good. Report in every two hours if you can. I have no idea how long I'll be. I'll leave a message with the desk sergeant whether I'll need to see you.'

'It's your money, old boy.' With that he turned to the barman and ordered a gin and tonic. A double. Jellicoe smiled and rose from his seat.

'Be sure to leave us something to pay the electric bill.'

-

Fifteen minutes later, Jellicoe was back in the police station. He met Burnett in the corridor outside the interrogation room. Through a window he could see DI Price and DS Fogg interviewing a heartily disgruntled Ronnie Musgrave. Beside Musgrave was a man who occupied the opposite end of the sartorial spectrum from the amusements owner. He was dressed in a dark three-piece suit and possessed a trim black moustache perhaps as compensation for the bald dome of his head. He even had a watch chain.

Musgrave, meanwhile, was a man that could sweat in an ice storm. His shirt was open far enough for the string vest to peek out proudly. Dark patches underneath his arms suggested Musgrave was as nervous as he was hot. The room was not particularly well sound-proofed, but one needed no skills in lip-reading to grasp that any feeling of forbearance had long since been abandoned by the suspect. That and the fact he was shouting.

'Go in and see if you can calm him down and get some sense,' ordered Burnett.

'What happened sir?'

214

A Time to Kill

'The Pemberton kid spoke. He told detectives that he did not see who took him but that they went straight to the place we found him. They had keys and they spoke openly about Ronnie being pleased.'

'He may have been set up,' pointed out Jellicoe. Just at that moment, Musgrave made a similar point, albeit at a different decibel level and interspersed with some colourful words to emphasize his dismay. 'Are we able to hold him?'

'Yes and no,' Burnett helpfully.

'Thanks, sir. Any other things you can help me with for the interview?'

'Do your best,' said Burnett with a shrug.

Jellicoe entered the room like a man tasked with making a factory workforce redundant. Somewhat dishearteningly, his arrival did not seem to raise anyone's spirits much. Maybe he'd forgotten how to make an entrance. His mother was the expert on that. Always stand framed in the doorway for a moment, she said, let people see you and wonder.

The only wondering going on that moment in the heads of those present was what Jellicoe was doing there. Jellicoe was of a similar mind. One thing was clear. They had no evidence. Just circumstantial items that made Jellicoe feel Musgrave was more wronged than wrongdoer.

'Another Keystone Cop,' said Musgrave, turning away in disgust.

Price and Fogg looked at Jellicoe and raised their eyebrows. They seemed, if anything, even less enamoured by his arrival than the suspect. Jellicoe could hardly blame them. It felt like he was trespassing.

'DI Jellicoe is joining us,' announced Price to the two men.

'Good afternoon, gentlemen,' said Jellicoe. It was never the worst idea to start civilly. He abhorred aggressiveness in interrogations. At least, explicit aggressiveness. If anything, his interview technique was more surgical strike than the saturation bombing. The gentle Welshman had his own approach which was probably based on the suspect under-estimating his antagonist. Not without reason, suspected Jellicoe.

'When can my client leave? You have nothing to hold him on.'

'Sadly, for your client, we have just enough, Mr…?' said Jellicoe calmly.

'Mr Elliot. Mr Elliot of Elliot, Elliot and Hardy.'

Jellicoe raised an eyebrow at the name and noted the look of dismay on the lawyer's face. The lawyer was younger up close than he'd expected. The moustache was not only an attempt to compensate for the premature loss of his hair but, perhaps, an attempt at *gravitas*.

'As I was saying,' continued Jellicoe, 'we are in between banging your client up and having to release him. Now, it would be best for both your client and our investigation if Mr Musgrave tells us more than he is currently so that we can get on with the real business of the day, which is to find out who did this, if it's connected in any way to the kidnapping of Stephen Masterson and the murder of his grandfather. Am I clear?'

Jellicoe's words were spoken with a quiet intensity. An additional thought passing through the lawyer's mind was that Jellicoe's accent was clearly not regional and, thus, gave pause for consideration. It suggested someone either more senior than the men he'd met or soon likely to be.

A Time to Kill

'Very. My client has nothing to hide.'

'The only thing your client is not hiding is his anger. He's keeping everything else very much to himself.'

Musgrave, who'd been staring angrily out of the office window at Burnett spun around and slammed the palms of his hands on the table. A restraining hand was placed on him by Elliot.

'What do you mean?' asked Elliot. The fencing had begun.

'Let's remind ourselves of three key facts. The boy was found in one of your client's properties. There was no sign that entry was forced. How did they get a key? Secondly, your client was identified by the boy in an overheard conversation. You may, of course,' added Jellicoe, holding his hand up to pre-empt an interruption from the lawyer, 'say that there are many people called Ronnie. True, but not many people called Ronnie are connected so heavily in terms of location and, shall we say, business, as your client. But even assuming that this is, indeed, a very obvious set up, it does beg the question who might do this and why? We'll deal with that in a moment. There is also the final point around Freddie Douglas who, I gather, has worked with Mr Musgrave in the past and who is currently sought after by ourselves, as well as your client. As you can see, Mr Elliot, there a host of things we need to understand. It will make all our lives easier if he tells us what he knows about these matters. You do see that don't you? Because I certainly do.'

Once again, Jellicoe's tone impressed in its seriousness and also something else. A note of tiredness with the verbal dancing, the never-ending cat and mouse. It conveyed that there was something bigger at stake if only the principals could see it. Elliot certainly did.

'Can I have some time with my client, please?'

Jellicoe glanced at Price. Moments later the three detectives stood up and left the room. Burnett looked at them and said, 'Well?'

'He's going to talk but I don't think he's a kidnapper.'

Burnett looked sceptical, 'Let him prove that. They found the boy at his place, so he'll need to have a bloody good explanation as to how that happened.' The Chief shook his head, and his eyes began to blaze. He glared at Jellicoe and Price. 'Find me a connection between Musgrave and Masterson. There has to be one aside from Freddie bloody Douglas.'

Elliot motioned for the detectives to return. Burnett held his hand up. He wasn't about to have his men subject to the whim of some lawyer. So, they waited for a couple of minutes and then returned.

'My client has indicated he will answer your questions,' resumed Elliot.

Jellicoe turned to Musgrave. He received a cold stare in return. Gone was the chumminess displayed with Clarke. This was an unhappy man and Jellicoe suspected he had a lot of reasons to be unhappy. Jellicoe said, 'Very well. Let's begin with the keys. How did someone get hold of the keys.'

Musgrave's face fell a little. Unless he was a good actor, and Jellicoe really quite doubted this, then the keys were a mystery to him.

'I don't know.'

'Don't be ridiculous,' shouted Price.

A Time to Kill

'I have no bloody idea, all right?' roared Musgrave, outraged at being interrupted and having his integrity questioned in the same sentence. Even Jellicoe was astonished by Price's outburst.

'Why not?' asked Jellicoe in a soothing voice.

'How difficult is it to steal a key, cut it and then return it? We haven't opened that stall up in nearly two bloody weeks. Not since Christmas. Anyone could've nicked the key.'

'You're saying none of them are missing?'

'Yes, that's what I'm saying. We checked, before you ask.'

'Could Freddie Douglas have taken one and returned it?'

Musgrave gave a curt nod. Is this why they were after Freddie or was there something else?

'Why are you after Freddie Douglas?' asked Jellicoe.

Musgrave looked even more on edge now. They were straying into the territory he'd wanted to avoid. Jellicoe could see a man wrestling with what passed for a conscience in a criminal mind.

'Does Freddie work for you?' pressed Jellicoe.

'In a manner of speaking. He's an associate, not an employee. I make sure no one hurts him. He's a delicate boy if you know what I mean.'

'I do, Mr Musgrave. The question in my mind is why you would act as his pimp.'

Musgrave was on his feet in split seconds. The chair flew back, and he put his fists on the table and leaned over to Jellicoe.

'I'm not his bloody pimp, all right?'

'Sit down, Mr Musgrave,' said Jellicoe calmly. He put a retraining hand on DS Fogg who'd stood up immediately.

'I'm not his pimp. Freddie does what Freddie does. I don't condone it, but I don't make his bookings if that's what you're suggesting or take a cut for that matter.'

'So, what do you use him for?'

Musgrave glared at Jellicoe.

'Not what you think, sonny boy. Some of us didn't grow up with a silver spoon. We had to fight for what we have. Your lot didn't help us. I've built up a business and sometimes I play a bit rough and sometimes I have to make sure your lot don't try and push me out. Freddie has his uses. I see him right.'

Jellicoe had guessed as much but Musgrave all but confirmed it. Still, it was worth twisting the knife a little further.

'Blackmail hardly seems your style.'

Musgrave's response was a cackle of sorts.

'It never gets that far, trust me.'

'I'm sure it doesn't.' Jellicoe sat back and contemplated the situation for a moment. Then he sat forward and asked, 'So, who is Freddie jumping into bed with, so to speak?' Musgrave's face turned into a mask of hatred, but Jellicoe suspected this was directed elsewhere. 'Warwick? Is that his new protector?'

The silence was its own answer. Yet this struck Jellicoe as wrong. Musgrave was obviously not aware of the Solomon connection.

'Why would Warwick get involved with someone like Freddie?' asked Jellicoe. He made no attempt to hide his scepticism. 'I mean, this is low rent stuff, isn't it? Warwick wants to be at the golf club quaffing G&Ts with his friends. Freddie Douglas? Definitely not his style.'

A Time to Kill

'Maybe he wants to put me out of business. Launch a takeover. Have you thought of that?'

'I had in fact. I rejected it seconds after it occurred to me.'

'Why?' asked Musgrave. There was just a hint of hurt in his eyes.

'Amusement arcades? Chip shops? Sweet shops? Bookies?' Jellicoe's tone was withering. The look on his face no less so.

'I think you'll find Johnny-boy has a lot more respect for earning money than you do, son. He had it hard enough too.'

'You seem a bit soft on him. I doubt you'll be playing a fourball with him any time soon.'

'Aye, maybe not but that doesn't mean Warwick wouldn't want a bit of what I have. What better way to go about it than see me in jail?'

'What use would that be? Surely one of your family would just take over.'

A look came over Musgrave's face. At first it was sorrow and then it turned to a cold anger. It came out as the snarl of a wounded animal.

'My boy was lost defending your right to go to your public bloody school and your university.'

Jellicoe and Musgrave stared at one another. The only sound in the room was the sound of the clock ticking.

'I'm sorry for your loss.'

With that, Jellicoe rose to his feet. There was nothing left to say. Without adding anything else he left the room. Burnett looked at him. A frown creased the gap between his eyebrows.

'He's not our man. There's more to this but whatever the truth is,' said Jellicoe, indicating Musgrave with his thumb, 'this is not a kidnapper.'

'So, what do we do?' asked Burnett, perplexed and angry in equal measure.

'I would let him go but keep some men on him. If he's convinced Warwick's behind this, then he may do something stupid. Last thing we need is a gang war.'

'Really?' said Burnett with all of the withering sarcasm that a cop of several decades could bring to bear on a relatively new and certainly very smart newcomer.

Jellicoe smiled at this and accepted that he'd probably been more than a little patronising. 'I should go back to our army friend. Find out more about Solomon.'

Burnett yanked his head back in an off-you-go manner. So, Jellicoe took that as his dismissal. He walked quickly down the corridor and into the foyer of the building. After a quick word with the desk sergeant, he headed straight for the exit. He felt for the car keys in his pocket. The liquid black body of the Wolsey beckoned him towards it. Just out of his line of sight a man appeared. His head was covered by a grey fedora and the lapels of his raincoat covered the bottom of his face. A sixth sense told Jellicoe to stop and face the man, but it was too late.

He felt a gun jab into the base of his ribs.

'Come with me.'

A Time to Kill

26

There was no one around. The street was as deserted as a ghost town. The journalists had taken the day off. Or they were very sensibly sleeping off a roast dinner. Either way, they were alone. Not a policeman in sight when you wanted one and here, they were, outside the police station. Jellicoe had no choice but to go with the man.

'Where are you taking me?'

'Actually, you're taking me. Don't turn around and don't do anything stupid.' They walked towards Jellicoe's Wolsey police car. The man with the gun sat in the back. Jellicoe felt the cold steel of the gun on the back of his neck. 'I doubt I should miss from here.'

Jellicoe started the car and pulled out onto the street in front of the police station.

'Which way?'

'Go past the bank and keep driving to the sea front. Pull in at the Funderland Amusements.

Funderland was another amusement arcade that belonged to Musgrave. The thought passed through Jellicoe's mind that he may have been wrong. Or perhaps it was just a coincidence. After all, Musgrave owned a high proportion of the businesses at the front. He drove slowly all the while considering his options. The voice of the man holding the gun was soft, educated and he was unlikely to be part of Musgrave's gang.

He glanced in the driver's mirror, but the gunman was keeping out of the way. He could just about see a dark coat. He drove on and decided against any rash action. One man had already been murdered. There was little point in adding to the tally.

The quietness of the streets meant the trip to the front took very little time. Jellicoe parked near the amusements. Then a hood was dropped into his lap.

'Put this on.'

'Do you think that some people may wonder why a hooded man is walking along the street at the point of the gun?'

'I expect they would. Perhaps we should avoid doing that.'

Jellicoe took off his hat and put on the hood. He wondered about putting the hat back on but thought better of it. He also left the keys in the car. This might alert someone to the fact that something was wrong. The gunman was out of the car. He tapped the bonnet and Jellicoe stepped outside, too. Moments later he felt himself being bundled into another car. Then they were racing off. It felt like something from a film noir. Not a very good one at that.

They had to be driving along the front past the harbour. He heard a boat horn that confirmed this. Minutes later they turned left and were heading up a hill. He felt his body pressing back against the leather seats. The gunman was beside him. No one spoke so there was at least one more man in the car, the driver.

The car turned again. Was it a left? It drove for another few minutes. They passed a church. It sounded as if it was on the right. The pealing bells told him it was three o'clock in the afternoon. Not much use that, he conceded but at least the church gave a sense of place.

Another turn, right, and now there was nothing that could provide any help as to where they were. The road appeared to twist and bend. They made another two turns, but Jellicoe was too disoriented to be certain which way they'd gone. They drove for only a couple of minutes though because Jellicoe felt the car slow down and eventually halt. Throughout the journey, Jellicoe's concentration had been so focused on gaining a sense of where they were heading that it came as something of a shock to realise that the real purpose of the journey might be to kill him.

Jellicoe congratulated himself bitterly on his sagacity. It was now time to consider what his plan for escape might look like. His options were limited. He had been cuffed and both arms lay uselessly behind his back.

Still no words were spoken until the gunman ordered him out. Jellicoe stumbled from the car. He felt a gun pressed into his back in a manner that suggested he walk forward. Then another pair of hands took his arm to frog march him ahead more quickly. He was walking over grass and twigs. They were outside now. The ground crunched underfoot where it was still frozen, but there was also some give in it. It was beginning to turn to mud. Then, just as he'd thought this, his foot squelched into a puddle. The muddy water invaded both his feet. It was bad enough that he'd been kidnapped and faced something much worse but now his feet were wet. He felt miserable but oddly not as scared as he thought he would.

He heard a door opening. Moments later he tripped over a doorway and fell the ground.

'Who's there? said a boy's voice. A very frightened voice.

-

Danny Lester wasn't a bad lad really. His problem was he liked messing around. Him and his mates just liked a bit of fun. They didn't mean any harm. Least that was what his mum would say. His dad worked at the big plastics factory. He used to give Danny a clip round the ear when he was out of line. No more, though; too big now. In fact, this had been the case since he was sixteen. He'd left school then, too.

Dad wanted him to work in the factory. It was always expanding; loads of work he'd say. Danny didn't want to, though. Part of him knew it would happen eventually. The town was shut half the year. Where else was there to go? He couldn't spend all his time playing the machines at Funderland.

But still, it was much more fun being with your mates, listening to music, chasing girls. He was only seventeen, sure. There'd be time enough to work in the factory. He'd have to earn money sometime.

Whenever he saw a dark Wolsey, it put him on edge. He'd never done anything seriously wrong. He wasn't a criminal; high spirited maybe. He and Jamie walked down the hill and passed by the police car. It was empty. Danny looked around and saw that the street was mostly deserted. There was some sunshine but, in truth, his face was stinging with the cold. No one would want to be out on a day like this.

He stopped by the car and glanced inside. The dark leather seats looked plush. These coppers didn't stint themselves, he thought. He saw the hat in the front seat and then his eyes saw a glint.

'Bloody hell, Jamie,' said Danny. 'The copper's only gone and left his keys in the car.' He looked at Jamie with a grin that his friend knew all too well.

-

'I was meant to be having a roast now,' said Yates sourly. He was sitting beside Wallace in a car outside a chip shop at the other end of the front from the harbour. The smell of chips had taken up residence in the car and would last for days. Wallace almost pitied the policeman who would have the car the next day. Almost. In truth he'd had better plans for the day, too. Instead, they were keeping an eye on a bunch of Musgrave's men who were drinking in a bar just around the corner called *The Smuggler*. The two men would have been within their rights to arrest the men. Drinking was not permitted at this time on a Sunday.

This, of course, would have been madness on their part and sparked something of a deterioration in relations between the forces of law and order and their natural enemies. Why poke the hornets' nest? Anyway, they had a job to do. Find the Masterson boy. If any of these men were connected with the kidnapping, then they would lie in wait for them and hopefully be led to the boy.

The car was parked on the front. Waves were beginning to froth and spew onto the sand. The weather was turning. The sunny skies of earlier were beginning to give way to something more ominous. Grey clouds were forming in the distance and looked like they were going to launch an attack soon. They sat waiting, crunching on the teeth-breaker chips that fell to the bottom of the newspaper wrapping. Yates looked at the vinegar-sodden paper and showed it to Wallace.

'Look. Freddie Douglas.'

Wallace saw the faded features of the young man that half the town appeared to want to speak to. He smiled and raised his eyebrows. Then something caught his eye. He looked up. He saw something he'd never seen before nor, he realised, was he likely to see again.

Framed against dark, forbidding sea was a black Wolsey car that looked very like one the police would have, like one he'd driven yesterday, driving at full speed along the deserted front, weaving from side to side. Yates had now caught sight of it, too. His mouth dropped open.

'What the…?'

-

Jellicoe rose to his feet. He ducked and tried to shake off the hood when he heard a voice behind him.

'Don't even think about it.'

'Who's there?' asked the boy again.

Jellicoe was helped up and bustled forward until he reached a point near the voice and then a firm hand on his shoulder forced him down.

'Why don't you introduce yourself, Detective Inspector?' asked the unknown man.

'My name is Jellicoe. Are you Stephen Masterson?'

The boy heard the muffled voice but could see nothing. He'd been blindfolded earlier but, at least the gag had been removed.

'What did you say?'

Jellicoe put his hand to the hood. He raised it slightly; no one stopped him.

A Time to Kill

'My name is Jellicoe. I'm with the police. The people who took you have taken me also.'

'I won't be going back with you?'

'I suspect not, Stephen. How are they treating you?'

'Horribly. They've tied me up, gagged me and now I'm blindfolded.'

'Food?'

'Yes, but I'm a bit tired of fish and chips.'

You and me both, thought Jellicoe. They hadn't blindfolded him earlier. A chill went through Jellicoe that had little to do with the cold. If they hadn't been worried about being seen, then the implication of this was all too clear. But why would they bother to keep him alive?

'We'll get you out of here soon, Stephen. Don't worry.'

Jellicoe wasn't sure he even believed this, but it seemed the thing to say in the circumstances.

'That's enough, Jellicoe,' said the man. He jabbed the gun in Jellicoe's shoulder although, noted the detective, it wasn't done to hurt. However, it was firm enough to indicate that the meeting was finished. Just for a moment Jellicoe felt a hand take hold of the hood. It was raised up giving him a brief view of the boy. It was certainly Stephen Masterson. As quickly as he had seen the boy, the darkness returned. He felt a hand gently push him.

'I have to go now,' said Jellicoe. 'I'll be back for you.'

This was met with a derisive laugh which Jellicoe ignored. Then he felt someone take his arm and then begin to hustle him away.

'Where are you? Come back!' shouted Stephen. There was an edge of hysteria in his voice. In no time Jellicoe was outside and the sound of screams grew louder.

'For God's sake, let him go. What earthly use can you have for the boy?' snarled Jellicoe as he fell against the car.

'You'll see,' said a voice. 'Help him inside.'

This was a different voice from the gunman. Jellicoe wondered if this was the man he was after: David Solomon. One other thought was now lodged in his mind. The walls of the prison were made of corrugated metal. He was being held inside a metal container or building. Like a farm building.

They were outside of the building now. The icy air folded itself around Jellicoe and he shivered. He felt a hand take his arm and he began to walk forward.

'Why are you doing this?' aske Jellicoe.

'Why not?' came the reply. This unaccountably irritated Jellicoe. It was glib and careless. Everything that the planning of the kidnap had not been.

'I don't understand how a man, an educated man like yourself has descended so low.'

'Try spending months in a foxhole. Try waking up, every day, thinking, no wait, wanting it to be your last. That's how you descend to this. Have you studied physics?'

'Not since school. You read physics, didn't you? Oxford.'

Jellicoe sensed his captor smiling. Certainly, he could hear the grin as he replied.

'Very good. Yes, I read physics at Oxford. I might still be there now, lecturing to bored students had it not been for the damn war. As if the world we live in wasn't a big enough mess without adding war to the ingredients. Insofar as we have any control over our destiny, and we don't, then war just provides you with a daily, hourly reminder that your life is not your own.'

'Very philosophical. How do you reconcile this with what you've become? A murderer and a kidnapper?'

'I didn't kill the colonel, by the way, you'll have to look elsewhere on that one, old boy,' said Solomon. It sounded genuine but then again, they always did.

'You're just a kidnapper, Mr Solomon, well that's fine then. We'll let you off with a warning. Don't do it again though.'

Solomon had the grace to laugh at this but there was a harshness to it, a bitterness born of fifteen years or so of jail. Jellicoe sensed his eyes boring into him.

'Do you really expect me to believe that Solomon? Two crimes committed in the same place, at the same time but by different people.'

Jellicoe sensed that Solomon was smiling.

'It may seem crazy but is it crazy enough to be true? You should study physics, Detective Inspector. Anything is possible. Let's take our friend, Major Masterson. He is both a victim of crime and a criminal. Is this possible? Of course, it is. Incidentally, he's the one you should be investigating, not me.'

'So, you are not a tawdry kidnapper but merely an informant?' replied Jellicoe. His voice was dripping with sarcasm.

'None of us are innocent but we are all bystanders. We have no control over what happens to us. One day you're smoking with a friend in the forest, next your blindfolded and lying in an empty building. One day you're studying for a

PhD, next you're told to go kill that man over there.' Solomon laughed mirthlessly. 'All we have is what happens now.'

Jellicoe felt himself being bundled into the car again. Solomon, he guessed, joined him in the back seat. The car started and they were off again.

'What happened back then that made you do this?'

'What do you think, Jellicoe? Even inside our heads we have no control. It's the story of our lives, believe me.'

27

15 Years Earlier

Lizette Giresse was twenty-six years old when she saved Solomon that day. She looked younger but her eyes had seen more than someone's twice her age. It was a whim. A recognition of someone who needed help: another lost soul. Hers had been lost years ago.

She motioned for him to come. He saw that she meant it. Seconds after he'd passed her the military policemen rounded two separate corners and almost crashed into one another like they were in a silent movie. It was funny. Another time she might have stood there, pointed at them, and laughed. But she knew she couldn't. They had rescued the city. It would have seemed ungrateful. Then, of course, she had to think of the poor soldier who was on the run. She stepped inside and turned to face him.

They were standing in a corridor that led to a small flat upstairs. The paint was peeling off the green walls. It was clean, though. She had that much pride. They stood looking at one another. The only sound came from the shouting outside. The military policemen were openly swearing at anyone who would listen. No one was.

Solomon saw a young woman who might have been a beauty in another world. Put her in finery and place her among the rich, she would have had many admirers. But this wasn't that world. It was a backstreet of Paris. She was poor and underfed. And frightened.

The man she was studying was young, perhaps her age but not older. He looked foreign but the policemen chasing him were British or American. There was fear on his face. His hair was matted with sweat, and he was breathing heavily. A voice upstairs shouted down.

'Maman.'

Lizette looked up, fearful at what she'd done. A man she had never seen before, a criminal perhaps, a déserteur certainly, was in her home. There were police outside. It would be so easy.

'Maman!' A child's voice. Female. More insistent.

The man sensed her doubt. Her regret. He put his hands up, palms facing her. In clear albeit accented French he said, 'Please don't tell them. I won't hurt you. I just need to stay out of their way. Just a little while. Please.' The dark eyes were pleading.

She ran upstairs saying nothing. He followed her. When he reached the top of the stairs, he saw he'd been wrong. It wasn't a flat. It was a room with a bed. A table with some old chairs. There was a fireplace and, in the corner, a curtained area which Solomon guessed was the toilet.

Solomon saw her cradling a young child of around six years. A little girl, with the same haunted eyes as her mother. The two of them looked fearfully at Solomon. A number of things passed through his mind at that moment. What could have brought such fear of men into their lives? He suspected there was only one answer. He walked forward towards them and then knelt down in front of the young girl, his head level with hers.

'Hello,' he said, 'I'm David. What's your name?' He looked directly at the little girl.

She glanced fearfully at her mother, who nodded, and then back to David.

'Sophie.'

Just behind Sophie was a photograph of a young man. He could see some of Sophie in him. He was in a uniform. Lizette saw him looking at the picture. The tears were stinging her eyes now.

A Time to Kill

'Paul,' said Lizette to the unasked question.

'Where is he?'

She shook her head and buried her face in both her hands. Her body shook with the anguish and a pain that would never go away. Solomon stood up and looked at her. His hands gripped one another tightly, unsure of what to do, wanting to do something, unable to do anything; playing the role of the tentative male in the presence of a desolate female, pitch perfectly.

A few days later there was a loud banging at the door. It was early morning. Solomon awoke from his makeshift bed on the floor. Sophie began to cry. Daylight peeked through the shutters giving the small room a dim light. Solomon could see the fear on the face of the young woman returning. Her nervousness, which had diminished over the last few days, was not completely his fault. Something else had been on her mind. The husband was dead, but perhaps she had a lover.

The voice downstairs was French. Solomon knew he would find out soon. It didn't sound like a lover. There was anger in the voice. More than that, there was hatred. The banging on the door continued. Lizette was sitting on the bed holding onto her knees. She looked very small at that moment: a fearful child.

'Who is it?' asked Solomon, eyes widening.

'Claude,' whispered Lizette. Nothing else was said. Solomon nodded and then headed downstairs. He opened the door.

'Who are you?' demanded a man of around fifty years, broad-shouldered, bearded, and angry.

'Who are you?' asked Solomon quietly. He stepped forward towards the man until his face was only inches away. Solomon was around six feet, but he still found himself looking up into a pair of dark eyes that knew violence. But then again, so did he.

The man's face creased into a smile. Solomon stepped backwards just in time to miss the full force of the head butt. It crashed into his chest and still hurt. But Solomon had anticipated well. His feet were now in a boxer's stance. He threw a sharp uppercut using the heel of his palm. He heard a grunt as the Frenchman's jaws snapped together painfully and his neck jerked backwards.

Solomon pushed the man out onto the street. All around them, people stopped and looked at the early morning entertainment. The man took a wild swing at Solomon which was easily evaded. He stumbled forward and received an elbow into the side of his head. The man fell to the ground, blood began to pour from an eye wound. Solomon stood over him poised but did not continue his attack. The man stared up at him, murder in his eyes.

Solomon saw the man knew he was beaten and stood up straight. Then he bent over and snarled at the man, 'If I see you round here again, I will kill you.' Solomon knew this wasn't the end. He was also more than prepared to kill the man.

'You need to leave, David.' said Lizette, when Solomon returned. His face seemed to fall. She knew he would leave if she asked him. The few days that he'd been in hiding with her had revealed a gentle man. He was respectful towards her and treated Sophie with nothing but kindness. She didn't want him to leave.

'I'm sorry, I've stayed too long. I should never have imposed.'

She shook her head and collapsed onto the bed.

'You don't understand. It's Claude. He's dangerous. He'll come, they'll come, David. They'll hurt you.'

'Does he hurt you?'

She answered with her tears. Sophie ran to her mother and cradled her like she was the child. Solomon moved towards her and knelt down.

'Lizette, I don't want to know what he is to you. But he'll only be bad for you and for Sophie. If he comes again, I'll deal with him.'

236

A Time to Kill

Lizette looked at Solomon. Uncertainty mixed with fear. She stared into his eyes. They were like her own: dark, full of secrets, yearning for assurance. What she wanted to embark upon would change everything. Yet she trusted this man for reasons that went beyond analysis and were unambiguously human.

Of course, he would come again. Solomon knew he would. The next time Claude would be prepared. So, must he be. He'd abandoned one front line and now he was engaged on another. Only this time the enemy wasn't in a uniform. They were all around, dressed like him.

He was careful. He never strayed too far from their room. If he did, the walk was short, watchful and took place in crowded places. A week passed and then another. It seemed maybe Claude was gone. Lizette knew otherwise. She heard things, rumours but there was no sign of her former 'employer'. She warned Solomon to stay vigilant. He promised he would.

But you can make all the promises in the world. Life is too ephemeral to make plans. Of course, Claude hadn't forgotten. The beating he'd taken was going to be avenged one way or another. He bided his time. Three weeks had passed when Claude struck.

Solomon liked to go outside the front door to smoke a cigarette or two in the evenings. This is how he began to get to know the people in the square. He liked the orange glow of the square and how it contrasted with the navy sky. Many of the square's inhabitants would sit out at the front of their houses and chat. Solomon often joined them and conversed while Lizette tried to put Sophie to bed. They liked him. More than this, he did odd jobs for them but asked nothing in return. Of course, they gave something. Food usually. He went through the pretence of refusal and reluctant acceptance. It was a game. A harmless game but it meant more for Lizette and Sophie.

Jack Murray

From time to time on these evenings he would see men, unfamiliar men, pass through the square. He was on his guard less for Claude than he was for military police. Then one evening a couple of men walked past chatting. They stopped for a light from Solomon.

He didn't see the punches coming. The first one across his eye sent him flying backwards, the second man followed up with a dig in the stomach. The pain blinded him momentarily, but he managed to roll away from one of the men. The screams of the women alerted Lizette. She ran to the window and saw two men attacking him. Nearby, she saw Claude smiling, smoking a cigarette. He looked up to her. She felt a chill descend. She grabbed a frying pan and sprinted downstairs.

Solomon was on his feet now. This wasn't the first time he'd been attacked in his life. He knew staying on the ground was death. The blows rained down on him, but he was on his feet and punched out wildly. One of his punches landed flush. It was one on one now. Then Claude joined in. The other man was on his feet, too.

With each second, Solomon's head was clearing but there were three of them circling him. Lizette flew through the door, weapon in hand. She attacked Claude, screaming with the hatred and the fear of someone who had reason to feel both. But something else was happening. Something unexpected.

Another group of men passing the square had heard the screams. They ran through the archway leading into the square and came across the three men fighting and a fourth attempting to punch a young woman. Choosing sides was not difficult. Within seconds Claude and his two accomplices were taken into the alleyway and received a form of summary justice.

One of Solomon's eyes was cut, and his ribs would give him hell for a few days, but he'd escaped serious harm.

'Merci,' said Solomon extending his hand to his benefactor.

The answer was something that passed for French, but Solomon immediately realised it wasn't. The man was not a local. More

238

worryingly, he was looking at him strangely. A silence fell between them broken only by the sounds of the man's friends working over Solomon's attackers. The two men studied one another warily.

Then the man said in an American accent, 'You're not French, are you?'

28

They were in the car now and Jellicoe forced himself to concentrate once more on the sounds and the turns the car took. However, it seemed his captor had suddenly realised that the detective might be able to pull off that trick so popular in dime novels and B-movies of using his memory of the sounds outside the car.

'Put the radio, on,' ordered Solomon.

Jellicoe heard an American pop singer crooning about a lost love. He couldn't remember the singer's name.

'Put something else on,' said Solomon. He clearly wasn't a fan. The driver found a station playing jazz. This was more like it as far as Jellicoe was concerned. Solomon, too.

'Keep it here.'

'You like Miles Davis?' asked Jellicoe.

Jellicoe sensed a smile on Solomon's face when he replied, 'Of course.'

'Why?'

Solomon was silent for a moment as if he wanted to find the right words to express his feelings on a subject that clearly meant something to him.

'I like jazz. I like people like Miles Davis and especially Ornette Coleman.'

'Ornette Coleman?'

A Time to Kill

'He's new. American of course. His is a different type of Jazz. All established rhythm and chords go out the window when he plays. It's pure; completely improvised. The ensemble reacts to what each other is doing in the moment. You should give him a listen.' There was a certain awe in his voice as he spoke. 'Do you like Jazz?'

'Yes, very much,' admitted Jellicoe.

'You sound more like a classical man,' pointed out Solomon.

'I like a lot of classical music, too. My wife was more of an aficionado. She never understood my interest in jazz. She felt there something feral about it. For people of dubious moral character.'

Solomon laughed at this. Then he said, 'If you don't mind me saying, I think your wife's prejudices have little to do with the music.'

This was perceptive. Sylvia wore her prejudices like a dowager duchess wore a pearl necklace. Jellicoe said nothing more about his wife.

Solomon became silent as if he'd decided Jellicoe had heard too much already at least about him, his character, rather than the narrative. This version of events he was communicating was meant to convey the idea that he was not evil, not a murderer. Interestingly, he still hadn't talked about why he hated Masterson so much. But they hadn't yet reached the part of his capture, the court martial and his imprisonment. What picture would emerge from this?

Jellicoe's arms were numb. He'd progressed through pain to cramp to numbness. His occasional requests to have the handcuffs removed were met with little sympathy. With his arms behind him, finding a comfortable position to sit in the car was increasingly proving a distraction.

'Why do you hate Masterson?' asked Jellicoe at one point. He'd interrupted Solomon but cared little for how rude it would have appeared. By now he'd earned the very British right to feel a little peeved at his treatment. The restrained agony in his voice would have been immediately understood even if commiseration leading to release was unlikely.

'Why? Let me ask you a question. Are you feeling a little uncomfortable at the moment?'

Jellicoe could not restrain himself from telling Solomon exactly how uncomfortable he was and his feelings on the matter. The laugh that followed was genuine if lacking in the requisite empathy that might have leavened the situation for Jellicoe. So, Solomon spoke a little more.

It was another ten minutes before the car came to a halt. It seemed that Solomon's story was finished if not quite complete, suspected Jellicoe. He heard the driver's door open. Moments later a blast of cold air told him Solomon was out of the car now. He felt a hand clasp his arm and he was helped out. By the sounds of cars around him, they had to be in town. Jellicoe 's feet were on a pavement then he was guided forward. A pair of hands pushed him down. They wanted him to sit at the edge of the pavement. The hood stayed, as did the handcuffs. Moments later he heard the car drive off.

There seemed nothing else to do but to sit there and wait for someone to notice that a handcuffed man with a hood was sitting on the pavement on a late Sunday afternoon. This was either a man with very particular erotic predilections or someone in need of help.

A Time to Kill

The former was certainly the first thought of Jackie Taylor as she walked back from an hour helping clean the church. At sixty-three, Jackie was not a prude, but she certainly had little time for the increasingly permissive values that were spreading through society like red wine spilled on a virgin-white dress. She glanced down guiltily at the stain on her pinny underneath her coat. A moment's lack of concentration while cleaning. Altar wine, too.

Jackie did not want for courage. She drew herself up to her full five foot one and approached the man seated on the pavement to have him explain himself, especially as it was the Lord's day. Such questions are best asked at a higher volume than normal social discourse allows and with an added peremptory top note to indicate censure.

'What do you think you are doing, young man?' asked Jackie. She was in no doubt it was a man and that he was young.

Jellicoe politely explained the situation to her. Jackie was sceptical but it was much too strange a tale to be just made up. She decided to give the man the benefit of the doubt. It would have been un-Christian not to do so.

'What do you want me to do?'

'Could you ring the police, please?'

This is what Jackie had always intended doing anyway. It was gratifying to have her instincts and her better nature validated simultaneously.

-

'I don't know why you're looking at me like that,' said Jellicoe defensively.

Burnett was glaring at him when he entered the office. Jellicoe had just been brought back in a police car. His body ached and he desperately wanted to go home and catch up on all the sleep he hadn't been getting for the last week. A dose of Burnett's sympathy was not what the doctor ordered.

'What the hell happened?' demanded Burnett. Loudly. Jellicoe could see a few amused faces in the outer office. Well, it was late Sunday afternoon and their weekend had been ruined. At least he was in a position to provide some modest entertainment even if he wasn't particularly enjoying his role in the show.

'Great security here. I was kidnapped outside the police station.'

'The cheeky devils,' said Burnett. His tone had changed to one of quiet admiration. Then a thought struck him. 'by who?'

'Whom,' answered Jellicoe before quickly adding 'Solomon.' Burnett looked witheringly at the detective and then shook his head.

'Solomon. What's his game?'

'He wanted to show me the boy.'

'And?'

'He's fine. Scared but fine. I should go to the major and update him.'

Burnett stared at Jellicoe to see if he was serious. The implications were pounding his head like a migraine. Could they not tell him? What would happen if he found out? It was all too complicated. And what about Musgrave? They had little enough to hold him on as it was.

'Any connection with Musgrave? asked Burnett hopefully.

'I have no idea,' he admitted.

A Time to Kill

'Warwick?'

'No, I don't think so.' He decided at the last moment against adding a shoulder shrug to emphasise the point. In the circumstances it may not have gone down well with the volatile chief.

'Holmes, you amaze me,' said Burnett with a shake of the head.

Perhaps he should have done the shrug after all, thought Jellicoe. He let that one pass. It was a stressful time and Burnett was not the sort of chief to deny his feelings of stress their rightful place at the forefront of his subordinates' minds.

Throughout Burnett had not inquired once if Jellicoe had recovered from his ordeal. There was a deficiency of sympathy from the senior officer that was actually quite endearing. Finally, Burnett agreed, in a manner of speaking, that Jellicoe should visit Masterson to update him on the latest events.

Jellicoe went in search of Yates and Wallace to get hold of the car keys. He saw Wallace and called him over. The younger policeman updated Jellicoe on their afternoon as they walked out to the police car that Jellicoe had been forced to abandon a few hours earlier. When they reached it Jellicoe's mouth fell open. There was a dent at the front and the paintwork was scratched all along the passenger side.

'What the hell happened here?'

-

'Watch it, Danny,' shouted Jamie who was now very worried that an innocent jape had turned into something far more serious. Danny had never been the most responsible of boys. Not that he could cast stones on that score. That would have bordered on hypocrisy. Danny always took a joke one step too far. By the time he'd finished, no one was laughing. This joke had certainly reached that stage and Jamie certainly wasn't laughing.

The Rubicon had been crossed two minutes previously when Danny had decided that rather than just move the car to a new parking spot, Jamie's original and rather funny suggestion, they would, instead, take it for a ride.

Fine.

Just down the street. Jamie could live with that because even if the copper came out to nab them, *they* had the wheels. But two minutes ago, that had changed. Jamie had detected this when he saw the speed rising to illegally high levels and his friend treating the Wolsey like it was a Dodgem car at the amusements. They were lucky the road along the seafront was deserted. Distant clouds rolling towards them suggested that things were going to turn nasty again.

Of course, Danny, being Danny, was having a ball. Another thing Jamie noticed about Danny was his capacity to enjoy things more when others were beginning to tire of the source of fun. Jamie was well past that point now.

'Watch it, Danny, you'll hit that car.'

Danny needed no second warning. He'd already decided where he was heading. What could be funnier when you're eighteen years old than raking the side of a parked car with your stolen police car.

It would be fair to say that Jamie was less than impressed at what Danny did as he'd been on the passenger side. Damn near soiled himself in fact, not that he'd admit as much to his idiot friend. It was then that they heard the police siren. That's when Jamie absolutely lost his rag with Danny.

A Time to Kill

However, even Danny recognised the situation had taken a turn. Coincidentally, that's what he needed to do. And fast. He crossed over the road, against the on-coming traffic, which, in this case, was a Morris Minor driven by a septuagenarian vet called Henry. They missed by a matter of inches but were now off the sea front. They roared up the hill, startling two nuns out for their constitutional, then pulled into a side street outside Colgan's Hairdressers.

Jamie did not need a second invitation to exit the car. The two boys abandoned the car in the middle of the street, thereby ensuring that the other police car could not follow them. They saluted the two policemen in the time-honoured fashion as they ran away to safety.

-

'Would you recognise them again?' asked Jellicoe as they drove up to the Masterson estate.

'No, 'fraid not.'

They'd all covered themselves in glory one way or another that day. Burnett would probably be on the receiving end of a carpeting on this double catastrophe from either the Super or the Chief. Even recovering one of the boys would do little to mitigate the sense of failure pervading their efforts. The stake out of the Musgrave gang had proved, as Jellicoe had suspected, a fruitless endeavour which had only diverted them from the real investigation. Jellicoe checked if Yates or Wallace had made any progress on the cases that Colonel Masterson had heard over the last few years as a magistrate.

'No, sir. He's heard over three hundred cases. I've discounted about eighty so far but then we had to do this stake out. They're all fairly low-level crime. Nothing that would have made anyone want to kill him.'

'Fair enough. First thing tomorrow I need a list of "possibles". We can't ignore this avenue.'

'You don't think it was this man Solomon?'

Jellicoe sighed audibly. In his heart, he had a feeling that Solomon was telling the truth but, equally, he accepted the balance of evidence, although circumstantial, pointed to him. Something was nagging at him. He wasn't sure if it was something he'd missed or if it was simply evidence that they were looking for that was not available. It was always this way, though. He detested detective work as much as he craved it. Until the case was closed his mind would not be at peace. Part of him wanted that restlessness; another part of him hated it. He could never be at peace.

His grandfather had been the same, and his father. But his father had his own solution. He left detective work and became a career man instead. He was good at it or, at least, at managing his ascent. He'd asked his father once, when he was a boy, why he'd stopped being a detective. His father had laughed but there was a look in his eyes he'd never forgotten. He understood that look better now.

Obsession.

He was afflicted, too. The need to finish the case. Nothing else could enter his thoughts. Sylvia had never understood this. She said she did. She was lying to herself. One of many lies, he realised. He'd read every one of them on her face, in her eyes, her voice. She even lied to herself that he knew she was lying. Then Jellicoe sensed Wallace was waiting for him to answer the question.

248

'We have to make sure that we're not missing something. But yes, it looks like Solomon. He denies it.'

'He would,' replied Wallace. Jellicoe grinned and said yes, he would. They pulled into the estate and drove towards the mansion. It was dark now and the purplish glow from the snow remained in patches. By tomorrow it would be gone. The first drops of rain were falling when they got out from the car.

'Can you think of a pretext to speak to Phillipa Masterson again? asked Jellicoe.

He didn't see the young DC colour slightly. He would be delighted to think of a pretext.

'Perhaps I can ask about her grandfather.'

'Find out about his movements since Christmas and just before.'

There was a police car outside the house. The man Burnett had agreed to have stationed there acknowledged their arrival. The two detectives said 'hello' to the constable before going into the house.

Fitch, as ever, disguised his delight at seeing the policeman behind a mask of benevolent antagonism. Policemen meant bad news in anyone's language, particularly for Gladstone Fitch. He'd never trusted them; never would. He led them through to the drawing room where, once more, Wallace excused himself and requested a few moments with the young lady of the house.

For once there seemed to be some hope in the eyes of Masterson. His features were less aggressive although he stopped short of providing a more welcoming countenance. Well short in fact. Jellicoe was unsure if he should deliver his message standing or sitting but Masterson had already sat down. Jellicoe did likewise and looked into the expectant face of the worried father.

'I've seen Stephen,' announced Jellicoe. 'He's unharmed.'

'Thank God,' said Masterson and, for the first time, Jellicoe felt sympathy for the man. His relief was genuine, and it was a close-run thing as to whether he might cry. He maintained his composure but could not speak so Jellicoe pressed ahead and gave an edited version of the events of earlier in the day. Whether it was relief or simply disbelief, Masterson did not question the extraordinary circumstances that led to the brief kidnapping of the policeman. This was a reprieve for Jellicoe. It was hardly his fault but, equally, he felt rather ashamed that it had happened.

'What does the kidnapper want? I don't understand. There hasn't been a ransom demand?'

'He didn't make any demands,' admitted Jellicoe. 'I think Solomon wants to make a point to you. Do you know why?'

Masterson looked up sharply at this. His eyes were filled with fury.

'What is that supposed to mean? Do you think I've brought the kidnap of my son on myself? That Solomon was entirely justified? How dare you. What's he told you?'

A Time to Kill

29

15 Years Earlier

Paris, October 1944

It was naïve really. Worse, utter negligence; not to anticipate a reaction from Claude. How could he be so stupid? Newton would have told him as much. All those years at Oxford. Wasted years if you could not learn the simple lessons that the physics lecturer was trying to impart.

Every action has an equal and opposite reaction.

Of course, it does. Claude waited. Bided his time. He had to, of course. The situation had changed. He recognised the threat that Solomon posed. It was only after, when it was all over, that Solomon realised what a fool he'd been. And what it had cost.

Yet if it had only been a few weeks later.

He and Lizette were going to move. They'd found a new place, larger. It was in the 5^(th) Arrondissement, the Latin Quarter. They would disappear there. A new life could begin for the three of them.

But that was to forget physics. We are all atoms. Life cannot be planned like a military campaign; one can try and guide it, but we are like a boat being tossed around on a stormy sea. Our existence is determined by our interactions with one another, with the elements and everything that surround us.

They came just after midnight. Lizette heard the loud banging on the door. She woke Solomon, who was beside her now. Solomon saw the frightened fawn eyes. Her first thought was that it was Claude with his gang.

He was out of bed immediately. It wasn't Claude, though. The voices at the door were assuredly not French. The banging grew louder, awakening Sophie. She flew over to her mother and they gripped one another. The door would be broken down. Solomon could hear them threatening to do this.

'Go down. Let them in,' ordered Solomon. He began to dress hurriedly.

Lizette frowned. Was he insane? Solomon was insistent. They would break down the door anyway. He'd long since accepted that someone would expose them. There was no doubt in his mind it was Claude who had revealed his whereabouts. But he was prepared. One could not control existence, but one could envisage the risks to be faced and what could be done about them. He'd mapped out his escape route. Tried it once, too: out of the bathroom window and over the rooftops.

'I'll see you soon. Trust me. I can hide for a while. I'll send messages to you.'

The banging on the door stopped. He kissed her. Then she shouted in French.

'I'm coming. Stop banging the door. I'm coming.'

Solomon climbed out the tiny window behind the curtained-off toilet. It led to a narrow rooftop. They were on the second floor. He looked down at his feet and then the pavement below. He could, perhaps, survive a fall but the injuries would be horrific.

As he began to inch along the narrow roof, he heard the sound of shouting coming from the tiny apartment. He reached the corner and swung around just as his pursuers looked out the window.

'He's on the roof.'

A Time to Kill

They'd seen him. He was on the roof of the adjoining building now. On the other side was the square. If he continued on this side of the building, he would be hidden from the square. He moved straight ahead. His route would take him over the roof tops of several buildings before leading to another square near the river.

The shouts behind him had died down. He wasn't surprised. This was a perilous route. He skirted across the slate tiles like a cat burglar. His progress was slow and inelegant. At times he was on all fours. His heart was exploding from his chest. The adrenalin washed around his body like a whirlpool. The sound of the air was deafening. Yet, oddly, he was exhilarated. He should have been frightened. But the insanity of the moment had heightened his senses to a pitch where the sound of a pin dropping on the ground would have been like the crash of cymbals in an orchestra.

He clambered over one apartment rooftop before jumping down onto a single storey house. He was nearly there. The street was clear of anyone who could have been military police. Not a moment to lose. He took a deep breath and pitched his legs over the edge of the building, holding on for grim life to the drain running vertically to the ground. Carefully, foothold by foothold, he began to descend. He was forty feet above the ground. Then thirty, around ten feet he felt it safe to jump. As he did so he heard a laugh. Out of nowhere around half a dozen uniformed men appeared. Then he heard a very English accent.

'Where do you think you're going?'

He was taken to a detention barracks just north of Paris. It was more of a stockade than a barracks. A wooden fence separated the prisoners from freedom. It would have been so easy to escape except each man was heavily manacled around the feet.

Jack Murray

A black belly of cloud hung heavy overhead as Solomon and a dozen other deserters stood on parade. This was more than a threat of rain. It would be a downpour. Solomon was in no doubt that they would be kept outside and denied cover. One of the men made the mistake of glancing upwards and received a smack on the side of his legs. He fell to the ground. The staff sergeant screamed at him to get up otherwise he would be put into a solitary cell.

The idea of being alone in a cell appealed to Solomon and he might have provoked such a punishment had he not had the suspicion that it might be even less hospitable than sharing with the men around him.

A captain arrived and regarded them with barely concealed contempt. It seemed to be requirement of the role. His sergeant was no more welcoming and, on the evidence of his capacity to dispense punishment, a sadist. Solomon wondered if he'd spent any time at the front. He doubted it. Yet the men around him, at least the ones he'd spoken with, had all been on the beach at Normandy, had all fought their way through France until something had snapped.

'You men,' began the captain, 'are deserters. Some of you are criminals. Those of you who have participated in criminal activities will be court-martialled, tried and jailed.' He stopped for a moment and a malevolent smile creased his lips. 'Expect hard labour. Some of you will be offered a last chance to go back to your battalion. If you refuse you will be court-martialled and jailed. You, too, may expect hard labour. Am I making myself clear?'

Silence.

'Am I making myself clear?' roared the captain.

A sullen 'yes, sir' murmured through the two ranks of men. As if to punish them, the skies opened up. At first it was light but within a couple of minutes it grew heavier. The men stayed still. Solomon felt like someone had thrown a bucket over him. As the officer and the staff sergeant stepped back under a roof, the rain battered the men in the yard. Water poured

A Time to Kill

down Solomon's eyes, blinding him. He'd never seen such rain. It was Biblical in its ferocity. It lashed the men like a cat o' nine tails. The symbolism was all too clear to Solomon.

The prison clothes he'd been given were soaked through within a matter of minutes. Every part of him shivered. Yet no one moved. For thirty minutes they stood there; all the time they were watched by the captain and the staff sergeant. All the time Solomon's hatred of this officer grew. Finally, the cloud passed slowly away until the rain became a light drizzle. The men were led to a number of cells. One of them was already coughing his guts out.

The next day at six in the morning the men were ordered to clean the barracks yard. It was still dark. Half the men were suffering from a fever. Solomon had a cold. A fever would follow. Some were given mops and pails. Others, like Solomon, were given nail brushes and ordered onto their hands and knees. He began to scrub. Slowly. He saw the captain looking at him. Then he turned to the sergeant who they now knew as Weir. A few words were exchanged. Seconds later the sergeant was marching towards Solomon. He knew there was nothing he could do. The sergeant stood over him menacingly and glowered. Solomon looked up nervously.

'Where do you think you are? Butlins?' screamed Weir down at him.

He steeled himself for the kick. A kick in the ribs would be disastrous. It was sure to crack something. He steeled himself. The kick came in his stomach. It winded him but the pain was less than he'd expected.

Solomon picked up the pace of his scrubbing. An hour and a half later they were finished, and he was starving. He'd have eaten anything at that point which was just as well because breakfast consisted of half a tin of congealed porridge, suspiciously stale bread, and tea. Solomon stared at the food and remembered wistfully the fresh bread he used to buy from the boulangerie, and the food prepared by Lizette. Tears formed in his eyes but the presence nearby of Weir stopped them dead. Any sign of weakness would be fatal. He needed to become invisible, to reach ground state.

Too much energy, especially undirected activity, anything observable by the guards, but not ordered by them, would attract their attention. The key to his survival or, at least, his sanity, was to disappear. Only through not being noticed could he exist. Only through disobedience could he be noticed.

Later that day, each man was called before the camp commandant. The name on the office door read Captain Masterson. The soldier accompanying Solomon knocked on the door; then they entered. Masterson was sitting at his desk writing. To his right stood Weir. As he expected, Masterson continued to write for another two minutes. The act of keeping him waiting was merely an emblem. A token nod to who was in charge, who had the power and who was captive.

Finally, Masterson looked up. His face twisted into a caricature of a gangster: an Aryan Edward G. Robinson. Solomon wanted to smile but managed, just, to keep his face neutral.

'You're here because you deserted. But that wasn't enough. You are a criminal as well as a coward. You should be with your comrades fighting the enemy, being a soldier, defending your country. But no, you ran. You thought you'd leave the dirty work to your mates. Well, you will regret the day you decided to let your friends face the bullets and bombs. You will not have an easy life Solomon, trust me. You're a smoker, I understand. Well, you won't have any cigarettes. You had a girlfriend, too, didn't you?'

Solomon stiffened as he heard this. He wanted to say something, but the words caught in his throat.

'Oh, we know all about that. Well, you won't see her. You will have no visits. You will have the right to send a letter once every two weeks. It will be censored of course. Don't expect your tart to write to you. She'll move on to the next one, trust me. I've seen it before. If you have any

complaints, *you must make them to me. You can imagine how sympathetically I will deal with them. There will be no communication with other prisoners unless so ordered. Any insubordination will be dealt with immediately. Any violence will result in constraint in body-belt and straitjacket. And solitary confinement.'*

A smile fell across the captain's face.

'Any questions?'

'No, sir.'

'Well,' concluded Masterson with a smirk, 'You made your choice. Doesn't say much for your wisdom if you don't mind me saying. Now you'll have to live with it.'

The afternoon that followed gave a clue to the days that he would face. They men were drilled to the point of mute exhaustion. Solomon's body no longer felt his own. Numbness replaced feeling as they marched around the yard endlessly. All the while he saw Masterson standing there. He and Weir would smoke cigarettes in front of the men as they ran, jumped, marched, and scrubbed away their humanity.

The physical torture was broken only by period breaks called 'Communication Parade' where chat between the prisoners was not just permitted but actively encouraged to the point of violence.

Yet, what was there to say to the hollow-eyed man facing you? Talk about the weather? Or perhaps the hatred. The loathing that burned deep within them: of war, of military justice and, most of all of the cowards in charge of the men who'd finally cracked after spending so long facing death, seeing death all around them and causing death to men they'd never met and who were every bit as frightened as they were.

30

'So, you're saying he was justified in killing my father and kidnapping my son?' The icy tones of Masterson could not disguise the fury and contempt in the tone.

'Of course not,' replied Jellicoe tersely. 'His motive is revenge. The truth of what happened is neither here nor there. It's what he believes the truth to be, however exaggerated, is what guides him.'

'You clearly haven't read the file I sent to you.'

'I haven't finished it,' acknowledged Jellicoe. 'I'll do so when I leave you.'

'Do that, Jellicoe. He's no saint. He was a coward who deserted his comrades and took up with some French prostitute in order to hide from the justice he so richly deserved. And now he has my boy.'

And still no ransom demand. Jellicoe was baffled by the direction they were heading. It broke the rules of all kidnaps, even murder. The gravitational pull of kidnaps was always towards a ransom demand followed by either payment or apprehension of criminals unknown. Yet Solomon had openly incriminated himself and asked nothing from Masterson. It was as if Solomon was toying with the intended victim whether that be the boy or his former captor, Major Masterson. None of it made sense. What was the end game?

A Time to Kill

'What happens now?' demanded Masterson.

'We will broaden the search to encompass all farm buildings in the local area. Stephen is being held in just this sort of building. It was less than fifteen minutes away from the centre of town.'

Of course, Solomon knew that Jellicoe knew this; yet another extraordinary feature of this case. He *wanted* Jellicoe to know. Either Solomon had a heightened sense of his own abilities or there was something else at play.

The meeting ended on this note. Masterson remained angry and dissatisfied; Jellicoe frustrated and utterly confused by the flow of events. They parted in the drawing room and Jellicoe met the waiting Wallace outside in the hallway. They went out into the dark night and over to the car.

'Have we anything new on Colonel Masterson?'

'Well, one thing was revealed which we weren't aware of or, at least, I wasn't.'

'Really? What?'

'Colonel Masterson is on the Parole Board of the county prison. His last meeting was just before Christmas.'

Jellicoe stopped and looked at Wallace. His voice was tight.

'Why didn't we know this?'

'I'm sorry sir,' said Wallace, downcast. He held his arms out.

But Jellicoe remembered it was Yates who'd been tasked with finding out about the colonel. This had either been overlooked or he hadn't checked. A wave of anger coursed through Jellicoe. He'd speak to Yates. Another failure.

'It's not your fault. Tomorrow, I want to know every case he's heard in this capacity.'

'What about his work as a magistrate?'

'Can you get a someone else to look at that? Let's get the hell home.'

-

The next morning, Jellicoe walked to the station. The snow had turned to slush with only the odd patch of white to be seen. The trees lining the street had shaken off their white robes leaving dark, wet wood and black branches reaching upwards. The sky was blue with white billowing clouds. Jellicoe stood frozen gazing at the scene outside the station. The stinging chill was relentless notwithstanding the sun. Perhaps he should join Interpol, he thought, and find a nice situation on the Cote d'Azur.

It was too early for the newspapermen, but he was gratified to see Wallace was an early arrival. Burnett arrived soon after seven followed by the other detectives working on the two cases. The arrival of Superintendent Frankie at seven thirty meant that they could discuss the events of yesterday as a group. There was a lot to discuss, not least the news of Jellicoe's abduction and release. What had been rumour the day before became fact. Frankie spoke first.

'As you may have heard, and I can now confirm, Detective Inspector Jellicoe was taken at gun point from in front of this police station to see Stephen Masterson. The good news is that the young man is alive and, if not well, being looked after and fed. Furthermore, thanks to an anonymous tip off, we were able to locate Tim Pemberton at a premises owned by Ronald Musgrave. So far so good. We have something positive to convey to our friends outside.'

Frankie's face looked far from happy though he continued. 'Alas that is where the good news stops.' He paused for dramatic affect and stared meaningfully at his adoring audience. 'The rest of it is an unmitigated disaster. No, make that humiliating disaster.' How is it possible for one of our men to be lifted from the very bosom of the constabulary?'

There was more ham in this performance that the average Gloucester Old Spot rolling around in its pigsty. The superintendent's voice lowered, and his finger pointed towards the group of officers.

'If any word of this incident gets out,' he whispered menacingly, 'I will fine each and every one of you irrespective if you were the guilty party or not. Then when we find the man responsible, he will be drummed out of the police service faster than you can say Jack Robinson. I mean it. This must not go further than this room. Understood?'

The response was a remarkably sullen, 'yes, sir.'

Frankie's eyes bulged and his face turned crimson.

'I said is that understood?' he roared. Flecks of spittle bathed the men in the front row. The response more vigorous this time but no less sullen. It would be fair to say that neither the superintendent nor the detectives were impressed with either what they saw or what they heard.

Burnett took over.

'As the super says, the boy is all right for now, but we still have no ransom demand. We still don't know who took the Pemberton boy or if it's connected with the Masterson kidnapping. Lastly, we're still no further forward on who the hell killed the colonel. In short, we know bugger all and it won't be long before this starts to get nasty. We've had to let Musgrave go because we've nothing to hold him on. I want some answers now. Anyone want to say anything or are you just going to sit there with your mouths open?'

Jellicoe looked around and it was true, there were a few mouths open. He stood up and all eyes turned to him.

'The boy is being held in a building with corrugated metal walls. What does that suggest to you?'

Someone shouted out, 'Farm building.'

'Yes. Anything else?'

Silence. Then Burnett spoke, 'Right, we'll concentrate on farm buildings in a five-mile northern eastern radius from the centre until DI Jellicoe has had a chance to retrace his journey. We'll do that at eight.'

This looked like Superintendent Frankie's cue to leave the men, but he felt a tug on his arm. Burnett pointed to his office. Frankie was not a man who liked to be told what to do, scowled by way of acknowledgement. Burnett closed the door behind them.

'Well, Burnett?'

'We need another man posted at the Masterson house.'

'Why on earth do we need anyone posted there? The horse has already bolted.'

'If this is about revenge then there's every possibility that the killer or kidnapper may strike again. I think having just the one uniformed man up there is a risk.'

Frankie dismissed this thought with a wave of his hand. His normal tone of querulous condescension seemed to rise an octave.

'Nonsense, man. He's army. Last thing he needs or would want is a bunch of our men patrolling the grounds armed with nothing better than a truncheon. Permission denied. I want all of our men concentrated on finding the boy and the killer.'

A Time to Kill

Frankie decided enough was enough. He opened the door to Burnett's office and left. His arrival in the outer office briefly silenced the low murmur of chat. Burnett returned and gave a curt nod to Price who stood up now and walked forward to join Jellicoe at the front.

'As yet we've established no connection between this man Solomon and Musgrave. If anything, Musgrave seems to be blaming Johnny Warwick for what happened. We'll look into any potential gang issues between these two.'

Burnett nodded and then turned to Jellicoe.

'What other avenues are you looking at?' asked Burnett to Jellicoe.

'Wallace and I will be in the car in the morning retracing what may have been the route I was taken on. It's a long shot but we'll give it a go. Then I'll check through the file on Solomon. I've asked Wallace to check on Colonel Masterson's recent work with the Parole Board. It turns out he's been on this board for several years. There may be the possibility that someone dispensed their own justice to the colonel.'

Jellicoe glanced meaningfully at Yates. The sergeant looked rather shame-faced at this. Another apology was heading his way, guessed Jellicoe.

'Sergeant Yates will lead a team of constables searching for the boy at the farms in this area.' Jellicoe walked towards a map of the county and indicated with his finger an area of ten square miles. 'Every inch, Sergeant Yates. Every inch.'

Yates nodded. He knew that he'd let Jellicoe down now on a couple of occasions. Worse, Jellicoe knew Yates had let him down. He tried to maintain eye contact with Jellicoe, and it was the hardest thing he'd ever done. The face of the DI was set to stone and he felt like a fallen idol. A failure to the new man, a failure to himself.

It felt like a last chance.

-

Wallace and Jellicoe were sitting outside St Peter's church waiting for the bell to ring. He was unsure whether to keep his eyes open under the blindfold or shut. In the end he elected to shut them.

'If you don't mind me saying, it seems a bit of a waste spending time looking through the Solomon file. We know he's guilty of the kidnapping,' said Wallace.

Jellicoe smiled and replied, 'You may be right. But I'm not certain yet about the murder. When we get back, clear your mind of Solomon. The only thing you should be thinking when you're looking through the parole cases is if this could have caused someone to murder the colonel.'

As he said this the church bell began to ring. Wallace started the car.

'Straight ahead,' ordered Jellicoe. The car moved forward smoothly, and they started on their journey. Behind them were two other police cars. Jellicoe tried to recall how long it was before they'd turned right. 'Is there a right turn anywhere near here?'

'Yes, just up ahead.'

'Take it.'

Wallace followed Jellicoe's instructions and they headed north. At this point they were in the lap of the gods. The road twisted and turned which Jellicoe remembered. The car slowed down and Jellicoe, sensing the change in speed, asked him what was wrong.

A Time to Kill

'Sir, we're at a crossroads.' It seemed like a metaphor. The two cars pulled in just behind them.

Jellicoe removed the blindfold. They were now in the middle of a wood. Just ahead was a bus stop. Oddly, there was a red telephone box near the bus stop. There were three directions the cars could go but Jellicoe had no earthly idea which they should take. He climbed out of the car and was joined by Yates from one of the other cars and Fogg from Price's team.

'I'm not sure,' admitted Jellicoe. 'This feels like the right area, but I can't be certain which way we went from here. I suggest you each take one of these roads and follow it for no more than a couple of miles. If you find a turn off, take it. Otherwise meet back here in an hour and proceed straight ahead. Fogg unfolded a map and the detectives looked it over. Fogg pointed to where they were on the map and the three men leaned in. What they saw was unpromising to say the least.

'Is this the best map we have?' asked Jellicoe.

'Sorry, sir,' replied Yates.

'It feels like a children's treasure map. I mean what's over here?' asked Jellicoe pointing to some large blank spaces. 'Are these all farms?'

There were a number of roads that seemed to branch off like the delta of a river. Jellicoe stared at the map hoping something would jump out at him. The wood was quite small and the land around it was almost certainly farmland. How many farms it was impossible to say. It was difficult to see from the map the location of individual farms.

'We need a better map. Yates, can you find one for tomorrow?'

Just as he said this, the group was startled by the sound of the telephone ringing in the box. Jellicoe nodded towards the phone and Fogg immediately ran over to it. He picked up the phone, but the line went dead as soon as he spoke.

'Well?' asked Jellicoe, still somewhat surprised at seeing the phone box in such a remote spot.

'They hung up,' explained Fogg, shrugging his shoulders. There was little else to be done about this, so they agreed to part company at this point. Wallace drove Jellicoe back to the hotel to see King before returning to the police station to follow up on the parole board angle. Jellicoe was keen to avoid the station as he knew he'd be running the gauntlet of the pressmen. This was a distraction he did not need.

-

'I wondered if you'd forgotten about me,' said King who was happily tucking into a breakfast that Jellicoe would never see at Ramsbottom's. All at the expense of the police force too, he thought enviously. The army man smiled when he saw Jellicoe looking at his plate of bacon, eggs, beans, toast, piled high like a mountain range. 'It's jolly good. You really should order one. Be my guest'

Jellicoe looked sourly at the army man and asked for the file.

'I'll read while you eat.'

'No point in blaming me for your lot's generosity.'

'Are you sure we didn't give you a daily budget?'

The response to that was mirthless laughter which made even Jellicoe smile. He quite liked the brazenness of the army lieutenant. The man was having a break from the army at someone else's expense. He was going to enjoy it.

'What did you do last night?'

'On a Sunday in a seaside town closed down for winter?'

Jellicoe grinned at this.

'Good point. Not much to do, I suppose.' The army man did not seem too put out, however.

'The bar was open here,' he said chirpily.

'Is there any gin left?'

'Well, I certainly did my best but there's a limit even to what I can drink.'

'That limit clearly wasn't based on any sense of budget.'

King's reply was lost somewhere in the mouthful of sausage and egg. The yolk dripping down to the plate felt like the wound from a knife being twisted into Jellicoe's envious stomach. To distract himself he reached into King's bag after receiving nodded permission and took out the file. He opened it up to where he'd left off.

15 Years Earlier:

Paris, France: September 1944

A week after saving his life, his new American friends took him to a hotel near the Arc de Triomphe. He'd seen them several times since that night. None of them spoke French beyond a very basic level. They were impressed by Solomon's command of the language. It was on their third night out at the café when one of them, Robinson, said, 'We could use someone like you.'

Solomon wasn't stupid. He knew what the men were. Deserter was no longer accurate, nor was Absent Without Leave. These men had become criminals. Paris was rife with deserters who'd turned to crime. Solomon had heard about this at the front. How supply trucks and trains were being robbed by their own men. His time in Paris had provided a more nuanced picture. Paris was full of senior officers and police. All of them seemed to be enjoying a life that would have been unrecognisable to the farm boys shivering scared in foxholes.

When the question came, Solomon knew there would only be one answer.

'Yes, I'll join you.'

Of course, they could not risk that he was an informer. The man he met at that crumbling wreck of a hotel just off Rue de Montenotte had been quite open with him. He was a former paratrooper. In fact, the men in the gang were all American. Some came from the Airborne; some were Artillery and others Infantry. They'd started out on cigarettes, stealing them from the supply trucks and then selling to the Parisians on the black market.

With each success their confidence grew, and they wanted to take on bigger prizes. None of them could speak like a local. Solomon knew where his value lay. But first there was a test.

'I like you, Sol. But you understand. We have to know if you're with us.'

Solomon nodded. He understood.

'We need a truck. American army. Can you get us one?'

At first Solomon was shocked. The idea of breaking into a barracks to steal a truck filled him with horror. On so many levels it would be a step too far. Just as he was about to refuse, he remembered that US army trucks were a common sight on the streets of Paris. Perhaps the task was not so unachievable.

'When?'

The men looked at one another and shared grins. This was exactly the right question. It felt like a validation. The man who Solomon knew only as Al leaned forward.

'Can you come here tomorrow with your new acquisition?'

-

Lizette hated the idea. This was less a moral question for her than one of risk. She made some money cleaning. They had enough to get by. She felt safer now. More than anything else Lizette craved normality, consistency, certainty. It had only been a matter of weeks, yet David Solomon seemed to represent all three. Friendships, relationships, developed so much more quickly in war time. They were all in the middle of a raging fire. Of course, the forging process would be more rapid, the bonds fashioned by the fire would be stronger; unbreakable. Wasn't this enough for him?

It wasn't enough. Getting by was not Solomon's idea of life any more than bullets flashing over his head. Lizette understood this just as Solomon understood that her worry was really that his new friends might pull him away from her. He gripped her hand and said, 'This is for us. For Sophie.'

He meant it, too. It was there in his eyes and she trusted him. Yet the risk was enormous. He'd tried to explain it all to her one night. How the world, the laws of science were anything but well-defined and solid. The idea that every object, everything around them had inherent and unchanging properties was not true. Instead, everything was in flux. The properties of an object changed depending on what it interacted with and if it was observed.

Lizette didn't understand at first then, Solomon explained in a way that was as beautiful as it was true.

'I love you, Lizette,' he'd said. 'I love Sophie. But if I'd never met you?'

Lizette had never studied physics, but she understood at that moment that both she and Sophie had been changed by knowing Solomon. Then she asked him the question that, strangely, had not occurred to him until she said it.

'If this is true, then what has changed in you or in us if you join the Americans?'

'Everything, Lizette. Everything including how I feel for you and Sophie.' He saw the tears form in her eyes, or were they in his? Then he said, 'That will only grow stronger.'

-

'What's your plan, Sol?' asked Al the next morning, when Solomon showed up at the hotel accompanied by Robinson and McKay.

'I'll need a gun.'

A Time to Kill

Al nodded. This made sense. However, the gang had, thus far, avoided any bloodshed in their activities. Solomon read the face of Al and smiled. They had spoken of having an impressive arsenal but had avoided testing out its capability.

'You don't have to load it. I want it more for show than anything.'

'I'll also need a US army uniform.'

'Fair enough, we have US, we have British, we have French. You name it, we have it. Do you need any help? Some of the boys have offered to come along.'

Al handed over the revolver as he was saying this. He let Solomon empty the chambers. The gun was now empty, and Solomon pocketed it.

'I can do this myself but by all means, happy to have an audience.'

Solomon led Robinson and McKay on foot to a street just off the Champs-Elysees. It was around fifteen minutes away from the hotel. He'd noticed the street before. It was often crowded with cars and, in particular, the six-by-six type of truck that the gang had requested.

The street was crowded but there was no sign of any military vehicles.

'Let's have a coffee,' suggested Solomon. They sat outside at a café. It was cold but they didn't seem to mind. Solomon's heart was racing, however. Blood was flowing through his veins. At that moment he was impervious to the chill in the air. His whole mind and body was in a state of heightened alertness. The first truck to match the description passed but Solomon left it. There were two men in the cabin at the front.

The second one had only the driver, but the lack of traffic meant it flew past them without stopping. They sat waiting another hour for a third truck to come. It was nearing lunch time and the street became more crowded. The traffic began to back up. Then they saw it. A big green six-by-six appeared at the top of the street. It immediately became bogged down in the traffic.

As it crept closer to them, Solomon could see that the cab at the front only had one occupant, the driver. He nodded to his two companions. The two men left their seats and walked around the back of the truck as it sat in the traffic. They came back a minute or two later.

'There's no one in the back,' confirmed McKay.

Solomon nodded thanks and remained seated. The two men looked at him expectantly. He waited as the truck slowly inched forward to the crossroads. Finally, it reached a point three vehicles away from the turn.

Solomon rose to his feet and walked quickly to the truck. He climbed inside the cab and pressed the empty gun to the driver's head.

'What's your name?' asked Solomon in a calm voice.

'Johnson.'

'Where are you from?'

'Peoria. Illinois.'

'Well Private Johnson. I want you to climb out from the truck and walk calmly to the neon sign over there. The red one. Then I want you to turn the corner and keep walking. Do you understand?' Solomon reluctantly pressed the gun more firmly against the side of Johnson's head.

'Yes, sir.'

Johnson did as he was told. He climbed out of the cabin and began walking at a steady pace towards the café on the corner. The traffic was beginning to clear in front of Solomon. He quickly climbed into the driver's seat and drove off to the left. He encountered more traffic. He stopped and noticed two military policemen standing on the side of the road. They looked towards him. Solomon saluted them. Out of the corner of his eye, he saw Johnson suddenly turn around. He'd seen the two military policeman, too. He began to jog towards them. Then he was sprinting.

Up ahead, the cars and trucks were growing impatient with a truck that had stopped in the middle of the road. Johnson was nearing the two policemen, shouting at them, but the sound of his voice was drowned out by the sounds of irate Parisians doing what irate Parisians do. The air was filled with the sound of vehicle horns being repeatedly blasted.

Johnson reached the military policemen just as the traffic began to move. Solomon watched him point to the hijacked vehicle. His heart was pounding by now. They turned towards him and started dodging in and out of the cars and trucks. Just as they were about to reach him Solomon pulled away. One of the MP's pulled out a gun and aimed it at the truck. He aimed the gun downwards. He was going to shoot at the wheels. The other MP stopped him. Vehicles were blaring their horns at them to get off the road.

Within seconds Solomon was around the corner and away from the gridlock. It had been a near miss. His head was matted with perspiration; his head and body swimming in the adrenaline surging through his body. Somehow, he managed to drive to the hotel. Along the way, he passed, what felt like, half the US Army in Europe.

The truck was stored in a garage a few minutes away from the Arc de Triomphe. Solomon returned triumphantly to the hotel. By the time he returned, Robinson and McKay were back. They'd shared the good news. Al greeted Solomon like a brother. In some senses they were now. Not only was he a deserter he was, by the act of hijacking, a criminal. Solomon had never once considered his desertion as an illegal act. Now, he was under no illusions about the path he'd chosen.

'What's the plan?' asked Solomon to his fellow gang members. They told him. He didn't say anything at first. Then he repeated slowly. 'So, we're going to hijack four US Army trucks carrying supplies of coffee, cigarettes, petrol, sorry gasoline, and booze by blocking the road they're travelling on and raiding them?'

Solomon could not hide his scepticism.

'Show him, Al,' said one of the men. There was smirk on his face.

Al stood up and went to a large wardrobe. He opened it and Solomon's mouth all but fell agape at what he saw. The wardrobe was full of 45's, rifles and sub-machine guns. They could have outfitted a small army. He even saw some grenades stacked at the bottom. The men around him began to laugh. So too did Solomon. However, his was a mirthless chuckle and he was shaking his head. All of the laughter stopped except Solomon's. A chill descended on the room.

'What's wrong, Sol?' asked Al. Solomon fixed his eyes on Al and slowly began to shake his head.

'People will die.'

'Are you afraid, Sol? I suppose you must be otherwise you wouldn't be here, I guess,' said Al. He smiled as he said this and the men beside him began to laugh. But Solomon wasn't laughing now. 'What difference does it make if the Germans kill you or one of our boys does?'

'This is suicide.' The anger in Solomon's voice was all too plain. It silenced the group immediately. But Al was angry, too, now. He stepped closer to Solomon and glared up at him.

'You got a better idea, Sol?'

'Yes, Al. I have a better idea.'

-

Three US Army trucks drove along Boulevard Voltaire, heading on a southern route out of Paris. They approached Place de la Nation, a circular square on the eastern side of Paris between Place de la Bastille and the Bois de Vincennes, on the border of the 11th and 12th arrondissements.

They passed by the central monument, a large bronze sculpture showing Marianne on a chariot pulled by lions. It was lit up from the ground and looked golden against the night sky. Sergeant Ed Temple gazed at it in wonder. Until the war he'd barely travelled a hundred miles outside of Wisconsin. What he'd seen in Paris was a marvel. Every day presented new and extraordinary sights of a world that was unimaginable to a boy who'd spent his life working on his father's dairy farm. He heard the driver utter an oath and begin to slow down.

'What's wrong?' asked Temple then he saw the military policemen up ahead at the check point. 'What the hell? You can't drive a mile without one these damn things. Have they nothing better to do? I'd like to see them when the bullets are flying.'

The fact that he had managed to avoid direct contact with the enemy through his role in the Quartermaster Corps was lost on Ed Temple at that moment. This was the third checkpoint they'd encountered on their way through the capital.

'I'll see what they want.'

He opened the door and climbed down from the truck. He was met by an MP. A small blond-haired sergeant.

'Everything ok?' asked Temple.

'We had another raid earlier. Some supply trucks were stolen.'

'Not again.'

The MP nodded. They were joined by men from the other trucks. Another MP strolled over and asked for a cigarette. Temple took a packet from his pocket and lit one for the MP. He was a lieutenant, but he seemed pretty relaxed, so Temple didn't bother saluting.

'What's happening?' asked one of the men from the other trucks.

Temple explained to them what the MP had said. The two MP's were apologetic. The taller one shrugged his shoulders and blamed the brass. Everyone laughed sympathetically.

'What was stolen?' asked Temple.

Solomon pointed his gun at Temple's head and replied, 'Whatever you're carrying.'

32

'I hadn't realised there was such an issue with crime during the war,' said Jellicoe, closing the file and writing a note in his notebook.

King chuckled at this. He took the file from Jellicoe and put it in his briefcase.

'Well, it affected the Americans very badly. They had something like eight thousand cases in the space of a year. Half of them were misappropriation of supplies.'

'Half?' said Jellicoe, eyebrows raised.

'Half. There was a lot of violent crime, too. As reluctant as they were to take on the Nazis, they'd no problem with murder, assault, and rape, never mind the robberies and house breaking. Oh yes, very brave when they were up against unarmed citizens.'

Jellicoe shook his head in surprise.

'Your chap was involved with one gang for a month or so before we nabbed him. Probably making a small fortune on the black market while his mates were dying at the front. For what it's worth, Jellicoe, I hope you catch him and throw away the key. Men like that sicken me.'

Jellicoe said nothing to this. The man who so sickened King had also been awarded a Distinguished Conduct Medal just weeks before he'd deserted. Solomon had not tried to justify his desertion but neither had he shown remorse. Of course, King was right to condemn Solomon the criminal but the real crime in the lieutenant's eyes was his desertion. Yet who, least of all King, was in a position to do this? Unless you had sat shivering, starved, sleep-deprived and shattered by the never-ending bombardment and the horrific landscape of death around you, who were you to condemn?

With King's mission effectively completed, the army man checked out of the hotel. They shared a taxi back to the police station before King headed on to take a train. The parting was brief but not without warmth. Despite King's sometimes supercilious manner, Jellicoe quite liked him. He had an odd regard for men who were eccentric, and King was certainly that. A soldier who appeared to have not a single fighting bone in his body. Such oddities appealed to him.

Even Solomon had seemed to him someone who, in another life, he would have quite liked. It was difficult to reconcile what he'd experienced directly with knowing what he'd done and what he was doing. Yet Jellicoe knew better than to fall for the *woe-is-me* story. Solomon was clearly highly intelligent, a man of science. Added to this was an undeniable charisma.

The telling of his story in Paris was compelling and convincing in equal measure. It had engaged Jellicoe's sympathy despite the detective's understanding that Solomon was unquestionably trying to manipulate him. However, its telling gave lie to his central thesis: that we exist, like atoms, only through the random interactions we have with others. Solomon wanted to be like an invisible hand, guiding, influencing, dictating those interactions. Yet once again

Jellicoe could not blame him for this. He'd gone to fight in a war he did not start, was given orders that he could not question, was expected to give his life without demur and had spent fourteen years in prison subject, Jellicoe had no doubt, to the harshest of regimes. Who wouldn't rebel against one's essential helplessness?

As he trudged towards the police station, his thoughts were interrupted by a familiar voice. His heart sank. London had finally caught up with him again. It felt like he was in a prison, too. He turned around and saw a face he knew all too well.

'Hello, Nick,' said Terence Singe, a crime reporter for… in fact Jellicoe couldn't remember who he worked for now. He'd been fired, rehired, and fired more times than Jellicoe could remember and that was only in the few years he'd worked at the Met. Singe was at least twenty years older than Jellicoe, so this pattern had most likely repeated itself over the previous two decades. Singe's brilliance as a writer was matched only by a self-destructive streak that was heroically Greek in its tragic impact on the man's Fleet Street career and, in all likelihood, his liver.

'Hello, Terry,' responded Jellicoe, shaking Singe's hand warmly. 'What brings you here? A bit of sea air?'

'I detest fresh air as much as I detest the cold, young man. Are there any pubs open where I can breathe in the vivifying atmosphere of friendly conversation and cheap tobacco and partake of the golden elixir while you relate this ghastly tale of murder and kidnap?' Singe's rich, fruity, slightly too loud way of speaking would have been right at home on the stage of the Old Vic.

'I'm sure you'll hear all about it at the press conference this morning.'

A Time to Kill

'I can hardly wait,' said Terry with all the enthusiasm of a husband hearing that his wife's family will be spending the summer with them.

Jellicoe evaded the other newspapermen and darted up the steps of the police station. On his way to the office, he ran into Superintendent Frankie and Burnett on their way to brief the press.

'Solved the case yet?' asked Burnett managing the improbable feat of sounding both hopeful and cynical at the same time. In fact, Jellicoe almost marvelled at this accomplishment.

'Not yet, chief,' answered Jellicoe. 'Do you need me in the briefing?'

'No, Jellicoe, I think that we can manage,' replied Superintendent Frankie with pious indifference.

Oh no, you can't, thought Jellicoe while imagining 'Widow Twanky' Frankie facing the gentlemen of the press, face beaming under his make-up. Announce the good news about the recovery of Tim Pemberton and enjoy the reflected kudos while leaving the communication of bad news to subordinates seemed par for the course for the Superintendent.

Jellicoe continued on his way. Yates was not back in the office. Clearly, he and Fogg were still following up on the farms in the area identified by Jellicoe. He spied Wallace on the phone. The young DC looked up and smiled. He waved Jellicoe over and ended the phone call.

'Sir, I've managed to find out more about the work that the colonel did on the Parole Board. It turns out that he was a deputy chairman. Not only that, in November last year he was present at a meeting where a number of prisoners were up for parole. One of them was the brother of Craig Woodward.'

'He was on Vince March's list, wasn't he?'

'Correct, sir. Bill Woodward was doing time for various misdemeanours.'

'Such as?'

'He's six foot six.'

'Ahh.'

'Anyway, he was due for parole last autumn but was turned down by the Parole Board.'

'Do we know why?' asked Jellicoe.

Wallace did not have to consult the volumes of notes he'd made.

'Apparently he was suspected of being responsible for a series of assaults over the years in the prison. He's very much Musgrave's man on the inside.'

'But no one ever pointed the finger,' chipped in Jellicoe.

'Exactly. Anyway, the Parole Board weren't buying it.'

'But is that a motive to kill?'

'As I understand it,' answered Wallace, 'the chairman was ill on the day that they sat. So, Colonel Masterson headed up the board that day. On the Woodward case, the board was split. It was Masterson's casting vote that saw Woodward denied parole for another year.'

Jellicoe frowned. This was still not enough but he saw Wallace wanted to add something else. There was a look on the young man's face which suggested there was a clincher.

'I think I can guess what you're thinking, sir, but I haven't finished yet. Soon after this meeting, Woodward was involved in a fight in the prison yard. Just before Christmas, in fact. The other man was killed. Woodward is claiming self-defence but the man in question was a member of Johnny Warwick's gang. This has upset things between the two gangs, to say the least. They're investigating it as we speak, but I gather from chatting just now to the prison governor, it's not looking good for Woodward. They reckon Woodward instigated the fight and took matters too far.'

Jellicoe's eyes widened slightly. This was more convincing, and he nodded at Wallace.

'Good work. If he's found guilty then it'll be life for sure. No wonder his brother is angry. If the Parole Board had let him go, as he thinks they should have, then none of this would have happened. He'd be free instead of facing life in prison.'

Jellicoe turned to the large board with all of the key players in the murder and the kidnapping. He stared at it for a moment, his eyes darting from one face to another. The news about Woodward's brother, was a key breakthrough. Woodward certainly had a motive for killing Masterson and, if descriptions of him were true, the capability for committing such a crime too. But this threw up another question. Was it really possible that two separate crimes were committed on the same night by two separate criminals at the same location at the roughly the same time?

Jellicoe had been on the police force for over seven years and had never come across such an unlikely occurrence. Although Craig Woodward had been something of an independent, he was more likely to favour Musgrave than Warwick, if only because of his brother. Could he be working with Solomon in trying to implicate Musgrave? Or was Solomon Warwick's man? If he was then it meant nothing less than a takeover bid by the Warwick gang. Yet Jellicoe did not believe this hypothesis. Everything about Solomon suggested someone who was his own man. That being so, what was his game?

He became aware that Wallace was looking at him expectantly. He asked Wallace to summarise the information about Masterson and pin it to the board. It would be better to wait for Burnett to finish the press briefing before bringing in Woodward. In the meantime, Jellicoe summarised the key points from the file on Solomon.

It was just after one when Burnett returned from the briefing. Frankie had left immediately, which was a pity because Jellicoe would've liked to let him know of the latest developments. He saw Burnett motion to him to come to the office. Just before joining Burnett, Jellicoe wrote out a couple of names on a piece of paper and handed it to Wallace.

'I need to know about them,' he explained before rising from his seat and heading towards Burnett's office.

'Close the door,' said Burnett ominously. Jellicoe did so and remained standing. 'Who is this character Singe, by the way?'

'Character is a good way of describing him. He should be on stage. Don't underestimate him though.'

'Don't worry about that. Frankie's loving the national attention. Wait'll you see. He'll be all over the case now if he thinks that he can appear on television or the national press.'

'It might be cases, sir.'

Burnett looked up sharply at Jellicoe.

'What do you mean, cases?'

Jellicoe updated Burnett on what Wallace had uncovered. Burnett's default reaction to anything new, Jellicoe was discovering, was anger that they had not known earlier. Yet he understood this, too. This had been missed: Yates was, once more, to blame. The detective sergeant was not rigorous enough on detail. Police work was all about the detail. It was increasingly obvious that Yates' interests lay more in career than cases.

'We need to bring Woodward in. Where is everyone? Are they still looking for the farm building that Solomon brought you to?'

'I daresay they are.'

This was another excuse for Burnett to vent his frustration. There was nothing else for it. Jellicoe guessed what would come next.

'All right, you, me and Wallace will find him. I'm fairly sure I saw Clarkey arrive earlier. Go find him. He can come too. Woodward's a big lad; we'll need all the help going.'

So is Clarkey, thought Jellicoe. It would make things interesting if Woodward decided to resist arrest. If Woodward was their man, then he would almost certainly put up a struggle.

33

Aside from Clarke, Burnett rounded up two other constables about to go off duty. The prospect of having to stay on a little longer was met a little less grumpily than the potential arrest of the six foot five Woodward. One of the constables, Dugdale, seemed to change colour when the name was mentioned. The presence of Clarke was strangely reassuring to Jellicoe, who was no more enamoured with having to tangle with the giant than Dugdale. Clarke radiated good fellowship and the possibility that Woodward might decide to come quietly. Wishful thinking as it turned out.

'Bring the van, Clarkey,' ordered Burnett when they congregated at the entrance to the station.

'We'll try his house first?' asked Clarke.

'House first then maybe *The Smuggler*, then *Bricklayers*.'

Clarke disappeared for a minute before returning with the keys to the Black Maria that had not moved from its parking space in the first week or so of Jellicoe's arrival. Two constables made for the van while Burnett and Jellicoe took the police car with Dugdale in the driver's seat.

'No siren,' said Burnett to Clarke as he climbed inside the car on the driver's side. 'Do you know the way to Woodward's house?' Dugdale nodded that he did.

A Time to Kill

The two vehicles were soon on the road to the harbour-side of the town. There were two large estates here that housed many of the men and women who worked in the plastics factory. Both estates, whilst not exactly lawless, were tough beats. No one liked being posted there.

It was a short drive to Woodward's house, a one storey, prefabricated house of the sort that had been thrown up immediately after the war. They were meant to be temporary but there was a permanence to them now. To Jellicoe, it looked like a corrugated tin box. There were around fifty prefabricated houses on the estate. It was like a beige sea, but the blandness was surface only. Many would have gone to ex-servicemen. Jellicoe had arrested countless numbers of such men in his relatively few years with the Met. Crushed men, immune to death and violence: conscripted, driven to face death then cast adrift on their return from war.

'Is Woodward ex-army?' asked Jellicoe as Burnett pulled up outside the house.

'Aye. Him and his brother. Don't let that influence you. He's made his choice. And if he's a killer then all the worse for him.'

The front of the house had a small garden with a footpath of paving stones leading to the door. Houses like this were often given specifically to servicemen who had a family.

'Does he have a family?' asked Jellicoe as they walked to the door.

'Did,' replied Burnett. 'The wife left him and took their kids. He's not a nice man, son, trust me.'

There were no lights on in the house. Burnett and Jellicoe split up. Burnett looked through the front window while

Jellicoe took the rear of the house. A cursory glance through a couple of windows suggested the house was empty. Jellicoe returned to the front. He saw Burnett had his face pinned to the window.

'No sign of him here. We'll have to check, though,' said Burnett irritably.

The Black Maria pulled up outside too. Its arrival prompted a few of the people living on the estate to come out and stand on the front steps of their house. Despite the cold, many of the men only wore vests. They looked ready for a ruck. Jellicoe glanced at Burnett. He had already noticed the attention they were attracting and looked far from happy about it.

'Natives are restless, I see,' he murmured under his breath.

Clarke stepped out of the Black Maria. Burnett pointed to the back of the house. Jellicoe led the two constables to the back while Burnett and Clarke went to the front. Burnett rapped hard on the door.

'Open up, Woodward, it's the police,' shouted Burnett. He thumped the door again. Jellicoe could feel the house vibrate as they banged on the door. He wondered what it must be like when the wind blew strongly. Moments later he heard shoulders barging against the door and the crash as it opened. Jellicoe ordered the two constables to stay where they were, and he ran around to the front.

The front door led to a narrow hallway. On the left was a door that led to a small bedroom. To the right was a door that led to a living room. The top of the corridor ended in two doors. The one on the left led to the main bedroom. The other was the bathroom.

A Time to Kill

The search of the house took minutes to complete. Burnett didn't want to hang around.

'Let's go. One of these houses is bound to have a phone. They'll ring the Bricklayer's and warn Woodward if he's there.'

The policemen ran from the house towards the two vehicles.

'What about Woodward's house? Are we just going to leave it open?' asked Jellicoe.

'He's six five. Who would steal from him?' asked Burnett, not unreasonably.

They left at speed for the pub near the front. It was less than five minutes away. The Black Maria went to the back of the pub while Burnett and Jellicoe parked immediately outside the front entrance. As much as Jellicoe had not been looking forward to encountering Woodward at his house, the prospect of tangling with him at the pub was even less enticing. If any of his friends decided to become involved, then they would very quickly be outnumbered.

Similar thoughts must have been coursing through Burnett's mind as he did not stop swearing from the moment, they left the estate until they arrived at the pub. It was a singularly impressive feat not just for its duration but also for the variety of expletives at the chief inspector's command and the relentless intensity with which he declaimed them.

Jellicoe's heart quickened as they stepped out of the car. Despite the cold night air, he was perspiring heavily. It probably would have been sensible to wait for more policemen. However, Jellicoe felt more nervous about suggesting this than confronting Woodward. The irrationality of this sentiment was all too clear to him as he and Burnett headed towards the pub like two US Marshalls entering a saloon in Tombstone.

'You first,' said Burnett with a something close to a mad grin.

Jellicoe rolled his eyes and pushed the door open. It felt like the inside was on fire. Cigarette smoke billowed from every table bringing tears to Jellicoe's eyes. He had no idea who he was looking for beyond the alarming descriptions of Woodward's physical dimensions. Burnett followed him in and then they stood shoulder to shoulder. The patrons of the pub were initially unaware of their arrival. This gave Burnett enough time to scan the small interior to see if their man was there.

'That's him,' said Burnett, nodding towards a man emerging from the Gents toilet. Jellicoe looked in dismay at the man they were chasing.

Craig Woodward seemed to fill the doorway. He had to duck his head as he came through the door. His imposing physique was matched by a face that would have had half the heavyweight division cowering in their corner. This was not a man to be trifled with and they were here to arrest him, thought Jellicoe with some dismay. Even Clarkey's unquestionable charm would have difficulty breaking through the aura of malevolence the man exuded. The crowded bar parted like the Red Sea as Woodward stalked forward, initially unaware of the policemen.

Within seconds he spied Burnett. Woodward's face became a mask of hatred. However, much to Jellicoe's initial relief, he turned around and headed for the back exit. By now

288

the other patrons had picked up on the unfolding narrative, at least if the sudden quietening in the bar was any indication.

Burnett grabbed Jellicoe's arm and pulled him towards the entrance they'd used. One man tried to step in front of Burnett. Moments later he was bent double with Burnett pushing the door open seemingly without a care in the world. The two policemen hurried around the side of the bar where they were greeted by a sight for the ages.

The two young policemen were lying spark out on the ground. Clarke and Woodward were facing one another like two boxers. Both men were nearing fifty. They looked like they'd seen their fair share of the rough and tumble of life. Woodward had height and reach advantage. Clarke was much shorter and considerably broader. It was an intriguing match-up. Jellicoe, with great reluctance it must be said, stepped forward to provide back up to his colleague. He felt a hand hold him back.

'I'd have paid good money to see this at the Harringay Arena.'

'Shouldn't we help him?'

'Clarkey knows what he's doing,' assured Burnett. The pub was now emptying like it was on fire. After the initial laughter at the spectacle of two policemen semi-conscious on the ground, it silenced in anticipation of what they knew would be a good scrap. Jellicoe followed Burnett's lead and held his arms out to create a de facto ring for the two combatants.

The two men circled each other warily as the crowd began to shout out encouragement to the home favourite. Woodward, emboldened by the support, sent out a few jabs. The second of which landed. Encouraged by this he sprung forward swinging wildly. Science went out the window, he was looking for a quick knock out. His arms became a blur, but Clarke covered up well and he landed his first couple of punches, two vicious digs into the ribs. Woodward kept swinging to the head. And missing. Clarke, meanwhile, kept covered up, bobbed, and weaved but barely moved his feet.

They clinched and Woodward grabbed Clarke by the back of the neck and began landing a series of blows to the back of the head. Jellicoe felt it was time to intervene. He glanced at Burnett, who was yelling encouragement to Clarke. The blows delivered by Woodward must have been hurting but their impact was limited by his close proximity to Clarke. The policeman, meanwhile, was using Woodward's body like a heavy bag. Jellicoe winced as he saw one nasty kidney punch delivered by the amiable copper.

Woodward threw Clarke off, probably realising, as most of the crowd had, that success for him would require better deployment of his reach advantage. That said, Clarke's face was showing signs of the beating he'd been getting. Woodward was breathing hard though. The body punches were beginning to tell. The next few seconds saw the two protagonists searching for a second wind like a drowning man for land. Clarke circled round to his right forcing Woodward to do likewise.

Woodward started popping jabs out that Clarke easily avoided. Woodward was now directly in front of Jellicoe and Burnett with two groggy policemen at his feet. Just at that moment, with all of the speed of a hunting hippopotamus, Clarke leapt forward, ducking under a swinging haymaker, he rammed Woodward in the chest. This caused his opponent to step backwards tripping over one of the policemen.

A Time to Kill

Woodward hit the deck, or at least would have, had he not landed on one the policeman. Clarke landed on top of them. The groan that split the air was from the flattened man underneath the four hundred and fifty pounds of human flesh. Even Jellicoe winced in sympathy. There was at least one cracked rib in that pile, and it probably didn't belong to the fighters.

Burnett was on Woodward in an instant. He had the big man cuffed before anyone realised what was happening. If his speed of movement had caught Jellicoe by surprise, then it came as a shock to everyone watching. However, the celebratory mood of watching a cracking fight between two evenly matched, albeit very different, opponents had worn off to be replaced by something uglier. The dawning awareness that Woodward had been handcuffed started as a ripple of anger before becoming something altogether more threatening.

Jellicoe leapt in front of Burnett and Woodward to face the mob. HIs eyes were wide, not with fear, but with anger. He shouted at the mob, 'The first person to interfere will be arrested for perverting the course of justice; the maximum sentence for which is life imprisonment.' This silenced the mob momentarily. Using the opportunity to speak he stopped shouting and his voice became a snarl. 'I mean it. We know who all of you are. If one of you obstructs this arrest, we will throw the book at you. There will be no hiding place from which we will not find you.'

Jellicoe became aware of the reassuring presence of Clarke standing beside him. To be fair, Clarke was showing the signs of battle and looked worn out. However, even a wearied

Clarke, a man the mob would hitherto have viewed with affectionate disdain, would have presented an unwelcome challenge to the men they were facing. The mob had been silenced but they were still faced with the prospect of putting the giant into the Black Maria. Thankfully the two injured policemen were now sitting up and vaguely aware that an arrest had been made thanks to their courageous efforts.

'On your feet, Woodward,' said Burnett at last. 'You are under arrest.' He turned to the two policemen, 'Up you two get. Holiday's over.'

This was not quite the two coppers' idea of rest and relaxation, but they let it pass and rose gingerly to their feet. They went either side of Woodward, truncheons in hand. Both men had been knocked senseless by the giant. He took one look at the foot long truncheons being wielded by two constables who had good reason to use them and accepted that retribution would be far from divine. He rose slowly to his feet and walked with the two constables towards the Black Maria. Woodward's body was in agony thanks to the pummelling received from Clarke. It was only some comfort to him to see that the copper was showing much more visible signs of their remarkable set-to.

Moments later, before the mob could decide on their best course of action, Woodward was shoved none too gently into the back of the police van. Clarke joined him in the back and the two constables went round to the front, slightly disappointed now that they could not spend some time with their handcuffed captive.

Burnett nodded to Jellicoe and they walked straight towards the mob who parted out of their way. The mood was surly, but Jellicoe felt sure that nothing would happen now.

A Time to Kill

They walked to the police car to the sound of pig noises from their admiring public.

-

'Where were you on the night of the 8ᵗʰ of January?' asked Burnett. Well, he didn't so much ask as scream at Woodward from a distance of several inches. He was standing in front of the suspect, two fists on the table propping him up. Jellicoe remained seated beside him taking notes. At least that's what Burnett thought he was doing until he spied what was on the notepad. He was making drawings of Woodward. Caricatures. He paused for a second and looked hard at Jellicoe.

Meanwhile Woodward sat stony-faced saying nothing apart from occasional requests to see his lawyer. Burnett did not deign to reply to this as he suspected the news of Woodward's arrest would spread quickly enough, resulting in the arrival of someone or other claiming to represent Woodward's interests.

'I was in the *Bricklayer's Arms* that night,' said Woodward at length.

There was little point in asking who could confirm this as Burnett and Jellicoe were completely certain that everyone would.

'Who were you with? What were you talking about?' asked Jellicoe.

Woodward made a face that suggested he would disregard Jellicoe's question. He turned to Burnett and smiled.

'Answer the question, Woodward. Who were you with? What did you talk about?'

'Can't remember. Ask the boys.'

'You don't seem to understand how this works, Mr Woodward,' explained Jellicoe in a dangerously soft voice. 'If you refuse to answer a question then you may believe, correctly, that you are not incriminating yourself. A bit like the communists in America who "take the fifth" with McCarthy. Unfortunately, those poor idiots were assumed to be guilty and blacklisted from working again. And that's the problem with what you're doing. Your refusal to answer the question and allow us to cross reference with those in a position to confirm your presence will be seen by any jury as an admission that you have no alibi. And if you have no alibi, alongside the fact that you have a rather big motive and, looking at you, the means to have killed the colonel, then this places you right at the centre of suspicion. I think it's important you understand this point, Mr Woodward.'

It certainly made a change from shouting, thought Burnett, but lacked the joyous catharsis, the purging of one's anger one experienced when looking at a suspect in the eye and venting your feelings at deafening levels.

The approach seemed to be having an effect. For the first time the cocksure arrogance was replaced by a discernible sense of uncertainty in the giant's eyes. Burnett sat back and decided to let Jellicoe wield the scalpel a little longer.

'You're an interesting man, Mr Woodward. It's rare to meet someone who keeps a foot in both camps, so to speak. You are a feared man, too, I understand. There will be a queue forming now to support your story. We understand this. I mean who wouldn't want to be in your good books?'

Woodward eyed Jellicoe warily. The new man was a different prospect from the well-understood approach of someone like Burnett. They'd had dealings before. Woodward had always evaded serious trouble. He sensed that this time it was different.

'Yes, they'll troop in, no doubt prodded along by your lawyer, or one of your paymasters. They'll line up outside and speak of your noble character, they'll talk about the fact that you were with them all evening. Then one by one we will peel away those who saw you from those who say they were with you. We will then narrow them down to those who say that they were with you when the crime was committed. We'll ask for witnesses to that. While we're doing that, we will of course be investigating these men. They will be warned against perverting the course of justice. They will be warned of the consequences of doing so. One of them will crack. And do you know why they'll crack, Mr Woodward?'

Woodward shook his head mutely. At this moment there was a knock on the door. All heads turned to the door as it opened. Mr Elliot of Elliot, Elliot & Hardy entered. He stood at the doorway and gave a thin smile to the three men looking up at him.

Jellicoe frowned as he saw the little lawyer step forward and assume a seat beside his client. Spying the detective's reaction, Elliot commented, 'It's a small town, Inspector Jellicoe.'

'You seem to have cornered the market among one particular class,' replied Jellicoe.

'That's to be proved, Jellicoe and I suspect that you are quite some way from doing so. Don't say a word, Mr Woodward. They have nothing on you. Absolutely nothing. Now, I gather we already are in a position to make a claim against you on police brutality.'

Jack Murray

34

Tuesday 13th January 1959

'We don't have enough to hold him indefinitely,' admitted Burnett. He was sitting with Jellicoe in front of Superintendent Frankie the morning after Woodward's capture.

Burnett's response, of course, was not what Frankie wanted to hear. Frankie pursed his lips and clasped his hands in front of, in Jellicoe's imagination, his fake bosom. Burnett and Jellicoe braced themselves. Frankie did not strike Jellicoe as a man who liked to face the press with bad news. Arresting someone and then releasing them without charge a day or two later was humiliating. It superseded murder because it reflected directly on the Super. The only thing worse than this would probably be the murder of the Super himself.

As Frankie slowly began his rant, a number of options ran unchecked through Jellicoe's head. Within a minute the Super had peaked both in terms of volume, the intensity of the redness of his face and the proportion of swear words of everyday nouns and verbs.

The performance petered out with an uplifting, 'Get out and find me the murderer.' Burnett dutifully promised that they would do just this. Outside the office, Burnett gave vent to his views on Frankie. They chimed mostly with Jellicoe's.

'You get more sense coming out of Dixon of Dock Green's ring piece than that man,' said Burnett. Elodie Lumsden was sitting nearby at her desk. She heard this and glanced up. Jellicoe noted the smothered smile at Burnett's comment. They headed back down to the office. The stairs echoed to their footsteps. When they reached the office, Burnett stopped and turned to Jellicoe.

'We need to get a grip on this, son. We're all over the place at the moment. If you've any more of your bright ideas, now would be a good time to share them.'

Jellicoe had some ideas at that moment but wasn't sure that he was yet ready to share them with the other detectives. One thought, in particular, was prominent in his mind.

'I need to see our friend Ronnie again.'

'What's on your mind?' asked Burnett, eyeing the new man closely.

Jellicoe told him and Burnett nodded. 'Take Clarkey, maybe. He'll see we mean business.'

'How is he? That was quite a scrap.'

'He's a bit sore. I think he's more unhappy at the cricket than anything. You should hear him moaning about Cowdrey poking around instead of trying to win the match.'

'Pretty serious, I agree,' said Jellicoe sardonically.

This earned Jellicoe a look from Burnett, but the chief had too many other things to worry about to waste time on recalcitrant school children.

Jellicoe left to go in search of Clarke. He was having a cup of tea with one of the other constables who'd tangled with Woodward. Doubtless sharing war stories. Clarke looked up and smiled at Jellicoe when he entered the office. Jellicoe wasn't exactly sure how he managed to smile never mind why. The policeman was sporting a shiner in one eye and a bandage over the other. These were just the visible signs of battle. Jellicoe had no doubt that the aches and pains extended beyond the face. Despite this, Clarke's 'good morning' to Jellicoe seemed cheerful enough.

After establishing that Clarke was able to come with him, they left for the car. Clarke passed off his battle scars lightly. He was not the belly-aching type.

'First ruck I've had in a long time.'

'It was quite a ruck, Clarkey,' agreed Jellicoe.

'So, I gather. Pretty even, I think. I doubt I'd have stood a chance if he'd caught me one, though. He's a big lad.'

'I'd noticed. They took him to the hospital, last night. Poor dear was complaining of chest pains. Suspected broken rib, I gather.'

This brought a wide grin to the big policeman. The news that he was being accused of an excessive and unwarranted use of force was less welcome. However, Clarke merely shrugged his shoulders.

'I wouldn't worry too much,' said Jellicoe. 'He was resisting arrest and if we can nail him on Colonel Masterson's murder then you'll certainly be in the clear.'

'Let's nail him then.'

-

The welcome from Ronnie Musgrave was decidedly colder than the other day. The warmth of the room, however, remained at tropical levels. Condensation dripped from the walls like a leaking pipe. Even the appearance of Clarke

signally failed to lift the mood of antagonism permeating like
sweat from Musgrave. Jellicoe decided that a little diplomacy
would be needed if they were to gain what they needed.

'We are not pressing charges on the Tim Pemberton
kidnapping,' said Jellicoe as an opening gambit.

'I didn't bloody do it, that's why. You should be speaking
to Warwick, not me.'

'We will. Anyway, that's not why I'm here,' said Jellicoe.

Musgrave laughed humourlessly. He folded his arm and
looked grimly at Jellicoe.

'We need to know why you were looking for Freddie
Douglas.'

'Why should I tell you?' replied Musgrave. His voice was
raised a little, the anger rising within him.

'We still need to find the Masterson boy and the killer of
Colonel Masterson. We've arrested Craig Woodward in
connection with the latter.'

Musgrave turned to Clarke. There was a ghost of a smile
on his face. Clarke shrugged modestly. Everything that
needed to be communicated was done so in those few seconds.
Jellicoe detected a degree of admiration in how Musgrave
looked at Clarke, affection even.

'So?' replied Musgrave, back to business.

'Why did you want Freddie Douglas?'

'I don't talk to coppers. Go do your job, son.'

'Are you protecting Craig Woodward?'

A hard glint appeared in Musgrave's eye. He leaned
forward and said in a low voice, 'He doesn't need me to
protect him. Time to go. Hop it. I don't help coppers.'

'Craig Woodward killed Masterson because he didn't give
his brother parole. Were you aware of what he was planning?'

A Time to Kill

Musgrave face remained still. Jellicoe let the silence last a little longer. He had no expectation that Musgrave would speak. He studied the face of the older man. Then he added, 'The murder was committed soon after Freddie Douglas helped abduct Stephen Masterson. Do you know what I'm thinking, Mr Musgrave? I think Freddie Douglas saw Craig Woodward that night. That's why Craig Woodward came to you. He wanted you to give him Freddie.'

Musgrave's pupils dilated. His eyebrows twitched into a frown. He was angry.

'Of course, Woodward didn't tell you what he'd done. But I think you'd put two and two together before now. You guessed Woodward had killed Masterson. And when Woodward came looking for Freddie Douglas you realised that Freddie could point the finger at Woodward. That's why you're after Freddie. You know what Woodward is capable of. The question in my mind is would you have handed Freddie over or would you have protected him?'

Jellicoe paused for a moment and then another thought struck him.

'Or maybe you were telling us something. Maybe you were trying to tell us that Freddie's importance extended beyond the kidnapping. That makes sense. That makes a lot of sense in fact.'

Jellicoe nodded to Musgrave and stood up. Clarke did likewise. The obvious respect Musgrave held for Clarke was clearly not going to be enough to sway him towards revealing anything more that would help the investigation.

The two policemen went down the stairs. As they reached the amusements, they heard, once more, the sound of jazz music. Sonny Rollins' saxophone accompanied by spinning wheels and bells. It seemed oddly appropriate.

'They don't rat on each other, sir,' said Clarke as they stepped out onto the sea front.

'I wasn't expecting him to,' confirmed Jellicoe with a grin. 'I just wanted to see his reaction when I said about Woodward's brother.'

'And?'

'I am pretty sure he knows now that Woodward killed Masterson. In a strange way, I do think he was trying to help us the first time we saw him. He might have helped us more if we hadn't arrested him. I think it'll be a while before he trusts us again.'

Jellicoe laughed as he said this. It seemed bizarre to speak of trust between the head of a criminal gang and the police, yet, incredibly, there was just such a belief implicit in the way each side acted. However, the situation was changing. Something Musgrave said alerted him to another problem.

'What did you make of the comment regarding Warwick?' asked Jellicoe.

'Not sure what you mean sir. They're hardly best friends but I wouldn't exactly describe them as enemies either. They tolerate one another but avoid direct entanglement usually.'

'A bit like Russia and America.'

Clarke laughed and replied, 'Well now that you mention it, yes. It's in neither of their interests to start a gang war. We haven't had one of those for years.'

'But do you think one is brewing? Didn't Woodward kill one of Warwick's men in jail? Perhaps Musgrave thinks that Warwick is trying to even the score by implicating him in the Tim Pemberton kidnapping.'

This set Clarke thinking. He frowned and then replied, 'You might have something there, sir. The week before you came there was an incident; a fire at one of Musgrave's arcades. They said it was faulty electrics.'

'Was it investigated?'

'No, I don't believe so. The place was gutted,' said Clarke.

'I know the one, I think we passed it the other day. I assumed it was an insurance job. Do you think Warwick was involved? A reprisal maybe.'

Clarke shrugged and said, 'There was some talk of it, but Ronnie didn't say anything, so I suppose it was either something he didn't want too many questions about, or he thought he'd deal with it himself. It's usually his way.'

'I'll bet it is,' said Jellicoe.

They got into the car just as a traffic warden passed by. The warden greeted Clarke like a long lost relative. This made Jellicoe smile. It seemed Clarke was known by everyone in the town. Jellicoe handed the keys to Clarke to let him drive. He wanted to think. Clarke, seeing that he was not in the mood to talk, remained silent all the way back. That Woodward was responsible for Masterson's death seemed almost certain. Solomon had clearly kidnapped Stephen. The only question that remained was if the two crimes were connected or if it was pure coincidence. If Woodward was after Freddie Douglas because he'd seen him at the estate on that night, then it suggested, incredibly, that it was a coincidence.

Burnett was not having it.

The chief inspector eyed Jellicoe with incredulity after he'd told him his suspicions.

'No bloody way. You know as well as I do how ridiculous it sounds. Two separate crimes taking place at the same time, at the same place. Trust me, if it sounds ridiculous to me, then it'll have Widow Twanky off on one, trust me.'

He had a point. Even Jellicoe could see how unlikely it was that two utterly unconnected crimes should happen in the same place at roughly the same time. Yet Solomon would, no doubt, enjoy the very arbitrariness of this. Time and again he'd expressed his belief in the absence of any structure or invisible guiding narrative to life.

'You'll need proof,' said Burnett.

'You mean I need Freddie Douglas.'

'That's about the size of it.'

Both men sat in a disgruntled silence for a couple of minutes. Jellicoe sensed that Burnett believed him. This was not a comfort to either man. Burnett was right; they needed proof, and, at that moment, Freddie Douglas was their only hope. Woodward was too old a hand to crack under questioning and Burnett had abandoned that soon after Jellicoe left. They did not have enough to take him to court and remand him in custody. This meant they had a couple of days and then they had to release him.

'I'll have to speak to Frankie. There's nothing for it. You can come with me, though. It's your bright idea,' snarled Burnett. Jellicoe smiled. Only Burnett could make praise sound like a reprimand. 'No point in waiting. Let's go and see him then we'll have another go at Woodward, for all the use it'll be.'

They ascended the stairs in silence. Elodie Lumsden smiled up at them.

'Can we see the Super?' asked Burnett.

A Time to Kill

'In a moment. He's just with someone,' replied Elodie in that strangely polished yet seductive mid-channel accent. The two men sat down on the two seats outside the office. Jellicoe tried to look anywhere but straight ahead. Unfortunately, this meant looking at the singularly less beautiful Burnett. The shrewd chief inspector was all too aware of Jellicoe's intention and a slow smile spread over his face. Jellicoe reddened slightly and a horrible thought struck him. Burnett would have fun with this.

The office door opened and out stepped Terence Singe. Jellicoe's mouth fell open.

'Catching flies, Nick?' said Singe cheerily as he spotted Jellicoe.

'Do you two know each other?' asked Frankie, anticipating Burnett's question by half a second.

'Oh yes, we go way,' back' said Singe as if he was speaking about an old school chum. The news certainly did not please Frankie, and Burnett was only marginally more understanding.

Frankie shook hands with the reporter and Singe went on his way receiving a look of censure from Jellicoe as he walked past. He smiled breezily and continued on his way.

'You wanted to see me, Chief Inspector?' asked Frankie

'Yes sir. Just some thoughts on the case we'd like to share,' said Burnett in reply. He turned to Jellicoe, an evil smile on his face, 'Come this way, Jellicoe, unless you'd rather keep Miss Lumsden company outside?'

Jellicoe gave Burnett a sour look which seemed to pep the chief inspector up no end. Jellicoe suspected, rightly, that any opportunity to put one over him would be grabbed lovingly in both hands by Burnett.

The meeting went as well as could be expected which is to say that Superintendent Frankie lost his temper not once but three times in the space of its four-minute duration. It was difficult to say who was the target of his disapprobation; it was certainly very clear he wanted action and he wanted it immediately.

One threat that was headed off was the prospect of him taking personal control of the case. That was likely to be postponed until such time as they were nearing its successful completion, predicted Burnett when they returned to his office. At current rate of knots, Burnett thought this would be days away. In fact, this prediction proved substantially incorrect.

They arrived back at the office. The office was empty. A phone was ringing. Burnett wondered out loud where everyone had disappeared to. Just as Jellicoe reached over to the phone it stopped. The two men continued on their way to Burnett's office. Just then Wallace appeared through the door. Jellicoe turned around.

'Did you get hold of a more detailed map?' asked Jellicoe.

'Yes, sir, I picked it up earlier,' replied Wallace and went to retrieve it. The phone began to ring again. Wallace, meanwhile, went to another desk and took the map from a drawer. He came towards Jellicoe. The phone, meanwhile, continued to ring.

Jellicoe pointed to the phone, 'See who it is and then bring the map into the office.' Burnett switched the light on, and the two men went inside. It was getting towards five now and it was dark outside. The shops were closing, and the streets were becoming more crowded. A distant siren made Jellicoe glance out of the window. The noise grew louder. A fire engine raced past the bank towards the sea front.

Just then Wallace burst into the room. His face was pale.

'Sir, that was the Masterson estate. A group of armed men came a few minutes ago.'

'What about the copper we had there?' asked Burnett.

'They tied him and the staff up. That was him ringing. No one is hurt but the Mastersons have been kidnapped.'

35

Burnett led Jellicoe, Yates, Wallace, and several other uniformed men out to the cars. The sky was black overhead, and rain was falling gently. The night was crisply cold and had the smoky smell of winter. Just as this occurred to Jellicoe, another fire engine came screaming past the police station. He stared as it went past. Then he heard a door slamming and it brought him back to what they needed to do.

Three cars set off towards the Masterson estate. It seemed like a futile gesture to Jellicoe. They'd failed once more. It would have been easy to blame Frankie, as Burnett was doing, at great volume, but the truth was even if they'd had half a dozen men up there, Solomon would have still taken the other two Masterson family members.

The car radio crackled to life as they sped up to the estate. Two fires were burning in the town. It seemed like the world was spinning off its axis. Burnett ordered Price to find out what was going on, or something like that. In his heightened state of anxiety, the order had contained little by way of instruction and had, instead, imparted a sense of his impotence in the midst of the maelstrom.

The police sirens wailed on the empty road. A few sheep ran away from the fence as they passed. The two cars reached the estate within ten minutes. Fitch greeted them at the door.

A Time to Kill

His face was pale, and he was clearly shaken. For the first time, Jellicoe felt a degree of sympathy for the aging butler. His face suggested that it was all a bit much and Jellicoe heartily agreed with him.

The young policeman who'd been overpowered appeared, rather shame-faced, in front of Burnett. For once the bluff cynicism that the chief inspector normally employed as an antidote to the task-mistressy condescension of the superintendent was missing. In its place was a more sympathetic reaction to a situation that had been beyond the young man's control.

Jellicoe smiled grimly as he reflected on this. Out of his control. It was the mantra that Solomon seemed to live by. Yet for all his professed submission to the chaos of life, Solomon was a man who had a plan. He ignored the uniformed men taking statements from Fitch and the housekeeper, Mrs Pickford, and walked back out to the car. He wanted to think.

His hands came into contact with folded paper. It was the map that he'd requested from Wallace. He put it out of his head for a moment and then, not trusting his instincts to concentrate his mind elsewhere, decided to look at it.

The radio crackled again as he unfolded the map. His eyes scanned over the lines and place marks, but it was difficult to make things out in the light. There was more traffic on the radio now. Jellicoe shifted his attention away from the map to pick up what was being said. His eyes widened a little as he began to understand more. Setting the map down he headed back into the house to look for Burnett. He was with the young policeman.

'Chief, I think you need to hear this.'

Burnett looked up, a trace of irritation on his face. 'What's wrong,' he said, rising from his seat.

'The two fires we heard about earlier. One of them was at a bookie's run by Warwick. The second was on the front at Nelson's Garage. Apparently, that's a…'

'I know. One of Musgrave's.'

'Price thinks that there could be fighting tonight. Superintendent Frankie left the office earlier so he's driving home now. Leighton is in London tonight. You're in charge, sir.'

'And we're here. This is a right bloody mess. Look get on the radio and tell Price to get onto County. We need more men. If there's going to be fun and games tonight, then we're royally buggered. Tell him to ring the home of Widow Twanky as well, while you're at it. He'll just have to drive back; that'll teach him for shipping off early.'

Yates and Wallace came out of the house and joined the two senior men. It sounded as if Price was going to need all the help available. There was nothing much to be gained by staying at the manor house. They went to the cars. Burnett spied the map laid out over the driver's seat.

'What the hell is that?' said Burnett.

Jellicoe assumed the question was rhetorical as it was abundantly clear what it was. He regretted laying the map out on the bonnet when he realised how wet it had become.

'I wanted to see a more detailed map of this area. We've been flying blind throughout. This is it,' said Jellicoe.

Burnett frowned and was on the point of responding when he paused. He was keen to return to the town, but he recognised that Jellicoe had unusually acute instincts. Instead, he reserved comment on the wisdom of studying a map at this moment. He glanced up at the rain falling gently on them and pointed to towards the house.

'Wait a moment,' he called out to Yates and Wallace who were climbing into the police car.

Jellicoe went back into the house accompanied by Burnett. He laid the map out on a table in the hall. Burnett pointed immediately to their location. From there, Jellicoe ran his finger towards the area that they'd searched the previous day when he'd tried to recreate the route taken by the kidnappers. Outside they heard someone running towards the house. Probably more news on what was happening in town.

'Sir,' called Yates, trying to interrupt them.

'What is it?' asked Burnett making no attempt to disguise his benign irritability. He wanted to see where Jellicoe's thought processes were leading but there was an urgency in Yates' voice.

Jellicoe's finger had traced its way past the wood they'd been to previously to a strip of land a few miles north. He read out the name.

'We've had contact from Solomon,' said Yates.

Jellicoe was only half listening. He was staring at the strip of land.

'He's told us where we can find the Mastersons.'

'What?' exclaimed Burnett. Even Jellicoe jerked his head around at this point.

'They're at Crook Airfield,' said Yates.

'Where the bloody hell?' started Burnett as he ransacked his memory for a familiar name. Then it hit him.

'Here,' said Jellicoe pointing to the strip of land on the map he'd been looking at not a minute earlier. 'They're here.'

Burnett was a man for a crisis. All at once his head cleared of the confusion and began to process what needed to be done. He glanced around at the raw material he had to work with. He saw Jellicoe, Wallace and Yates looking at him expectantly. Just behind them were a couple of the uniformed men. All in all, it could have been worse.

'Right, let's go,' said Burnett. 'You two,' he shouted to the policemen in the corridor. 'Come with us.' The three detectives ran outside to the cars. Wallace was waiting.

'Sir,' said Wallace. 'We've had unconfirmed reports that Ronnie Musgrave was seen with twenty men outside the *Bricklayer's Arms*.'

Burnett stopped and stared at the young policeman caught between shooting the messenger and utter disbelief at the rapid deterioration in events: both here and in town. He collected himself immediately and turned to Jellicoe.

'Twenty? Has to be an exaggeration.' He shook his head and then gathered himself. He pointed to Jellicoe and said, 'You, me and boy wonder here will go to the airfield. Yates, you, and the other men get back into town and assist Price. He'll be having kittens if I know him. And have an ambulance sent to the airfield. Heaven only knows what we'll find there. And I want an update on what the hell is happening in town. Musgrave no more has twenty men than I have two wives.'

A chill that had nothing to do with the climatic conditions went through Burnett as he said this. Yates, meanwhile, looked like he'd stepped on something soft. He was distinctly put out at the prospect of missing out on being in at the kill for the Masterson kidnapping. Then another thought struck him that was even worse. He'd be slap bang in the middle of a potential riot. And it was raining more heavily now. He felt like howling to a moon hidden behind a black curtain in the night sky.

Wallace took the driver's seat. One uniformed man joined him in the front while Jellicoe and Burnett sat in the back.

'You know the way, son?' asked Burnett. Daft question. He knew the boy was local, but still, he had to be sure.

'Yes sir. Ten minutes. Less probably.'

'You're not at Le Mans,' warned Burnett who thought ten minutes would be a touch optimistic. 'Make sure we arrive in one piece.'

Notwithstanding the chief's warning, he fell backwards in his seat as Wallace tore down the driveway of the estate. Wallace was a young man who, like most young men, was predisposed to believe in his almost supernatural ability behind the wheel. He was also probably in love. And the object of his adoration, at least this month, was potentially facing great peril. Just the thought of this sent his foot to the floor.

As they sped towards the airfield, they heard more of what was happening in town. Another shop was on fire. This was another one of Warwick's, this time on the outskirts of town near the plastics factory. There was no question in anyone's mind now that this was not just an arson attack but a concerted series of attacks.

'What was the exact message from Solomon?' asked Jellicoe in an attempt to keep his mind off the suicidal speed at which Wallace was driving and hoping that it might slow him down.

'We weren't told what the message was, just that the three Mastersons were at the airfield.'

'Why didn't we look there?' asked Burnett. He was angry and probably with good reason.

'The airfield's not been used since the war,' said Wallace. 'It wasn't even on the map we had.'

'I want a review of all the maps back at the station,' said Burnett. 'We can't be caught like this in future.' His voice was tight with frustration. This was probably aimed as much at himself as the others around him. They'd all missed this and, to be fair to Jellicoe, he was not to know of the airfield.

They drove through the forest. The only light came from the rather inadequate headlamps of the Wolsey. At the rate they were travelling, any deer that was out for its nightly constitutional would be in for a nasty surprise.

The journey of ten minutes was made in something closer to five. This was either a result of an overestimation by Wallace or, more likely, a wilful ignoring of Burnett's orders. They drove at speed down a long track. Ahead, Jellicoe could see the black outline of an aircraft hangar. It was at least fifty feet high and wide enough to accommodate the wingspan of a Spitfire.

As they approached the hangar, two things were apparent. The hangar was made from corrugated metal. It was entirely conceivable that this was where he'd been taken by Solomon. The surrounding area was deserted. If Solomon had been here with his men, then he'd clearly abandoned ship. This was less of a surprise to Jellicoe than to Burnett if the chief's oath-laden rhetoric was anything to go by.

A Time to Kill

The question occupying Jellicoe's mind was why Solomon had chosen to reveal the whereabouts of the Masterson family. Especially now after going to the trouble of kidnapping the major less than an hour previously. Something else was at play. He had little doubt they would find the Mastersons inside. Had he killed them? It did not ring true with the profile he'd built in his mind of Solomon. Thoughts were whirling around his head, however. As incredible as it seemed, he could see Solomon's hand in the events unfolding in town.

The car skidded to a halt which also served to interrupt Jellicoe's line of thought. They were out of the car immediately and running towards the hangar. The front door was bolted and had a lock. To Jellicoe's eyes the lock seemed cursory, an afterthought. Moments later it was in bits thanks to the constable's mallet.

Burnett pulled the door open, and they piled inside. The first man in, Burnett, appeared to trip over something but managed to avoid falling entirely. It was black inside. It took a moment for Jellicoe's eyes to adjust. He could discern some shapes, pillars at the side of the hangar. Behind them, Wallace found a light switch. The lights came on a moment later.

'Bloody hell,' said Burnett.

Bloody hell, all right, thought Jellicoe.

'Pippa,' shouted Wallace, who was the last through the door. A second later, he flew past Jellicoe and Burnett, headed for the rear of the hangar.

Jellicoe, glancing at the ground and what Burnett had appeared to stumble over. Then he realised what had Solomon had set up for their arrival.

'Stop' shouted Jellicoe at Wallace.

36

DS Yates would have required no lessons from DC Wallace in the art of driving like a reckless boy racer. That he did so with as much reluctance as Wallace had done with overwhelming motivation was no small tribute to the unavoidable feeling that he'd been letting the side down on a number of occasions. He needed to set things right with Jellicoe. This thought gave impetus to the way he drove back from the Masterson estate along with a number of very nervous bobbies.

They passed a large army truck on the way to town, sped past the police station tore around several hairpin bends nearly taking out a black cat who'd strayed too long in the middle of the road.

They arrived just in time to see an extraordinary sight. A line of policemen was advancing towards two groups of men, each numbering around a dozen. The atmosphere was almost palpable. Clouds of vapour surrounded the men. They seemed like a black beast emerged from the depths. To the side of the policemen, he saw DI Price and DS Fogg. They had taken the rather foolhardy step of trying to act as peacemakers between the two sets of men.

'Out of the car,' ordered Yates, parking about a hundred yards away from the scene. He didn't want the police car to become collateral damage if a riot ensued. He also wanted a potential escape route. A Black Maria was parked further down the street. It was unlikely to be sufficient if they had to start making arrests.

Yates jogged behind the other constables trying to delay the inevitable when he would be in the middle of this disturbance. There was no sign of violence.

Yet.

Yates was by no means a coward. He was not the tallest of policemen, but he could handle himself when push escalated beyond shove. Under normal circumstances, he would have felt that the odds were favourable standing alongside half a dozen truncheon-wielding uniformed men and a couple of plainclothes. However, neither Price nor Fogg inspired much confidence or, he suspected, much fear in the people they were advancing towards. This was a problem. A big problem, in fact.

However, given the circumstances, it seemed the reasons for unrest lay not, for once, with anything to do with the police. Price's efforts seemed as naïve as they were foolhardy in Yates's eyes. The sensible thing would have been to let the two bands of ruffians have their fun and then round up the detritus afterwards. But it was too late.

So, Yates, screaming silently inside, jogged forward towards the three groups facing one another at the crossroads outside the *Bricklayers Arms*. As he neared the scene, he saw for the first time, Ronnie Musgrave, and Johnny Warwick at the head of their respective groups. They were exchanging greetings of a sort. Both men seemed to be carrying weapons in their hands whose size and heft would make the truncheons of the coppers somewhat redundant.

'Hello, DS Yates,' said Price with a smile. Was he insane, thought Yates? 'Bit of a set-to here, isn't there?'

A colourful exchange between Musgrave and Warwick confirmed that 'set-to' was one way of describing it. Oddly, neither side had yet pulled the pin out of the proverbial grenade. Yates wished he'd used another metaphor as it wasn't entirely beyond the realms of possibility that some of the ex-army men here might have kept some souvenirs from their time at war. This alarming prospect did little to calm the rather troubled thoughts of the sergeant.

He listened in on the abuse being hurled between the two sets of men. They had moved closer to one another. In between the expletive-laden rants, it was clear that both sides were blaming one another for the fires that had been started over the course of the late afternoon.

Price was grinning weakly and appealing for calm. However, his high-pitched entreaties were not so much falling on deaf ears as being picked up by the wind that had whipped up suddenly and thrown into the ether. To Yates's mind, the presence of the police was only likely to make matters worse. He sensed that although both sides were talking aggressively, the desire for a scrap was diminishing with the increasing intensity of rain in their faces. All it would need, though, was for some damn fool to do something stupid.

-

The army truck, at Solomon's insistence, kept well under the speed limit. The last thing they needed at this critical point was for the 'peelers' to nab them on a speeding charge. He glanced at Clive 'Desperate Dan' Weir. His eyes were fixed on the road ahead. There was a steadiness to him that commanded trust. He knew the score. Like an extension of Solomon, he understood instinctively what the boss wanted without having to ask.

Nothing was said. They drove into town in what might have passed for companiable silence were it not for the palpable tension. It was there in the air they breathed, in Weir's grip on the wheel, in the nervous fluttering Solomon was experiencing inside.

And then they heard a sound that caused two men's stomachs in the front and the three in the back to lurch, a wailing siren. At first it was faint, then it grew louder. Solomon focused on the rain splattering the windscreen. Little pearly drops lit by the lamplight streaked down the window before being swiped away. The sound of the siren was now very loud.

'They're behind us?' asked Weir, unable to hide a trace of nerves in his voice.

Solomon glanced at in the rear wing view mirror. There were no cars behind them at this point. The road ahead and behind was empty. Suddenly a black Wolsey appeared. They were driving at great speed. Solomon glanced at the speedometer and saw that Weir was well within the speed limit.

'It'll be the fires. Relax, sergeant.'

Sergeant.

He'd always be sergeant. Since the first day they'd met all those years ago when he and Masterson had forced the men to stand in the rain. One of those men had died from pneumonia ten days later. Masterson couldn't have cared less, of course. But not Weir. The look of shame was all too apparent. But by then it was too late. Not for the dead man, but for Solomon. They were to leave for England that day. The same day they announced poor Lyle was dead.

He'd seen the look on Weir's face and realised then that he should have gone to him and not Masterson. Things might have been different. He felt a sickness in the pit of his stomach that little to do with the police car overtaking them. Soon the police car was out of sight and they were in the centre of town, opposite the police station, in fact. Two men appeared on the street. They waved at the army truck. Solomon waved back.

'Boys did a good job by the looks of it.'

In the distance he could see the night sky lit up by what appeared to be a fire. Weir meanwhile had slowly come to a halt. Solomon was already opening the door.

'Good work,' he said to the two men as they approached.

'That'll keep the cops busy for a while,' said one of the men.

Three other men appeared from behind Solomon.

'Right,' said Solomon. 'Let's hurry.'

-

'No good will come of this, see,' shouted Price. He turned his head left and right. No one was listening. There was more than a hint of desperation in the Welshman's voice. He turned to Fogg and Yates.

'Not sure this is working.'

Damn right this isn't working, thought Yates. They were sitting on top of a powder keg and it wasn't going to take much to set the whole damn thing off. And they were stuck in the middle.

A Time to Kill

'Sir,' said Yates, 'I know this will sound strange, but I think we should pull our men back.'

It did sound strange. Price's face darkened in disapproval.

'What? Have you gone mad?'

Yates coloured a little but forged ahead with what he wanted to say. He felt certain about the situation and, in a strange way, knew he was right.

'I'm not sure they want to fight. They'd have started by now. But something may set them off. Pull the men back and you and I can talk to Musgrave and Warwick. Try and set them straight. Tell them about Solomon. Tell them he's the one who set off the fires.'

It was out of his mouth before he realised that this is exactly what had happened. It was Solomon who'd set off the fires. Who else could it have been? Warwick and Musgrave had co-existed for nearly a decade without any major eruptions. Along comes Solomon and all of a sudden, they were at each other's throats.

'It has to be Solomon, sir. There's no other explanation.'

Price nodded. It made sense or, at least, it was plausible enough. He turned to the two groups of men and then back to Yates.

'All right. Go to Musgrave. I will speak to Warwick. Fogg, tell Sergeant Uprichard to pull the men back a little.'

The look of relief on Fogg's face was barely disguised. He turned and jogged towards a short, uniformed, officer with stripes on his arm. Uprichard seemed surprised by the order. He glanced over at Price. Typical Ulsterman thought Yates. Think they're above it all. Only take orders from the Almighty.

Price waved them away. That'll go down well, thought Yates sourly. By the look on Uprichard's face it hadn't, but he turned to the uniformed men and motioned for them to retreat.

'Come on,' said Price, his voice was tight.

Seeing the police pull back seemed to quieten the crowd. At first no one had noticed but then, slowly, it dawned on the two groups of men that the police were leaving the field clear to them. Somewhere in the distance, at the town hall, the old clock was chiming. It was seven o'clock.

The crowd now noticed Yates and Price approaching them. Their footsteps seemed to be in time to sound of the bell chiming. The silence of the crowd was its own presence. Yates's heart was racing so much his head began to swim. He felt giddy with nervous tension.

Musgrave glared at the approaching Yates as much in amusement as anger. He recognised the nerve the young policeman was showing but the sound of the clock ringing and the copper's sombre-slow walk towards them seemed like something from a western. Musgrave liked westerns. Randolph Scott and some baddies; that was him, happy. Finally, the bell stopped. The only sound that could be heard was sound of the policemen's footsteps.

Until the explosion.

A Time to Kill

37

Wallace stopped and turned desperately to Jellicoe. There was no fear in his eyes, just desperation. Jellicoe understood so much in that moment but now was not the time. His attention was gripped by what he saw in front of him.

The three Mastersons were handcuffed hands and feet to the back wall of the hangar. Their hands were over their heads. All three were gagged. But that wasn't what concerned Jellicoe at that moment. His eyes were fixed on the dynamite that was strapped to the chests of both Stephen Masterson and his sister. Beneath them was a box with a timer. Wires extended from the box to the dynamite. The timer was a simple alarm clock.

A horrible feeling gripped Jellicoe as he stared at the scene. He turned to Burnett. They looked at one another for a second and then they both turned to the doorway. There, on the ground, was a wire. It had been strung across the doorway.

'We've set off the timer,' said Burnett. He was in shock.

Jellicoe looked at the wire. It did not seem to be connected to anything. He shook his head.

'Misdirection,' he said simply. He turned to the clock.

It was three minutes to seven.

Wallace was by Masterson now, the army major's eyes widened in fear. Wallace yanked the gag away from him. He coughed and tried to speak. Jellicoe had sprinted over by now and was examining the bomb mechanism. Unfortunately, he hadn't a clue what to look for. The major was speaking breathlessly now.

'Solomon has booby trapped them. Don't touch anything.'

That much was obvious, and Jellicoe was certainly not going to touch anything, yet. The wires all went into a black box with a strange design flowing around the middle. Red and blue wires stretched up to the sticks of dynamite.

'He said it's going to go at seven.'

Jellicoe had guessed as much. The call had deliberately been timed to lead them here just as the bomb was to go off.

'He's left the key in the major's handcuffs,' said Wallace in surprise. He crouched down and released the legs of Masterson and then used the key to do likewise to his hands.

Jellicoe glanced at Masterson's two children. Each had keys in the handcuffs attaching their feet to a pole that had been screwed to the wall. Why would he do this? Jellicoe glanced up at the faces of Stephen and Phillipa. Their eyes were wide with terror. Both were crying, shaking their arms and legs as if trying to escape.

Two minutes to seven.

Burnett helped release Masterson. He was over in an instant to the bomb.

'What can we do?' asked Burnett. He hoped the army man might have some clue about disarming the bomb.

But Masterson was crying. There was nothing he could do. He tried to speak but no words would come. Wallace was frantic. He shook the major so much that Jellicoe had to grab his arms. Finally, Masterson said something that they could understand.

'You can disarm one of the bombs but not the other. He said one of them would die. I had to choose and live with that choice.' He started to sob again. A memory passed through his mind of something he'd said long ago.

'When?' demanded Jellicoe.

'Seven,' said Masterson. It came out like the cry of a wounded animal.

Burnett pointed to the keys locking the handcuffs. Wallace and he immediately set to work releasing the handcuffs, careful not to disconnect the wire. This risked setting of the bombs. The gags were removed. Phillipa screamed. It cut through the air of the building and scorched the ears of the policemen. Stephen was crying hysterically, demanding to be released.

Masterson looked from Stephen to Phillipa frenziedly. Solomon had given him a choice. Which child to save? Jellicoe was struck by the biblical parallel that Solomon had imposed on Masterson and wondered what could have made him contemplate this.

Masterson stumbled forward and grabbed both his children. His body covered the two sets of explosives. It was as if he wanted them all to die together. His desolation rendered thought obsolete. He wanted to die. His sobs and those of his children woke Wallace up from his inertia. He turned to Burnett and Jellicoe.

'We can save one of them.'

One minute to seven.

Jellicoe and Burnett grabbed Masterson and tore him away from his children.

'No!' screamed Masterson. He began to fight them. 'Let me go!'

'Daddy,' screamed Phillipa.

Stephen was beyond speech. His head hung low. He'd long since accepted he would die. 'Save her,' he whispered to Wallace. 'Save her,' he pleaded again.

Wallace needed no other invitation. He ripped the two wires attached between the dynamite and the black box. Phillipa screamed again and began to fight Wallace as he tried to move her away.

'No! I won't leave him.'

Masterson had stopped fighting and collapsed to the ground sobbing. Jellicoe and Burnett each grabbed an arm and began to drag him away from his son. Wallace draped Phillipa over his shoulder although she was still putting up a spirited fight to remain with her brother. He sprinted towards the two policemen.

The clock's hand moved inexorably towards the 12. Moments later the shrill alarm began to ring, then…

Boom!

-

'What the hell was that?' said Musgrave staring at Yates as if he was to blame. Yates had no idea and said as much.

Warwick and his men seemed in no doubt that another firebomb had detonated. More pertinently, if the sound was anything to go by then it was in *their* part of town. They surged past the hapless Price towards Musgrave and his men. Yates spun around, horrified at the prospect of being caught in the middle of a riot. He yelled at the top of his voice.

A Time to Kill

'Stop!'

Incredibly, they did.

Yates had both his arms out as if he was crucified. If he didn't get this right, he realised, that would be the least of his worries. 'Stop,' he shouted once more. 'You're being set up. Someone else is responsible for the fires.'

Warwick put his arm up to still his men. He walked forward towards Yates and Musgrave.

'What's all this about?' HIs voice was wary. He was ready to call his men forward. But, to Yates's ears, he wanted to understand.

Yates took a deep breath and walked forward towards Warwick and into the middle of the two groups who were now barely five yards apart.

'A man called Solomon is responsible for the fires and the kidnappings. He's ex-army.' Yates turned desperately to Musgrave and then to Warwick. 'I mean it. This is a set up. this is what he wants. You two killing each other.'

A curious silence fell on the street as the two gang leaders pondered what Yates had said. It was clear the detective was in earnest. Warwick looked from Yates to Musgrave. The fire was still in Musgrave's eyes, but he saw something else too. Doubt.

'Why would he do this?' shouted Warwick. Of the two men, he seemed the most sceptical. The most on edge. Yates knew at that moment he was just a few words away from a riot.

-

Jellicoe and Burnett had ducked instinctively when they heard the explosion. This meant they'd dropped the major none too gently to the ground. All three looked up. Wherever the explosion had taken place, it certainly wasn't in the hangar. Everyone was still intact.

Wallace was lying on top of Phillipa Masterson and showed little desire to move from this delightful position until she threw him off and scrambled onto her feet. Masterson was on his feet too and running towards his son, who remained in one piece and still sporting the explosives around his chest.

Jellicoe and Burnett followed the two Mastersons and Wallace towards Stephen. The boy had his head down and he was quietly sobbing. They all arrived together. Stephen looked up at them with red-rimmed eyes. He smiled weakly and said, 'Can someone remove this blasted thing from me?'

Burnett nodded to Wallace who moved round to Stephen's back. He tried to remove the dynamite belt not helped by the fact that the father and sister were hugging Stephen tightly.

Jellicoe knelt down to the black box. It was now revealed for what it was. A Jack-in the-box. The Jack in this question was a jester with a red nose and red circles for cheeks. It had a manic grin. Jellicoe wondered what evil parent would consider this an ideal gift for a child. The jester was clutching an envelope. One word was written on the envelope.

Boom!

The bombs were carefully removed from Stephen. Wallace carried the belt away from the group. Meanwhile Burnett crouched down beside Jellicoe. They both looked at the envelope.

'Well, are you just going to stare at it? Open it,' ordered Burnett.

A Time to Kill

Jellicoe tore open the envelope. Inside was a folded piece of paper. A swift glance to Burnett and then he unfolded the paper. It was a letter. It was addressed to him.

'Bloody hell,' said Burnett, looking at Jellicoe strangely.

'What's wrong?' demanded Masterson who was slowly recovering his senses if not his manners.

Jellicoe had quickly scanned the letter as had Burnett. They both looked up at Masterson. The major's recovery was in full flow now and his temper was rising.

'Well? What the bloody hell do you have there?'

'A letter from Solomon,' said Burnett.

'Give it to me,' shouted Masterson, stumbling forward, rage in his eyes. Burnett stood in his way. A firm hand was placed on the major's chest.

Jellicoe began to read from the letter.

'Dear Inspector Jellicoe,' he began. 'if you are reading this then you will doubtless be aware that I have not killed any of the Masterson family. Yes, I may have taken them for a short time against their will. They'll be shaken but otherwise none the worse for their experience.' Jellicoe glanced up at Stephen Masterson who had collapsed to the ground and was being consoled by his sister. Solomon was, perhaps, being a little disingenuous on this point.

'The question that will doubtless be uppermost in your mind is what was this about? Why did I kidnap the boy and then his sister and their vile father? As you may have surmised, revenge. Ask Major Masterson why I would do this. No doubt he will deny everything, but I shall tell you.'

Masterson made another attempt to grab the letter from Jellicoe. 'Let me have that,' he screamed.

Wallace was now standing alongside Burnett. His was an onerous position. On the one hand he had to ensure he was seen to do his duty. After all, his immediate boss and his boss's boss were beside him. However, he didn't want to set the major against him either. Not if he was to see Phillipa Masterson again. All in all, it was a decidedly tricky path he had to negotiate at that moment.

'A few days after my arrest I went to see Captain Masterson as he was then. My purpose was to hand over my ill-gotten gains. In return, I begged him to see that some of the money went to Lizette and Sophie. Inspector Jellicoe, I literally begged him. I believe he took all of the money for himself. I believe that none of it went to Lizette and, I suspect, none of it was returned to the authorities. You may wish to check this.'

'That's a damned lie,' erupted Masterson. 'You can't possibly take the word of a coward, a deserter and a criminal. The man would say anything to smear me. Surely you can see that?'

'It continues,' said Jellicoe, ignoring Masterson. 'I was a deserter. I did turn to crime. But I never killed anyone then and I did not kill Colonel Masterson. Major Masterson, however, is a despicable individual who has blood on his hands. I offer my apology to Stephen and to Phillipa and my heartfelt commiserations that they have such a loathsome parent.'

Jellicoe looked up and fixed his gaze on Masterson.

'The letter is signed, Lieutenant David Solomon, DCM.'

Phillipa and Stephen Masterson slowly walked over to the group. Masterson turned away from the detectives and embraced his children. Then he said with repressed fury, 'It is all lies.'

Burnett was having none of it, though.

'Lies? Lies? Then why would he do all this? Make no mistake about this, Masterson, I will be investigating this. After the weekend I've had, that's a promise.'

Why would he do all of this? This was a pertinent question as far as Jellicoe was concerned. Jellicoe rose to his feet, still clutching the letter. His mind was racing. Solomon had kidnapped the Mastersons. But yet, it had all been staged. Staged for a reason. The messages. The tip off where he'd hidden them. And then there was the loud explosion they'd heard two minutes ago. Not just this explosion. The fires in town. The potential riot happening at the *Bricklayers Arms*.

Solomon had the police and the fire brigade running here, there, and everywhere. Random particles clashing in the ether. But why? And then it hit Jellicoe. He turned to Burnett.

'We have to get back into town. Now. I know what Solomon's doing.'

Burnett frowned. It was his way of asking why.

-

A hush had descended on the street. Yates was breathing hard. Clouds of vapour escaped from his mouth. Beads of perspiration popped up on his forehead. The combination of cold air, fear and his rapidly beating heart made him feel as if he was drowning. It crossed his mind momentarily that he might faint. None of this was helped by the conspicuously malevolent presence of the two gang leaders who stared at him, expectantly.

331

The silence only served to emphasise the electrical atmosphere. For the first time, somewhere in the distance he could hear the faint sound of an alarm. Rain beat against the brim of his hat then dripped down past his eyes. He focused on the rain. It interrupted the conflicting thoughts buzzing around his mind like planes in a dogfight.

Why was Solomon creating havoc all around the town? Takeover? It seemed too far-fetched. How did revenge on Masterson require the firebombing of shops in town? He could almost feel the thoughts rushing around his head in a maelstrom. Thoughts appeared and then were submerged in a vortex of confusion. He needed to think straight but his mind was spinning out of control.

'He's not after you,' repeated Yates. He looked desperately at the two men. He was buying time. He knew it. They knew it. 'He's not after you,' he repeated, desperately. Musgrave's face was slowly contorting like he was building up to do something. Something violent.

Then it hit him. Solomon really wasn't after the two gang leaders. Of course, it was a ruse.

'It's us,' shouted Yates. 'Solomon is distracting us. The police, I mean. He's using you, the fires, the kidnappings to do it.'

'Why?' snarled Musgrave, his patience exhausted. He stepped forward towards the policeman until he was barely inches away. Yates turned away from Musgrave and gazed in the direction of where the loud bang had come from. The alarm was still ringing. Out of the corner of his eye he saw a policeman running from one of the cars towards him and Price.

There could only be one place that explosion had come from.

38

Four men emerged from the bank clutching holdalls filled to the brim with money. Weir looked on in satisfaction. It had taken less than three minutes from the initial breaking open of the front door to their departure from the bank. The practice runs that Solomon had insisted upon in the woods had worked. They had been drilled and honed into a formidable unit. An army unit.

Solomon was grinning as he climbed up into the passenger seat. The sound of the bang had finally attracted the attention of some passers-by on the street. A constable appeared then disappeared. He was too late.

Weir already had the engine running. Two thumps from the back of the truck and they set off.

'Not too fast,' warned Solomon. 'Don't want an accident.'

'Relax,' smiled Weir. They'd done it. Just as Solomon had predicted they would. He felt light-headed. He wanted to ask how much but that would come later. Enough for his pension. Enough for a country house.

In France.

Ridiculous really. Clive Weir, military policeman, a man who'd served in various detention centres for years would soon become what he'd spent his career incarcerating. And he didn't care. He glanced at the man who'd changed everything. A man who did not believe in fate, only chance. On this, Weir disagreed with Solomon, but he hadn't Solomon's intellect. There was no point in trying to argue with him.

Chance had brought them together in France. Chance had seen them reunited a few years later in the prison where Weir had become a warden. No, fate existed, whatever Solomon claimed. And planning, too. For all his reasoning about the unpredictability of life, he was a meticulous planner. The goal of good planning, he maintained, is operational simplicity. Solomon's plan was as simple as it had proved effective. Use army men, material, and training to rob a bank.

It struck Weir, as they headed down the hill towards the sea front, that it was Solomon's fear of the haphazard that drove him; the unforeseen event that would change *everything*. This is why he organised so thoroughly.

'What are you smiling at?' asked Solomon, glancing towards Weir.

The answer died in Weir's mouth as they heard the sirens for the first time. Three police cars were racing up the hill. There was no way they could avoid passing them.

'Just keep going,' said Solomon calmly. 'They've no reason to stop us, believe me.'

-

'It has to be the bank,' said Jellicoe.

Burnett needed no further explanation. He was convinced. 'Right, out to the car. We'll have to take them with us,' he said, indicating the Mastersons. 'Nothing else for it. There's no time.'

They rushed out to the police car. Burnett glanced at Wallace who was brandishing the keys. There was a just a hint of apprehension on his face. Confronting a possible bank robber like Solomon seemed an altogether safer prospect than being driven by a young Stirling Moss. The frustrating thing was that, for once, he couldn't caution him on his speed. They had to get back to town quickly.

It was a tight squeeze in the back; Burnett and Wallace were in the front. Burnett wasted no time in using the radio.

'Burnett here. All units get to the bank.'

The radio crackled in response.

'Yates here. On our way there now. We think Solomon has robbed the bank.'

Jellicoe was pleasantly surprised that Yates had reached this conclusion. So too was Burnett.

'What about the situation in town?' demanded Burnett.

'It's calmed down,' lied Yates. He'd left Fogg and a couple of uniformed men with the gang leaders while he, Price and the majority of the uniformed officers raced towards the bank.

Jellicoe stopped listening to the radio traffic and tried to think about what Solomon's next move would be. Two thoughts hit him simultaneously. If Solomon and 'Montgomery' were working together then it made sense that they had other ex-army people helping them. That being so, they were facing not only men who were, potentially, armed but also men who were well-drilled.

They were no longer at the bank.

He leaned forward and indicated to Burnett that he wanted to speak to Yates.

A Time to Kill

'Yates, they'll have cleared out from the bank. We need to send men to block their potential escape routes. Send the cars to the roads leading out of town. And the harbour, too.'

-

They went past the army truck while Yates was communicating with Jellicoe. At first, he didn't register the truck, so intent was he on reaching the bank. Then, just as Jellicoe pointed out the obvious, they wouldn't be there, he remembered the army truck.

'We've just passed them. They're heading towards the front.'

Jellicoe replied immediately.

'The harbour.'

Yates responded immediately to the uniformed man driving the car.

'Turn around.'

Burnett, meanwhile, ordered all units to proceed immediately to the harbour. He forgot to take his fingers off the radio button. Six police cars heard the chief inspector say to Jellicoe, 'I hope to hell you're right.'

The three police cars accompanying Yates turned immediately. Yates's car narrowly avoided a catastrophic accident with a Morris Minor driven by Lydia Sackville, a retired schoolteacher from Cheam. Miss Sackville careered off the road, braking just in time to miss by a margin of inches the front window of Norrell's Butchers. She opened the front door and climbed out of the car. She leased off a few comments in the direction of the disappearing police cars before spying a joint of meat in the front window that would be perfect for the

337

visit of her sister and brother-in-law. The vicar's daughter concluded that the Lord works in mysterious ways.

-

Dead meat was at the forefront of Burnett's mind as the police car careered around yet another blind corner at a speed that British engineering had never intended for the sturdy old Wolsey. If any car had been coming the other way, it would be the end for all of them. By the sound of the swearing emanating from the back seat, he and Masterson were, for once, of a like mind. Wallace was a menace and would never be allowed near a driver's seat again if Burnett had his way. Assuming they survived the journey into town, that is.

However, as terrifying as the journey had been, he'd managed to make it into town within a matter of minutes. The sea was now visible in the distance and the lights of the harbour, too. There were around a dozen boats visible. The road leading to the harbour was hidden behind a row of buildings so they could not yet see if the army truck had, indeed, taken this route.

The other thought uppermost in Burnett's mind, aside from surviving the car journey, was the possibility that they were heading out of one highly perilous situation, courtesy of young Wallace, into another equally health-endangering position. A problem shared while not, in this case halved, at least meant Burnett could get something off his chest.

'What if Solomon has guns?'

Jellicoe had been pondering something similar and had no ready answer. The British police were not well-equipped to deal with armed confrontations. Even the average bobby knew you could not take a truncheon to a gunfight. He turned to Masterson.

A Time to Kill

'Do you think that Solomon could be armed?'

The gist of Masterson's succinct response was that he was unlikely to know. The major, realising he was being somewhat unhelpful, or perhaps just embarrassed at his use of language in front of his children, apologised unapologetically and sat with his arms folded while the car hurtled down Sycamore Hill towards the harbour.

Moments later they rounded the corner, on two wheels, Burnett was to swear later. One hundred yards ahead was the harbour.

There was no army truck.

-

Solomon's exterior calm could not hide from Weir's eyes the way he was gripping the holdall. They passed the police cars and both men instinctively turned their eyes to the rear wing view mirrors. Both men held their breath. Then they saw the lead car suddenly brake and turn sharply against the oncoming traffic causing a Morris Minor to swing violently off the road.

The other two Wolsey's turned as sharply as the first one had done. Solomon swore out loud. The two men looked at one another and then back to the mirrors. The police were coming after them.

Without waiting for an order, Weir put his foot down on the accelerator and the truck roared down the hill. A smile suddenly appeared on the lips of Solomon. He almost wanted to tell Weir that he'd told him so. Now wasn't the time.

'What do we do?' asked Weir

Good question thought Solomon. The original plan had been to head to the harbour and take the waiting boat. That

339

was out of the question now. They couldn't head there directly. That was too obvious. But they could delay their flight across the Channel. Misdirection would be key.

'We can't go to the harbour. They'll either have that covered or they'll catch us before we're even out of this truck. We can't outrun them in this crate. They'll be on us in a minute. Get onto the front and then we'll have to escape on foot. Every man for himself. We'll try and meet up at the main boat around midnight. We'll leave then. Whatever happens, whoever is on the boat at midnight goes.'

Weir nodded. Solomon banged the wall behind him and shouted to the three men in the back to listen up. He relayed the instructions and told them to get ready to abandon the truck.

-

'They're not at the harbour,' shouted Burnett into the radio.

Yates's reply was immediate.

'They've abandoned the truck. I can see three men running now. No, four. One is making for the pier. The others have ducked off the front.'

Burnett motioned with his finger to Wallace to keep driving.

'Roger,' said Burnett before colouring a little in embarrassment. He sounded like a bit-part player in a B-movie. 'We're near the pier. We'll head there. Go after the other gang members.'

Yates appeared to decline the opportunity to say 'Roger', opting instead to say nothing. Wallace, meanwhile, appeared intent on blowing up the already strained Wolsey engine such was his rush to reach the pier. Burnett listened with alarm at the Wolsey's screaming protests. They reached the pier less than a minute later.

'I can see someone,' said Jellicoe, opening the door before the car had finished moving. He was out of the car and sprinting along the front towards the steps of the pier before Burnett could issue any orders to that effect. Wallace brought the car to a halt and quickly jumped out. Burnett decided the best policy was to stay put. No, not quite. One other thing needed to be done. He stepped out of the car in a more dignified manner, walked around the bonnet to the driver's side and climbed in.

'About bloody time,' said Masterson sourly. 'That boy is a madman.'

Burnett didn't have the heart to argue a point he sorely agreed with. Instead, he, like the three Mastersons in the back, peered through the gloom in the hope of seeing what was happening at on the pier.

-

It's difficult to keep your natural poise when you're sprinting down a pier, at night, wearing an overcoat, carrying a holdall filled to the brim with bank notes, heart thumping through the effort and adrenalin. The surfeit of clothes and the lack of running shoes was, in retrospect, a mistake. However, uppermost in his mind was how tawdry it seemed. There was no escaping the fact, he was a common little robber. He smiled at the thought.

Behind him now, he could hear several sets of footsteps. Cops and robbers. He'd played it as a child. Now here he was, in real life, playing the game once more. Back then he'd always been one step ahead of his friends. Unlike them, he thought ahead. He always had his escape route mapped out. Of course, this could never take account of chance. That lesson had been learned well in Paris. Claude's face swam into view and he felt a wave pass through him. Hatred drove him forward towards the end of the pier.

He passed two fishermen. They didn't look up. There were more sirens blaring in the distance. How were the others doing? Not his problem now. There wasn't enough air in the seaside town for him. The strain was telling. Limbs slowing, muscles tightening. Stay relaxed he told himself. How could he? The footsteps behind were louder. They were gaining.

Past the stalls now. A smile broke out on his face. He thought momentarily of Tim Pemberton. So easy. He'd had them running here there and everywhere. A stab of guilt for this man Musgrave. He hadn't met him, but he sounded a good, bad sort. Not the worst according to Freddie.

The end of the pier was in sight. Seconds later he was there. he turned around. Lit by the lamplight he could see two men about thirty yards away. One of them was Jellicoe. The other he didn't recognise. At the far end of the pier, he could see the uniforms arriving.

He was cornered.

-

They had him. Jellicoe could see that the man they were chasing had reached the end of the pier. And he recognised the man in front of him from the prison photograph. He began to slow down. The sprint down the pier had left him a little breathless. Anyway, where could Solomon go now? They were over two hundred yards out to sea. The jump was fifty feet into a sea that was far from calm. He'd be dashed against the cast iron columns. The race was run. Solomon had lost.

A Time to Kill

Jellicoe was walking now. Wallace, too. Behind them they could hear the uniforms running towards them. And Solomon was facing them. There was a smile on his face. An easy smile. Jellicoe almost felt sorry for what he had to do. There was something about the man. He was likeable.

'There's no escape,' said Jellicoe. He felt a stab of embarrassment at having to utter such a banal statement of the obvious. 'You can't go anywhere.' Bloody hell, he felt tired. This was ghastly. He refrained from saying 'come quietly'. That would have been beyond the pale.

Suddenly Solomon climbed up and over the iron railing. He was now standing on the other side of the railing. He was still smiling.

'Sorry, Inspector. I can't let you take me. A bank robbery, fire bombing, two kidnappings. It doesn't look good, does it?' Solomon was smiling now. 'I daresay they'll bang me up for life after that little lot.'

Solomon let go of the railing now.

'Solomon, stop.'

Jellicoe put his hands up, palms facing their quarry. His legs seemed to seize up. He couldn't run. He looked at Wallace. A shake of the head. The young constable stopped. Behind them the uniforms were now almost upon them.

'You'll find Freddie at his flat, Inspector. He knew nothing about all of this. We forced him to do what he did. He's not an accomplice. Do you understand?'

Jellicoe nodded. He saw Solomon look down and then back at him.

'Don't, Solomon. Either you'll be killed by the fall or you'll drown, or you'll die of exposure. You won't last minutes in that sea. It's too cold.'

'Bloody freezing here, too, I can tell you,' agreed Solomon with a chuckle.

Jellicoe edged forward slowly. Wallace did the same. They were less than twenty feet from Solomon. A strange silence descended on them. The uniforms were right behind Jellicoe now.

'Don't, Solomon. Please. No one was killed. It doesn't have to end like this.'

'Alas, Inspector Jellicoe, it does.'

Solomon dropped into the sea.

38

'No, Solomon!' shouted Jellicoe, sprinting forward to the edge of the pier. He peered over. Below him the sea frothed and surged angrily against the cast iron columns. Floating on top of the sea was an overcoat and some bank notes. Then the sea took them into itself and they were gone.

Jellicoe turned to the policemen behind him. There was a frantic look in his eyes.

'Is there a way down to the sea from here?'

No one knew.

He gazed over the edge again. A part of him wanted to jump down, too. It would be so easy. He'd be with Sylvia again. He shivered and it wasn't just the cold. All of the policemen were looking uselessly over the edge of the railings. The wind blew rain into Jellicoe's face, stinging his eyes. He looked out into the English Channel and felt an overwhelming sadness descend upon him. Then he heard a familiar voice. He turned around.

Burnett ambled up alongside him. He'd walked the whole way.

'I take it from the way all our men are looking down at the sea that someone jumped.' There was little sympathy in his voice and absolutely no expectation they would survive.

'Solomon,' answered Jellicoe.

'The man himself?' replied Burnett. 'Pity I'd have like to have met him.' There were two ways to read such a statement, but Jellicoe detected a degree of awe in the curmudgeonly chief's voice. Solomon had led them a merry chase for nearly a week now and damn near pulled off an audacious bank job while the town's police were tied up keeping two rival gangs apart, dealing a with a handful of fires and a kidnap situation.

'Where are the Mastersons?'

'A uniform is going to take them to hospital.'

'Perhaps Wallace can take them back,' suggested Jellicoe. he turned to the young policeman. There was just a hint of gratitude in the young man's eyes.

'They'll certainly arrive quickly,' growled Burnett. Then pointing at Wallace, he added, 'Tomorrow, son, you're on a driving course. Bloody maniac.'

Wallace had the grace to smile rather sheepishly at this and he set off back down the pier.

'There's no way down there, I suppose?' asked Burnett, walking to the edge, and gazing down at the waves. Jellicoe joined him and the two men looked down at the dark lead-grey water. Waves exploded against the columns. The foam-frothed water bubbled and gurgled until the next crash of wave against the pier.

Then they heard it.

The whine of an outboard motor cut through the sound of the rolling sea.

'What the...?' started Burnett.

The motorboat emerged from beneath the pier moments later. A man dressed in a black trawlerman jumper and ribbed woollen hat was driving it. He rose and crashed against the

346

incoming waves. The man turned to the policemen who had all advanced towards the end of the pier.

It was Solomon.

There was a broad grin on his face. He offered a salute to the audience above and then turned away. The boat started out moving forward again. They watched it disappear into the night. The sound died away until it was only a distant buzz.

'Cheeky bugger,' was Burnett's only comment. It was neither angry nor resentful. The two policemen looked at one another. Neither could think of anything to say. Instead, they turned and began walking back down the pier towards the front.

They passed the two fishermen on the way back. Neither turned to look at them. Burnett glanced at them for a moment and shook his head. Behind them, trooping dejectedly were half a dozen uniformed men.

Jellicoe felt, for the first time, the chill infiltrate his clothing. His coat was fighting a losing battle against the rain which fell more heavily now. He wondered about Solomon. Was he really going to sail a small boat over the channel to France? He'd escaped but the journey ahead would be perilous. The channel could be dangerous in bad weather for fishing boats. How could he seriously contemplate travelling across this stretch of water in a small boat with outboard motors?

But they were dealing with Solomon, weren't they?

As iron sharpens iron, so a friend sharpens a friend.

It was cold comfort, but Jellicoe knew he would be a better policeman despite their failure. Yet he hadn't failed completely. They had Masterson's killer. They'd rescued the family. Perhaps Solomon's accomplices would be caught. However, letting Solomon escape would rankle. The coast guard would be informed, of course. A futile gesture like trying to get the last word when you've lost the argument. On a night like this the chances of finding him would be remote.

Superintendent Frankie would gripe in private about Solomon's escape while accepting, in public, the acclaim for their success. Burnett was a sore loser, too. Jellicoe glanced towards him. The chief, eyes straight ahead, ploughed forward towards the police cars in a sombre, rather than angry, silence.

They reached the cars. Wallace had already taken the Mastersons away, so the two men rode back with the uniformed men.

'Back to the station,' said Burnett as if he was speaking to a taxi driver.

'No sir, we need to go one other place first.'

The chief inspector eyed Jellicoe warily.

'Oh aye?'

-

Two uniformed men led the way up the stairs followed by Burnett and Jellicoe. The block of flats wasn't in good enough condition to be called low rent. Jellicoe suspected that those living here shared their accommodation with all manner of rodent life. They ascended the wooden staircase trying to avoid touching either the bannister or the walls. The smell was a head spinning cocktail of nicotine and ammonia.

They reached the second floor. Flat six's number was hanging upside down. Jellicoe wondered if this was deliberate misdirection on the part of young Frederick. One of the police officers banged on the door. There was no response.

A Time to Kill

'Police. Open up.'

Still no response. Burnett nodded to the two uniformed men. Two burly shoulders met with a very cheaply made door and door frame. There was only going to be one winner in this battle. The door flew off its hinges sending the two policemen sprawling inside.

Lying on the bed was a body. At first it was still then it started when Burnett put the light on. Despite the large gag and blindfold, Jellicoe guessed he was looking at Freddie Douglas. His hands and feet were tied with rope. One of the policemen went to untie him when Jellicoe motioned for him to stop.

Instead, he went forward and removed the blindfold and gag. He looked at the knot on the rope and noted that his hands hadn't been bound too tightly. A similar story with the feet. But what could he say? Solomon had thought of everything. The gang would have had no more use for Freddie. The problem of what to do about him could have been resolved in two ways. Solomon had chosen the least violent.

Freddie would, no doubt, have been well rewarded for his efforts. He would have to contend with a charge of conspiracy to kidnap but he could, no doubt, claim he was duped and then kidnapped himself. If there was any custodial sentence this and the fact that he was relatively young would be taken into consideration.

'I'll have you free in a jiff.'

'Took your bloody time. I hope you caught 'im.'

Jellicoe looked archly at Freddie Douglas.

'Do you, Freddie?'

-

Despite the spraying rain, a crowd had gathered outside the police station as Jellicoe's car pulled up outside. Aside from a few of the local pressmen he now recognised, he noticed Singe had made an appearance. He was propped against a lamp post and evidently a little squiffy as he was wont to say. Singe saw Jellicoe looking at him from the passenger seat of the car. He waved a cigarette at him as he passed.

A few uniformed men stood at the front of the police station although their presence was somewhat redundant. The crowd, though certainly quite large given the time of night and intemperance of the weather, was well-behaved and there out of a curiosity that would soon dissipate.

Jellicoe used his coat to cover Freddie Douglas as they made their way into the station. Once inside they took him upstairs. They hadn't bothered to handcuff him. He'd had enough of that already.

Much to Burnett's surprise, both Chief Constable Leighton and Superintendent Frankie were there to greet them. The news of the events in the town had obviously been enough to prompt them to come in. Both seemed in a good mood which even the news of Solomon's flight did not dampen. Three other men had been captured, the bank's money had been mostly recovered save for what Solomon had taken and they had rescued the Mastersons.

'Great work, Chief Inspector, great work,' said Leighton effusively. He was like a big Labrador whose owner had reached for the dog lead. He eagerly shook the hands of both Burnett and Jellicoe. Frankie, inevitably, was more reserved in his reaction but he appeared happy enough although a faint trace of disapproval was never far away from his mouth. Perhaps aware that Leighton might think him ungracious, he attempted a smile.

Freddie Douglas was led past the two senior officers to be interviewed. This was another point in the favour of the operation. It wasn't quite a neat bow but, for the moment, the two senior men had a story to tell the waiting press and they were clearly eager to tell it. Burnett declined Frankie's reluctant invitation to join them at the press conference.

Burnett wandered over to Jellicoe who was peering through a window into an interview room where three men were being questioned. They were all sitting stiff-backed at a table. Facing them were DI Price and DS Yates. Yates glanced out of the window and saw Jellicoe. Their eyes met briefly. Jellicoe nodded to him.

'Do you see your friend from the guest house?' asked Burnett.

Jellicoe shook his head. None of the men were 'Monty'.

'Masterson thinks it might be a man called Weir. They were stationed together in France when they first encountered Solomon. Masterson left the military police a few years later to join another section. According to Wallace, Weir left the army just after that and became a prison officer.'

The two men looked at one another for a moment and then Burnett wondered out loud, 'I'll bet you two bob that he was at the same prison as Solomon.'

'I was thinking the same,' smiled Jellicoe.

They were silent for a few moments. Jellicoe studied the three men they'd arrested. All had the look of army about them: their haircuts, the way they held themselves, the merciless look in their eyes. He sensed Burnett was looking at him. Jellicoe glanced at the chief inspector.

Burnett turned away. Then, almost reluctantly, he murmured, 'I suppose Yates did well.'

'I'll let him know.'

'And for heaven's sake do something about that young lunatic. Bloody idiot took years off my life.'

Jellicoe laughed and then they went inside the room to join Yates and Price.

A Time to Kill

Epilogue

Paris, France: 19th January 1959

Things had changed so much since he'd been here last. He walked through the centre of the city. What struck him first was the absence of uniforms. The traffic was heavier, too, but not with army vehicles. He smiled at a memory of his nerve-shredding drive through Paris in one such truck.

He would visit the centre later. For now, there was only one place that he wanted to go. He wiped some imaginary dust off his new suit. Such a difference from when he'd first arrived in the city looking like a member of Fagin's gang. The suit was dark grey in colour. It would do until he could find something better in the city. Something tailor-made.

His French was rusty, of course. Speaking it wasn't a problem. As ever it was understanding spoken French which was the challenge. It wouldn't take long, though. And he would be here for a while.

The other thing he noticed was how much warmer it was given it was mid-January. Not quite the stinging wintriness of Britain. He passed near a café by the station playing Jazz music. They loved it here. He smiled as he listened to John Coltrane's saxophone. However, he couldn't stay long. His arm shot up immediately to hail an empty taxi. There was no point in hanging around. He had to go there. Now.

For the first time since his arrival at the Gare de Nord he felt a fluttering in his stomach. The warm feeling of hearing the French language, of seeing the Gare du Nord again and the Art-Nouveau Metropolitan entrances gave way to a sense of expectancy that tightened his heartbeat.

He climbed into the taxi and gave an address. Three times he had to repeat it before the driver understood where to go. Nerves strangled his voice; no wonder the poor driver couldn't understand him or, perhaps, he was just being French; demanding perfection of tone and inflexion. It would have been funny had he not been melting inside.

The drive was like a tour through his memories. The happiness he'd felt here with Lizette and Sophie overpowered him. His eyes became moist at seeing the street where he'd first encountered the military policemen who'd chased him into the square.

'*Ici*,' he said pointing to the spot where the chase had begun.

He paid the taxi driver and gave a generous tip. The taxi driver looked at it indifferently. I'll take it back if you want. Then he hopped out of the car and retraced the footsteps he'd taken fifteen years earlier. His heart was beating fast, like it had then. The sun beat on his back until he turned into a narrow street with high-sided walls. The shadows gave the passageway a distinct chill.

Another turn and he was walking through the archway that led to the square. All at once he emerged into the bright sunlight. Honey-coloured walls greeted him like the long-lost son that he was. Just ahead he saw the small fountain. He walked over to it first and sat down. The sound of water gurgling brought some calm to the turbulence inside.

He was facing the door now.

The street seemed to have stayed exactly as he remembered. Old people sat on old chairs with old friends repeating old conversations. Children laughed and ran around enjoying the late afternoon sunshine. He looked up at the blue sky and closed his eyes.

The door opened.

A young woman emerged. A younger version of Lizette. Tall and lithe, she seemed to glide across the cobblestones. The dark eyes were not the haunted ones he remembered but there was no mistaking Sophie. He rose to go to her but paused; uncertain whether to go or just simply enjoy that moment. Then she glanced in his direction. She looked away immediately. Something, however, made her look back. This time she held his gaze.

It took a few moments; her eyes widened. She walked backwards as if in fear for her life. A frown creased her forehead. She turned towards the doorway.

'*Maman*,' she shouted. She was crying now.

It must have been the tone of her daughter's voice, for Lizette soon appeared. Older yet still the same. The eyes betrayed the fear lurking forever within. She clutched her daughter wanting to know what was wrong. Sophie was saying something. Pointing.

Lizette turned towards Solomon. Her hand touched her throat. But Solomon could barely see her now through his tears. A cloud had passed over the sun, darkening the square; a chill descended upon him.

He opened his eyes. The vision was no longer there. The dream of five thousand nights evaporated into quanta, into particles, into atoms. Bent double, shoulders shaking, the sobs wracked his body; a howl of desolation, of anger, of hatred, caught in his throat.

-

Across the English Channel, Jellicoe gazed out of the window down to the street in front of the police building. The sky had drained away the colours of the buildings. For the first time since the case had begun, there were no pressmen in front of the police station. The murder of the colonel and the kidnappings and the bank robbery had become yesterday's news. Shoppers and office workers patrolled the street like worker ants. The front door to the bank was repaired and people were entering and leaving. An old woman was pointing out the front of the bank to a friend. Two Miss Marples discussing the case. It was probably the most exciting thing to happen to the town since the war.

In all they had recovered around ten thousand pounds; three of the robbers were captured, four if you counted Freddie Douglas but there was little doubt that he would claim he was more wronged than wrongdoer. Certainly, Burnett was of a mind to go easy on the boy, partly as a sop to Musgrave who was still sore at his treatment by the police, partly in recognition that Freddie might say things that were best left unsaid. It was surprisingly nuanced approach from the chief inspector.

The bank calculated that Solomon had managed to take around five thousand pounds. Jellicoe thought some creative arithmetic had been used to reach this amount.

A Time to Kill

Burnett sidled up alongside him and joined Jellicoe in gazing down at the street. They stood in silence for a few moments. Then Burnett broke the silence.

'There are eight million stories in the Naked City; this has been one of them.'

Jellicoe's eyebrow arched and he turned to his chief.

'Eight million?'

Burnett shrugged and replied, '*Naked City*. Barry Fitzgerald.'

'I know the reference.'

'You would. Anyway, if not eight million then, half a dozen stories at least.'

Jellicoe pondered this for a moment.

'I preferred him in *Going My Way*,' said Jellicoe after a while. Burnett looked confused so Jellicoe continued. 'Barry Fitzgerald. More believable as a priest than a cop. Too kindly.'

Burnett's face had what-do-you-know written across it.

'Are you suggesting I'm not kindly?'

'Heart of gold, Chief,' said Jellicoe. 'Speaking of which, do you mind if I leave a little earlier this evening?'

This was never going to pass unchallenged. Burnett went through the motions.

'Why? On a promise?'

Jellicoe shook his head. There was a sense of guilt in his reply.

'I'm looking for a place to live. I can't stay in Ramsbottom's forever.'

Burnett studied Jellicoe for a moment. The red-rimmed eyes of Jellicoe betrayed the fatigue of the new man or perhaps he was experiencing a wave of grief. The intensity of the last few days had made Burnett forget that Jellicoe was recovering from the loss of his wife. There was a fleeting moment of sadness in Burnett's eyes. His thoughts, though, were not, at that moment, for Jellicoe. Instead, they were for a woman he'd known for forty years; a woman who was likewise in mourning and always would be.

'Aye son. I suppose so. Elsie will understand. Do what you need to.'

Elsie? Jellicoe had never asked for her name. She'd always been Mrs Ramsbottom. The guilt returned. It was a conversation he was not looking forward to.

A thought struck Burnett. He frowned momentarily, a more business-like tone in his voice. 'Have you spoken to Aldershot yet about the bank robbery they had?'

'Yes, I did. Same *modus operandi*,' replied Jellicoe. 'An army truck was seen in the town. There was an explosion. They didn't connect the army truck to the robbery though and no one checked because…'

'…Aldershot is an army town. Bloody hell,' said Burnett finishing the sentence. His dismay blazed through his eyes. A silence descended on them again. Both stared down at the world below them.

'Do you think Masterson stole the money?' blurted out Burnett. It was out of the blue. Neither of them had spoken of the accusation levelled by Solomon. But now that matters were being settled it seemed as good a time as any.

'Of course, he stole it. Might have been a few thousand in that account.'

A Time to Kill

'No way we could ever prove this, of course,' said Burnett angrily. 'What became of Solomon's woman and her daughter. Do we know yet?'

Jellicoe turned away and reached for a telegram sitting on his desk. He handed it to Burnett.

'From the Sûreté in Paris,' said Jellicoe.

Burnett glanced at it and then he looked up at Jellicoe. His voice was taut with disapproval.

'It's in French.'

Jellicoe took the telegram back from Burnett. His voice was barely more than a sigh, 'According to this, there was a fire at the apartment of Lizette Giresse. The police are convinced that she and her daughter were killed in the blaze. They charged Claude Aubert with arson but in the end, they had to let him off. There just wasn't enough evidence.'

Burnett nodded and turned to the window. Outside, rain fell steadily from a grey velvet sky.

'I know what I would do if I was Solomon,' murmured Burnett picking up his pipe and tapping it against the edge of the table.

-

It's all just physics; matter that moves in time and space. However, our existence is relational. No man is an island said Donne and it's true. We are atoms that live in relation to other things. That relationship defines us. A mother is a mother only because she's had a child, sadness cannot exist without happiness, a hunter must have its prey, a murderer requires a victim. More than that, each must observe and recognise who they are. But the act of observation makes us a participant. Then it becomes real. We interact and by doing so we leave traces of *our* presence.

It was odd to think about such things while skulking through the shadows. The feeling that he was being hunted overwhelmed him. Yet he knew, at that moment, it was not entirely accurate. In another's reality, he was the hunter. That other person would not know this, of course; at least, they would not know this until the very end. Their final act would be this observation.

He moved forward, collar up, initially towards the front door but then round the side of the building and then the back. The sky was a deathly black. As black as a heart set on murder.

The window at the back gave way easily. He was inside now and moving through the house. He heard a radio in another room. His heart was beginning to race now. Breathing became shallower. Light-headed he clutched the table. Sadness enveloped him, not for what he would do but for what had been done already. It emboldened him, though and air began to reach his lungs.

The sounds of the other man were all too human, yet this made his hatred all the greater.

He waited.

His senses were at a pitch now, the clock's ticking, deafening. Then the man came at last. An old man. Stooped like an old man. He grumbled like an old man as he moved. He reached for the light and missed it. Never mind. He felt his way forward and found what he wanted on the sideboard.

He was still unaware of the other. A movement perhaps, or a sound? And then he saw him. He stopped. Fear in his eyes.

A Time to Kill

His legs turned to stone. The other man came to him. A shaft of light fell across his face.

'Remember me?' asked the man.

A slow shake of the head. Decades of memories as vast in number as the stars in the heavens or grains of sand on a beach or atoms in a body raced around inside his head. Then he knew who it was. He knew why he was here. And he turned away.

The man came at him. Something was in his hand. It was raised over his head now. And it came crashing down. He stared down at the fallen man; a halo of blood encircled his head. And then he whispered venomously parting words to a dead man.

'Remember me…Claude? That's for Lizette.'

He hit the man one more time.

'And that's for Sophie.'

The End

Jack Murray

About the Author

Jack Murray lives just outside London with his family. Born in Ireland he has spent most of his adult life in the England. His first novel, 'The Affair of the Christmas Card Killer' has been a global success. Four further Kit Aston novels have followed: 'The Chess Board Murders', 'The French Diplomat Affair' and 'The Phantom' and 'The Frisco Falcon'. 'The Medium Murders' is the sixth in the Kit Aston series.

Jack has also published a spin-off series from the Kit Aston mysteries featuring a popular character from the series, Aunt Agatha. These mysteries are set in the late Victorian era when Agatha was a young woman.

In 2022, a new series will be published by Lume Books set in the period leading up to and during World War II. The series will include some of the minor characters from the Kit Aston series.

A Time to Kill

Acknowledgements

It is not possible to write a book on your own. There are contributions from so many people either directly or indirectly over many years. Listing them all would be an impossible task.

Special mention therefore should be made to my wife and family who have been patient and put up with my occasional grumpiness when working on this project.

My brother Edward and John Convery have helped in proofing and made supportive comments that helped me tremendously. I have been very lucky to receive badly needed editing from Kathy Lance who has helped tighten up some of the grammatical issues that affected my earlier books. She has been a Godsend!

My late father and mother both loved books. They encouraged a love of reading in me. In particular, they liked detective books, so I must tip my hat to the two greatest writers of this genre, Sir Arthur, and Dame Agatha.

Following writing, comes the business of marketing. My thanks to Mark Hodgson and Sophia Kyriacou for their advice on this important area. Additionally, a shout out to the wonderful folk on 20Booksto50k.

Thanks to all the healthcare professionals the world over and those involved in developing the vaccine against this terrible virus.

Finally, my thanks to the teachers who taught and nurtured a love of writing.

Printed in Great Britain
by Amazon

13714039R00215